CIRCUS OF SHADOWS

KIMBERLEE TURLEY

SWEETWATER BOOKS
An imprint of Cedar Fort, Inc.
Springville, Utah

"The gaslamp fantasy setting is brilliantly detailed. The story itself is passionate and irresistible. Fans of dazzling, action-packed adventures will not be disappointed."

—JORDAN ELIZABETH, author of *Cogling*

This is a work of fiction. The characters, names, incidents, places, and dialogue are products of the author's imagination and are not to be construed as real. The opinions and views expressed herein belong solely to the author and do not necessarily represent the opinions or views of Cedar Fort, Inc. Permission for the use of sources, graphics, and photos is also solely the responsibility of the author.

ISBN 13: 978-1-4621-4153-1

Published by Sweetwater Books, an imprint of Cedar Fort, Inc.
2373 W. 700 S., Springville, UT 84663
Distributed by Cedar Fort, Inc., www.cedarfort.com

Library of Congress Control Number: 2022933522

Cover design by Shawnda T. Craig
Cover design © 2022 Cedar Fort, Inc.
Substantive by Rachel Hathcock
Edited and typeset by Spencer Skeen

Printed in the United States of America

10 9 8 7 6 5 4 3 2 1

Printed on acid-free paper

For Jennifer

In size 20 font, per your request.

CHAPTER I

GRACIE HART took a quick glance around the corner before stepping out of the shadowed alley. A persistent mist hung over the rooftops of the brick buildings towering all around her. So far, the only other people on the streets of Albany were the newsboys and the morning sweepers. She held her chin high, even though her heart crashed against her ribs.

No doubt there were worse things a young woman of seventeen could feel after murdering a man. Like regret. She'd done the world a favor, but a judge would never see it that way.

How many times had she been warned that her stubbornness would get her into trouble? Too many, and yet not enough. Gracie certainly had a lot more experience causing problems than resolving them.

With every step, her battered leather steamer case banged against her ankle. She'd been stupid to bring it. Besides slowing her down, it marked her as a runaway. While the case contained only the barest essentials of a working drudge's wardrobe, she hated to think of leaving it behind. It was the only thing she had left from her old life—from England.

Fear told her to abandon the case, but the blisters on her heels would appreciate dry socks when—or rather, *if*—she reached the train station.

As she continued walking, the clattering of window shutters and the clanging of bells on street trolleys filled the air. She knew that the factory's morning shift workers would soon be lining up to turn in their time cards. At any moment, someone would find the foreman's body and alert the police. She didn't have much time.

A shaggy-haired messenger boy ran past. Gracie reached out and stopped him. "Boy, is this the way to the train station?" she asked.

He held his hand out, palm up. "I'll tell you for a dime."

"Oh, shove off." She let go of his arm. She'd walk an extra mile before she trusted the directions of a boy who presumed she had pocket change to spare.

Gracie reached the Albany train station by late afternoon. The tightness in her chest had eased a little after several hours of uneventful walking. No one had given her a second glance. Running errands for the orphanage headmistress, Mrs. Levenson, had taught her to expect to be ignored. Gracie supposed people feared that if they acknowledged her existence with a friendly smile, it would encourage her to beg for a handout. She'd never wanted their money, or their pity, and that turned out for the best, since people didn't give her either.

Gracie entered the station through the large keystone doorway. Coal smoke drifted, mingling with the thick, acrid scent of hot engine oil. Tired, aloof people sat on wooden benches lining the edges of the room. A husband and wife and their six children begged their pardon of the station patrons as they rolled a towering cart of trunks and suitcases toward the barred ticket window.

"Stay close and keep up," the mother said, taking her youngest daughter's hand and pulling the girl along.

Gracie stepped to the side as the family passed by, tightly clutching her steamer case handle. How nice would it be to have someone to hold her hand and have all the answers to her problems? With a self-satisfied nod, she decided that keeping it was a smart decision, as now it helped her blend in better.

Turning toward the chalkboard of ticket fares, she brushed a tendril of walnut brown hair from her damp brow. With a huff, she set her steamer case down. Tiptoeing her fingers on the map of train routes next to the chalkboard, Gracie traced a line from Albany, New

York, to Chicago, Illinois. Eight steps. Each step equaled a hundred miles of travel.

Gracie didn't know why her aunt and uncle had never come to claim her, but she refused to believe Mrs. Levenson's explanation that her aunt and uncle simply hadn't wanted her. Clinging to hope hurt a lot less than accepting she was unlovable and destined to be alone for the rest of her life.

If her aunt and uncle were still alive, and still in Chicago, she intended to find them. Never mind the eight long years she had spent in the orphan asylum, the last three months at the poultry factory, or that she'd murdered a man last night. Family was family, right?

Picking up her steamer case again, Gracie entered the ticket queue. Once at the front of the line, she slid a gold coin under the barred window toward the ticket master. "I'd like one ticket on your next westbound train, please."

The ticket master's upper lip was hidden by a thick mustache with waxed ends that hooked on the edges of his mouth. "Where are you going?" His voice was gruff, his tone similar. As his gaze shifted back and forth from her to the coin, she wondered if it was normal that he hadn't scooped her money into his till yet.

"As close to Chicago as I can get. The sooner the better." She smiled, though in reality the gesture was more akin to baring her teeth in self-defense. Her clothes might be ill-fitted and outdated, but he had no business treating her money like it was secondhand too.

He stared at her a moment more before dragging a large book of distance tables, fares, and time charts in front of him. He flipped it open to the well-worn Albany fare schedule.

"Do you need a private cabin?"

"No, thank you."

He strummed his fingers on the countertop as he read, twisting the end of his mustache with his other hand. The pendulum on the large wall clock behind him counted the seconds aloud. What was the matter? She'd given him a half-eagle—*five dollars*—all her savings from the last three months. She wasn't sure if it was enough to reach Chicago, but it should certainly get her *somewhere*.

He finally lifted his eyes from the page and cleared his throat. "It seems the best I can do for you is a second-class ticket on a train headed to Rochester at the top of the hour."

Rochester wasn't nearly far enough. "Do you have anything like a steerage-class ticket?"

To his credit, he answered her question with perfect courtesy. "We don't allow steerage travel anymore. The Cleveland train has a third-class car, but it won't be leaving until 9:25 tonight."

She couldn't afford to wait around that long. "I'll take the Rochester ticket, please."

Gracie shoved the ticket and change into her left pocket and then backed away from the window. She scanned the station, her gaze lingering on an elderly railroad attendant in pinstripe overalls by the rear door. If she had to make a run for it, kicking him in the shin and then scampering through the door seemed to be her best option. She stooped to pick up her case and felt something brush the folds of her skirt.

A glance over her shoulder revealed a young gentleman standing beside her. Spanning his broad shoulders was an ink-black frock coat that could not have looked better on a shop window's wicker mannequin. The crispness of his high collar and the gold watch chain across his red brocade vest indicated he worked for a respectable company. However, he lacked a hat, giving his dark hair a windswept appearance. His brown eyes regarded her with intrigue rather than disdain. She breathed a sigh of relief—he wasn't a policeman.

"Allow me to carry that for you," he said, extending a gloved hand toward her. The lilt and soft *R*s of his accent reminded her a little of the way people spoke in southern England, though something made her doubt he was an Englishman. No dandy would think of leaving home without a hat, even if his short, tousled hair *did* emphasize his strong jawline and straight nose.

Across the station, the yardmaster stared in her direction. *Just act normal. Pretend you're on a day trip to visit an ailing relative.*

"Thank you, sir. Very kind of you." Hesitantly, she handed the gentleman her steamer case, hoping he'd interpret her pause as polite restraint. She struggled to remember if her English governess from so many years ago had ever told her if it was improper to let someone escort her without an introduction. Etiquette training at the orphanage had only prepared her for plucking feathers off dead chickens.

She followed him toward the baggage area on the far side of the station. He walked at a leisurely pace, his shiny black Oxfords gliding along while she did her best not to trip on the hem of her too-long dress.

Weighing her case with two extended fingers, her escort noted, "This isn't at all heavy."

"I'm not going very far," she said.

"I see. So you're not headed back to England? That is home for you, if I'm not mistaken?"

Gracie studied the ground, frantically scheming how to turn the conversation from herself. If the authorities ever questioned him, it was best he knew as little about her as possible.

She tilted her chin up and increased her stride. He wouldn't be so interested in her if he knew he carried her dowry in his hands—the case, a toothbrush, tooth powder, a nightgown, a comb, and an extra pair of stockings. The comb was missing so many teeth that it resembled a picket fence trampled by a stampede of wild horses.

"England hasn't been home for quite some time. What about you? Where do you call home? Your accent sounds familiar, but a little exotic."

"I was born and raised in Australia, but I've been traveling across America for the last several years." The faint wrinkles next to his lips became more grooved, and his shoulders hunched. "I guess you could say my home is where I work."

He set her steamer case down among the stacks of other baggage and crates to be loaded onto the 2:00 p.m. Rochester train.

"Do you need any other assistance, miss?" His manners flattered her. At the factory, courtesy didn't extend beyond calling someone by their real name.

"No, thank you. You've helped enough already."

His kiss to her knuckles was quick and soft. She blushed for a moment and then quickly squashed the sentiment. He'd only offered to carry her trunk because gentlemen were expected to show charity to women. Gracie knew the type of young woman likely to be found hanging on his arm. A sweet, delicate flower who would never talk back but would graciously nod and do as she was told. A young woman who was nothing like herself.

With a tilt of his head and another one of his charming smiles, he walked away. Gracie wrung the fabric of her skirt, the sensation of his lips still a cool spot on the back of her hand. She looked down, almost expecting to see a lip-rouge mark, and felt the color drain from her face. There, on the side of her sleeve cuff, she did have a rusty-red stain, but it wasn't rouge—it was dried blood.

She hid her soiled sleeve behind her and instinctively searched for the yardmaster. He had left his post by the door. Her stomach squeezed to a pinhole and remained that way until she saw him again. He was walking toward the train yard, away from her.

Stupid. Stupid. Stupid. What if anyone had noticed the blood? She needed to find a place to wash up. With less than an hour until the Rochester train departed, maybe she could scout the streets for a rain barrel and buy something to eat with her last fifteen cents. She reached into her pocket to give her coins a reassuring squeeze. Blood rushed to her face as she realized her pocket seemed very deep. Did it have a hole? Terror gripped her as she clawed at the seam lines and then turned both pockets inside out.

She danced around, shaking her petticoat and hoping for her ticket to appear. Onlookers must have thought a rodent was in her drawers.

Nothing else fell out. No coins and no ticket. A sick feeling rose from her stomach to her throat.

I've been robbed.

CHAPTER II

J ACK KICKED his shovel into the crunchy pile of black coal and then tossed the load into the firebox. Beside him stood a wizened man dressed in the sooty pinstripe coveralls of a train engineer. The engineer checked his pocket watch and then turned to Jack with a smile that stretched the wrinkles out of his baked cheeks. "You can quit stoking the firebox, Jack. This next stretch is straight, long, and level."

Jack threw in one more shovelful and closed the furnace door. Mopping his forehead with a rag, he set the shovel aside and seated himself on the tender's coal pile. The inferno inside burned a ton of coal for every fifteen hundred gallons of water that it vaporized into steam pressure. Hell had a back door, and it was the belly of a steam engine.

Jack allowed himself ten minutes of rest before picking up his shovel to start moving the coal from the back of the tender to the front. Using the shovel for support, he picked his way to the top of the slippery pile.

Standing almost as tall as the train's chimneystack, he threw a few loads forward and then stopped, his attention fixed on the line of train cars behind him.

He squinted at the dark shadow on one of the passenger cars. It couldn't be one of the brakemen since the next stop wasn't for a while. That meant one thing—a stowaway.

He turned to the engineer and nodded to the throttle lever. "Wilson, think you can keep your mitts off the Johnson bar for a while?"

The engineer set the steam throttle to the lowest cut-off position and wrinkled his bushy eyebrows with curiosity. "What's the matter, Jack? You've got another fifty miles before your shift is over."

"I think we've got a leech on one of the sleeper cars."

"It's the rear crew's job to keep an eye out for that. The next time we stop I'm certain they'll take care of it."

"I don't think they can see him."

The engineer rolled his eyes and returned his focus to the track ahead. "Then the next time we stop, *you* can be the one to tell him he's reached his final destination."

Ignoring this advice, Jack threw his shovel on top of the coal pile and crossed the gap between the tender and the first stock car.

"Hey!" Wilson shouted after him. "What do you think you're doing? Why don't you leave the acrobatics to the trapeze artists and get back here before you get us both in trouble?"

With a devious grin, Jack called over his shoulder, "I'm just gonna have a little fun."

"It's only fun until someone gets hurt," Wilson tossed back.

JACK'S disappointment when he approached the sleeping stowaway could only be surpassed by his surprise. It was a young woman. Sprawled in the center of the train roof, the sheila slept with her arms pulled tightly into her chest. Soft curls of brown hair lay strewn around her face. He estimated she couldn't be more than seventeen at most—three years his junior.

Unfortunately, the fact that she *was* a woman ruined his plans to tie her shoelaces in knots before waking her with a crack of his heel on the car roof.

He knelt beside her, wondering when she had snuck aboard and if bravery or foolishness had prompted her to travel alone. His eyes fell on the row of undone buttons down the front of her bodice. He shook off the temptation to let his gaze linger. "Miss," he said. "Excuse me, miss." He reached for her shoulder. "Are you all right?"

She bolted upright with a sharp breath, knocking him in the face with her granite head. Jack flinched backward and cupped his hands over his nose. *"Mince alors!"*

"No! Stay back!" She kicked her feet in a mad scramble, confusion and wild fear in her eyes.

As she continued to back herself closer to the edge, Jack shot forward to grab her before she slipped over and fell to her death.

Yanking her to safety by her waist, Jack felt her tumble on top of him in a tangled heap of limbs. He held her tightly to his chest, panting and waiting for his pulse to slow. He huffed against the tickling sensation of blood from his nose dripping down the back of his throat. Why did that cocky engineer always have to be right?

He felt her heart pounding through the folds of her clothes. "Don't hurt me," she begged.

Hurt her? Who was the one with the bloodied nose? "Calm down, you ninny, no one wants to hurt you."

Her voice grew more confident. "If that's true, then let me go." She planted her palms on his chest and pushed.

"I'll let you go, but you'll break both your legs if you try getting off this train while it's moving." He slid his arms out from around her waist. She pushed off his chest, her hazel eyes as hard and cold as the metal roof she knelt on. He sat up more slowly, pinching the bridge of his nose. Thankfully, it didn't feel crooked.

The young woman quickly began buttoning the top of her dress, concealing a mottled blush on her neck in the process. He continued watching, determined not to lower his guard again around her. With a snort, he released his nose, the bleeding staunched. If she truly cared so much about propriety she should have bought a ticket for herself and had an escort. "You mind telling me what you're doing here?"

She looked up from buttoning her bodice and went rigid. "It's you!" she cried and then slapped his bewildered face.

He leaned back, rubbing his cheek. Of all the young women he'd been slapped by (with or without sound reason), this one carried a brick in her glove.

He could understand why she was mortified. After all, he'd seen her with her dress partially unbuttoned. However, when she began pounding on his chest with her fists rather than fixing her bodice, he realized her gracious thanks for his gallant rescue had been indefinitely postponed.

Grasping her wrists, he kept her at arm's length long enough to get to his feet. "The next town is Rutland, but if you keep causing problems your stop might be the next tree we pass."

That settled her a bit. "Where's Rutland? Is that east or west of Rochester?"

He turned from her, ignoring her question, and began the walk down the length of the car toward the caboose at the rear. He should have listened to Wilson and let the rear crew do their job. Then she would be *their* problem and not his.

"Is that east or west?" she repeated, getting to her feet.

"Rutland, Vermont, is *north*. This train is going to Montreal." He stopped at the edge of the car. "When you next go to find work, I suggest you don't apply for any positions as a cartographer's assistant."

"Don't mock me!" She followed him to the gap. "If you hadn't stolen my ticket, I wouldn't be here in the first place."

Whoever this girl was, she had quite the fire burning in her—not a prim trait, and unusual for someone who sounded like she was from across the pond. "What's this about me stealing your ticket?"

She narrowed her gaze into a cold scowl. "You stole it from my pocket when you offered to carry my steamer case at the train station."

With a laugh, he jumped the gap between the cars. "Miss, I have never seen you before in my life."

CHAPTER III

GRACIE STARED at the gap and at the man's outstretched hand, inviting her to join him on the other car. No matter what he claimed, he was undeniably the pickpocket from the Albany station. It didn't matter that he now wore work clothes covered in coal dust or that the silk cravat around his collar had been replaced with sweat stains. No amount of moonlight or shadow could lessen the handsomeness of his angular jaw, the straightness of his nose, or the whiteness of his teeth. She would recognize his face through a kaleidoscope just as she had recognized his accent even with a nasal nuance from the knock to his face.

"You've got some nerve." She jumped the gap behind him, refusing his hand. Landing, she tripped on the hem of her too-long dress. With a loud ripping sound, the fabric ripped in a steep split several inches up from the hem.

He raised a curious brow. Gracie thought that was worse than if he had laughed outright. Straightening her shoulders, she smoothed her skirt and did her best not to appear too upset by the long tear.

"What are you going to do with me?" she asked, rubbing her goose-fleshed arms as they crossed the length of the car. She told herself it was just cold from being on the train roof. It had nothing to do with feeling cornered and helpless.

"Stick you in the caboose. It's got a small stove, a bed, and a chair. You can warm up while I inform Vincenzio of the situation. He'll decide what to do with you, whether he's going to hand you over to the authorities or turn you loose."

The speed of his answer and the details of his plan suggested that this wasn't the first time he'd dealt with a stowaway. Well, it wasn't like this was her first time trying to talk her way out of a mess, either.

"I haven't caused any harm. Please, can you just let me go? I'll get off at the next stop and you'll never see me again." She fluttered her long eyelashes and ventured what she hoped was a demure smile.

"You bloodied my nose, so I wouldn't say you're entirely harmless. You owe me a clean shirt at least." He jumped the gap at the next car and didn't offer to assist her.

Indignation swept over Gracie. Her ruse to sway his devotion to duty hadn't worked. In matters of confrontation she preferred first, to seek out a tactical advantage; second, to run away if the odds were stacked against her; and third, negotiations. Surrender ranked last on her list—beneath a second attempt to run or fight. Disadvantaged by his bigger stature and the remote location, she would have to handle this situation out of order.

She resignedly crossed the gap. "I'd say a bloody nose is a fair trade for scaring me awake," she muttered to his back. He might have the upper hand over her now, but that didn't mean she had to be happy about it.

He glanced at her over his shoulder, eyes narrowed. She reckoned she might have said that louder than she'd intended. He turned forward again, jaw clenched.

"Speaking of scaring things awake—you should step lightly so you don't disturb the animals."

"Of course," she said. "Because pigs need their beauty sleep before they're slaughtered."

"That would be true if we had any pigs, but we don't. Instead we have lions and tigers, and they're definitely persnickety about noise."

"Tigers?"

He scoffed. "Maybe you really did get on the wrong train. Didn't you notice the paintings on the side? This is the train of Vincenzio's Circus Troupe & Menagerie."

A circus train! Of all the trains she could have boarded tonight, it seemed that she made a poor choice. Even in the dark, she should have realized this wasn't a meatpacking train headed to the slaughterhouses in Cleveland. Despite the many livestock cars, it hadn't smelled foul enough.

Trying to avoid disturbing the circus animals, Gracie attempted to tiptoe, but it made the blisters on her feet hurt. So she switched to a half shuffling, limping sort of gait.

"What are you doing?" His tone marked the statement as an accusation more than a question.

"Sorry," she mumbled, walking normally. Truth be told, though, the thought of the animals beneath her stampeding and trampling everything underfoot suited her mood. Everything up to this point had been miserable. Why should the remainder of this evening be anything less than brutal?

She followed him all the way to the rear of the train. He spoke openly about the circus's last performance in Albany and the train's departure this evening, but he would not admit that he'd met her at the station. Her resentment grew. She *knew* it was him.

What were the odds of there having been another gentleman at the same train station with the same handsome eyes, flirtatious smile, and lilting accent?

She hated that she still found his features attractive while wanting to despise him. Perhaps if Mrs. Levenson had not spent so much time ingraining in Gracie and the other girls the importance of having a male figure to provide for their safety, she wouldn't have trusted him so easily at the station. And if Gracie had not helped herself to Mrs. Levenson's secret stash of romantic dime novels, she wouldn't have this ridiculous sentiment that a young man's physical attractiveness alone qualified him to take care of a young lady. At least she knew better now. Men, whether as handsome as the gentleman from the train station or as course as the foreman, were only to be trusted at arms' length.

CHAPTER IV

G RACIE'S BODY ached the next morning like she'd slept on a pile of bricks instead of the pull-down cot in the back of the caboose.

Flattening her cheek against the train window, she watched lamp-posts and streets, crowded with carriages and horse-pulled trolleys, rush by. People on the platform tucked their chins to their collars against the sudden gust of wind and grabbed for their hats as the train chugged through the station.

The sign hanging over the platform read "Montreal."

Canada. The crewman who had found her had said Rutland, Vermont, was the next town. Whoever was in charge must have decided not to put her off. Montreal, Quebec. French-speaking Quebec. Now she regretted not having a single French lesson since her family died, eight years ago.

The train, screaming like a boiling tea kettle, crawled to a stop on a stretch of track next to a large dirt lot. Gracie turned from the window and tried the handle of the caboose door. Still locked.

She fought the urge to start pacing like one of the caged circus animals.

There was no other door or roof hatch. Because the caboose served as a breakroom and office for the crew, its furnishings were sparse. Besides the cot, there was a small desk, a stove with a pot full of stale coffee, and a three-legged stool.

She wrapped her arms around her knotting stomach and flopped back onto the cot.

With stiff fingers, she undid the top few buttons on her dress, reached into the front of her corset, and pulled out a worn postcard. Thank goodness she'd not had it in her pocket yesterday, with her ticket. She gazed at the picturesque view of Manhattan. Crowded city streets pushed their way to a harbor full of sailing ships. The recently completed Brooklyn Bridge spanned the background. White cracks where the brick-red ink had flaked off the cream paper added extra streets to the dense cityscape. Mr. Levenson's sloppy cursive filled the space for the recipient's address: St. Patrick's Orphan Asylum, New York City, NY.

The day she left the orphanage, he'd given her the postcard to mail back after she'd found her family. There was no stamp on the postcard—his final snub, an assertion that she'd never succeed.

With her luck so far, she was beginning to think he might be right.

She refolded her postcard and let her thoughts wander down the worn path they'd been traveling since she'd drifted asleep late last night. Many of the details of the evening two nights ago were sharpened in her memory, while other parts had blurred and dissolved.

The factory foreman had locked the office door. At some point she must have unlocked it to get out, but for the life of her she couldn't remember where she'd found the key. Had she filched it out of his pocket, picked it up off the floor, or removed it from a wall hook?

She knew with certainty that the room had been dark when she'd fled for the train station because every time she closed her eyes, the darkness called her to go back to the room and to relive the nightmare again.

After about an hour, the creaking of the caboose's floorboards drew her attention to the rear door.

The handle jiggled, and a moment later the door slammed open to reveal a man with a barrel waist and grizzled hair. He wore a checkerboard vest with a long-sleeved white shirt and charcoal gray pants.

"So, you're the stowaway everyone's talking about," he said.

Gracie jumped to her feet and clumsily worked to button her bodice to her throat, and then rake the loose curls of her brunette hair into a bun. "It's polite to knock," she scolded. She shoved her postcard into her right pocket.

The heavy-set man stared at her with narrowed eyes. "This is my circus, my train, and I'll do whatever I please."

She dipped a curtsy, causing her hasty bun to untwist and topple from her head. *Mind your tongue, Gracie. If you're smart about this, he might let you off easy.* "My apologies. I didn't realize you were in charge."

The stern lines on his forehead smoothed. "You can call me Vincenzio."

She dropped her gaze, something she knew Mr. Levenson had demanded whenever he was giving one of the orphans a stern talking to. "I'm very sorry for the trouble I've caused. I'd purchased a ticket to Rochester, but—"

"I don't care what your excuse is," he interrupted. He took a seat on the edge of the small desk. "We get runaways all the time—boys, usually. We toss them off at the next tree when we find them. Since you are a young woman though, it seemed more reasonable to wait until the next major town. I could hand you over to the authorities and not even lose a wink of sleep."

If he tried to hand her over to the authorities, she'd fight tooth and nail. Her life depended on it. Her heart beat quicker, but her voice betrayed no anxiety. "I would be most grateful if you didn't. I haven't caused any harm. Please, can you just let me go?"

Vincenzio folded his arms over his gut and shifted his weight, causing the desk to groan. "The problem is, you crossed the border on my train. If you get into trouble later, they'll hold me responsible."

"If you let me go, I'll find work shortly, I'll apply for papers, and I won't ever mention I came here on your train. I promise I won't cause further trouble."

That was a lie. Gracie would stay hidden until dusk and then sneak aboard a different train heading to Chicago. Next time she'd be more careful not to get caught.

"You were caught on the roof of my train; that makes you a troublemaker. But, if you're interested in work, it just so happens I have a position open—one which I think you'd be well suited for."

His eyes slid over her a second time.

"What do you have in mind?" She'd rather be locked in a jail cell than lose her virtue to anyone, but especially to a such a slovenly pig.

"You'll be the new assistant for my magician, and it's so easy a monkey could do it. But the costume looks much nicer on a young woman—and it helps that you're about the same size as our last girl." Vincenzio peeled himself from the desk. "I'll pay you a dollar a week. You'll have Katherine's old room, and you'll eat meals with the performers in the pie car. So, what do you say? You want the job, or should I send for the police?" He glared at her with leveled eyebrows, his mouth pressed in a firm line.

This isn't a choice, it's blackmail. Did he somehow know what she'd done? News of the foreman's murder could already be in today's paper. Perhaps she should be grateful she was found by someone selfish enough to turn a blind eye to her crime.

"Can you tell me if the circus will stop in Chicago at any point?" she asked.

"We'll be spending a few days here in Montreal while the locomotive has its boiler washed out, then we'll head west. We perform in every major city from here to Omaha, Chicago included."

Gracie sucked in her cheeks and chewed on the sides. Any job with the circus had to be better than going to jail or working sixty hours a week in another factory. And not only was Vincenzio going to house and feed her, he was giving her a salary. Having some money saved up before she reached Chicago *would* make it easier to find her aunt and uncle.

She extended her hand out to Vincenzio. "I'll do it."

"Wonderful." He shook her hand. Oddly, rather than letting go of her hand, his grip slid up and tightened around her wrist. "Come with me. It's time for you to get to work." He half-dragged her out of the caboose behind him.

The moment she stepped down from the rear porch of the caboose, the heavy smell of hot engine oil and unwashed bodies assaulted her. Men, with broad, square shoulders tossed bundles of canvas down and pounded tent stakes into the ground with sledgehammers. The red and white striped tents of the canvas city were going up all around the dirt lot. Six elephants formed a brigade to pass support poles from the flatcars to the workers. Other workers assembled a corral for the camels and horses. Gracie swore she could already smell the candy apple glaze in the sweetshop frying pans.

Her stomach complained and her mouth tasted worse than pig slop. Her last meal had been cold coffee and stale bread. But breakfast would have to wait. Vincenzio kept a firm hold on her wrist.

Amidst all this busy activity, it'd be easy enough to slip away.

If she did manage to shake him off, then what? Her lack of a reference letter from the poultry factory would surely come up at her next job interview—here or in the States. If Vincenzio was willing to add her onto his books, and feed her . . . well, she ought to at least stay until they reached Chicago.

She pulled her wrist out of his grip, which he acknowledged with a sideways glance. Clutching her skirt, Gracie stayed close to Vincenzio's side, doing her best to not get in anyone's way. Performers in jumpsuits, sequined headdresses, and short ruffled skirts circled around the mushrooming tents like fairies playing tag. A handful of clowns grabbed buckets of water and flour paste to begin wallpapering the town with flyers.

Vincenzio's Circus Troupe & Menagerie. Lions from the wilds of Africa, camels from Egypt, and crocodiles from the Amazon river. Trapeze artists performing death-defying stunts. Wolfman & the Bearded Lady.

Nothing about a magician, she noticed. Maybe the magician was half-rate. So easy a monkey could do it, right?

"There's someone you need to meet," Vincenzio said, guiding her to a large canvas mountain in the center of the lot.

The tallest points of the big top were the twin peaks above the tightrope towers. Trapeze ropes, strung like a ship's rigging lines, occupied the right ring. Wood planks were set up for the spectators in tiered rows on both sides.

A large crowd of performers was already gathered for morning rehearsal. The dog trainer, in his tights and glorious teal cape, had his nine terriers bounding rambunctiously around his legs. The aerial artists climbed up and slid down the ropes, like spiders spinning red silk. They paused in their activities as soon as Vincenzio and Gracie entered. The low buzz of their hushed voices was drowned by the deep thuds of her pounding heart.

The anonymous gazes of the circus performers brushed her skin as Vincenzio escorted her to the center ring. Drifting fumes from the kerosene lights mingled with the wet smell of the straw floor.

Vincenzio stopped in the center ring and turned to her. "What did you say your name was?"

"Gracie Hart," she said, immediately regretting she'd not told him a lie.

"All right then, Miss Hart, allow me to introduce you to your partner." Vincenzio cupped his hands to his mouth and shouted to a young man holding an anchor rigging line. "Jack! Get over here!"

The young man didn't even turn at the mention of his name. He was tall and broad-shouldered and she couldn't help but notice how his biceps strained against his rolled-up sleeves as he hoisted a counterweight high into the air. His dark hair, that indiscriminate color between brown and black, was short on the sides and slightly mussed on the top. "Sheeze! I'm busy, can it wait?"

That accent . . .

"Let the other stagehands handle that. You've got a performance to get ready for tomorrow."

"Cripes," he muttered, turning his attention fully away from the rope.

The moment his gaze met hers, Gracie's stomach twisted itself into a string of sausage links.

Not the pickpocket again!

The young man's dark eyebrows jumped high on his forehead. "What's she still doing here?"

"Jack, I'd like you to meet your new assistant."

Jack's jaw went slack along with his grip. The rope slid through his hands and the pulleys, hissing like an angry viper. Before the counterweight crashed to the ground, he caught the line with a yelp—and a strong French swear word.

Jack handed the rope to another stagehand before blowing air across his palms.

Gracie arched a brow. First stealing, and now swearing (even if it was in French) in front of a young woman—was there no end to his vulgar ways?

He turned to Vincenzio "What's the meaning of this?"

Dread and confusion filled her. "*You're* the magician? I thought you were one of the train crew." She wondered if he styled his hair or if it he let his nights on the windy train roof do it for him.

Jack glanced at her before returning his pointed stare to Vincenzio. "You can't be serious. You really want *her* to be Katherine's replacement?"

"That's right."

"She's unsuitable for the stage. I've seen stray dogs with better manners!"

Vincenzio scratched the back of his neck and twirled the tufts of hair over his ears, looking a bit lost. "She'll have to do. No one else is willing to take the position. You've already had a week off to sort things out. People want to see every act, and it's my job to give them what they want. I'm not changing my mind." Vincenzio illustrated his authority by pounding his fist into his palm like a gavel at a court hearing.

Jack unrolled his sleeves and drew his shoulders back. "Katherine's role as my assistant entailed a lot more than putting on a costume and smiling for the crowd. She guided the audience's attention and directed them to the illusion." He gestured to the empty stands and pointed at Gracie. "How is this guttersnipe supposed to distract the audience when she doesn't have allure? By making them count her ribs? She's too skinny—almost sickly."

Gracie's cheeks prickled and she knew that a splotchy blush had bloomed on her face, neck, and chest, as it always did when she was upset. "You insult and judge me based on my figure. Yet yesterday, you were parading around the station in your fancy suit, picking pockets!"

Jack threw his arms up. "Flaming galahs, what are you on about? Why would I steal a train ticket when I work for a traveling circus?"

"Maybe you just wanted the leftover change in my pocket and the ticket was in the way?"

His dark eyes scanned her from head to toe, his gaze lingering on the tear near the hem of her dress. "More likely I'd have found a big hole."

She pointed an accusing finger at him. "If there's a hole in my pocket, then it can't be bigger than the one in your heart."

At this, Jack's face went stark, as though she'd blown out his inner candle and cut him to the quick with the expertise of a cook fileting a fish.

Vincenzio's lips curled upward slightly. He stepped between them, folding her finger back into her palm and pushing her arm down. "Is it possible you might be mistaking Jack for—"

Jack coughed loudly, cutting Vincenzio off. It was impossible to miss the arrows flying from Jack's eyes—sharp points looking for a target. Surprisingly, they found their mark between Vincenzio's eyes and not hers.

Vincenzio cleared his throat. "Is it possible you might be mistaking Jack for *someone else?*" he said, matching stares with Jack, figuratively raising the pot another nickel.

"I doubt it." There was no mistake, or rather, the chance she'd admit she was mistaken was about as low as that of finding her mother's lost rosewood trunk, with her aunt's address still inside, after all these years. With a sigh, Vincenzio shoved one hand deep in his pocket and hooked her around the shoulders with the other. She leaned away, but he seemed determined to breathe right down her neck. "Here's how I see things: It doesn't matter what happened or who's at fault because you've got a ride to Chicago on my train, so you've no use for a day-old ticket. However, that means you and Jack need to have the magic act and the knife act ready for tomorrow's performance."

A huge stone dropped in her stomach. She pushed Vincenzio's arm off her shoulder.

"A knife act? I thought you said the job was for the magician's assistant."

Jack bristled. He had a hundred-man firing squad behind his brown eyes, and all their muskets were fixed on Vincenzio. "You didn't tell her?"

She looked to Vincenzio and then back to Jack. "Tell me what?"

Jack swallowed, and his confident expression turned repentant. "Katherine's role as my assistant was part of a two-hat gig." He avoided looking at her. "She was my assistant during the magic show, and my target girl for the knife act."

Gracie no longer wondered whether it had been an oversight that Vincenzio had kept her on his train all night or that he'd not let her leave his sight since he unlocked the caboose door. Vincenzio took her hand and patted it. "Not to worry my dear. Except for his last show, Jack has had a perfect knife-throwing record. But if you'd like to reconsider, I can have him escort you to the police station since he won't be busy getting ready for the show." Vincenzio turned to her with a leer that spread from cheek to cheek. "The choice is yours."

CHAPTER V

GRACIE'S GAZE shifted between Jack, Vincenzio, and the tent flaps leading out of the big top. She knew better than to think she'd get far making a run for it, which was why she'd act like a patsy for now and then slip out when the crowds arrived. Vincenzio's troupe wouldn't be able to search for her because they'd be too busy with the show. She might even wait a day or two to lower their suspicion that she'd run off when she got the chance.

"I'd rather work than go to jail," she said. In her head, the decision sounded more like, *I think my odds are better in front of your knife board than in front of a jury. And they'll probably feed me better at a circus than in a prison.* Her stomach rumbled, settling the deal.

Vincenzio clapped his hands. "Perfect. I'll tell the ticket vendors to let people know they can expect to see your acts tomorrow."

The wrinkles on Jack's chin deepened. "She needs a costume. The acts will look cheap if we can't even dress our performers."

"I'll tell Miriam to start on that right now. It'll be ready by tomorrow."

Jack raised his voice, and his accent almost slipped into a drawl. "It needs to be done sooner so we have time to rehearse."

"You let me worry about that. Keep an eye on her so she doesn't run off."

Vincenzio strode away from the big top with his hands in his pockets, like he might start whistling a tune.

Jack's gaze turned from the tent flaps Vincenzio had left through to a point just behind her. He approached, knocking her shoulder with his as he passed, and not in an accidental sort of way.

She patted her right dress pocket, making sure her postcard was still there, before turning to follow him. "Thief, train crewman, stagehand, magician, and knife thrower. Is there anything you don't do here?"

"I don't do actual magic, which is what we'll need to get you ready in time for tomorrow night."

His skepticism of her abilities and appearance stung and fueled her feelings of inadequacy. Jack was no different than the stuffy shop owners who had made her knock at the back door for an order pick up, instead of the front.

Gracie stiffened her upper lip and took a few deep breaths. Her worth was more than the value of the clothes she wore. Also, Vincenzio was the person who would be paying her salary, so only his opinion mattered.

"Where will we be rehearsing?" she asked.

"We can't rehearse the knife act until your costume is ready, so I guess we'll have to start with the magic act." He turned toward the side exit. "Follow me."

Jack led Gracie to the lineup of circus wagons, some featuring gold leaf animal carvings and whitewashed wagon spoke wheels. Gracie easily picked out Jack's prop wagon—the painting of his caricature on the side was a bit of a giveaway.

Along the inside wall of the wagon stood an oak trunk and a cherry dresser with juggling pins, a mini unicycle, and a collection of spinning plates all stacked haphazardly on top. Jack's magic act props created a cluttered maze on the floor, but Gracie's attention was drawn to the tall, rectangular shape, draped in black velvet, which stood towering in the middle of the room.

"Sorry it's a bit of a mess in here," Jack said, clearing a small space by picking up a knotted length of scarves. "The police took me into custody after the accident, and the stagehands just shoved everything in here. It's been a week, but I haven't had a chance to clean up yet."

He continued to apologize, picking up various items around the room and explaining what each was used for, but his voice sounded like it was coming from far away. Gracie couldn't take her eyes off the black cover.

The image, so similar to the setup in the foreman's office on the night of his death, made Gracie's stomach clench and twist. She clung to the rear door of the wagon as the nightmare replayed.

The foreman had forced Gracie to work through dinner. She'd swept the floor for the better part of an hour before he called her into his office.

When Gracie entered the office, she immediately noticed that the desk had been pushed to the side wall, and that some sort of easel, draped in a heavy black curtain, had been put in its place.

The foreman had started as usual—outlining Gracie's faults and pressing buttons on his adding machine to determine the deductions to her weekly wages. Based on his current calculations, her wages for the week wouldn't be enough to cover the company housing and food expenses. Further, her default on this week's payment gave him the legal justification to demand another seven dollars as a security deposit for next week.

She'd argued the impossibility of coming up with so much money in so little time.

That's when he'd removed the black covering on the easel to reveal a camera tripod and a thick folder of his "French postcards."

One dollar per photo.

Things had escalated quickly after she'd refused his offer. Apparently she'd been mistaken to think he was giving her a choice in the matter. She got up to leave and found that the door was locked. Frantically, she turned back to the desk for the key, but only found a letter opener. He ripped her away from the drawer and somehow she knocked over the tripod. Swearing he'd cut the price of the broken camera from her skin, he chased her around the room. She fell, entangled with him and the letter opener.

She wouldn't have thought such a small thing could kill a man, but he didn't get up after she crawled out from beneath him. He stayed on the floor, gasping like a fish out of water, the letter opener sunk to the handle in his neck. "Are you listening? Miss Hart?"

Gracie jumped, surprised to see Jack, and not the foreman, standing beside the large, tarped object.

She shook her head. "No, sorry, I wasn't. Can you say it again?"

Jack sighed. "I said this is the vanishing closet for the magic act. For the performance, the prop handlers will unload it and bring it out into the ring. But since they're busy setting up the other tents, you can pretend we're already there."

"Yes, right. Of course." She took several deep breaths, willing her pulse to slow down. She'd been in a bad situation, but she'd made it out alive. The foreman hadn't.

As Jack tugged on the covering, the fabric slid off the cabinet like falling water.

The magic closet looked like a grandfather clock someone had steamrolled flat then reassembled inside out. Cold-pressed designs of clock faces, watch parts, keys, locks, and cogwheels, overlapped one another. The intricate detail of the etchings on the closet rivaled that of the north apse of Westminster Abbey back in London.

That trip to London with her family had been the summer right before they'd boarded the steamship to go visit her aunt and uncle . . .

Jack began to fold the covering for his magic closet, but stopped after a few seconds. "Are you ill?"

"Pardon?" His comment about her health made her realize that she had let her thoughts drift too far. Again. "Oh, I'm fine." The only weakness she ever planned on admitting to him was hunger.

He raised a brow in disbelief and then switched it for a knowing smile. "Oh, I see what's wrong. You're claustrophobic, aren't you?"

"What?" She'd half expected him to say he'd seen a newspaper with her name in the "wanted" section.

"It means you're afraid of small spaces."

"I am not scared of your box, it's just—" She thought about telling him a lie, except considering he knew such a fancy word like "closet-fobic," she suspected he'd see through her half-brained explanation.

"It's just what?"

"Nothing," she replied. While the angels had graced Jack with good-looks and brains, they had compensated with arrogance. Jack was obviously flaunting his superior education with his extensive vocabulary—who really was the one without manners?

She stepped deeper into the wagon and circled the box, inspecting the sides. "How does this magic vanishing trick work, exactly?"

"I'll lock you inside and chant a few 'magic' words. When I open the door the second time, it will appear to the audience as though you've vanished. To reverse the illusion, I repeat the words backwards and open the door a third time to present you to the audience."

She picked up the velvet covering, rubbing it between her fingers. Up close, she could see it had patterns of stars and crescent moons pressed into the fibers. "I can't imagine where Vincenzio would have gotten such a nice prop."

"Actually, everything in here is mine."

If Jack came from a background of money and fancy furniture, what was he doing performing as a traveling magician and pickpocketing unescorted young women at train stations? She had one theory, at least.

"You must be a poor gambler. It would make perfect sense—why you resort to petty thieving. You *do* seem like the overconfident type who would drive himself to ruin just to continue satisfying his own ego."

He snatched the covering from her. "You couldn't be more wrong."

He kept saying that, yet she'd not seen anything that suggested otherwise.

Jack recited the entire script for the magic act and their cues and then finally opened the closet door and invited her to step inside. Three wooden walls faced her, the scent of cedar nose-scrunchingly strong. She knocked on the back panel and had to rub the ache out of her knuckles afterward.

"Where's the secret door? I slip out the back and then what?" Gracie investigated the walls, sticking her fingernail into every crack.

"That's not how it works," he said, pulling her hand away. "You won't be leaving the closet. I have to set the device, and then after I close the door, there's a panel that swings in front, hiding you so that it looks like you disappeared when you haven't gone anywhere." He opened the closet door and gestured inside. "If you're ready, we can practice once."

That was the trick? No wonder she only needed to practice it once.

"Go ahead, make me disappear."

He nodded. "Stand there at the back of the closet, and whatever you do, don't leave that spot unless you see me open the door. Understand?"

She rolled her eyes. "Maybe you should draw me a picture?" Still, she wished he'd be more explicit in explaining the mechanics of the box. She had a knack for making bad situations worse and could see no reason why Jack's magic box would be an exception. Where was this panel that was going to move in front of her, and how could she be sure she wasn't going to be in the way even if she did as he said and stood there, doing nothing? For once, she wanted to prove she was a capable young lady instead of a burden on society.

She pressed her back against the wall as Jack shut the door.

Blackness darker than coal enveloped her and she could no longer sense where her nose was without touching it. Something solid moved in front of her—the hidden door for the secret compartment. The air in Jack's box pressed in on her, thickening in her chest. Her lungs turned to hard rocks in her ribs, threatening to drag her deeper into the darkness if she took a single breath. She imagined this was exactly how it felt to be buried alive in a nailed-shut coffin.

The darkness made it impossible to judge time. Seconds or minutes might have gone by. Again and again, she considered calling out for Jack, but kept her mouth clamped shut. This was supposed to be the easy part.

Finally, the whirring of parts in Jack's box ceased, and the panel slid to the side with a soft thump. A sliver of light appeared at the left side of the box, followed by Jack's firm hand pulling her toward him. She strained to identify the familiar shapes and colors of the props in the back of the wagon as her eyes adjusted to the light.

"How'd it go?" He continued to hold her hand, a bit tight for her comfort.

Unable to think of the appropriate word to describe the whole experience, she settled for something inferior. "Suffocating, but not unbearable."

"Did it seem like you were in there very long?"

"I don't suppose so." Even if it had felt like a long while—a terrifyingly long while—she'd wait as long as it took. Hiding in a box and smiling to an audience beat plucking feathers off dead chickens back at the poultry factory, and it certainly beat hanging from a noose.

He sucked in his cheeks, an expression Gracie recalled Mr. Levenson wearing whenever he was upset about something. "Did you notice if anything unusual happened before I opened the door?" Jack released her hand.

Why all the questions? Did the trick not work?

"Well—" she twirled the ends of her hair around her finger. Jack's head was tipped to the side with curiosity, as if he was actually interested in what she had to say.

The lie rolled smoothly off her tongue, so preposterous she knew it'd give his straight-forward intellect a rise. "Right before you opened the door, there was this sorceress who appeared and told me there was a magic sword hidden in the bottom of the lake, and that if I found it, she'd make me queen of the Britons."

Gracie thought injecting herself into the story of King Arthur was a good farce, but instead of laughing, Jack's mouth turned into a straight line and his face paled. She laughed dryly, Jack eventually joining her chortle with a bit too much gusto. Guess he wasn't the joking sort.

"The closet—it's not really magic, is it?"

His tense, serious expression cracked and he laughed, sincerely this time. "Flaming galahs! What are you on about? There's no such thing as magic, and I just showed you how the trick works." His laugh died down. "Be serious now. Did you notice anything that felt out of place before I opened the door?"

Gracie marveled that he didn't have more wrinkles on his forehead from how quickly he switched from mirth to austerity. She bet if he ate something, it'd fix that—people were always grumpier when they were hungry. Or at least she was. "How would I know if something was off if this is the first time you've locked me in there?"

He closed the closet door. Then, with almost too much deliberation, he flexed his hand open and closed as though soothing a cramp in his wrist. "Yes, I guess you're correct in this case. Just remember to smile when you walk out during the performance."

"Is your hand all right?"

He tugged his jacket sleeve down. "It's nothing."

"You burned it on the rope earlier, didn't you? Does it still hurt?"

"My hands are fine." He flashed both palms to her. They lacked a shiny burn or even a red welt. "I just have to keep my muscles loose. You know, so my knife throwing stays the same."

Gracie's gaze dropped. "Yes, that makes sense." When she looked up, Jack had begun covering the closet.

"You should go see if Miriam has finished your costume while I clean up here," he said, dismissively. "I'll meet you in the big top in a half hour so we can rehearse the knife act."

With a small nod, she stepped out of the back of the wagon.

"Wait," Jack called. "If anyone ever asks about the secret of the closet, tell them I hypnotize you during each performance and you don't remember. It's important a magician never reveal his tricks. If the illusion is ruined, we'll need a new act. And I know Vincenzio would love a show where I pretend I'm King Solomon and cut you in two . . . Of course, I've never done it before, but I imagine it wouldn't be too hard to figure out."

He grinned wickedly, the sides of his mouth raised at uneven heights. That unsettling smile was all it took to guarantee her silence.

CHAPTER VI

Jack waited a long three minutes after she left before rolling up his sleeve cuff. On the back of his hand and all the way up his forearm, he had purple and black rosette bruises as numerous as the spots on a leopard's pelt. The secret of a good illusionist was to play off the predictable nature of people, to train their eyes to follow the distractions and overlook the deceptions. Gracie had been looking for a burn on his palm, and so all she'd seen was that he didn't have one. Never mind his darkened veins and swollen arteries.

Holding his wrist tightly, he rubbed the bruises until they disappeared. At least his *real* secret was still safe. Gracie hadn't remembered a thing. But how long could he keep it that way? How long until she ended up like Katherine?

CHAPTER VII

SINCE GRACIE had no idea where to find the seamstress, she asked around for Miriam and was informed that she could find her with Vincenzio in his stateroom in the second-to-last train car. A gentleman on his way out of the car, bald as a stone, introduced himself as Vincenzio's bookkeeper. "They're just finishing up in there," he said.

"Who is?"

"Vincenzio, Richard, and Miriam." Noting her blank stare, he continued, "Richard is our ringmaster and Miriam takes care of all the costumes."

Gracie nodded and then climbed the steps onto the train car and knocked on the door.

"Come in," Vincenzio said.

The room smelled like burned toast and cigar smoke. The three circus heads were gathered around a grass-green card table. Vincenzio sat next to a wiry woman with stooped shoulders and straw-pale hair. Across from him was a man with a broad, golden face, tawny hair, and a pronounced nose—Richard, by her estimation.

A pair of women's high-heeled shoes sat in the middle of the table. The amber jewels adorning them sparkled and reflected little golden suns onto the table.

Vincenzio gestured to the woman. "Miss Hart, this is Miriam, my seamstress. She's going to take care of your costume."

With languid grace, Miriam stood and swept the golden shoes under one arm. "This way, *s'il vous plaît*." She pressed a bony hand into Gracie's back and ushered her from the train car.

Miriam seemed content to walk in silence to the dressing tent, but Gracie wasn't about to miss an opportunity to learn a bit more about the trouble she'd gotten herself into.

"What happened to Katherine? Why couldn't Vincenzio find anyone else for this position?" Gracie didn't believe that her ability to fit in Katherine's costume without splitting the seams was Vincenzio's primary concern when he'd offered her the job any more than she believed that justice was blind, or that life was fair.

Miriam's lips tightened. "I suppose it's better for me to tell you than for you to hear it from someone else." She leaned in closer. "For the first feat of the knife act, Jack put the blade between *Kathereene's* eyes." The seamstress pronounced the girl's name like it was a French wine or an exotic appetizer.

Gracie wilted in her boots. Jack's last toss hadn't maimed his assistant, it'd outright killed her. "It was an accident though, right?"

Miriam's eyes darted from side to side, searching the shadows and sliding over the scenery of canvas tents, horse corrals, and sunbaked men. "The risk of a bad toss comes with the job, but everyone else knows something was going on between them."

"Like a tryst?"

Miriam halted mid stride, so sharply it made the ruffled tiers of her dress's layered bustle bounce up and fan out, similar to a cat bristling its tail. The seamstress turned to Gracie with a much softer expression. "I'm sure you are only curious and did not mean to be disrespectful, so I will warn you that many here do not feel a week is a long enough mourning period and to not repeat what I tell you."

Heat pooled in Gracie's cheeks. The moment the words had left her mouth she'd wished she could pull them back in. It was rude to indulge in gossip, especially outside the bonds of friendship. One rehearsal with Jack had plainly not yet earned Gracie the right to be "in the know." She muttered, "I'm sorry."

Miriam resumed walking, at a slower pace. "It's true Katherine had many admirers, but this was something different. In the last month Katherine had stopped eating meals with everyone else and was jumping at shadows. There were whispers she had secret plans to quit the circus and catch a train to the South. It was Jack who convinced her to wait until the circus reached New York. 'More opportunities to start a new life in a big city,' he'd said. She died the next show."

Gracie tucked her arm to her side to hide the bloodstain on the sleeve. "Didn't the police do an investigation? I'm sure if they knew all the circumstances, they'd realize it was an honest mistake."

"They did. He proved to the police that it was not his fault because Katherine had just bought new shoes. If she'd worn her old, shorter shoes, his knife would have missed."

The seamstress's gaze dropped to the shoes under her arm, which told Gracie all she needed to know—those were the shoes Katherine had died in.

"So, it really was an accident then?"

Miriam leaned in. "No one will ever know for sure, but I will tell you this last thing: the satin on her old pair of shoes was smooth and shiny, the soles barely scuffed. Katherine bought those new shoes with her own money, when it has always been my charge to provide her with new shoes when her old ones wear out. Why would she buy new performance shoes if she intended to leave the circus?"

They arrived at the dressing tent. Rugs and trunks were strewn over the floor, and clothing articles were draped on numerous coat and hat racks. Miriam pulled back the tent flap and handed the shoes to Gracie. "Here, let's see if they fit."

THE shivers of doubt Gracie had fended off earlier made their first impact on her resolve when she saw her costume. All Miriam gave her was a pair of stockings, something resembling a ruffled child's diaper, and a blue satin corset.

Cleaned and pressed, the satin looked as though no human hand had ever touched it. Could this be the outfit Katherine had died in?

Miriam hovered over Gracie's shoulder, her sharp eyes squeezing Gracie's chest with her invisible tailor's tape. The lines beside her mouth deepened when Gracie continued to poke at the costume. "The costume is very nice, yes?" Miriam took the garment back and loosened the lacing cords.

Sure, if the new height of fashion includes wearing your bloomers in public.

Following Miriam's instructions to undress down to her corset and underwear, Gracie stepped behind the fanfold divider. Reaching in her pocket to check on her postcard, her fingers sunk into something gritty and thick.

Black soot dripped through her fingers in thick clumps as she removed her hand.

"My goodness!" Gracie searched the small changing area for somewhere to dispose of the muck besides shoving it back into her pocket.

"Do you need help dressing?" Miriam invited herself behind the divider before Gracie could answer.

Gracie turned to Miriam, trailing soot in one hand and holding the costume in the other.

"Quel Malheur!" Miriam grabbed the costume and clutched it to her chest. "What is that?"

"I don't know." If Gracie had to guess, she'd bet Jack dumped it in her pocket with one of his fancy magician hand tricks. This must be his idea of punishing her for being distracted when he'd been explaining how his tricks worked.

"Do not move an inch!" Miriam said, with a *tsk* of her tongue. "I will be back with a bath."

Miriam returned shortly with a large, galvanized scullery bucket, a smaller bucket, and a pail of water. "Strip and wash. When you are clean, I will help you dress."

Gracie dumped the soot into the small bucket and then dug in her pocket for the postcard. She found it in her other pocket, the *left* one, clean and free of soot. Thank goodness. She must not remember having moved it—likely because she'd hardly had a bite to eat in the last thirty-six hours.

She set the postcard off to the side where it wouldn't get wet while she bathed, but picked it right back up. On the front of the picture there was a black smudge across the cityscape.

More soot? She tried to wipe it away with her thumb and realized the black smudge was not soot but ink letters.

She unfolded the postcard. The word "KNOSSOS" spanned the picture in a bold, heavy hand.

She scraped the ink with her nail, holding back tears. She couldn't erase the message without damaging the postcard. Whatever "Knossos" meant, she didn't think it was a good thing. It was probably another one of Jack's fancy words meant to insult her, like how he'd pointed out her fear of small spaces.

She traced the letters, committing them to memory, before folding the postcard and tucking it away in the pocket of her skirt. Having grown up as a waif, she'd been well schooled in the saying: Sticks and stones may break my bones, but words can never hurt me.

She knew the rhyme wasn't true. Cruel words hurt a lot, even if she didn't necessarily know what this one meant. The note almost made her miss being at the orphanage where differences were settled in the open with fists and force instead of this skullduggery.

She tucked the postcard into her dress's pocket for safe keeping.

Her feelings of anger hardened into resolve as she washed up. She may have spent the last eight years in an orphanage, but for the first nine years of her life, she'd had a governess and a proper education. She just needed some time to prove to Jack that she wasn't some floozy lacking decorum, manners, or any education. She had learned to read, and if she could get her hands on a dictionary, she'd look up the word herself.

Though Gracie's last real bath was just before she'd left the orphanage for the poultry factory, she still couldn't believe how dirty the water was after she was done. Neither could Miriam, who loudly voiced her disgust as she carried the tub away to dump it.

Dressed in the costume, Gracie stepped out from the divider and faced the standing mirror, her lips pressed in a stern line.

The black silk stockings called too much attention to her lean physique. Should a tribe of cannibals invade the canvas tent at this moment and have nothing to feast on except her thighs, they would starve to death. At least they were dark colored so she didn't feel entirely naked.

She did, however, love the feel of the royal blue satin curving around her waist—her own chameleon camouflage amongst the other colorful circus characters.

"You will need some *soufflés*. Katherine was bigger up top." The seamstress approached, holding two miniature pillows, flat like pancakes.

36

Turning her back to Miriam, Gracie inserted the cushions down the front of her corset. When she turned back around, Miriam handed her a second pair. "In France, these would not be necessary. French men focus on the *rondeur*. They prefer women with large hips to bear their children."

Gracie didn't have those either. "How many children do you have?" Gracie hoped some friendly conversation would distract Miriam from realizing the trouble she was having getting the second pair of pads in place.

"I have three daughters. All are married now."

The results of the pads earned her Miriam's approving nod, and spared Gracie the humiliation of needing a third set.

Stealing another glance in the mirror, Gracie's breath caught. Every curve was perfect. The costume highlighted a thin waist and her chest rounded out nicely to match the swell of her hips. Was it a sin to like what she saw? She dismissed the feeling as mistaken pride because for once, she was wearing something clean, expensive-looking, and fitted.

Miriam hovered over her shoulder, a wry smile on her lips. *"Tu es magnifique."*

Gracie blushed at the compliment, but wondered if, maybe, there was some truth behind it. "Yes, thanks to *you*."

Katherine's golden, jeweled shoes completed the ensemble. In the slanted afternoon sunlight coming in through the cracks between the tied canvas panels, the shoes looked like they were made of liquid fire. *Beautiful. And deadly.*

It really was a shame Katherine had only worn them once. Any superstitious concerns Gracie had that the shoes would bring bad luck were buried in the same place as her belief in Father Christmas. Poor people couldn't afford to care who wore their clothes before them or why they were donated.

Miriam took Gracie's wrist and pulled her away from the mirror. "Come with me. You are ready to go rehearse in the tent now, yes?"

"Hold on. You want me to wear this outside?"

"Bien sûr." Of course.

"Is there something more I can wear over it on my way to the big top?" Even if she did warm up to the idea of wearing it for the performances, casually strolling around in it was an entirely different matter.

Rolling her eyes, Miriam handed Gracie a thin robe embroidered with cranes and oriental calligraphy. "I will need that back: it is not to keep." She then picked up Gracie's old dress and began to wad it in a tight ball.

"Wait, what are you doing with my dress?"

"This is garbage. I will find you another dress to replace it."

"No!" Gracie dashed forward, but Miriam pulled the dress away. "I just need the postcard from the pocket." Since she hadn't been able to reclaim her steamer case from the baggage area of the Albany train station, the worn, defaced card was now her only possession.

With pinched lips, Miriam fished out the postcard, holding it by two fingers as one might hold a dead rat's tail. "This is not garbage also?"

"No, it's important to me." Gracie tucked the card into her garter for lack of a better place to put it.

A breeze blew across the circus lot, pulling taut the brightly colored flags on top of the tents. Flittering tassels and scalloped drapes hanging from the sides made the tents look like wedding cakes.

Inside the big top, the chairs and tiered planks were empty. By tomorrow evening, they'd be filled for the performance. They approached Jack where he'd set up a large, red and white target board in the third ring. Splintered wooden scars indicated the spots where he'd thrown his knives countless times before. Not one of the clusters was wider than three fingers. Gracie clutched the folds of the robe and wished she could relax.

"Here we are," Miriam said, grasping the robe by the collar. The fabric recognized the touch of its master's hands and slid off of Gracie's shoulders.

She hadn't had this much skin exposed to any man since her birth. She crossed an arm over her chest and pulled the corset hem lower with the other, backing behind Miriam.

Tsk. Tsk. Tsk. Miriam clicked her tongue and then reached for the ruffled diaper and goosed her.

Gracie dropped her hands and rubbed her sore bum. This woman was way too comfortable touching her, or maybe it was the way of the French?

"Come find me in Katherine's room when you're done," Miriam said before heading back out.

Gracie walked toward Jack and the target board, arms stiff at her sides.

He looked her up and down once, his expression painfully neutral. She would have preferred him to laugh.

"That was Katherine's costume back when she was a soloist in the aerial ballet," he said. "It seems Miriam was able to alter it without trouble."

Gracie squeezed her arms to her sides. Miriam had promised to sew in the pads later, but until then, Gracie was certain they'd fall out the first time she bent over. The seamstress had also mentioned something about finding the misplaced hairpin and necklace that belonged with the costume. Gracie didn't mind the loss of the hairpin, but she wished she had something to hide the mottled blush that was spreading from her neck to her chest.

Jack stood beside the knife board, arms crossed over his chest. "Are you sure you want to do this?"

"You're going to throw knives at me, and I might die. I know that."

Jack cradled his head in the palm of his left hand. He massaged his temples before dragging his hands down the side of his face and resuming his hardened gaze. "Are you really so naïve?"

Gracie swallowed, pinching her lips together tightly.

It didn't surprise her that Vincenzio hadn't found Jack a replacement yet. Who'd want to be partnered with someone so condescending and rude? What was more shocking though, was how she found herself surprised each time his character disappointed her. She should know better already. Unfortunately for Jack, she'd put up with much worse. Mr. Levenson had broken no less than four yardsticks across her legs during the eight years she'd spent at the orphanage. And the foreman—well, Jack would have to do a lot more than insult and humiliate her if he wanted her to leave.

Jack's jaw tightened and relaxed, pausing before he broke the silence. "Yes, there's a risk that one of my tosses could go wrong and you'll die." He scratched and pulled his collar away from his neck. "What I meant though is—I doubt anyone has told you that Katherine also played hostess for Vincenzio's after-dinner gatherings for cigars and brandies. There's a reason she had her own room, and it's not from the quid Vincenzio paid her."

"I can take care of myself." Her voice trembled as she tried to sound flippant instead of intimidated. She hadn't realized it would be so difficult to keep her virtue safe.

"For your sake, I hope you're right." Both his voice and his eyes were hard. He left her side and went to grab a small jar of white paint and a narrow painter's brush from the side of the ring. Unscrewing the lid, he dabbed paint over a few of the smaller scars on the edges of the target board.

She pinched her lips together and took a deep breath. "If you really cared about me, you'd have let me go last night instead of locking me in the caboose. So please stop it with the concerned gentleman act, you're not fooling me."

"It's not an act, I assure you. I'm legitimately concerned that you're unqualified to assist me." He screwed the lid back on the jar, already finished with the touchups.

"Rubbish. You're trying to get me to resign before giving me a chance, but I think I know the real reason you're so eager to be rid of me." Gracie watched Jack's eyebrows rise, daring her to name it. Emboldened, she continued, "You're trying to save your own face. Why don't you just admit that *you're* scared to do the show because of the accident?"

Two steps brought him close enough for her to see the dark pores in his face where his stubble was growing in. "You think I'm scared?"

"I do."

"Fine then. I'll prove you wrong. Right now. Stand against the board."

Cursing her stupid mouth, Gracie stepped up to the knife board and planted herself in the shadow of Katherine's ghost.

CHAPTER VIII

JACK'S FINGERS traced the lip of his waistband, reaching for one of his knives. Only feeling the fabric of his pants and shirt, he realized, with some embarrassment, that he'd left his knives in his prop wagon. This was actually a good thing, since throwing in haste or with unsettled emotions increased the risk of a bad toss.

He swallowed the sticky saliva pooling in the back of his throat and then undid the top two buttons of his shirt. "Wait here for me. I've got to grab my knives and change into my costume."

Gracie shifted her weight to one side and crossed her arms. Her expression danced on the tightrope between confidence and trepidation. "Take your time, I'm not going anywhere."

Forcing his gaze from Gracie, Jack exited the big top and made his way to his room in the fourth-to-last train car. He grabbed one of his performance shirts from his trunk and shook the folds out.

Why does it matter if you're dressed for the part? She'll never see you as a gentleman. There's no such thing as a "second impression."

Or maybe there was. His first impression of Gracie had been that she was impulsive, naïve, and malnourished. All cleaned up now, he'd label her as passionate, ingenuous, petite, and even pretty. While she wasn't an equal match for him in education, her intellect seemed adequately developed—at the least, she was cultured enough to know the story of King Arthur. She'd also sniffed through his pretense of confidence with shocking precision.

Jack quickly changed shirts and replaced his cufflinks. He'd have to do better at masking his feelings around her before she unraveled something he didn't want her to see. In a traveling circus, there were few places private enough to hide a secret, and Jack had enough of them to be buried in.

He checked the knot of his cravat in the mirror, and then he went to his prop wagon to fetch his knives. For the hundredth time, Jack checked the edges for blood, but they were clean.

Why was he remotely entertaining the thought of training Gracie as his assistant? Young, determined—she belonged in a classroom with a strict nun, in a dress store ringing up customers, or ironing bedsheets as a housemaid—somewhere safer than in front of his knifeboard. If she were less argumentative and independent, he could easily see her married in the next few years.

This last thought made him pause. He was scarcely older than Gracie, but still young enough to make decisions that would have lasting consequences on his life. What else could he be doing with his time if not performing with the circus? Would he ever get married? Stop traveling? Start a family?

The ideas appealed to him, and yet he wouldn't let them take root. Such joys were meant for people without blood on their hands.

He closed the back doors of his wagon and returned to the practice ring, channeling all his emotions out of his thoughts as he had conditioned himself to do before a performance. Dust clouds swirled around Gracie's ankles where she'd been pacing. "I'm still here. I haven't run off," she said.

Unfortunately.

She posed for him in front of the knife board, resting her hands on her angled hips and smiling slightly.

"Don't get so excited," he said. "I need to measure you first."

Gripping her shoulders, he extended her slender arms and legs, and compared the reach of her limbs to the scar clusters on the board. Tucked into her garter, he spied a folded postcard addressed to St. Patrick's Orphan Asylum. *Typical.* A runaway orphan.

He had a chalk line of extra space to work with around her sides and nothing extra above her head. Gracie was shorter than Katherine, so the taller shoes, which had caused Katherine's death, made Gracie the correct height for his marks. He would see Gracie wearing the shoes every performance—and be reminded of Katherine, bloodied and crumpled in them.

Why had he thought he was ready for this? Vincenzio had told him to make sure Gracie was ready, but how could Jack do that when he didn't know if he was prepared to resume the act himself?

The night after Katherine's death, he'd stayed up until morning, practicing his tosses over and over. The rhythm and movements had still felt comfortable and natural, mechanical even. He'd perfected his routine to the extent that he'd mistaken a repetitive pattern for excellence. It had been his intent to repaint the entire knifeboard the next morning and retrain his technique to focus more on his assistant's safety and less on exactness, except the stagehands had packed the knifeboard away and not unloaded it until now.

In order to perform with Gracie, Jack would have to stop viewing his rigid technique as a jinx, but instead as a reliable tool. This rationalization eased the trembling in his hands. As long as Gracie didn't change her shoes, he'd be fine.

He shook his head. *Focus on the task in front of you.* "I think we'll start with the standing tosses first. If you've got the board against your back, that'll help with your stability."

He helped her create a diamond with her arms and had her cross her right leg over her left at her ankles. Taking a step back, Jack wiped his forehead on the back of his sleeve. Stepping toe to heel, he marked his paces away from the backboard. His gaze turned to the trapeze bar where Maria was doing warm-up drills. In the left ring, Barty lined up his tigers. They appeared focused on their activities, but he knew the truth—they were watching him, waiting to see his first knife toss with an assistant since Katherine's death.

He turned back to Gracie. "What if I told you I am afraid?"

Gracie dropped her arms from the diamond pose. "I'd believe you."

He drew a line in the dirt with his toe then went back to reposition her arms again. "Well, you needn't fear. Because, while I am scared, it's not about the act."

Gracie shifted her weight from one hip to the other. "What are you afraid of then?"

He tried to coax her into a more natural-looking pose. "Miss Hart, would you say you're superstitious?"

"Not more so than anyone else. And please, call me Gracie. You're not fooling me with the 'miss' thing."

He agreed that calling her "miss" hardly seemed fitting.

"Gracie," he said, "in the circus there's a belief that bad luck comes in threes. In a string of unfortunate events, Katherine's death has been labeled the 'First Act.' From now on, bad luck will plague everyone until the omen has been satisfied. None of the other women wanted this position because they fear what's still to come."

"Poppycock. If I had any money left, I'd bet it all that no one wants to be your assistant because you're a cad and a thief."

He'd told her already he hadn't taken her stupid ticket. However, he *did* have an idea of who else might have stolen it. While Jack couldn't speak for the other pompous strangers at the Albany station she'd run into, he did know one other circus performer who rivaled his charisma and intelligence, and who also preferred brunettes over blondes. She could stew in her stubborn ignorance until he confirmed his suspicion. If she insisted on staying in his act, he'd serve her a huge slice of humble pie later.

Jack positioned her arms out to the sides in a new pose. "I guess that means we're well matched for each other as I can imagine few reasons that a young lady of sound mind would be desperate enough to let someone they thought was a villain throw knives at them."

A disconcerted frown replaced her self-satisfied smile.

"I didn't exactly leave my last job on good terms." Looking up at him through her lashes, she explained, "I'm worried about what will happen if I apply for another job without a referral. Besides, it might take me a while to find my aunt and uncle when I get to Chicago. I figure it'd be smart to have a little money saved up."

Gracie might not be as sane as he'd originally assumed. "You don't even know where they live?"

"My mother had the address, but she died eight years ago on the crossing from England, along with my father and brother. There was a cholera outbreak that killed a fifth of the passengers, requiring the ship to be quarantined when we arrived. By the time they got done shuffling everyone around and disposing of the bodies, my mother's rosewood trunk with all of our travel papers had vanished." She dropped her head, delivering the next phrase to the dirt in front of her, refusing to meet Jack's eye. "I know there's a chance my aunt and uncle aren't even in Chicago anymore. They might be dead too, but at least it's a place to start."

Jack quit fussing over her posture and took a step back. All kinds of people could find themselves without food or a home. But being alone—that was true tragedy. Since he'd come to Vincenzio's circus he couldn't say he was lonely. However, the things he used to fill the hole in his heart from his own parents' deaths didn't really feel like they made the hole smaller, just more jagged. His thoughts shifted as his eyes drifted back to her postcard. "If not your aunt and uncle, who sent you that postcard in your garter?"

"You Peeping Tom!" Her hands flew to her thigh and snatched the folded paper. The postcard disappeared under the front hem of her corset so quickly that she might have given herself a paper cut in the process. He hadn't been able to identify the image, only that it featured a harbor and it had some word written across the picture.

"Is it from your hometown in England?"

"Nothing like that." She raised her arms back over her head.

"Is it a place you'd like to visit?"

"It's from a bet I made a long time ago—which is of no importance to you."

Her eyes narrowed, and suddenly she was no longer just some helpless orphan standing before him, but a young woman capable of dark, vicious things. In the sneer of her mouth he felt as though he had a sense of the misfortunes she'd experienced as an unwanted orphan, and her willful determination which had saved and brought her to this exact moment in time. He nodded. His curiosity was far from quelled, but he was well aware that if he pushed any harder, he might be the one with the knife stuck in him.

"You shouldn't keep papers hidden in your costume. It could ruin my magic act if you slip me the wrong card or prop," he said.

"I'll put it in a safe place later. You can be assured I'll never put it somewhere you can touch it again."

Again?

Her expression remained guarded as he resumed correcting the alignment of her shoulders. After a minute her scowl softened. "What about you?" she asked. "Where are your parents?"

Dead. It was all my fault too.

He shrugged. There was little point in opening up to her if she was only staying until Chicago, and yet he didn't hate the idea of her knowing something true about his past to counteract the wildfire of false gossip Katherine's death had ignited. "Both my parents died, about three years back. We were with another circus at that time. That's actually how I started this act. There was a period of time when I wasn't performing, and I didn't know if I ever would be able to again. To earn my keep, I shoveled coal to help the train engineer. During the breaks, I threw knives into the tinder pile until I got good enough to make it an act. About that time, Vincenzio's circus crossed paths with my old circus. He liked the idea of getting two acts for the price of one performer, so he signed me on."

Her left eye twitched ever so slightly. "How long have you had this act?"

"A year and a half."

"I think I agree you didn't intentionally murder Katherine. The mistake of an amateur seems more plausible."

If she hadn't bought new shoes or if he hadn't done the "star" formation for his first feat, she'd still be alive. For the star feat, he'd thrown five knives left-right-left-right-top. The risk came from the quick switches between the two sides of her body. He'd been so focused on his lateral movements he hadn't noticed the vertical difference until the last one went into her head.

He'd trade anything to hang her star back in the sky and return the light to her eyes, but both were faded and gone forever now. Maybe he *was* an amateur, for thinking the work he did for his circus job was important enough to risk the life of another young woman.

He wiped his hands on his pants and then pulled his sleeve across his brow. "You should be careful that you don't lose sight of your dream, or else you might end up like the rest of us—stuck in this sinkhole and addicted to the false sense of family the circus creates."

"At least you're contributing to the happiness of others. Making all those people in the audience feel joy and a sense of wonder, isn't that worth something?"

The brief smile which followed her statement caught him off guard. While open and inviting in its appearance, it made him more wary, like she was tugging at something fragile inside him.

Do you mean, worth something besides money? Though it wasn't money that tied his fate to the circus, he was just as trapped here as she was. His father's death had left him with a whole wagon full of magic tricks and a huge burden to carry. It wasn't a financial burden, as Gracie accused, but one that Jack imagined he could spend his whole life with and still never fully unload. How was he supposed to continue his family's legacy when he hated himself for existing? How could he ever forgive himself for his role in their deaths and now Katherine's?

He guided her through the next set of positions in silence. When she assured him she could recreate the poses on her own, he took his place behind his mark in the dirt.

Jack wrapped his slender fingers around a knife hilt and cocked it back. The silver blade shimmered. He felt something tingle up his spine, but it wasn't fear. Anticipation? Expectation? Excitement? Yes, the last one was it.

The swirling in his head reminded him that he needed to breathe again. Jack lowered his arm. "Perhaps I should practice a few more times."

"You'll be reinforcing your own doubt if you do. When you fall off a horse, the thing to do is to get right back on, isn't it? Not walk it around the ring a few more times."

For some reason, her encouragement meant more to him than any he'd gotten from his circus "family." If his new assistant didn't doubt his skill, he needed to give himself the same credit.

"You don't have a rag, do you?" He knew very well what had become of his. Stained with Katherine's blood and still in the pocket of his ruined performance jacket.

Gracie shot him a glare that could melt stone. "I sure hope you don't mean a blindfold."

"You're the one I'm worried about. Once you see the daggers flying, I don't want you jumping and hurting yourself."

She took a deep breath. "Throw it, I'm ready."

"If you truly think that, then let me ask you this—do you trust me?"

"I'll let you know in a few seconds."

He ran his finger along the edge of the sharp blade. Scratching the back of his neck with the blunt edge, he shrugged and coiled, a cobra ready to strike. Stillness spread across the circus lot.

Jack stepped forward, muttering before he flung the knife, "You shouldn't."

CHAPTER IX

THE THUNK in the knife board echoed across the circus lot like a guillotine blade hitting a wooden block.

Gracie's heart leapt in her throat, and her lungs felt like they had been turned inside out. She released a slow breath. *I'm still alive.*

He'd really just thrown a knife at her. And it wasn't like he'd thrown it into a far corner of the board or that he had only pretended to throw it. The handle of the knife stuck out next to her thigh, the scrunched lace and satin of her garter reflected in the gleaming blade.

"Should I continue?" Jack asked.

"I'm fine." Her heart beat in her throat, but she'd done it. She'd stood still.

Jack nodded and wiped the sweat from his brow. "Let's proceed to the first feat then."

Her breath hitched to her pulse. The arc of spinning silver landed low in the backboard, next to her calf. With the speed of gunshots, his knives traced her side. Thigh, hip, waist, chest, shoulder—

She didn't have enough time to form the word "head" in her thoughts before the knife crashed next to it. A sliver of wood exploded from the backboard, spinning across her vision.

Gracie flinched, eyes clamped shut, as it grazed her nose. "Ouch!"

"*Zut!*" Jack crossed the distance to her in half a second. "Are you okay?"

She pushed his hands away from her face. "It's just a splinter." She rubbed her nose, even though it was her arm that smarted, like she'd brushed it with a recently doused candle wick.

His brow un-knit and he stiffly turned to collect his knives from the board. "If one of my knives grazes your skin during a performance, you must resist crying out or moving until I come to collect the knives. If you're bleeding, you may inform me at that point."

"I'm bleeding."

His head whipped to face her, gaunt and hollow.

She rubbed at the red mark on her arm. It smudged, but then a drop welled up and rolled down. "It's not that deep. I think I grazed one of your knives when the splinter made me jump."

A bit of wood tore as Jack wrenched the last knife free. "Go clean yourself up and change." He dumped his knives hastily into a box. "I'll find you later to rehearse our entrance and exit." He rushed out, not sparing her a second glance.

THE cut had stopped bleeding before she'd climbed out of the ring, so she didn't bother going to look for a bandage to cover it. Instead, she made her way to Katherine's room.

Everything inside the room not bolted to the train car had a numbered tag slapped on the front. In another life, Vincenzio's bookkeeper might have worked as a cataloguer in the Library of Congress or a junkyard foreman. Among the fine silk gowns, ostrich feather fans, and Kentucky Derby hats, a ruddy brown trunk caught Gracie's attention.

She traced the raised ridges and chiseled corners of the roses carved in the top, mindful to stay out of Miriam's way as the seamstress searched for a suitable dress for Gracie to wear.

Miriam let out a sharp breath. "Harold says he numbered everything, but what good is it if the numbers are not in order?" The seamstress moved a stack of hats from the nightstand to the bed. "*Il pourrait être un babouin, si ses fesses manquaient tant de cheveux que sa tête.*" Something about a baboon's buttocks and hairless heads.

Gracie didn't ask Miriam to translate, far more fascinated by the trunk than by Miriam's criticism of Harold's organizational methods.

The odds this trunk could be Gracie's mother's lost rosewood trunk were practically non-existent. The rose motif was even more popular now than it had been a decade ago. Still, she wanted to believe this trunk had once belonged to her mother and that fate had reunited her with it.

Two numerals stood in the way of her happiness. Lot number "56."

"What are these numbers for?" she asked Miriam.

The sinewy woman looked up from the hatboxes she was sorting. "For the auction. Katherine had no will and no family to claim her belongings or pay for her burial."

Gracie stepped back from the trunk, but the temptation to rip the tag off remained. "When is this auction?"

"Saturday. It will include everything except for the jewelry. Vincenzio will appraise the pieces with real gems and sell them privately." Miriam restacked the hatboxes and nodded to the trunk. "That trunk is hand-carved rosewood. Very nice." Gracie's shoulders slumped so low her height shrunk by an inch. Nice meant expensive. The faces of her mother, father, and brother had blurred over the years and grown murkier every day. She needed something to hold on to, something real that would keep the memories from fading further.

She stared at a tower of feathered hats, plotting how she'd come up with the money. She might get enough if she asked for several advances on her salary or took to begging on the street corner when she wasn't at rehearsal. Lifting her skirts was the obvious answer, but she refused to consider that.

"Here, wear this." Miriam handed her a dress that smelled like expensive French perfume. Its gray and black pinstripes created an optical illusion at every dart and seam line where they intersected. A black ribbon trim, woven through Chantilly lace, decorated the neckline and sleeve cuffs. Sixteen ivory buttons were sewn down the front, and six dotted each sleeve.

Gracie traced the lace detail. "This is too nice for me."

"If the towners see you in those rags from before, they will assume the circus is poor and our acts are bad. You can wear it until you can afford something new."

"Towners?"

"Townsfolk," Miriam explained, "People not from the circus."

Gracie changed, noting the lingering smell of perfume on the dress. She was about to leave the room when Miriam handed her a dainty umbrella. "Here, for protection."

Protection from what?

"Now off with you. I must move everything out before you sleep here tonight."

Clutching the parasol, Gracie walked back to the big top to meet Jack. With Katherine's bustle tied in place over her hips, a three-layered petticoat, and a volcanic eruption of fabric on her backside, Gracie felt like an ox yoked to a wagon.

She didn't see Jack anywhere and was about to make herself comfortable on the front-row bench when a man shouted to her from across the tent. "Hey, you there!"

A teal cape hung on his narrow shoulders and rippled over a small satchel on his waistband. His wrists and ankles were too long for his suit and his neck too short for his thin, square-cheeked face. He jogged across the tent to her, accompanied by a small, barking terrier with white fur and brown ears.

Gracie gripped the parasol tighter and braced herself as the dog raced ahead of its trainer. It still barked, though it did so with an open mouth and wagging tail. The man waved his arms, calling it back, but it ignored him and leapt into her arms.

She dropped her parasol, needing both hands to keep its kicking paws from clawing her dress as it licked her face.

The dog trainer stopped a few feet from her and ran a hand through his dark, oiled hair. His eyebrows were set low in a scowl, which he directed alternately at her and his dog. "Miss, I need you to leave. This area is closed until the show tomorrow."

"I'm here for rehearsal," she said, squirming under the torture of the dog's wet tongue. "I'm Jack's new assistant."

The creases around his eyes softened. "My mistake. You were dressed so nice, I thought you were one of the towners." He clapped his hands twice and raised his voice. "Shiloh, that's enough. Come!"

This time, the dog twisted and squirmed, wheeling around until Gracie set it on the ground. It returned to the man's side, eyes fixated on the satchel. When the man reached in the bag, the scent of bacon and rawhide wafted into the air.

"I'm sorry he jumped on you. He's usually more well-behaved." He dropped a small chunk of pork skin, which the dog snatched in midair.

"No harm done." Gracie picked up the umbrella from the ground and tapped the dirt off with her toe. If his dog had torn her dress or gotten mud on it, that might have been another matter.

He put his hand out and took hers. "My name is Jonathan Detweiler. Allow me to welcome you to the circus, Miss—?"

"Miss Hart."

"Pleased to meet you." He bent over her wrist and pressed a wet kiss onto the back of it. The level of restraint she needed to avoid immediately wiping her hand on her dress was the same that she'd called on earlier when resisting the urge to jump as Jack threw his knives.

"Usually he growls at strangers," Mr. Detweiler said, leaning over to scratch the dog behind its ears. The dog's tail wagged a bit, though it didn't look up from its earnest task of chewing the piece of pork skin.

Gracie patted it on the head, not wanting to test the limits of its temper. Stray animals usually turned more vicious and territorial when food was involved. "He still hasn't growled at me. He must like something about the way I smell."

She hadn't meant the statement as an invitation, but it prompted Mr. Detweiler to lean in closely. His nostrils flared as he sniffed the air. He leaned back with a smile. "Yes, it's your perfume. I thought I recognized it. Miriam fixed you up with some of Katherine's things, didn't she? I suppose that makes sense if you're taking over her act."

Gracie jumped on the chance to excuse herself. "We'll see if I'm ready in time. I should probably go find Jack so he can go over our entrance and exit."

He nodded. "Yes, and I need to get back to work as well," he said with a smile. His teeth glistened with saliva and her grip on the parasol tightened. "I look forward to seeing you around more. Jack is very lucky to have such a beautiful assistant."

"You flatter me." She hadn't known if that was the proper way to respond to his brazen compliment. It seemed like something one of those dime-novel heroines would say.

"I hope so." He clapped his hands and returned to the other side of the tent, Shiloh trailing after him.

Gracie scanned the big top again for Jack and spied him on the trapeze rigging, now dressed in a white jumpsuit trimmed with golden suns and silver moons. He hung from the bar upside down by his knees, in the catcher's position, and used his arms to increase the momentum of his swing.

He must owe someone a great debt if he's involved in this many acts and still doesn't make enough money.

His flying partner was a petite, middle-aged woman with dark brown hair. Her costume was a nude body suit with flames of pearls and teardrop crystals streaked over her torso.

A guttural shout from Jack signaled the woman to jump off the trapeze platform. They swung in tandem, two clock pendulums ticking side by side. Jack shouted again. This time the woman let go of the trapeze bar, her body flipping like a coin. Jack was on the backswing—too far away to catch her.

Time slowed to a snail's crawl as the woman reached for Jack's absent hands and began falling.

Gracie looked for a safety net, a scream rising in her throat when she didn't see one.

The next second lasted an eternity.

Jack's swing reversed. His arms stretched like taffy and he caught her by the fingers at the last possible moment. Her fall converted to a graceful swing.

Gracie let out a long breath and fanned herself with her hand. Surely they didn't do something so dangerous every performance? She squinted as she walked toward the third ring, looking for a hidden safety wire. Ah, there it was—black and dark enough to blend in with the shadows. Still, even if Gracie excluded the degree of danger from the equation, the feat still required an enormous amount of talent and skill. The timing alone was—

"Watch out!" a shrill voice cried from the ring beside her.

A horse, which had been running laps in the center ring, reared and almost tossed the female rider off its back. The brown haze at the border of Gracie's vision formed into thrashing horse limbs. Distracted by Jack's performance, she'd wandered too close to a practice ring.

Gracie threw her arms over her head and tripped on her train in her scramble to get away from the horseshoed brain-smashers. As she fell, the headlines of tomorrow's paper flashed before her: "Act Two: Girl Trampled by Horse."

She'd counted halfway to eternity while waiting for the impact before arms hooked around her waist and dragged her away from the ring. The horse's whinnies ceased as the girl regained control over the Arabian mare. Gracie looked up as two sets of hands helped her onto her feet.

Jack, in his celestial jumpsuit, had offered his hand. But so had another Jack in a pair of pressed black pants and a dark shirt. Perhaps she had hit her head and was now seeing double.

The puzzle pieces rattling in her skull fit together immediately.

Identical twins. Her gaze shifted between the two men. She brushed the straw from her dress and beat the dust off her skirt. "Jack?"

Jack in the black pants answered, "I'm Jack."

With Jack and his doppelganger standing side by side, Gracie scrutinized them for any differences. The two men combed their hair the same way, longer on the top than on the back and sides. They had their weight shifted to the same leg while standing, and she couldn't find one misplaced freckle. How ridiculous. She must not be searching hard enough. Young men in their line of work couldn't make it through so many years of life without a few scars to show for it.

"Is this another one of your magic tricks?" She wondered if the identical faces would be equally handsome if one had longer hair or a mustache.

Jack stepped forward, his expression haughty. "Harris is my twin."

She whirled to face Harris. "*You* stole my ticket!"

"Not this again." Jack rubbed the bridge of his nose.

Harris studied her with fresh eyes. "Have we met before? You do look a little familiar."

"Yesterday at the train depot—you pick-pocketed my train ticket and money after you carried my trunk to the loading platform."

"What use would I have for your ticket when I travel with the circus?"

Gracie wanted nothing more than to wipe the smile from his face with a slap. "You might have resold it to someone else, or maybe you just wanted the money." She pulled herself straighter. "Even though you are obviously not a gentleman, I insist you repay me the value of my ticket."

"Good luck collecting on that, since I'm not admitting guilt. Though if you should happen to stop by my room this evening in your costume from earlier, I might reconsider."

Gracie raised her hand to strike him, but he caught her wrist in midair. "Slapping someone isn't very ladylike, is it?"

She bet Harris wouldn't expect her to crush the arch of his foot with her heel. Jack stepped in front of her before she could act on the impulse and expose her subpar upbringing even worse. Physical violence might be the language of the working class, but civilized society preferred quick retorts and witty banter. Her disappointment over Jack's intervention matched her regret that her efforts to prove herself a lady hadn't survived past noon.

Jack took Harris by the shoulder, tightening his grip until the twin released Gracie's wrist. "You disgust me," Jack muttered, his fingers digging into Harris's skin.

Harris winced. "Yeah? At least I'm not a murderer."

Jack balled his fist and threw it into Harris's jaw. Gracie almost clapped.

Harris stumbled, but caught himself. He rubbed his jaw, and with a wide grin, spun around, shoving Jack to the ground. He knelt down, hands forming a collar around Jack's neck. Jack broke the choke hold with a quick jab to Harris's sternum. Harris grunted, falling backward.

Jack jumped at Harris and they rolled on the ground, limbs flying so fast that it was hard to tell who was winning.

Gracie briefly thought to call for help, except the few fights she'd gotten herself into at the orphanage had given her an extreme dislike for snitches. It seemed that the rest of the troupe preferred watching a fight to stopping it, as a small crowd of men had gathered, amusement on their faces. She might actually fit in here better than she'd thought.

Harris and Jack continued to scuffle on the dirt floor, clawing at each other's backs. Bets were called out on who would win.

Gracie took a few steps back. What under heaven could possess two brothers to hate each other so much?

Someone shouted for Vincenzio and Richard.

A man wearing red jodhpurs ran into the big top first, with Vincenzio shuffling in after—a penguin racing an ostrich. Richard hooked his arms around Jack's waist while Vincenzio pulled Harris back by the shoulders. Harris pushed his boss to the side and kicked Jack solidly in the stomach, sending him and Richard toppling backwards.

"Josef, Hugo, Victor!" Vincenzio called. "Get over here and grab these two!"

Three large men stepped in and succeeded in restraining the brothers.

Vincenzio stood between Jack and Harris, chest heaving. "What am I going to do with you impetuous pups? I don't want to fire you since we'd be short three acts, but if you behave like savages, I won't have a choice, will I?"

Harris muttered, "He started it."

"Quiet. The both of you. I've got a circus to run. If you two aren't going to act like men, I'll have you caged with the animals for the rest of the week. Think about that, and get back to work!" Vincenzio signaled for Jack and Harris to be released.

Jack crossed his arms over his chest with a mutinous glower. Harris spat on the ground then returned to the trapeze equipment, rowing his shoulder in circles.

Ringmaster Richard declared the "show" over and called for the crowd of performers and stagehands to disperse.

Gracie stormed up to Jack, chin jutting out. "Why didn't you say you had a twin?"

Jack rubbed what appeared to be a cramp in his forearm. "Do you believe me now when I say I didn't steal your ticket?"

"How can you blame me? I'll bet your own mother couldn't tell the difference between you two."

He studied her for a moment, the features on his face as sharp as the edge in his tone. "I wouldn't know, but I'll ask next time I see her."

Gracie folded her hands in front of her and stared at the ground, her face, neck, and chest suddenly hot and itchy. If she wanted Jack to think of her as a refined young lady, she should stop acting like a spoiled child who never listens or thinks before opening her mouth. *Jack already told you his parents were dead.*

She spoke softly, "I'm sorry. That was a careless thing for me to say. Still, I think you should have mentioned earlier that you had a twin."

Jack wiped his mouth across his sleeve, despite having no sign of a bloodied lip. His sleeve cuff slipped up his arm, and Gracie noted it was covered in dark purple bruises from the fight already.

When he caught her staring, he quickly tugged his sleeve back down. He glanced over his shoulder at Harris, a snarl curling on his lips. "How about I just put my relationship with my twin this way: I wouldn't piss on him if he was on fire."

"Rubbish. You obviously care more about him than me because you didn't rat him out when I accused you of stealing my ticket."

"I didn't do that for his sake," Jack said.

"What should I assume then? That you wanted me to keep thinking you were a liar?" She could think of no other explanation he might have for withholding the information from her, except that he wanted to be cruel and mock her.

Several deep wrinkles appeared on Jack's forehead. He fixed his scowl toward a group of performers near the trapeze towers, bunched in furtive conversation with Harris.

Jack turned back to face her, jaw still clenched tight. "Half the rotten circus thinks I murdered Katherine, and I'm supposed to care if one ragamuffin thinks I'm a liar? I figured you'd wise up and take off, or if you stayed, you'd see us together sooner or later."

Gracie stiffened. She would have apologized had he given her any sort of reasonable explanation, but he'd resorted to name calling instead. She matched his dour tone. "Spoken like a true two-faced Gemini."

"You believe in fortune-telling and zodiac signs? I thought you weren't superstitious."

"I'm not." Or maybe she was a little, but she wasn't about to let him railroad the topic. Even if he wasn't a liar and thief, he was still condescending and rude. "Why does Harris upset you so much? I'll bet if you ignored him, he'd get bored and leave you alone."

Jack dusted his shoulders and straightened his shirt. "I'm not as different from Harris as you might wish to believe, but I'm definitely not a liar, thief, or murderer. Katherine's death *was* an accident. But there's still time before tomorrow's show for you to change your mind about the act."

He stomped out of the tent wearing his temper like a second skin and rubbing his bruised arm.

Quit? Right when things were getting interesting? At least she didn't run from *verbal* confrontation, as he preferred to do.

A shield provided the best defense when carried in the front, which is why Gracie looked for weaknesses in a person's armor from the sides or the rear. The set of Jack's shoulders as viewed from behind— pulled back, level, and stiff—revealed his largest chink. The fact that he made an effort to appear nonchalant and indifferent indicated that he felt the opposite. She'd often seen Jack's hollowed cheeks and his not-a-care-in-the-world disregard on the faces of new orphans, claiming they didn't miss their mum and pop.

Lies. Always.

Jack *did* care what Gracie thought of him, what others thought of him, and she sensed he desperately needed someone in this "sinkhole" to trust and believe in him.

Jack hadn't lost his parents as young as she had, but they were still gone, which made him a kindred soul. Gracie never thought herself a sympathetic type, yet a strong part of her wanted to wrap her arms around him and tell him he wasn't alone, that they could be sad together—or she *would* want to, if he wasn't such a dolt.

Taking care to avoid dragging the hem of Katherine's dress through any muck, Gracie picked her way out of the big top.

Jack wasn't a child, so she shouldn't pity him like one. Neither was Harris, which meant she could be as relentless as she wanted in demanding restitution for her stolen ticket. She might have considered sneaking away from the circus at the first opportunity, but now that fate had placed the true pickpocket in her path, there was no way she was leaving until she collected her losses from him.

Until then, she wasn't going anywhere. Plus, it was lunch time. And she was starving.

CHAPTER X

THE PLATE of food weighed heavily in Gracie's hands, much more than she knew it would in her stomach. Unfortunately, even after she'd licked the plate clean, she couldn't banish the rosewood trunk she'd seen in Katherine's room from her thoughts. Asking Vincenzio for an advance seemed her best chance of getting it, though this idea seemed ridiculously stupid considering how things has gone the last time she discussed money with her employer. After an hour and much deliberation, Gracie found herself waiting in the narrow hallway outside Vincenzio's stateroom.

She set the tip of her parasol against the ground and spun the handle. First clockwise, then counterclockwise.

A husky voice preceded the footsteps of its owner. "Careful there with that brolly. If you spin it too fast, you might drill a hole through the floor with the point."

Gracie flipped the umbrella and pressed the tip into the soft spot in the neck of her guest. He raised his hands in surrender. The twin before her wore neither the black knife-throwing outfit, nor the white acrobatic one. He also smelled of pine trees and mint, which Gracie guessed meant he'd bathed recently.

"Harris?"

He pushed her imaginary sword blade away. "Good guess, but it's me, Jack."

A good guess would have been if she'd guessed right, or if she'd had less than a fifty percent chance of success. In this case, she'd set the odds more like seventy-thirty since Jack had been in quite the sour mood leaving the big top.

She tucked the parasol under her arm. "Is there any way to tell you two apart?"

"Yes, several. Though for someone like yourself, who only has average perception skills, you're better off just asking each time we meet."

The weight of the insult dragged the corners of Gracie's lips down. While Jack did enjoy belittling her, she felt the barb lacked its usual sting. "Unless you two are willing to make your differences your priority, I see no need to make them mine. Until then, I will call you by whatever name I believe is most fitting at the time. And right now, I believe you are still Harris."

"If I agreed with you, we'd both be wrong."

She hated being wrong, nearly as much as she hated arrogant men. Her mother may have named her "Gracie," but that didn't necessarily mean she had a forgiving or compassionate personality.

"I don't think your word should be any more valid than mine. Prove you are not Harris and tell me something about myself only Jack would know—which one of my hands has six fingers?"

Harris's gaze dropped to her folded hands. As soon as it did, Gracie hit him over the head with her parasol.

"Bloody Hell!" Harris pressed his hands against his head. "Sheeze! What's your problem?" His accent almost sounded Cockney, it was so thick.

Gracie bounced the shaft of her umbrella in the palm of her hand. Katherine's nice dress had infused her with the confidence of a knight wearing a suit of armor. "That, *Harris*," she said, "is your punishment for lying to me. When you're through playing games, I'd like to discuss the matter of repayment for yesterday's ticket."

He snatched the parasol out of her grasp. With a single downward stroke, he broke it over his thigh and threw it on the ground. "Don't you think I know who I am?"

She eyed him with the same scowl she would give a hairy fly in her teacup. Was he still trying to pretend he was Jack? Could she possibly have been mistaken? Her gut said no.

"You owe me a new parasol now, too."

"Blast the brolly." He kicked the broken pieces down the carpeted hall. "I'll buy you a dozen of 'em if you can name one, genuine difference between me and Jack."

Gracie pulled herself taller. She did have one theory. "Jack prefers to swear in French."

"On t'a bercé trop près du mur comme une enfante?" Were you rocked too close to the wall as an infant? Gracie's French teacher had used the phrase whenever Gracie assigned the wrong gender to a noun.

She held out a scolding finger. "It doesn't count if you're not caught unawares."

Harris's shoulders rolled back. "You'd already decided you didn't believe me before you hit me."

"It could easily have been a lucky guess, as you said before." She shrugged, hopefully to irritate him further. She strolled down the hallway to retrieve the poor umbrella. "I might have been convinced by your flawless acting had you not been so eager to glance at my hands in hopes of preserving your lie. If you were really Jack, you'd have seen during our rehearsal that I don't have six fingers on either hand."

She picked up the umbrella and carried it back with her. Maybe Miriam would be able to fix it. Gracie met Harris's leering face. "What I find most curious, more than your enjoyment in beguiling me, is why you'd be bothered if I knew a way to tell you two apart. Someone else must know, despite your reluctance to tell me."

Harris laughed. "Everyone here has only gotten used to the clothes we wear and the jobs we do. If we wore the same thing, they'd be helpless."

"Why the intrigue? At the station, when you offered to carry my trunk, you seemed like a man able to present himself well to a lady. Is copying your brother really how you wish others to know you?"

"Jack is the one who copies me." Harris folded his arms across his chest.

The door to Vincenzio's office opened suddenly.

Gracie jumped as though she'd been caught out of bed after hours, while Harris rocked back on his heels casually.

Vincenzio stood in the doorway to his room, his arms on the jambs like he alone held the wall up. His attention fixed on Harris. "Is there something you need?" Gracie noted he didn't call him by name.

"Yeah, Katherine had something important of mine before she died. I believe it's been misplaced among the auction items. With your permission, boss, I'd like to search her room for it."

He'd better not stop by any time while she was using it to change or sleep. To her relief, Vincenzio shook his head. "Harold has catalogued every item in the room. You'll need to ask him."

"Thank you, I'll go see if he's around." Harris bowed and excused himself, squeezing to the side wall as Mr. Detweiler entered the train car.

The dog trainer was a half head shorter than Harris but almost as wide in the shoulders. He had his teal performance cape hung over the crook of his arm. The scent of overcooked bacon filled the narrow hallway.

Harris briefly raised a hand to his mouth, as if to stifle a sneeze. Nose scrunched, he made for the train car door.

Vincenzio turned to her and held the door ajar. "You need something from me?"

"If you have a moment to spare—"

"We can speak inside my stateroom." He gestured for her to enter and then turned to the dog trainer. "I'll be with you in a moment, Mr. Detweiler."

"Gracie!" Harris called her attention back to him from the train car doorway. "Jack likes two spoons of sugar in his coffee, and I prefer three. Also, I'm the better kisser."

Gracie held her tongue until she was certain another second of silence would pop her like an over-inflated balloon. "I would never let my lips touch anything of yours! Not even if it was dipped in cheese or rolled in sugar!"

"That's a shame since I know of a fantastic bakery here. If you want me to take you to it, you'll have to shed your snake skin and ask nicely." He winked at her and disappeared outside.

Her cheeks burned. She could've set the carpet on fire just by staring through a magnifying glass while picturing his face. Go out to a bakery with him, after he'd robbed her? She'd sooner kiss a real snake.

Vincenzio coughed into his hand and had the decency not to say anything as she seated herself in the creaky wooden chair. He sat across his desk from her, his chin resting on his palm and his head tilted to the side with unreserved scrutiny. His eyes were cold and sharp, difficult to stare at for more than a few seconds. He listened quietly while she asked about getting an advance and explained her reason for wanting the trunk. Then, without the least bit of sympathy, he turned her away empty-handed, citing her lack of history with the circus as a reason not to trust her with an advance.

On her way out, Mr. Detweiler caught her wrist. He shoved a crumpled bill and several coins into her hand. "It's a loan, not a gift," he said, his coffee-black eyes never meeting hers. "I expect to be repaid, with interest. Vincenzio isn't always a good judge of character, but my dog is, and he likes you."

The tight parts of her dress—her corset, sleeve cuffs, and high collar—all pulsed. With the modest salary Vincenzio paid her, she could put every spare dime aside and wouldn't have enough to repay Mr. Detweiler for a few weeks. By that time though, the circus would be in Chicago.

Or, if I don't wait for the auction, I could run away with this money tonight. His dog was wrong about her. It only recognized Katherine's familiar scent and perfume.

Knowing she'd probably regret it, Gracie closed her fist around the money.

GRACIE exited the train car, Mr. Detweiler's money in one hand and the broken parasol pieces in the other. Although Katherine's dress had pockets hidden under the fabric folds, Gracie didn't feel safe carrying so much money around.

Stopping a few cars past Vincenzio's stateroom, she rapped on the door of Katherine's room.

"Yes?" Miriam's voice answered from the other side of the door.

Gracie stepped into a near-bare room, concealing the broken parasol behind her back. Miriam had already removed the trunk, hat boxes, and dresses. Only the vanity, bed, and oil lamp remained—all permanent fixtures of the room. Sundry hygiene items littered the bed.

"I came to drop off a few things and see if you needed any help," Gracie said.

Miriam considered her a moment, one arm folded and a slender finger curled under her chin. "I thought you were supposed to be at rehearsal."

"I was, but Jack and Harris started fighting and then Jack stormed out." She revealed the parasol pieces. "Also, Harris broke this."

Miriam *tsked* her tongue and took the pieces. "Like wolves, those two. In the time they've been here, I don't think a month goes by when they've not been at each other's throats."

"Why doesn't one of them quit if they don't get along?"

Miriam appeared thoughtful. "People born into this life rarely leave it. When they get tired, they simply find a different circus. If another circus has an opening, it's possible one of them might leave."

Gracie shuffled her feet as Miriam tested the fit of the broken parasol pieces. A frown formed on the seamstress's face, one that showed more in the creases around her eyes than the curve of her lips. "Did you find the costume hairpin and necklace you were looking for? Or do you still need help emptying the room?"

Miriam dumped the parasol pieces into a small wooden box. "I don't need help. I already had Victor assist me—he's our strongman and was able to carry it all in one trip." She picked up the box by the handles. "I did find the hairpin and costume necklace, so you will have them for the performance tomorrow." She crossed to the door. "My work here is done."

"What about this smaller stuff?" Gracie pointed to the mess on the bed.

"Those items won't fetch a price. They're yours." Miriam held the door open with her hip.

Luckily, Gracie was in the market for a hairbrush, a dowdy night gown, and a near-empty jar of perfume. She'd even make use of the lone sock by turning it into a coin pouch.

After Miriam was gone, Gracie stuffed the money and coins into the sock and stashed it under the mattress along with her postcard.

The rest of the evening was uneventful. Jack found her after dinner to make sure she hadn't skipped town. She hadn't, so he'd given her a simple rundown of her role in his magic act and their entrance and exit cues. He stressed that during this next performance her main role would be to walk the props he handed her back to the prop handlers.

He warned her about a few other circus superstitions:

"Always enter the ring with your right foot first. Never count the audience. Don't whistle under the big top or the tents, since someone might mistake it for their entrance cue. Don't eat peanuts in the dressing room or move someone's trunk once it's been put into place," and so on.

At the end of his lesson, Gracie practically fell into her bed. That night, she had the best night of sleep she'd gotten in months, even though the last two days were the worst she'd had in years. She was on a path to Chicago and finding her family.

CHAPTER XI

R EADY OR not, at five o'clock the next afternoon, the rope in front of the marquee opened, and a chorus of lemonade venders caused the lions to start roaring. By the ticket wagon, the cash registers clinked as hundreds of towners streamed into the big top.

The circus's sixteen-piece band played a fanfare of medleys while the Montreal spectators added to the percussion with their noisy cracking of peanut shells. The clash of cymbals marked the cue for the grand opening parade around the hippodrome. The small dressing tent Gracie was waiting in vacated to the tune of a patriotic march. The show had started.

In the next few acts, acrobats climbed precariously-stacked furniture or balanced candelabras and dinner dishes on their feet and heads. Carpet clowns told jokes and sent the audience into peals of laughter.

Gracie's favorite act, even over Harris's trapeze performance, was the group aerial ballet.

Women wearing newsprint sheets, accordion pleated into skirts, performed arabesques and spins on their partners' heads. Crow feathers ornamented their hair and covered their arms to give the illusion of wings. The men were fish, also with newsprint tunics, and had gills and shark teeth drawn on their cheeks.

The band played four songs meant to represent the four seasons: a galop, a cotillion, a mazurka, and a waltz. The performers tossed souvenir origami flowers and cranes to the audience during the summer song, and confetti snowed from the trapeze rigging during the winter waltz. Gracie's stomach plummeted at the end, even though she clapped so hard it made her hands sting. She was outclassed and had to be the least talented person here. When her job entailed standing still and hiding in a box, it was hard to consider herself a performer instead of a prop.

Still, putting up with Jack and Harris's teasing and wearing Miriam's scandalous costume would all be worth it when she reached Chicago.

A piccolo trilled, the cue for her and Jack's act to begin.

Jack took her hand and escorted her into the big top. By some miracle, he was smiling and gentle as he did so.

The crowd hushed, and the limelight turned on. The evening sun spilled gold across the canvas sides of the tent. Gracie took her place in front of the colored backboard. Even after Jack walked to the far end of the ring, she could still feel his grip squeezing her hand. A force with similar strength tightened around her chest.

Breathe. Just breathe. She'd made it through practice with only a scratch, which meant she could make it through the performance.

Jack turned and addressed the audience. "Ladies and gentlemen, as you enjoy my spectacular exploitation of impalement artistry tonight, I would like to call your attention to my new assistant, Miss Gracie Hart. We picked her up off the streets yesterday morning, and this will be her first performance." Several chuckles echoed throughout the crowd. "Watch her silhouette with a close eye," Jack continued. "Should she flinch at all, the knife will strike her fatally!"

A few people clapped with mild enthusiasm as Jack turned back around to face her. Inwardly, Gracie cringed. He'd said her name aloud.

She scanned the crowd, listening for someone to shout, "Murderer!" Her heart jumped as high as her throat when a man stood. Thankfully, all he did was remove his coat. She released a shuddering breath when he sat down again. It seemed that if anyone was going to report her, they intended to wait until after the performance.

Gracie spread her arms and legs for the first pose, her jaw clenched tightly enough she could have cracked walnuts between her teeth if she didn't have to keep a smile plastered on her face.

A light flashed and Jack's first knife struck the board beside her waist. The knives outlined her figure with sounds like the pops of champagne corks. Jack had already finished the first feat.

The applause from the audience pounded her ears worse than a thunderstorm. The women and men cheered, while the children hollered and shrieked for more. From the sound of it, Jack might have been throwing gold coins into the audience instead of knives at her.

She locked eyes with him as he approached to collect his knives. "You could have warned me you were going to throw them so fast."

His smile didn't waver during his reply. "That's why we practiced earlier. I already gave you a chance to quit. The time for cold feet is past."

From the start of the next feat to the end, he didn't blink once. Neither did she.

It was as though Jack had issued her an informal challenge. Never mind the temptation to run away with Mr. Detweiler's money. She'd either make it to Chicago as his assistant or die trying. Her pride fueled her courage until the last of Jack's knives landed one inch over her head.

On to the hard part, the magic act—though she was sure Jack didn't see the act as difficult.

Hardly needing her assistance, Jack entertained the audience with a few sleight of hand tricks. He caused a toy ball to float over his hand and roll along the underside of his arm, and he pulled fresh roses out of old ladies' ears and then made the blossoms disappear in a puff of smoke. When he was done with a prop, he'd hand it to Gracie and she'd run it to one of the prop handlers at the side of the ring.

Soon the stagehands moved the vanishing closet into place, and she joined Jack in the center of the ring.

The solemnity of Jack's words before shutting the door to the vanishing closet tightened the knot in her stomach. "Stay in the closet, and whatever you do, don't come out until I open the door."

"Like I have a choice." She rolled her eyes.

In the cramped rear compartment, her neck itched as though ants crawled beneath the costume necklace Miriam had given her—the tightness verged on asphyxiation. Sweat beaded on her temples while she hummed the tune of "London Bridge Is Falling Down" to count the passage of time. She reached the fourth verse and faltered. Something tickled in the front of her corset.

The itch might be an untrimmed thread, or it could be something more. The stanzas of "Incy Wincy Spider" danced through her thoughts. Gracie didn't remember seeing any cobwebs during rehearsal, but spiders were good at hiding like that.

She wiggled and squirmed, which only made the tickle worse. Hang the audience—if Jack didn't open the door soon, she was going to scream.

The disgusting spider got washed down the spout two more times before light burst through the crack in the door and Jack reached in to escort her out. *About time!*

With a forced smile, she nodded to the audience and took a step to the side to present Jack for recognition. He bowed; one arm crossed in front, the other folded behind his back. Linking his arm around hers, he escorted her from the ring. Gracie heard Ringmaster Richard behind them, stirring up excitement for Sandra's blindfolded walk across the tightrope with peach baskets on her feet.

The moment they'd left the big top, Gracie shrugged her hand out of Jack's and began digging in the front of her corset for the irritant. It couldn't possibly be her postcard. She'd made sure to leave that in her room before the performance.

Her fingers grasped something crisp and thin, a band of paper cut small enough to be used by a carrier pigeon.

Find Katherine's key. Keep it secret or you'll die next.

The words were crammed together to fit as many as possible across the paper. The handwriting style itself was shaky and nonuniform, indicating the note might have been written in a hurry or with the author's non-dominant hand to disguise his or her identity.

Find Katherine's key. Could that be what Harris was looking for too? Gracie didn't think the object of his search was a secret, though, as he'd asked Vincenzio about it.

"What's that?" Jack nodded to her note.

Gracie crumpled up the note and tossed it over her shoulder. "My size measurements. From when Miriam checked the fit of the costume."

Someone must have slipped the note in the front of her corset before the performance. Before the show, Helena, the girl whose horse had nearly trampled Gracie in the big top, had taught Gracie how to fix her hair with Miriam's hairpin and had given Gracie some crimped pins to tuck in her stray curls. But if Helena didn't want Gracie around, then why had she bothered to be nice to her?

With no audience around to see the two of them underdressed, Jack loosened his cravat and opened the top two buttons of his dress shirt. Next, he unscrewed the backs of his cufflinks. Gracie had not paid much notice to them before, but now she found the accessories quite curious as she realized they were mismatched. One was a little glass cylinder filled with a bright blue fluid; the other, a cobalt gem-stone in the shape of an octagon. A dark inclusion in the stone stared at her like the pupil of an eye.

The eccentric cufflinks disappeared into Jack's vest pocket. He rolled his cuffs up twice, exposing his wrist and part of his forearm. Gracie gaped in astonishment. Where were the dark bruises she'd seen earlier? His skin looked completely tan and flawless. It must have been dirt he'd washed off and a trick of the light that had made her think they were purple.

Jack turned to her with stern eyes. "If something strange hap-pened in the closet, you'd tell me, wouldn't you?"

She searched his eyes for a hidden meaning. Was he worried the secret compartment mechanism was about to break?

"I suppose I would."

"And did anything unusual 'appen tonight?"

Gracie noted that both his and Harris's accent regressed when their tempers flared. Was Jack trying to get her to admit to the sudden tickling feeling in her costume because he'd been the one who slipped the note into her costume? It certainly seemed plausible that Jack had used his sleight of hand to slip it in when he'd come to collect his knifes. *Lecher.* He was also her biggest opponent in the circus troupe, calling for her to quit.

She turned to face Jack, her shoulders pulled back. She had resolved not to let him see that he'd struck a nerve. "Nothing unusual happened in the closet that I can think of, though it did get a little warm and humid. I suppose that's because the closet is airtight."

"Katherine complained as much."

Gracie whipped her head forward and lengthened her steps, disappointed that Jack's facade as a concerned gentleman was little more than an act that corresponded to the costume he wore. "I wasn't complaining, and if you aren't going to respect my opinions, don't ask for them."

"I believe you're a strong-minded young woman who'd impose her opinion on whomever she wished—whether invited to or not." A burst of laughter followed his statement.

Such an infuriating man. To protest his accusation would prove his point, and to remain silent would mean she didn't deny it. Why couldn't he be hideous and beastly so that the parts of her body below her neck would agree with the portion above it? She reached to draw back the curtain to the women's dressing tent.

Jack grasped her arm, his face contorting into a strange mixture of anger and concern. "Gracie, I need to know if anything different happened during the vanishing act than during practice yesterday morning."

She met his eyes and wrenched her arm free. With a smirk, she put on her most bland face. "I don't remember. I'm under hypnosis during each performance."

He leaned in close, his eyes sharp. "That's not funny, Gracie." He clutched the folds of the curtain closed.

"I didn't *ask* if you cared if it was funny." She ducked under his arm and through the divide in the curtain into the women's changing area. He wouldn't dare follow her in here.

Gracie changed out of the costume, but rather than leaving through the front flaps, where Jack stood waiting, she ducked under the back wall and returned to Katherine's room. Gracie had nothing more to say to him. To think she'd felt sorry for him after his fight with Harris.

Luckily, she had an idea about how to get square with Jack for his note and for ruining her postcard. His fight with Harris in the big top had revealed an easy trigger for her to squeeze. The only downside was she'd have to make a significant personal sacrifice to pull the trigger—by appearing to forgive Harris and becoming friends with Jack's hated twin.

CHAPTER XII

Jack paced outside the door of the women's changing tent, waiting for Gracie to emerge. He pulled out his pocket watch and flipped the lid. The filigree hands twitched like a weathervane and then corrected and resumed ticking normally. He snapped the watch shut. He'd settle things with Gracie later. Right now, he had more pressing matters to take care of.

Guided by his intuition, which tonight bordered on clairvoyance, Jack soon found himself outside his prop wagon. Behind the colorful mural of his caricature holding a top hat and card fan, the sound of trunk lids opening and closing alternated with the slamming of dresser drawers.

A dull *thump* followed by a string of lazy-voweled curses revealed the intruder's identity. In the back of the wagon, Harris crouched underneath the open drawer of the dresser, holding his head with pale-knuckled, interlocked fingers.

Jack leaned against the door frame, relieved to see his closet was still covered. The anomaly he'd seen on his watch must have been because Harris had slightly disturbed the covering while opening one of the dresser drawers.

"Fancy finding you here, Harris. Up to your usual tricks, or have you come to help yourself to some of mine?"

"What kind of question is that?" Harris winced, standing. "Naturally, the first statement entails the latter." He continued to apply pressure to his head.

"Yes, I suppose it would've been more considerate if I'd asked if you've hurt your head seriously or if you're cradling it because it feels cold."

"Gracie put a hen fruit on it earlier with her brolly. I've now had the misfortune to be reminded of it."

Jack picked his way over a spilled deck of cards and slammed the drawer shut. "Serves you right for fossicking through my things uninvited."

"Considering how everything in here belonged to Father, I hope you can understand my offense to the possessive tone you've used while referring to *our* inheritance."

Jack gritted his teeth. A twisted smile formed. "Yes, of course. Let me rephrase: clean up your mess when you're done or I'll give you a third lump on your head, one you can ring a horseshoe 'round."

"Whoever tied your cravat this morning made it too tight. I haven't heard your accent this strong since the incident with the skunk." Harris nudged a colored scarf on the floor with his foot. "Besides, Vincenzio's threatened to throw us in the animal cages if we start fighting again. Although . . ." Harris looked up from the floor, eyes sparkling. "I'm beginning to think that sounds like a fair deal."

Even if they moved the fight to the edge of the lot, if word got back to Vincenzio later, he'd still punish them.

Harris hunched and balled his fists, ready for a blow. He held the pose for ten seconds before realizing Jack wasn't going to attack. He shrugged. "What's gotten into you today? You're no fun at all."

"Interestingly enough, I'm having a bit of trouble with Gracie as well."

Harris laughed patronizingly. "Was it something you did or something you said?"

Jack considered if Harris could use his answer to make the situation worse and then concluded he didn't care either way. "Perhaps both? Had she red hair, I'd mistake her for the Protestant wife of a Catholic Irishman—and I'm the husband. Most despicably, she's too opinionated for the heaven of any god, and hell should fear she'll take over."

"I'll keep that in mind when I call on her tomorrow."

Jack's breath caught in his lungs as though someone had tossed him a bag of potatoes when he'd thought it full of feathers. "You're gonna what?"

"Call on her tomorrow. Now that Gracie is one of the crew, I figured I should make more of an effort to patch things up with her and maybe introduce her to a few of the ladies so she doesn't feel like an outsider here." Harris reached for the lid of a trunk that Jack kept scarves, hats, and extra toy balls in. "What did you do with the black umbrella—the one you used to turn into a flock of pigeons?"

Jack sat on the trunk, almost sandwiching Harris's fingers in the lid. "What do you want with it?"

"Does it matter? All your bird cages are empty, so I know it's not something you're using for your act."

True. When Katherine died, Jack had released all the birds, grateful to no longer have the messy chore of cleaning their cages. Turning umbrellas into pigeons was an overdone trick among professional magicians, one he wasn't necessarily eager to bring back to the show with Gracie.

Jack sighed, standing back up. "It's in the top drawer of the dresser." *Which you already know because you hit your head on the opened drawer.*

"Thanks." Harris retrieved the umbrella from the drawer and hooked it over his arm. He moved toward the door as if to leave, but Jack shifted his weight to block him. Since when did Harris ever use common courtesies with him like "thanks?"

"What were you really looking for? And don't lie, we both know I can read your poker face."

"Something I don't want you to find first," Harris said, squeezing his way out with a muscled shove.

JACK sat heavily on the trunk and moaned into his hands. Ever since Gracie had shown up, things only seemed to be getting worse. He had a small idea what Harris might be looking for and prayed he was wrong.

Groaning inwardly, he stood. With a gentle tug, Jack removed the covering from his closet. In the lower left-hand corner on the west side of the box, Jack depressed a small button in the center of one of the cogwheels and then turned it counterclockwise three rotations. The closet door unlocked with a muted *click*.

A glance over his shoulder reaffirmed he was alone. Squeezing into the cramped space behind the closet, he dug through the piles of boxes and baskets until he came across a worn steamer trunk. He brought the case out and set it flat on the floor.

Checking one more time to ensure Harris hadn't doubled back, Jack raised the lid and removed his particle extractor from the case.

While someone else might mistake the boxy device for a portable telegraph unit from a distance, up close they'd likely notice the four carat diamond bracelet through the fuel chamber's small round imbedded window on the back. Also, the extractor's firing component could hardly be mistaken for anything but an oversized revolver.

He'd already heard enough theories as to why he'd murder Katherine. He didn't need to invite more wild accusations by adding the diamond bracelet and his conspicuous device to the pot.

Jack slung the box over his back, fastened the chest strap loosely, and buckled the thigh holster around his leg. Holstering the gun, he entered his gloomy magic closet and shut the door. He braced himself before opening it again.

The scene in front of him had become dark and cavernous, the temperature hot and humid. He blinked, waiting for his eyes to adjust to the dim light provided by a hanging string of flickering, oblong light bulbs. Instead of the back of the wagon, he stepped into a stone corridor.

It wasn't a trick and it wasn't magic: it was science. He'd been transported to a time-augmented reality, self-contained in a floating fortress anchored somewhere over Russia.

Jack flicked the power supply button of his particle extractor to the "on" position. The unit on his back whined, finally quieting after a lengthy warm up. Digging his pocket watch out and checking the time, Jack noted the centi-second hand hadn't yet ticked one increment in all the time he'd been here.

Shoving his watch back in his pocket, and with his particle extractor humming on his back, he proceeded forward into the maze of identical, intersecting corridors.

He made a few turns and arrived at a set of heavy, rusted doors. His nose scrunched at the musty smell of rot and decay as he stepped into a long, dimly-lit hallway. Soggy leaves carpeted the ground along with shards of glass. The vaulted ceiling sagged in several spots and the cabbage-rose wallpaper peeled like dead skin. Dark green and gray spots grew on the surface of the fabric armchairs.

Things had gotten rather run-down since his last visit several months ago.

Jack continued deeper into the fortress until he reached a section where the doors no longer hung askew and he didn't need to fear for his clothing if he sat on the furniture. He checked the time on his pocket watch. The milli-second hand of his pocket watch spun slower. Only thirty-seven centi-seconds had passed in total. Back on the circus lot, this amount of time would hardly amount to a blink.

He stopped in front of a mahogany door and let himself into a bright room full of heavy, dark-grained wood tables, spindly scientific instruments, and bookshelves loaded with documents and thick tomes. It was only slightly cooler here than in the cloisters and halls; the tall windows in the back of the room were closed behind gauzy white drapes.

Jack paused in front of the refractometer. His gaze turned to the large-windowed slide cabinet on the table beside it. Instead of slides, the drawers contained confirmed gemstone samples. A thick layer of dust coated the top of the box and even the small knobby handles on the windowed doors.

It seemed as though it had not been disturbed recently, but this was not enough reassurance. He opened the small doors and scanned the labels of crystal structures on the narrow drawers until he found the one titled "Hexagonal."

Jack pulled the drawer out and dread filled his entire person. The key was gone.

In a flurry, he tore out the other drawers above and below it. He next emptied all the drawers and shook the cabinet to make sure nothing had fallen to the bottom. Still no benitoite key.

Had Harris already found it? Was his search in the wagon a ruse to distract Jack from realizing that his twin had already returned from the closet by the time Jack had found him searching the drawers? Had *she* found it?

As if on cue, her arrogant, high-pitched flutelike voice cut across the room. "Nice to see you again, John, how long has it been?"

Clarice.

Clarice was beautifully statuesque but had the cutthroat heart of a butcher and the white coat to match. Her eyes narrowed behind her oversized safety goggles and her smile had all the warmth of a January morning. She swept the blonde strands of her hair to the side and hoisted the telescope-like cannon of her particle extractor onto her shoulder.

He patted his thigh to make sure the gun of his particle extractor was ready. He replied with a level voice. "I just thought I'd check on you, see what progress you've made—not much from the look of things. The fortress is falling apart."

"I could fix that with a junior assistant, or a new specimen. For which would you like to volunteer?"

Jack stepped out from the table, not bothering to clean up the gemstone cabinet drawers. "I have no desire to play with you and your toys."

Clarice raised the orifice of the cannon and fixed it on his chest. "People often say that, but no one ever says it twice."

Jack froze, a few paces from the door, but not close enough to push his way past her if he needed to. "If you kill me, you'll be stuck here forever."

Clarice huffed, pushing her goggles up onto her forehead. "I don't need to kill you, just to make your life as unbearable as you've made mine. I think it's only fair that you spend a few years imprisoned here for lying to me."

He imagined that would be quite awful—mostly because he'd have her for company. "Our prior agreement was that I'd tell you what I knew about the location of your heartstone. It's not my fault you looked and it wasn't there."

"My conniving sister used a benitoite key to lock the drawer she hid it in. You may not have lied outright, but I'm certain you knew I needed that key. Gladys left it with your father before she died, so you must still have it somewhere."

"Maybe." He shrugged, the movement so tense it might be mistaken for the involuntary convulsion that comes with the hiccups. As of ten minutes ago, it was the truth. He'd *had* the key, but now it was missing. Jack knew he should've hidden it better.

"Maybe?" Her voice turned shrill. "You'd better have it. Benitoite is rare and can't be synthetically created. How am I supposed to visit jewelry stores and get another benitoite stone when I can't leave this place for more than a day and you insist on hauling the closet from coast to coast? Even if I found a shop that would inquire overseas for a stone, your circus would be gone the next day and not back for months!"

There was another option—one that he refused to consider and that he knew she had no qualms about. One of them could use their particle extractor on a living person and cross their fingers that the gemstone it extracted was the one Clarice wanted. Based on the notes in Gladys's journal, there was a five percent chance that the process of having all their light particle-energy extracted would kill them immediately.

Jack unholstered the gun from his thigh and raised it to his chest level. "Gladys did leave the key with my father, *Aunt Clarice*, because she trusted him to know when you'd paid penance for the lives of all those people you killed. Since he died it's my key now, and it's up to me when I think you're ready to be released. That time is not now, so put your gun down, and let me through."

Her tube began to whine, a good indication she was getting ready to fire it. "I don't think so. You don't have the backbone to kill me. You need me alive because my research is your best hope for reversing our last experiment together."

Anger came to him, like a spigot turned to full as he recalled the botched experiment. Jack tapped the receiver area above the trigger with his finger, itching to curl it and obliterate her existence. If only he had the technology to go back in time and stop all this mess before it ever started.

Jack ground his teeth like he had gravel in his mouth that he wished to chew to sand. It seemed they were at an impasse.

He let out a heavy sigh. "I guess you'll just have to drop your weapon and see what happens."

"I think you should go first."

Jack might have rolled his eyes if the gesture wouldn't have left him vulnerable in the split second his eyes shifted away from her.

"Enough," he said, holstering his gun.

Clarice relaxed her stance and lowered her extractor. He stiffly walked past her, his nerves on fire.

"Keep your extractor handy," she said. "The lighted areas in the fortress are shrinking as the chandelier crystals burn out, since you won't let me replace the gemstones. A few shades ventured out of the attic." Her last statement should have sounded cautionary, but coming through her smiling lips, he thought it menacing instead.

He walked from the room as quickly as he could without actually running. He'd almost made it back to the cloisters before he saw them.

Thick, murky shadows flooded the hallways, though the lights hadn't dimmed or blown out. Inky black rivers seeped from the ceiling, washed down the walls, and collected in large puddles on the floor. Hands formed from the black pools, clawing their way out of the ground along with the beastly appendages and bodies attached to them.

"She calls this a 'few?'"

He unholstered his particle extractor and ran, dodging the grasping hands and claws. He squeezed the trigger and a bright flash discharged from the muzzle toward one of them. The door beside the shade ripped from its hinges, splinters chasing Jack down the hallway in slow motion. The pieces hovered in the air as though floating on water instead of moving through air.

Interesting.

The balance of sub-atomic energy in the room must have caused a hiccup in the time-compression field.

The pack thinned quickly, as he continued to shoot. He dared to hope he'd gotten the last of them when he turned the corner leading to the cloisters and saw it was empty. Or so he thought, until he realized that the tall mass of shredded fabric by the window wasn't drapes.

This shade was a bit more defined than the others—one of Clarice's last victims. Filthy and dressed in a robe of rags, the shade turned from the window and lumbered toward him, its eyes fixed on him like a hungry dog in search of a bone.

Jack wound his fingers tightly in the shade's clothing, and slung it in a half circle, flinging its hollow, bird-like body into the wall. Shoving the barrel of his gun deep into its chest cavity, he pulled the trigger. The shade shuddered once and imploded with a loud cracking noise.

"I'm sorry. Be at peace." Jack said to the charred wall.

He'd find that key and then throw it in the ocean. What Clarice did to these people . . . It was unforgiveable. She could rot here until the fortress fell out of the sky for all he cared.

Turning at various intersections to avoid the remaining shades, Jack made it to the closet without getting lost or injured. He hurried inside and pulled the door closed tightly.

When he opened it, a shaft of sunlight streamed through, growing wider. Everything in the back of his wagon was in its place, exactly where he'd left it. A glance at his watch indicated only four seconds had passed since he'd entered the closet.

His heart hammered. He took several deep breaths until it slowed back to normal. Over the past few years, Jack had trained himself to compartmentalize his visits to Knossos. Clarice hadn't found the key yet. Four seconds had passed. He could go back to his business as usual.

Well . . . maybe not exactly. He looked through the fuel chamber window, disappointed to see only the skeletal remains of the bracelet. Cripes, he'd have to find some more gemstones for it.

He shoved his particle extractor back in its box and secured it under the boxes in the back corner again. *Blast*, where was that key?

CHAPTER XIII

S OMETHING THAT *I don't want you to find first.*

Harris's comment stuck in Jack's thoughts all night. He'd have slept better with a rattlesnake for a pillow. He was also troubled by Gracie's manner at the conclusion of the evening performance—she was annoyed with him again.

It hardly seemed fair that she could attack his character with constant accusations of thievery, yet he couldn't make a modest observation that she was assertive and outspoken. If she was still angry that he'd called her a ragamuffin the other day, he'd have expected her to say so during rehearsal or when he went over their entrance cues.

He'd have to watch his mouth around her. She had a way of bringing out the worst in him—sort of like Harris.

Jack rolled off his pull-down bed and tucked the bedsheets under. The bed across from him was empty and unmade, indicating Harris had gone out for breakfast, but that he'd be back shortly. Sharing a room with Harris was the only everyday activity Jack did with his twin. They had a mutual understanding that the room was strictly for changing and sleeping in, and that they would ignore the other if they both occupied it.

Jack dressed in a rush, hoping to be gone before Harris returned. He contemplated approaching Vincenzio again about changing rooms, except Jack knew he'd rather have Harris under his nose than behind his back. Petty thieving and seducing young women didn't fit Harris's usual penchant for mischief, and Jack was wary of what Harris might be up to.

Jack especially didn't like the idea of switching rooms if Harris truly intended to call on Gracie.

Jack let out a heavy sigh before closing the door to his stateroom. The next time he caught Harris rummaging through his prop wagon, he'd be sure to ask Harris if he'd seen his spine somewhere. Jack didn't exactly know why Gracie was upset with him, but he feared her scorn enough to put aside his pride and apologize to her anyway. His sense of honor insisted he protect Gracie from his rotten twin by starting over on a better foot with her—and Jack could really use a better night's sleep this evening. At least tomorrow was Sunday. If he could make it through today, he'd catch a little break on the circus's day off.

For the entire morning, Gracie could not be found without a gaggle of women around her. Jack probably had Harris to thank for that. And she took a circuitous route wherever she went, further hindering his chances of finding an opportunity to deliver a private apology. Jack had considered giving up until Harris and Gracie entered the big top, her small hand tucked in the crook of his elbow. She wore a pale pink dress trimmed with white bows and black ribbon—one of Katherine's older dresses. In her free hand, she carried a familiar black umbrella.

If Gracie could forgive Harris enough to let him escort her to the auction, it seemed reasonable that she could overlook whatever Jack had said to offend her yesterday and last night. Squaring his shoulders, Jack marched in after them.

The tent was filled with a brown fog from the fine dirt kicked into the air by the patrons who'd come for the auction. Jack signed his name to a wooden bidding paddle while the Colonel stamped his hammer to close the sale of a gilded mirror.

The small herd of auction attendees stirred a little in the break before the next item was brought out. With Harris standing at Gracie's left side, and now carrying the umbrella for her, Jack placed himself on her right. She greeted him with a curt nod and condescended to murmur a painfully polite, "Good afternoon," in his direction.

Undeterred, he bowed his head. "Miss Hart, you look very fine in that gown. Are you here to model the lot items or acquire them?"

Gracie blushed, raising her paddle over the lower half of her face to cover it. "There is one item in particular I hope to bid on, though I doubt I'll be its only contender," she said. "And I've told you before to call me 'Gracie.'"

"If it's a dress, I should think it will fit you very well."

"Yes, I'm sure any of Katherine's dresses would fit my *sickly* figure better than your lumberjack one," she shot back, deflecting his intended compliment.

Jack sighed. He should just invite Harris to jab him in his nether regions with the stupid umbrella. The circus would be in Nebraska before he got in Gracie's good graces. However, the thought of being so easily outwitted and outmaneuvered by Harris was demoralizing enough to keep Jack from returning the paddle.

He settled into his seat as the auction continued. Gracie clutched her paddle to the front of her chest with both hands like a shield, getting steadily more agitated. The lot numbers moved into the fifties, and two men carried a reddish trunk out and set it in front of the Colonel's podium. Gracie bounced the fan end on her palm then wrung the handle in both hands. Jack suspected the paddle might not survive the auction.

The auction colonel shuffled the papers in his hands before announcing, "Our next item, lot 56, one rosewood trunk, is now open for bidding at one dollar."

Harris turned to Gracie. "This is the item you want, right?"

Gracie's paddle flipped up. A crone with hoary hair, dressed in shades of gray and lavender, raised her paddle. A gentleman with a brown bowler hat increased the bid. As Gracie fought to be the highest bidder, Jack found himself being fanned by her paddle like he was the sultan of a Middle Eastern country.

The allure of the trunk grew among the patrons as a few more paddles went up and the bid passed $1.50. Gracie chewed on her lower lip and upped the bid to $1.70.

Jack leaned toward her. "Why do you need such an expensive trunk?"

She switched her paddle to her right hand and he had to lean back to avoid getting smacked in the face. "When I want your opinion on how to spend my money, I'll *ask* for it."

Harris stroked his chin with two fingers. "You said I stole your money at the station. How can you afford it and also claim you're broke?"

Her stiff shoulders sharpened, as did her tone. "Mr. Detweiler gave me a loan."

A flush of heat ran from Jack's collar to his ears as though he'd backed up too close to an upright furnace. When had this exchange occurred? And what was it about Harris and Jonathan Detweiler that made all the young ladies turn a blind eye to the fact they were disagreeable as hornets?

Stealing a glance at Harris, Jack noted that the news seemed a bit surprising to him as well. But a moment later, his twin resumed smiling without comment, no doubt buoyed in spirit because of his quickly formed friendship with Gracie. Something was amiss. Gracie must be clowning him. She hadn't even cringed when Harris mentioned stealing from her just now when previously, each time she'd accused *him* of stealing her ticket, her eyes pled, "Please die painfully."

The old woman raised the bid to two dollars. A splotchy blush crept high on Gracie's cheeks and spread to her neck. Whatever money Mr. Detweiler had given her, it wouldn't hold out against the widow's estate. At around $2.25, Gracie's paddle took a break. The old woman and a gentleman increased the bid to $2.90. At that point, Gracie jadedly rejoined.

Jack turned to face her. "You realize you could probably buy a new dress with that much money; that's a whole day's wages!"

"Three *weeks'* wages," she corrected him.

With a small shake, Jack lowered his head. Now he better understood Vincenzio's eagerness for him to take on Gracie as his assistant. He was paying her nickels on the dollar of what he'd paid Katherine.

At $3.70 Gracie's arm lowered and her head drooped in defeat.

The Colonel called for any last bids. The gentleman shook his head and held his paddle in a downward position. Gracie's arm twitched. The old woman turned around with a quelling stare, perfected by half a century of practice. Gracie's arm turned limp.

"I'm sure you can find another trunk you like that's cheaper," Harris offered his condolences.

"Going once . . . Going twice . . ." the Colonel sang. Jack noted the brown portion of Gracie's hazel eyes had dulled enough to resemble dirty pennies. She had a pocket full of borrowed money, and yet this trunk was so important to her that she'd stayed for the auction instead of fleeing for the train station. She wanted this *more* than she wanted to get to Chicago, which he knew she wanted bad enough to become his assistant—to put her trust in a hack of a knife thrower.

Jack shot his paddle in the air.

"I have $3.75 from the gentleman in the back, thank you." The Colonel reopened the bid.

"What are you doing?" she asked, her eyes suddenly alert, searching his.

"Spending my money."

With an indignant scowl, the crone raised her paddle to counter. Gracie pulled on his arm.

"You're not going to spend that much on a trunk, are you?"

Why was she protesting? If he bought the trunk for her, she'd be getting exactly what she wanted without spending any of her money. Did she despise him so much that she wouldn't accept the trunk as a gift?

"You were, and Granny over there seems to think it's worth more," he replied. "Clearly, this is a fine piece of furniture a young lady would be proud to own."

Gracie lowered and folded her hands. He had her full attention now for the first time since he'd entered the tent, and especially since they'd brought out that ruddy trunk. Having her stare hopefully at him, like he was the answer to her prayers, was a bit burdening . . . and a little attractive.

The value of the chest to the old lady didn't exceed $4.50. Jack held the high bid at $4.60.

"Going once . . ."

"$4.70!" Jack heard his voice shout on the other side of Gracie. He whirled toward Harris and frowned at his raised arm.

"So now you want the trunk?"

"Of course not. *I'm* gonna win it for Gracie, since she's always saying how it's my fault she lost her ticket."

Jack raised his arm stiffly. Whatever his twin was plotting, he would put an end to it.

"$4.80. Will someone offer $4.90?" the Colonel asked.

Harris grinned unctuously and bid. "You know I hate it when we do this."

"Then stop it." Jack bid again.

Gracie squirmed in her seat between them. "You two aren't seriously going to compete with each other to win this for me, are you?"

Harris created a small landmark for the auction by raising the bid to five dollars. "Let's say we make this a sweeter deal? Whichever of us wins also gets a kiss from Gracie."

Gracie's mouth dropped open. "What? You can't promise things like that!"

"Six dollars!" Jack shouted.

The crowd hushed and the Colonel paused, his rhythm broken. Jack hiccupped in his chest as well. Why had he raised the bid so steeply? He couldn't let Harris win, so Jack justified the impulse.

"I have s-six dollars! Will anyone beat six dollars?" The Colonel found his voice.

"You drive a hard bargain, Jack." Harris smirked. "Seven!"

"Stop this now, both of you." Gracie clung to Jack's shoulder. "Jack, let him win. Just stop this nonsense before you send yourselves to the poor house!"

Her eyes, darkened with distress, smothered the flame of his ego. If she wasn't happy, was there really a point for him to keep going? The voice of the Colonel echoed in the background. Seven dollars. Seven dollars . . .

His hand twitched. Her fingers curled around his hand, pushing it down. "Please, Jack. Stop this."

"If you want Harris to give you the trunk, I'll stop."

"I do."

The paddle he held felt like a dirigible waiting to take flight. Only the weight of Gracie's hand wrapped around his kept it anchored. It had been his idea, and he deserved the recognition, but his twin had swindled it away from him.

"Sold!" The hammer cracked like a falling boulder on the podium.

Her hands slid off of his, and her cherry blossom lips murmured, "Thank you."

She drew Harris, the winner, to her chest in a firm hug—without even a Bible's width between them. Leaning toward him, she planted a soft kiss on his cheek. From Harris's wry smile, with his nose pressed into the soft curls of her hair, Jack knew her touch was everything Harris had imagined it would be.

Jack stood, spun on his heel, and returned to the collection's table, throwing his bidding paddle against the wood with a sharp smack. He shouldn't have given up. That should've been his victory.

CHAPTER XIV

Inside her room, Gracie clicked open the lock on the rosewood trunk with a single turn of the brass key. The left half of the trunk had five pullout drawers. The right side featured a mirror and two small drawers.

She'd sold her forgiveness for seven dollars and a peculiar black umbrella, a great bargain considering she had thought she'd settled the score yesterday with her parasol. Though the purchase of the trunk had secured her forgiveness, Harris hadn't earned her trust yet.

Gracie leaned back and pushed her palms down the skirt of her dress. She released a long, heavy breath. The trunk was empty, as she'd suspected it would be, which made her all the more chagrined for hoping she'd find something more than dustballs to soften the finality of the gaping truth that now faced her.

No fashion accessory, piece of clothing, or furniture item would ever bring back her mother's plucky laugh, the freshly-laid-egg feel of her father's face after he'd shaved, or the sound of her brother's marbles clacking in his hip pouch.

Gracie pursed her lips in disappointment. She could have bought a wicker laundry basket to store her meager belongings in for a half-dollar, but that wouldn't have helped preserve the memory of her family. And it would be ungrateful, untrue, for her to say she wasn't happy with the trunk. Yet how else could she describe this feeling of being poorer for owning it, without having spent a penny to win it?

Harris had insisted she didn't need to repay him, but she couldn't possibly accept so much charity and not feel indebted somehow. And she still needed to return Mr. Detweiler's money, plus interest.

Gracie placed her postcard in the top drawer and covered it with her threadbare nightdress. She pushed the drawers back into their compartments. If she hurried, she might have a chance to thank Jack before he began his pre-performance preparations. Because of him, that grandma hadn't made off with her trunk.

The trunk lid rattled as she attempted to lock it. Something was preventing one of the drawers from closing completely. Gracie opened it again and inspected the interior. The bottom drawer protruded nearly half an inch out from the others. Had a loose button fallen behind it?

The back of the drawer appeared normal, sending her to search the dark space of the empty compartment. Her fingers wrapped around a cold, slender object with protruding edges like the teeth of a gear. She pulled it out.

Another key?

Despite its size, hardly longer than the length of her pinky, its weight led Gracie to believe it must be solid silver rather than pewter. On the handle were several jewels, small circles of milky white and blue surrounding a large, deep, clear blue stone. She scrutinized the furniture in the room, especially the tiny vanity affixed to the cabin wall, looking for signs of a keyhole. Except for her trunk, which she'd already opened with the larger brass key, she saw none.

Find Katherine's key. Keep it secret or you'll die next, the note had said. Had the note meant this key?

"Finders keepers." She shrugged and tucked it down the front of her corset. But with one look at her two mole-hills of a chest, she thought better of it and fetched the old sock from beneath the mattress. She'd keep it safe alongside Mr. Detweiler's money, just in case the bookkeeper somehow came asking for it; if he didn't, she'd consider pawning it.

As Gracie approached the big top, she had to fight against the riptide of the stagehands, constantly entering and exiting the big top with scaffolding seats for the evening performance.

She found Jack's vanishing closet already unloaded off his prop wagon, but saw no sign of him. The door hung ajar, inviting her to step inside.

Certain the secret panel came from the side, she ran her fingers over the seams. She couldn't even find a space large enough to wedge a coin into.

"You mind telling me what you're doing?" One of the twins asked.

Gracie spun around. The twin's accusing glower, paired with his rigid posture and the way he clasped his hands behind his back, reminded Gracie of the way Mr. Levenson carried his yardstick around during class.

Definitely Jack. Harris had been in a good mood at the end of the auction.

She scrambled out of the closet. "I didn't mean any harm."

Jack shut the door firmly. Only then did his expression soften. "This closet was custom made. Any piece would be difficult to replace if something gets buggered. I'd appreciate it if you wouldn't poke about."

"The door was open. I was just curious."

"You found it open?" The lines in his forehead furrowed into dismal ruts as his eyes jumped to the closet door. "I'll have to inspect it then and make sure no one's tampered with the secret compartment mechanism while it's been sitting here like a public fountain," he said, reaching for the doorknob. "Either way, don't let me catch you in there alone again." He shot her a cautionary glance. "You should go change into your costume before it gets any later."

Hesitantly, she approached him, set her hands on either side of his collar, and stretched to the tips of her toes until her chin brushed his jaw. "Thank you for the trunk," she whispered and then pressed her lips into the shadowed area of his cheek. She felt a slight tickle from a patch on his jaw that hadn't been shaved as close as the rest.

Jack pulled away. "Thank Harris, not me. He's the one you wanted to win it for you."

Her face was hot as she turned back toward the big top. Whatever feelings of gratitude or affection she thought she had for him, he had no such feelings for her. She slapped her cheeks, embarrassed by the silliness of her own thoughts. She'd be leaving the circus once it reached Chicago, or sooner if things went smoothly at the border crossing. She couldn't afford to have any sort of sentimental feelings that might attach her to this life.

In the pad room just outside the big top, Gracie dusted the shiny parts of her face with the talcum powder she'd gotten from Elizabeth. Her left hand fumbled for the stub of a kohl stick which Olivia, from the gaggle of girls she'd met earlier, had given Gracie to help her outline her eyes. She was mindful of Jack's occasional glance in her direction, but aside from their conversation after the auction, he'd not said a word to her.

"You seem a lot more relaxed today."

The voice belonged to a woman with long dark hair and warm brown skin. It took Gracie a moment to recognize her as Harris's flying partner since her hair wasn't piled on her head like a mushroom. Maria.

"I survived my first performance yesterday, and since Harris introduced me to a few of the other girls, I don't feel like such an outsider."

"That's good to hear." Maria smiled, creating long dimples in her cheeks. "I've been with the troupe since before Vincenzio took over, so if you need anything, just let me know."

"Not at the moment," Gracie returned Maria's smile, "but once I get paid, there are a few items I'd like to go out and buy." All the items she'd had in her steamer case which Harris had carried over to the train's luggage loading platform. She doubted she'd ever see that case again.

Maria nodded and then patted Gracie on the shoulder. "I'm here if you need me. Break a leg!" And with that, she left Gracie to finish getting ready.

The phrase still seemed strange to Gracie, but she recalled the contortionist had told her to "break a leg" as well. It must mean something different in the circus, something only known to insiders, something Maria would be well aware of. After this thought, Gracie realized she should've asked Maria for her tips on how to tell Jack and Harris apart. If anyone knew, she would.

Jack's melancholy still lingered during the evening performance, reinforcing Gracie's thought that his capability to hold a grudge was definitely a force to reckon with her own. Twice, during the knife act, she thought he'd scathed her with a paper-cut sized scratch. But when she examined herself afterward, she couldn't even find a snag in her tights.

Before she stepped into the vanishing closet, he warned her again. "Don't touch anything, and don't come out until I open the door."

Could she even get out if she wanted to?

Once he shut the door, she began humming. After the third verse of "London Bridge is Falling Down," the panel for the secret compartment closed in front of her.

The hairs in her nose burned from an astringent scent. The good news was that if she fainted, the smell would revive her immediately. Midway through the eighth verse, light penetrated the closet. Fresh air—thank goodness.

Jack's nose and forehead wrinkled when he escorted her out. He must have gotten a whiff of the noxious odor too. "Can you smell that?" she asked through her forced grin. The crowd under the big top clapped with vigor.

Jack bowed. "It's the solvent I used to oil the closet's mechanical gears. It's not something you should be concerned about."

Unless I pass out inside the closet during the act.

As the sound of applause faded, he led her out of the big top by the crook of her arm. She whispered as they walked, "Could you *please* have the decency not to oil the closet so soon before a performance?"

Jack was silent as he parted the flap leading out of the big top. He studied her for a moment as he let the flap close behind him. Then, turning his attention to unbuttoning his cufflinks, he asked, "Has my twin asked you to look for anything among Katherine's things?"

"Excuse me?" What did Harris or Katherine's things have to do with the smell of oil?

He shrugged off his costume jacket. "Has Harris asked you to search Katherine's room for anything?"

Her comprehension wasn't the problem. His question was as unexpected the second time, but at least he was talking to her. "Yesterday he wanted to look for something, but Vincenzio told him to ask the bookkeeper," she replied.

"Harold?"

She thought that was his name. "He's bald and Miriam doesn't like him much."

Jack smiled at this. "Miriam hardly likes anyone." He refocused their conversation. "Did Harris say what he hoped to find?"

Her thoughts turned to the key she'd found. *Keep it secret or you'll die next.* Surely if that was what Harris wanted, he would have hired a locksmith to tool the lock for him.

"I only recall him saying he believed Katherine had it last."

"That doesn't help much."

"What did he lose?" If it had something to do with their rivalry, she might spend some time searching for the item herself.

Small lines etched Jack's forehead, countered by the clenched muscles in his jaw. Was he hiding fear, disgust, or masking anger?

"Something he doesn't want me to find first," Jack said.

She pouted, wishing that her trust in him during their act was reason enough for him to confide in her now. "That's not much to go on."

Jack fussed with the buttons of his shirt and his cummerbund. "Either way, there's no need for you to get involved." He slipped into the men's dressing tent.

Inside the women's dressing tent, Gracie helped herself to a seat on the corner of one of the costume trunks. Flexing her feet to soothe her arches, she let Katherine's shoes teeter on the end of her toes. A folded strip of paper fluttered out of the left shoe. Gracie scooped it up.

Stay away from the shadows. Run or you'll be dead next.

Stay away from the shadows. What shadows?

Run or you'll be dead next. She felt her blood run cold, but the threat actually wasn't the part of the prank that Gracie found most disturbing. Rather, it was the fact that the handwriting had a striking resemblance to her own hand.

Who was trying to frighten her? Jack had said everyone else was too superstitious to agree to be his assistant, so then what was the point in trying to scare her away? Jack also openly didn't want her there, so there was no reason for him to be sneaky about the notes, but this could be Harris's type of mischief.

Maria had spent a fair amount of time just being chatty, and the fact that she was Harris's flying partner might suggest that Maria would be disposed to hate Jack, and possibly Gracie by the extension of her partnership with him. While Gracie hadn't removed her shoes in front of Maria, could she have been distracting Gracie while someone else somehow took Gracie's shoe off, planted the note, and then replaced it? Highly unlikely.

Aside from magic, Gracie was running out of plausible explanations.

She checked the insoles of her shoes for any other notes and slipped them back on.

She shook her head, as if the physical action could somehow dispel her distress.

Someone in the troupe was unhappy with the fact she was here.

CHAPTER XV

GRACIE CHANGED into one of Katherine's old sarcenet evening gowns, less sure of her prior belief that a person shouldn't care about the clothing's previous owner. She wondered what Miriam would charge to sew a new dress.

Absorbed in her thoughts, she hung her costume on one of the dressing racks and set off across the circus lot to find Miriam. She was abruptly called back to the present when she cornered the ticket stand with her head down and bounced into Vincenzio's gorilla chest—or rather, his gut. Jack flanked him, still dressed in his performance outfit. His knives winked at her from his waistband.

Vincenzio gave her an unctuous smile, and Jack looked as if he wanted to harpoon the pompous whale. "Gracie, I'm glad I found you," Vincenzio said. "I'd like you to accompany me to dinner tonight at the Chateau Versailles hotel." He looked her up and down for an uncomfortably long moment, and then added, "Have Miriam find you something more suitable to wear."

The air around Gracie turned stifling, as though she'd been over-laced in a Turkish bath house. She picked at the buttons on her sleeve cuffs, testing the strength of the thread holding them on. "Actually, if you don't mind, I was planning on washing my stockings tonight."

Vincenzio threw his head back laughing.

She looked to Jack for encouragement. He had none to give her, too focused on crushing peanut shells into the ground with his heel.

Vincenzio smoothed the frizzy wings of hair over his ears and hitched his vest down so it covered his waistline again. "Wash your socks? You can do that sort of a thing on a Sunday. Tonight, I'm giving you a chance to eat a fine meal with civilized company."

"But—"

"The socks can wait. Dinner is at seven," he said with finality.

He left without waiting for her reply. Sadly, even in these few extra moments, she'd yet to think of a better excuse besides telling him she was due for a headache that hour.

Jack gave her an uncertain smile as he passed, which Gracie could not be sure was meant in sympathy or annoyance.

She squared her shoulders and searched for the courage she'd had when Jack first told her of Katherine's alternate duties as a hostess at Vincenzio's after dinner parties. She found just enough of it to face Miriam.

Miriam procured an ecru foulard dress with a low cut basque from the few dresses she'd withheld from the auction. The seamstress folded the elegant dress into a large box and tied it with a ribbon.

"If it gets soiled, you'll have to pay someone else to clean it. I am a seamstress, not a laundress. You know this, yes?" She shoved the box into Gracie's chest.

Hugging the box, Gracie headed back toward the dressing tent, taking the shortcut through the menagerie and sideshow as there were still a fair number of towners filtering out of the big top now that the show was over.

The sideshow resembled the streets of Coney Island. Instead of a large, single tent, two lines of canvas booths lined the dirt walkway. The fire-eaters, sword swallowers, and other eccentric circus characters performed here. Additionally, there were the shriveled remains of a mermaid: "$100 reward if not absolutely real."

Although the sideshow was closed and the front flaps of the tent doors were laced shut, Gracie's inner child couldn't resist sneaking a peek at the mermaid. Half hitch knots weren't too difficult to retie. No one would ever know she'd stolen a peek . . .

"Miss Hart!" someone shouted from the far side of the sideshow.

She dropped the rope to the tent flaps and called out, "The knot was loose so I'm retying it!" It was always better not to fess up right away.

"Look out!" the voice cried, more panicked than before.

She spun around. Instead of a person charging toward her, Gracie faced four hundred and fifty pounds of muscle beneath an orange pelt with black and white stripes—one of the menagerie tigers. Far behind the big cat was Mr. Detweiler. "Don't move!" he shouted to her, waving his arms frantically.

"Don't move" implied she should remain still. Too bad fear had already taken control of her body. Her legs, which had been frozen, reacted like horses at the crack of a whip. She sprinted in the opposite direction, her feet hitting the ground faster than typewriter keys hitting a page.

She threw the dress box behind her as a decoy. A stolen glance over her shoulder confirmed that tigers still preferred fresh meat over evening gowns. She dashed out of the side show and into the section of the circus's utility and storage tents.

Movement near one of the tents drew her attention from the tiger. She screamed as something large crashed into her. *A second tiger? A lion?*

The impact compressed the air from her lungs, cutting off her voice. A pair of muscular arms seized her. Her legs treaded water in air and she felt like a fish snatched from the river by a hawk.

A deep voice whispered in her ear, marked by an accent that spoke of time spent in places populated with koalas and kangaroos. "Don't break eye contact," the twin said, lowering her to the ground.

The twin's hold around her, tight and firm, kept her heart from pounding out of her chest.

The tiger's glowing amber eyes, highlighted by circles of black and white eyeliner, locked with hers. It slowed to a creeping stalk, its shoulder blades shifting up and down as it edged closer. Gracie didn't dare blink.

The tiger drifted to the side of one of the tent rows. The twin pressed his weight against her hip, coaxing her to sidestep with him. His heart raced through the folds of his shirt and something that felt like knife hilts dug into her back. She could barely hear Jack's voice over her own whimpering. "He'll only attack if he thinks he can surprise us."

Jack moved with calculation, his weight balanced like a dancer. With her legs shaking and knees locked, she pivoted more like a drafting compass from one point to the next. They circled until the tiger was positioned in front of the tent Jack had emerged from.

His grip loosened and Gracie felt his hand slide down her back to withdraw a knife from his waistband.

"On the count of three, help me scare it into the tent."

She didn't think she could send a bird flying from a birdbath, let alone the king of the jungle running with his tail between his legs.

". . . Two."

Barking spiders, he'd already started counting.

"Three."

She squeaked a cry of terror a rabbit wouldn't have perked its long ears up for. Thankfully, Jack bellowed louder than a fog horn. His body seemed to double in size as he threw his arms up and leapt at the tiger.

The cat pinned back its ears and bolted into the tent, tail clamped between its legs. Jack wasted no time kicking out the supports and collapsing the canvas panels over it. The tiger, a large lump under the canvas sheet, snuffed around while Jack circled the deflated tent, using his knife to cut the anchoring cords. His actions were so calm and methodical that Gracie half expected him to sling the bagged feline over his shoulder and carry it back to the menagerie. But there was no need, as Mr. Detweiler and a few stagehands had arrived to take over.

Breathing loudly through his nose, and with a sheen of sweat on his forehead, Mr. Detweiler gathered the tent cords while one of the stagehands rang a small bell and tried to get the tiger to "lie down" under the canvas.

Gracie wondered why the cat trainer wasn't here to help, though she didn't feel she was in a position to assist either.

Her hands trembled despite her efforts to hold them still and her palms stung from the indentations her nails had left. Her thoughts slowly collected, starting with shame for panicking. The easiest way to forgive herself was to pretend that nothing out of the ordinary had happened.

The tiger had been loose. Now it was caught. She'd thought her life might end for nothing. How silly of her. And with everyone else cleaning things up, she should grab the dress and be on her way. The shakes would soon pass.

She took two steps and was overcome by the feeling that she'd wandered into the hall of mirrors. Distorted persons of all forms and shapes surrounded her: tall and skinny, short and fat, and people with oversized heads attached to tiny baby doll bodies. The floor waved and swirled, the sight nauseating and dizzying. Jack caught her the moment she swooned.

In his hold, she felt the same protection and comfort she had years ago in her father's arms. She remembered their trip to Wiltshire to visit Stonehenge. Her father carried her on his back while her brother, Robert, ran ahead through the arches. Her mother twirled her parasol in her blue and pink bustled dress. Beautiful, laughing, smiling.

Gracie smiled for moment, and then realized that seeing her parents meant she'd slipped into a dream. Suddenly, the scene dissolved into a cloudy white fog. Gracie squeezed her eyes shut, savoring the memory. Her head felt like it'd been packed in wool and holding onto the details became a challenge, like carrying sand in her hands. The tighter she squeezed, the more the grains slipped through.

"Gracie, snap out of it."

Her eyes opened to their widest. The fog cleared, and an array of canvas tents and circus performers came into focus. Jack hovered over her, his lips and cheeks the same pale hue. "You passed out for a second."

Gracie's throat fluttered. Her voice broke its way through, small and pinched. "Yes, it seems I did."

Jack pushed her shoulders forward, easing her into a sitting position. "Hang tight here for a moment. I'll get you some water."

She grabbed his sleeve and held him back. "That's not necessary, I'm fine." Heavens, he was making such a fuss over her—and at a time when she just wanted to melt into a puddle and evaporate. If she'd ever fainted at the orphanage, she would have woken up with her eyebrows shaved off and a new nickname like "Fainter-Face-Grace." She didn't know what type of social hierarchy existed within the circus, only that she had failed its initiation test by overreacting to a loose animal. This sort of thing probably happened monthly.

Gracie turned her gaze to the pack of stagehands hauling the tent-wrapped tiger back toward the menagerie. Her scowl fixated on the newly arrived cat trainer. Bartholomew, or Barty as everyone else called him. He was a man of less than forty, dressed in a red coat and canary yellow bowtie. His eyes were hidden beneath bristling eyebrows and his lips were buried by a thick mustache. Was it possible he'd let the tiger loose on purpose? Of anyone who might have, he would've had the most opportunity. Plus, she'd always thought men with facial hair were a bit suspicious, like they had something to hide even if it was nothing more than bad teeth.

As she sat up further, she felt Jack's hand on her back, supporting her. "How did the tiger escape?" she asked.

Jack's lip curled up to his nose, exposing a snarl. "That's a fair question. Why don't we find out?" He left her side and jogged to the group. "Hold up, Barty!" Snagging the lion tamer by his long whip, Jack tore him away from the others and dragged him to her side and helped Gracie to her feet. He gestured toward her. "I think Gracie deserves to know. How did Semaj escape?"

Barty mopped his brow with a handkerchief. "It's all my fault. When I went to feed Semaj after the show, he was cowering in the corner. I opened the door wider and was trying to coax him to come eat. Then I saw—"

He paused, his eyes darting around. Gracie followed his gaze and realized their conversation had been joined by several other troupe members. She recognized Miriam, Harold, Olivia, Mr. Detweiler, one of the clowns, and she thought the muscular man with log-sized legs must be Victor.

Barty ran his finger around his collar and tugged at his yellow bowtie.

"Saw what?" Harold prompted.

The cat trainer wrung his handkerchief. "I don't know if I dare say. It might get angry."

Miriam's fine eyebrows shot up into her forehead. "It?"

Jack set a hand on Barty's shoulder and pulled him close, though it hardly equated to a private conversation. "Barty, if you can't describe it, people will think you're making it up and you let the tiger out on purpose."

The cat trainer pulled away from Jack. "People are going to think I'm making it up anyway, but I know what I saw." He spat the next words out. "It was a ghost!"

"Katherine's ghost?" said a woman wearing a white pleated smock with a beaded Egyptian necklace. With her heavy eye make-up, it was hard to tell if she was outraged or afraid.

Jack's tone was careless when he spoke again to Barty, but there was a set to his shoulders that revealed his underlying nervousness. "I'm sure there's a logical explanation. Could it have been a trick of the light?"

Barty shot Jack a sideways glance. His next words were very much for the benefit of the crowd around them. "Can't say. It was dark and shadowy. I thought it might be from a fire smoking somewhere, but then it moved as if to grab me."

"Dreadful!" The Egyptian queen pressed her hand to her scarab necklace.

Barty nodded. "I've never considered myself a coward until that thing charged me. I dropped the bucket of meat and fled. I ran into Jonathan, told him what I saw, and we both went back to look for it. It was gone, along with Semaj."

The cat trainer then turned to Jack and pulled him into a full, firm hug. "I can't begin to say how thankful I am that you managed to detain him before someone shot him. Poor thing was just scared."

Jack peeled the man off. "Let's be thankful this didn't happen before the show when the towners were around." Everyone seemed to agree on that point, though the general mood remained dark and gloomy.

"My apologies, Miss," Barty leaned over and kissed her hand just below the wrist before taking his leave. "I must catch up with the others and make sure Semaj gets back in his cage without trouble."

Vincenzio arrived a minute later, which made Gracie wish she'd waited to get up. She might have gotten out of dinner if she'd had the foresight to feign shock. He circled the dirt patch where the tent had been pitched. "Seems we'll need a new laundry tent." He said, twirling the wings of his hair. "Why didn't those idiots roll the tiger cage over here? By the time they haul Semaj back to the menagerie the tent'll be ruined."

The man had been born with an abacus for a brain and a coin scale for a heart. Compared to the price of a new tiger, Gracie thought he'd gotten a bargain. As for the going rate of stowaway orphans—she knew Vincenzio wouldn't bat an eye for her sake.

"Jack, clean up this mess," Vincenzio said.

The circus owner was about to leave when Miriam stepped forward with folded arms, her fingertips pressed against the insides of her elbows. She stared down her long, remarkable nose at the overweight man. "Is that all you have to say? What if it had killed someone?" She looked at Gracie briefly. "Jack saved your circus. You can at least thank him." The authority in her tone straightened Gracie's spine.

Beside Gracie, Jack's face twisted into confusion, as though he'd expected Miriam to call for the crowd to throw rocks at him, and instead was showered with rose petals.

Vincenzio prodded one of the tent cords with his foot. "Jack, I guess I owe you for saving my tiger before someone called the police to come shoot it." Vincenzio raised his eyes from the ground. "As a reward, why don't you accompany me to dinner at the hotel?"

Vincenzio turned to Miriam, eyebrow raised as if to say, "There, happy now?"

Jack bowed, the movement much stiffer than the way he bowed after a performance. If it wasn't for Jack's polite smile, Gracie would've thought him injured. "Thank you, but I didn't act alone. Jonathan Detweiler and Barty assisted as well."

"Barty will be lucky if I don't fire him for letting the tiger escape! But of course, Jonathan," Vincenzio's eyes found where Mr. Detweiler was standing amid the small group of performers and nodded his acknowledgment, "you are invited as well. But you three—" Vincenzio's gaze turned from Mr. Detweiler, to Jack, finally resting on Gracie, "—will have to get your own carriage to the hotel. I'm not waiting around for you to change clothes."

There went her plan to get lost on the way to the hotel.

The group seemed satisfied with this outcome and dispersed. Gracie dragged her feet back to her dress box. Despite the box's crushed state, the dress remained unharmed. Her thoughts turned again to the note she'd found in her shoe. Miriam had had the fore-sight to wrap her dress in a box. She also had access to Gracie's cos-tume. Could Miriam be the one leaving the notes as part of a twisted publicity hoax to increase ticket sales? Who wouldn't be more excited to see a show that claimed to have man-eating tigers compared to one that just had tigers?

Gracie tucked the box under her arm and turned toward the train cars, her mind abuzz with suspicions and unanswered questions.

GRACIE took her time changing into the ecru dress, which was cut so much smaller than Katherine's other dresses that she filled it with only one set of pads. Self-conscious, she regretted not asking Miriam for a wrap. She threw the extra pancakes into her trunk before heading to meet Jack and Mr. Detweiler.

She found them on the street corner beside Vincenzio's hired car-riage. Jack was dressed in a well-tailored evening coat, a red brocade vest, and a clean white fitted shirt.

Although Jack and Harris were identical twins, Gracie couldn't help but think Harris had worn the ensemble a little bit better at the Albany train depot. Harris's arrogance fit the profile of an opulent businessman more than Jack's modesty. And while there wasn't any solid evidence to support this observation, it seemed to her that when Harris walked, he did so with his chest thrust out, whereas Jack's stiff posture came from the heavy load on his shoulders, pulling them back.

Mr. Detweiler wore his performance outfit, minus the teal cape. White and black dog hair covered the lower half of his legs.

Jack opened the carriage door for her before the team master stood from the driver's seat. With the tips of his fingers, he held her elbow to balance her while she climbed in. She felt a little flush of pleasure at his touch, but quickly stamped it out. He was merely being polite.

Jack dug a coin out of his pocket to pay the driver and Gracie silently cursed that she hadn't thought to bring the sock with Mr. Detweiler's money so she could return it.

Once Mr. Detweiler and Jack were seated on the other side, the driver whipped the horses. The carriage rumbled onto the street with the other wide-wheeled drays and hackneys. Gracie leaned closer to the window, using the view to try and drown the memory of her last carriage ride—a one-way trip from the Castle Garden immigration office to St. Patrick's orphanage.

The streets of Montreal were bustling with people and dense with shops. The spires of the town hall, hospital, and local church rose up over the tree line, similar to sharpened pencils standing on end. The wheels of the carriage rolled through puddles, spraying droplets of gray water behind them.

Gracie retreated from the window. "Jack?" He looked up from fiddling with his cravat, a snowy expanse of ruffled linen. "You told me that bad luck comes in threes, and that all sorts of things would go wrong before the other omens were fulfilled. Did the tiger escaping this evening count toward one of the three?"

Before Jack could speak, Mr. Detweiler grabbed her hand and stroked it, much like she imagined he'd pet one of his dogs. He winked and flashed her a warm smile fraught with significance. "Don't be afraid Miss Hart, you're quite safe with us."

In that moment, if the air between Jack and Mr. Detweiler were passed through a distiller, the result would be pure acid. Gracie pulled her hand free and rubbed it on the side of her dress.

"No one got hurt, so I'm inclined to think it's just one of those smaller misfortunes," Jack replied, barely moving his lips.

"I'm certain if you hadn't been there, the tiger would've mauled me. I suppose it was good luck you also managed to trap it before someone shot it."

A frown stretched across Jack's face. "If I were being honest, I should admit it wasn't my intent to save its life. Things just happened that way."

"Oh?" Gracie leaned forward. "You had your performance knives, didn't you? I know you could have hit it."

Jack shook his head. "I'd no sooner try to slit my enemy's throat with a fruit peeler than hope my knives could take down such a beast."

Gracie leaned heavily into the seat. She clung to the side wall for support from what she hoped Jack and Mr. Detweiler would mistake for the roughness of the road, and not the illness she felt when her thoughts were forced to the letter opener protruding from the fore-man's neck.

Letter opener, fruit peeler, or knife—all these tools could be deadly if wielded intentionally or accidentally. Could it have been the foreman's ghost Barty saw and not Katherine's?

Mr. Detweiler rubbed his chin with his forefinger and thumb, hardly sparing her a second glance. His eyebrows leveled, he turned to Jack, and his lips became a razor thin line. "The death of a tiger would be better than a tragedy involving a performer. Perhaps you should've killed the beast, so we could count it as the second omen."

The muscle in Jack's jaw twitched. "If there truly is some mysti-cal, evil power that honors the 'rule of three,' then I would expect it'd want the satisfaction of causing the mischief itself. Its craving for blood wouldn't be appeased by an orchestrated event."

Mr. Detweiler leaned forward. "Do you really think the thing Barty saw was Katherine's ghost?"

"No." Jack rearranged himself toward the window and offered no further explanation.

Mr. Detweiler next looked at her, words of silent prodding written in the lines on his forehead. She shook her head. Gracie didn't want to speculate what it wanted, as there really could only be one thing: revenge.

Ghosts were souls with unfinished business on earth, who had yet to ascend to heaven. If Katherine hadn't died in peace, it was entirely possible her ghost might decide to haunt the circus—or the girl who had replaced her—until her death was avenged.

With a shrug, Mr. Detweiler crossed his legs slowly, one over the other. "In any case, I'm sure Vincenzio will do everything in his power tonight to spin it as foul play so it ends up in the paper."

Gracie hoped not. The last thing she wanted was her name printed in the paper for someone in Albany to make the connection that the circus train had left the same day she'd disappeared. And if this was all really a publicity hoax, wouldn't the headlines be bigger if she'd been mauled and not saved?

Mr. Detweiler, who'd called out to her and alerted her of the danger, had told her to hold still. But fear had made her run. Had running been a genuine instinct, or did she do it because of the note's warning? *Stay away from the shadows. Run or you'll be dead next.*

CHAPTER XVI

THE CARRIAGE stopped at the front of the hotel and let them off under the tasseled awning. A jaunty bellhop led them to a small lounge with wainscot paneling and windows as tall as the ceiling. Gracie curtsied to each gentlemen Vincenzio introduced her to, unable to keep their names straight. From behind, they all looked alike. From the front, the only distinguishable difference was the style in which they waxed their mustaches.

The call to be seated for dinner was a relief to her cheeks, which were aching from too many fake smiles.

They sat in deep, sloping armchairs around tables draped in linen and topped with china. The chefs served chicken braised in red wine with sides of button mushrooms, chopped onion, and bacon. She dawdled like a turtle, delaying the end of dinner for as long as possible. Although there were other women from the circus in the company, she imagined she was the only one who hadn't made her debut doing a hoochie coochie dance in the doxy's tent. They laughed absurdly loud, making it unthinkable that anyone in the hotel could not hear them.

After dinner, Vincenzio found every excuse to keep Gracie close to him. He'd have her hold his glass of brandy while he spoke with someone, or he'd send her to get him another bottle. When he didn't require her service as his personal waitress, he thrust her back into the company of all those mustachioed gentlemen, insisting she recount her frightening experience with Semaj.

The men would listen with interest and then kiss the back of her hand and invite her to call on them if she found herself in need again. She didn't mind their well-wishes until the empty bottles grew crowded on the serving platters. That's when they began to shove room keys into her palm or offer her private tours of their collections of taxidermy or Wedgwood porcelain.

It hadn't proved difficult to decline most of their invitations. Mr. Detweiler, however, had an unattractive streak of stubbornness. As far as she'd counted, he'd also had the most to drink. The nearly empty bottle of scotch she held, which she slopped into his cup each time he took a step closer, seemed the only thing keeping his hands at bay.

She searched the room for Vincenzio and Jack. Vincenzio had left and Jack remained preoccupied with an older gentleman. She failed to catch his eye before the bottle ran out. Gracie turned the bottle over in her hands, wishing it had been filled with wine instead. A full-bodied red stain would look beautiful on Mr. Detweiler's shirt—noticeable enough for him to excuse himself to go clean up. She wondered how much it would cost to have her dress cleaned if she poured the last serving of scotch on herself.

"Let me go find another bottle for you." She tried to maneuver around the jumble of coffee tables and chairs Mr. Detweiler had cornered her behind. The bustle of this particular dress, which held a striking similarity to the rear-end of a horse, made moving rather difficult.

"No, I think I've had enough to drink tonight." Mr. Detweiler downed the rest of his glass. He disarmed her of the bottle and set it on the fireplace mantle. "But I wouldn't say no to more of your company. I,"—he hiccupped—"shall get a room for us. We may take a fancy carriage ride back in the morning if you'd like."

What she'd like was to kick him in the shins. Gracie tucked her elbows tightly to her side before he could slip his arm through hers. "You'll have to excuse me, I have a headache and a tickle in my throat which I'm certain is going to develop into a whooping cough at any moment." She chanced a look in Jack's direction but didn't see him. "I think it's best if I spend the rest of the evening alone."

"Then please allow me to escort you to the lobby." His greasy, matted hair fell into his eyes. Underneath the tangle, his coffee brown eyes winked at her with lust.

She choked back a nervous laugh and fought the sour taste rising in her throat. "I'll be fine on my own."

As long as he can't get you alone, you'll be safe. He won't try anything in public.

But one look at him reminded her just how intoxicated he was, and she realized that this room wasn't public enough to discourage him. If she could just make it to the front foyer . . .

She banged her shin on the settee stepping around him and hurdled the footrest in a manner unbecoming for goats, let alone a young lady in a skirt. Behind her, the furniture scraped the floor as Mr. Detweiler followed.

She made it as far as the door before he caught her by the arm. His grip tightened until it seemed he intended to carve his name in her skin with the stubs of his chewed fingernails. He leaned in close, speaking in a voice only she could hear. "Perhaps I haven't made myself clear. You owe me a favor,"—he hiccupped again—"and now I want to collect it."

A trapdoor beneath her stomach opened. The fireplace poker and all other blunt or club-like objects were confoundedly out of reach. If it came down to a fight, she'd have to make do with her bare hands.

Gracie thrust her chin high and wrenched her arm free. The memory of her last physical struggle still haunted her, and she was desperate to avoid making a scene. "You can have your money back. Every penny of it."

The alcohol in his breath hit her face. "When someone gives you a loan, you don't get to specify the terms of repayment."

"Whatever I owe you, you're grossly mistaken if you think you'll get anything more than a firm handshake from me tonight."

Her gaze instinctively sought Jack again. Since he was half a head taller than most of the men present, she quickly spied him across the room. His attention was glued to his conversation partner. A dull pain in her chest blossomed. A secret part of her had hoped Mr. Detweiler's self-appointment as her escort might have attracted Jack's jealous interest. Chagrin made the pain in her chest throb and spread it to every hollow space in her body. Earlier this evening, when Jack had caught her as she fainted, and when he'd helped her into the carriage, she'd somehow confused his idle touches for signs of growing affection instead of etiquette.

Her attention lingered too long on Jack, drawing Mr. Detweiler's notice.

"You wouldn't be saying no if I were Jack, would you?" Mr. Detweiler stepped closer, blocking of her view of Jack.

"Of course I wouldn't—would!" Her face burned, and she knew that the neckline of her dress wouldn't hide any of the mottled blush.

"Since you seem like a nice girl, I suppose this once I'll forgive your loan in its entirety if you return my money. You have it in full, don't you?" He reached out and patted her cheek, his smile tight.

Even though she already knew she didn't, she dug into her pocket, cursing silently. "I don't have it on me at the moment," she said, trying to steady her rapid breathing. "But I promise, every cent is accounted for."

He held his chin in his fingers, appearing thoughtful. "In that case . . ."

Her head cracked against the wall as he shoved her against it. His dry, thin lips mashed into hers, cutting off her scream. She gagged on his unsolicited tongue as it forced itself between her lips, floppy and fitful—an oversized frog trying to swim in her mouth.

Dizzy for breath, she thrashed and squirmed, her focus divided between swatting his hands away from her chest and poking him in the eye at the first opportunity.

Thankfully, before she had to seriously consider biting off his tongue, he broke away.

"That was for interest," he said, the left side of his mouth twisted in a leer. "I'll be by your room tomorrow to collect, and you'd better have every penny."

Gracie slapped him. Hard. Then once more for good measure.

"You're despicable." She shoved him back and wiped her mouth and lips, leaving them raw and pink.

He laughed, rubbing his cheek, still red from her strike. "Here," he said, handing her a white, round lump of fabric, "this is yours.

Lucky for you, I prefer real women over little girls and dinner rolls over pancakes."

She glanced down at her front, immediately drawn to the mushed appearance of her left breast. Seconds earlier, she'd wanted to retch and eat a bar of soap—now that he'd handed her one of her bust-soufflés, she'd settle for nothing short of instantaneous death. She'd never be able to look anyone in the face again.

He'd exposed her as a fraud of a woman. She was nothing more than a little girl in a costume—the emperor out on parade in his "new" clothes.

Mr. Detweiler reached for the door handle to let himself out but was torn from it with a violent jerk. There was a crack of colliding bones, and he stumbled backwards, falling to the floor in a heap. Jack stood over him, fists balled and teeth bared. His eyebrows were angled so sharply they almost touched in the center. If this was what the tiger had seen earlier, she didn't blame it for running.

Jack's shoulders heaved and his breath rasped like a broken radiator. With a final hiss, he smoothed his hair, and then brushed some invisible dust from his squared shoulders.

Among the sea of black frock coats and bowler hats, several haughty faces turned in their direction and then quickly turned the other way. Whispers were exchanged and then conversations resumed at full volume as though the incident was no more interesting than if someone had changed the cylinder on the phonograph mid-song.

Mr. Detweiler was still huddled, unmoving on the floor. Jack tugged once at his own coat lapels and then extended his arm to her. As she accepted it, she noted the heightened contrast between the white knuckles on his left hand and the glowing pink on his right. "You're looking a bit overheated," he said, his voice surprisingly even. "I believe we should take a turn through the corridor."

If he'd said she should stick her head in a lion's mouth, she'd have done that too.

CHAPTER XVII

J ACK DIDN'T beg Jonathan Detweiler's pardon as he stepped over his sprawled figure on the floor. It took every ounce of self-control not to give the man a new nose. His blood boiled so hot it threatened to cook him from the inside out.

One minute. I looked away for one minute!

All night Jack had fought the constant bubbles of envy that boiled up whenever a well-to-do, so-called "gentleman" engaged Gracie in conversation. In exchange for the comforts desired by lonely, unmarried men, Gracie easily could've found a traveling partner to take her to Chicago. Nine men at the gathering had solicited her, and true to her strong-willed nature, she'd dismissed each on her own. So, when Jonathan had approached her, being poorer and less impressive than his predecessors, Jack had let his guard down.

Detweiler sat up, nursing his split lip. "You had no right, Jack. She owes me."

Jack reached deep into his pocket and dropped several bills on the floor, keeping only the coins he needed for the carriage ride back. "I suggest you take it, and I'll consider this matter settled." The intoxicated man made his first wise decision of the night and scooped up the money. Remembering to be gentle, Jack touched the inside of Gracie's elbow and led her into the hallway. He slammed the door behind them.

He hadn't walked ten steps down the hallway before Gracie pulled her arm out of his grip and took a crystal flower vase from a small table. Dumping the roses on the floor, she glanced hesitantly into the bottom and then tipped it toward her lips.

"Don't drink that, you'll get sick!" He grabbed the vase from her.

"But he—" She reached for the vase again.

Jack turned it over, drenching the carpet and his shoes in the process. "He stole a kiss, not your dignity." Or had it been more than that? Gracie had slapped Detweiler twice. How much mischief could one man cause in a single minute? And in public view?

Gracie made a noise that sounded like a hiccup. Her shoulders shook from the effort of holding back her tears—society dictated that young ladies should never make a scene, no matter how embarrassed they felt. Calmness and serenity were the only acceptable ladylike expressions.

He patted his coat pocket, searching for a rag. No luck. He'd meant to get a new one after his first rehearsal with Gracie, but his fight with Harris had put it out of his mind. There was something small and white in one of her hands, though she hadn't wiped her face with it yet. Should he untie his cravat and offer it to her?

She scrubbed her mouth against her sleeve, the effort turning her lips quite red.

Unsure of how she'd receive a more intimate gesture from him, Jack set a hand on her shoulder. "Don't let it bother you. Your worth isn't going to be diminished because of something like that."

She surprised him by turning into his touch and throwing her arms around his waist. Leaning hard against him, she buried her face into his shoulder. "That horrible, vile, rotten scoundrel! I wish I could have broken one of those bottles on his face."

With a nod, he held her to him. As much as he regretted what had happened to her, he couldn't deny he liked the way she felt in his arms. Gradually, she stopped trembling.

"Thank you." She pushed on his chest to release herself from his embrace, but not in a manner that suggested she was disgusted by his touch. "I'm sorry for making a scene."

He wasn't. The best part of his evening was that he'd gotten to hold her like this.

"It's all right, Gracie. I won't let him touch you again. You can cry if you want." People didn't always cry because they were weak—sometimes they were just strong for too long. Gracie had withstood more excitement in one day than some girls got in their whole lives.

Gracie smiled weakly. "I think I've disgraced myself enough for one night." She sniffled once, "I just wish I had a handkerchief. My nose feels like it's about to start running."

Wasn't she holding one in her hand? He peered around her head and saw that both her hands were unclenched and empty now. A small trace of the white fabric poked out from her sleeve cuff where she'd hastily concealed the item, the way he performed some of his magic tricks.

"Just wipe your nose on my sleeve. It's the only reasonable thing to do."

She stepped back, pinching her nose with her cuff, a weak smile on her lips. The shadows underneath her eyes glistened with unshed tears. He had to suppress the urge to take her face in his hands and wipe the skin there with his thumbs.

Her smile fell away under the weight of his stare. With her gaze on the floor, she said, "Please don't look at me. I'm such a mess." She angled herself away from him, her left arm clinging oddly to the side of her chest.

"Did he hurt you?" Forget what he'd said earlier about considering the matter even with Jonathan. Jack had half a mind to march back into the room and break both Detweiler's arms. The other half of him wanted to break Detweiler's arms *and* legs.

"It's nothing. I'll be fine. I'm sorry I ruined your evening." Her eyes fell on his clenched fist. "What about your hand? Does it need bandaging?"

It hurt like he'd slammed it in a door. But he wasn't going to tell her that. "I'll be fine. I think it's time to get you back to the lot." He extended his elbow to her.

She took his arm but followed a step behind him, hunching inward and avoiding his eye. He'd never seen her so uneasy, or her blush so dark. Though he wasn't exactly himself, either. Until tonight, no one except Harris had ever made Jack angry enough to strike them. And Jack had never held someone so tenderly as he had held Gracie.

He escorted her in silence into the grand foyer where a huge staircase spilled cinnamon-speckled carpet onto the marble floor. Near the large fireplace, Vincenzio stood in a circle of men.

Jack and Gracie had almost made it to the front doors of the hotel when Vincenzio detached himself from his conversation and shuffled over to them. "Hold up there! *Filer à l'anglaise?*"

Yes, Jack did intend to take a "French leave" and not say goodbye to the host.

Vincenzio jerked his head toward Gracie. "What's the matter with her?"

Jack cleared all traces of anger from his face. "One of the gents offered her a taste of his grog. She misunderstood and downed the whole thing in one gulp."

"Will she be all right?" Vincenzio asked.

"She'll be apples. I'll see to it that she gets back to the circus lot." Jack led Gracie the rest of the way to the doors.

Once outside, he hailed a coach, helped Gracie onto the seat, and paid the driver with a few coins. As he was about to enter the coach, Gracie fled to the far side, continuing to clutch her arm oddly to her side.

He hesitated on the step, holding the door. "Shall I ride back with you?"

"You've done enough for me already," she said, and yet Jack couldn't shake the feeling that her words, body language, and facial expression were at odds with each other.

He nodded, trying to conceal his disappointment. "You'll be fine once you get back to the lot. And if anyone gives you trouble, shout for Victor."

"The dumbbell lifter?"

"He looks tough, but he's quite friendly. He's one of the few people who testified on my behalf in Katherine's murder investigation. You'll be safe with him."

"If you say so, I'll trust your word." She remained seated on the far side of the coach, leaving Jack feeling like he'd somehow offended her. No, he'd *definitely* offended her. He'd led Vincenzio to believe she had tried—and failed—to stomach a glass of alcohol. On his figurative scorecard rating her affection, she probably fancied him more than taxes but less than their breakfast gruel. He started closing the coach door.

"Jack . . ." She slid across the bench and rested her chin on the side rail, gazing down at him. His shoulders straightened.

"Yes, Gracie?"

"Go ahead and say it."

Say that I should accompany you? That I want to hold you close until you feel like yourself again? Say that I've never felt stronger than when you wrapped your arms around me?

"Say what?" he asked, forcing his voice to stay moderated and level. Her closeness flirted with his restraint and required his full concentration to resist sweeping her to him.

She stared at the cobblestones in the sidewalk. "You warned me this would happen, remember? During our first rehearsal. I dismissed your concern, so why don't you go ahead and say, 'I told you so.'"

Is that really what she thought he wanted to tell her? He chewed his lower lip and slowly closed the door. "I'd rather have been wrong."

"Will you go back to the party?"

In her voice, Jack thought he heard disappointment. He dismissed the observation, certain his own emotions were interfering with his good sense. If she'd wanted to spend more time with him, she would have let him escort her back to the lot.

"There's something I still need to do here before I return." He finished closing the door and pounded on it twice to signal the driver to take off. "Take care, Gracie."

Once the carriage clattered around the corner and disappeared, Jack set to twisting off his cufflinks and rolling up his sleeves. He returned to the hotel foyer and waited. If Gracie wanted to be alone, then Jack would stay behind to ensure no other woman suffered the same mistreatment before Jonathan sobered up.

It was a good two hours before Detweiler emerged from the dining room, completely rotten.

Jack followed several paces behind Jonathan down the hotel steps. He moved surreptitiously from one dark spot on the street to another, until Jonathan passed an alley. Under the cover of darkness, Jack ambushed the drunken fool and dragged him into the passageway.

Jonathan tottered on his feet like a harbor buoy in the wake of a cargo ship. In his tipsy state, he mistook Jack's hold around his collar for aid.

Rage washed over Jack, tearing down the walls of control he'd built to contain his darker side. Hoisting Detweiler by the collar, Jack slammed him into the side of the building.

"Jonathan!" Jack slapped the man's face, coaxing the dog trainer's rolling eyes to look at him. Jack's next words were cold, calculating, and absolutely sincere. "Tonight is just a warning. If I ever see you near Miss Hart again, I'll leave your body so beaten that the next time you go to use the dunny, you'll have to pinch your nose to make sure everything comes out the right hole."

Detweiler shouted for help, but the only thing in the alley with him was his shadow.

CHAPTER XVIII

THE ECRU dress Gracie had worn last night lay discarded on the floor like molted snake skin. The morning sun shone through the window, spotlighting the bustle's collapsed frame beside it. She should have hung the dress over the back of a chair to prevent wrinkling, but the dress reeked of Mr. Detweiler's grubby bacon-grease, and the thought of touching it made her cringe.

If Jack hadn't intervened—if Mr. Detweiler had tried to carry her from the room by force . . .

Like she'd have let *that* happen while she still had breath in her lungs. She'd killed a man already for much less, hadn't she?

You're really not so brave. You couldn't even tell Jack you did want him to ride back in the carriage with you, all because of a piece of stuffing.

Jack might not have even noticed her lopsided breasts in the dark. Why should she be so concerned if anyone besides Miriam knew she had to stuff her bodice to fit Katherine's dresses?

Because, despite what you want to believe, you care what Jack thinks of you as a woman.

Gracie jumped from the bed, refusing to let her skirmish with Mr. Detweiler haunt her like the fight with the foreman did. She trampled the dress as she dug under her mattress for the sock holding Mr. Detweiler's money. She would use the money to repay Jack immediately after breakfast.

Of the two men, she'd prefer Jack as her creditor. Still, she was not entirely comfortable. Jack had helped her out of difficult situations so many times that she couldn't believe he had done so without self-interest. People didn't just do things for nothing.

Gracie counted the bills and coins, dropping them back into the sock, along with the silver key. Maybe she should keep the money unless Jack specifically asked to be repaid? If she did keep it, would she be able to say she'd earned this money honestly, or would someone think she'd stolen it?

She hoped to have at least another night to think things over. Vincenzio wouldn't dine out two nights in a row, would he? Gracie didn't think so. This small comfort allowed her to organize her thoughts for the day—and to realize how late she'd slept.

Gracie wadded the dress and bustle into a compact bundle, tucked it under her arm, and set off for the dressing tent.

Usually, the background noise around the circus lot reminded Gracie of a flock of ducks let loose in a donut shop. This morning, everyone huddled in groups and murmured in low, reverent voices. No one honked bike horns, shouted, or paid her any mind.

Miriam's cheeks grew hollow and her lips pinched together as Gracie approached.

Did I do something wrong? Why is everyone so serious?

With a nervous smile, Gracie unrolled the bundle.

Though no sound could possibly escape Miriam's lips, Gracie could hear the seamstress's voice as if she were speaking aloud. *Have the ecru dress back here clean and folded in one hour, or I will sew your eyelids shut while you sleep.*

Gracie gathered the dress into her arms. "I just realized I forgot the box. I'll go fold this and bring it back."

The seamstress's eyes softened. "I heard from Vincenzio what happened to you last night. I'm glad you seem to be feeling better."

At least the gossip about her was only that she had a weak stomach. It could have been much more scandalous. Although the orphanage and the factory had hardened her spirits, they hadn't lifted her skirts. She still clung to her mother's ideals of proper etiquette and chastity.

Gracie left Miriam to finish her sewing work. She feared if she said anything about what really happened, Miriam might think she was fishing for pity. Pity was useless. People only used it to say, "I'm relieved things are unfortunate for you and not me." She'd trade any amount of pity right now for a hot cinnamon bun.

Unfortunately, by the time Gracie had retrieved the box, folded the dress, and returned it to Miriam, the pie car had stopped serving breakfast. She stomped her foot. Everything was against her today.

She rooted through the pantries, finding dishes, bags of coffee beans, and condiments—useless stuff of no real substance. Counting the hours until lunch, she clutched the money in her pocket. Dare she spend any of it to buy breakfast somewhere else? She stopped by the pie tent to see if any of the crew was still eating.

All but two tables under the tent were cleared, the benches stacked neatly to the side.

One of the twins sat alone at the table, with a steaming cup of coffee and the sugar bowl close at hand. One spoonful—*shovelful*. Two . . . three. Harris—unless he'd been lying when he'd told her he liked more sugar in his coffee than Jack.

She approached Harris and gestured to the seat across from him. "May I join you? Harris, right?"

He nodded. "You can, but I'm sorry to say I got the last cup. If you want any, you'll have to brew a fresh pot.

With her luck, she'd burn the tent to the ground lighting the fire and satisfy the second omen. No thank you. She slid onto the bench opposite him. "I know I slept late, but I didn't think they'd have breakfast put away so soon."

"That's because it's Sunday—everyone gets the day off, including the cook. There's no show and no meals."

She didn't mind not having a performance, but no meals? Her stomach gave a low growl. Mortified, she folded her arms over it to muffle the beast.

Harris chuckled and set his cup off to the side. "Why don't you come to breakfast with me? That bakery I spoke of isn't too far, and by now we should be late enough that we'll have missed the morning rush."

She considered his offer. Even though he had bought her the trunk yesterday, could she trust him without a chaperone? With her poor sense of direction, it *would* be nice to have his company to visit the downtown district. And she was so hungry.

Gracie glanced across the lot toward the town. Approaching, she saw an official-looking figure, leading a horse-drawn cart behind him. The cart didn't look like the sort of wagon for jailing prisoners, but she didn't want to chance it.

She turned back around and leaned forward on her elbows, chin resting on her interlocked fingers. "That sounds nice I'd like that," she said in a single breath.

His eyebrows rose. "Great. I'll grab my coat and meet you by the street corner on the west side.

HARRIS took the crook of her arm and led her downtown. They crossed through Dominion Square, a public park. A line of churches formed a divide between the neighborhoods to the northwest and the business areas to the east and south. The square was an obvious focal point of the city. Hundreds of people were out enjoying their morning amid the grassy areas and park paths that came together to form the Union Jack.

The bakery was north of the square, on a street dominated by restaurants, smoking parlors, and taverns. The buildings varied in size, height, and hue. Intricate wrought iron decorated the lower windows.

"Here we are, La Patisserie," Harris said.

In the little time she'd been at the circus, Gracie didn't think she'd yet seen his expression so kind or his smile so sincere.

The inside of the bakery featured cozy brick walls, timber beams, and a hammered metal ceiling. A flight of narrow stairs led up to the second floor. Only a few patrons occupied the intimate space. Harris led her to a small table near the front window. She studied the menu, her forehead creased.

"What's wrong?" Harris asked, his menu untouched on the table.

She set her menu down and studied his open face, wondering what he'd think if she told him. Her thoughts continually drifted to how handsome he looked in his dark coat. She decided it didn't matter what she said to him because she was never going to be his type. Her faults weren't going anywhere, so she might as well let him see them. "My French is rusty, and these prices are a bit more than I was expecting."

He pushed the menu back toward her, his long fingers brushing hers in the process. "What sort of gentleman would I be if I invited you on an excursion and didn't pay?"

"If you mean by 'excursion' that we're sharing a moment where I don't want to slap you, then I suppose we are. Though I don't think I could possibly accept any more charity from you since you bought that trunk for me."

He shifted in his seat and signaled for the aproner to roll the tea trolley over. "I actually hoped I'd get a chance to ask you the reason behind your interest in the trunk."

Gracie selected a tea from the trolley—Earl Grey. The aproner scooped the leaves from the tin into a strainer with a smile and took it to the kitchen to prepare it.

"My mother owned one just like it." Gracie savored the perfumed smell from the open tea tin. "It was lost before I disembarked and was never found. I like the thought of being able to pretend it was hers."

Harris poured himself a cup of coffee. "I'm glad I bought it for you, though I don't think it was worth seven dollars." He took a swig and his cheeks and lips puckered as if he'd swallowed a starfish. Wincing at the cup with narrowed eyes, he added several spoonfuls of sugar.

Gracie raised both eyebrows and pushed the creamer to his side of the table. "If you thought seven dollars was too high a price, then why did you outbid Jack so steeply?"

"If Jack had won the trunk, there's no guarantee he would've given it to you without wanting something in return."

"Like a kiss?" She rolled her eyes.

"Guilty as charged," he said with a wink.

Her cheeks turned hot. When was she going to stop letting these unprincipled men catch her off guard? She'd read about men like him in dime novels—charismatic and genteel, but no matter how sweet his words or how soft his touch, his favorite girl would always be whoever was in front of him. Gracie buried her face behind the menu, hoping it would mask her blush. She remembered that outside of Vincenzio's stateroom Harris had said he was a better kisser than Jack. Was that true? Or was all kissing as disgusting as her experience with Mr. Detweiler?

The menu featured open-faced smoked trout sandwiches, crumpets, and Eccles cakes. She didn't see any cinnamon buns. "What do you recommend?"

"I know just the thing." Harris called the aproner back over and ordered several items in rapid French. Gracie caught the words "*tarte*" and "*merci beaucoup*."

She set her tea aside to let it cool. "Where did you learn French? You're very good." She craved for him to reveal every little thing he could about his and Jack's childhood.

Harris's eyes darkened, clouded by something Gracie guessed was anger or misery. "My mother, but don't flatter me. I know my accent is terrible." The corner of his mouth rose slightly in a rueful expression. He gave a short laugh. "It's funny you noticed that Jack prefers to swear in French. Our mother had this philosophy—if you want to do something, do it with passion or not at all. She knew all the swears in English, French, Italian, German, even Chinese, so when she wanted to be crass, the words came marching out. My father only swore in French because he said it was more 'polite.'"

Gracie's heart pounded fast. This revelation was hardly something "personal" about his and Jack's past, yet it excited her. It revealed that Jack wasn't the only person with a vast knowledge of foreign insults. This outing with Harris might be what she needed to make sense of those notes she kept finding in her costume.

"If I wrote a foreign word down for you, would you possibly know what it means?"

"That likely depends on how you spell it and what the word is." He sipped cautiously at his ceramic cup.

Gracie spelled the word from her postcard. "K-N-O-S-S-O-S."

Harris spit his last sip back into his cup. He wiped his chin on his sleeve. "Where did you learn that word?"

His reaction confirmed it must be vulgar. She looked around the room to see if anyone else had overheard. No one met her eyes or seemed to care. She glanced back to Harris and saw he'd cleared his face of emotion. His dark brown eyes regarded her with curiosity, but his other features revealed none of the shock he'd just displayed.

Bored—he looks bored now. She regretted asking, but she needed to follow through. "I think Jack wrote it on my postcard sometime during my first rehearsal. What does it mean?"

With his napkin, Harris wiped up the small drops of spittle he'd gotten on the table. Then he raised his eyes to meet hers. His lips were pressed together, his eyes stern. "I assure you, Jack isn't the one who wrote that, and if you don't want more trouble with him, I wouldn't mention it."

Gracie knew Harris was inclined to be elusive, but in this case he was more annoying than coy. "Does it have something to do with Katherine?"

He stared deep into his coffee cup, as if deciding whether he wanted to finish it or get a new cup that he hadn't spit in. "You could say that."

The sound of a shoe scraping wood pulled her back from her confusion. The aproner had arrived with their order.

The pastries between them turned to empty plates as they talked about their favorite foods, songs, and circus acts, avoiding the topic of the postcard.

Gracie chided herself for having eaten so much, but Harris had pushed the plates toward her and insisted she try everything. She folded her napkin and set it in her lap. "Thank you for bringing me here. This was lovely."

He signaled the aproner for the bill. "I'm glad my brother hasn't entirely poisoned you against me."

She set her tea cup down. "Why is it that you and Jack don't get along? It's sad to see brothers quarrel." She'd treasured her brother Robert. It would've been awfully lonely to have the nursery all to herself, with no one to play pretend.

The playfulness left Harris's eyes and his demeanor changed from cheeky to solemn. "No one knows Jack better than I do, and I swear he wishes more than anything that I were dead. If you really want to understand, ask him what happened to our parents. Or better, after the next performance, ask him to show you his hands."

Gracie lost interest in finishing the last pastry and placed it carefully on her plate. While chewing, she sifted his words and compared them to his ominous tone. "I noticed that after performances, he tends to get cramps in his wrists."

"Do you honestly think someone with Jack's physique would get muscle spasms from throwing a few one-pound knives?"

"No, I suppose not." Shame on him for making her feel like a fool.

The corner of Harris's lips turned up into a smirk. "Why do you suppose that is?"

How obnoxious of him to make her beg. She pushed her tea and the plate aside. "Why don't you just tell me?"

His eyebrows rose thoughtfully as he scooted to the edge of his seat. She tensed as he reached toward her, but he only took the bill. "I'd like to, but that's not how this works. If you want the answer to this secret, you'll have to give me one in return."

CHAPTER XIX

HARRIS SAID little to her on the way back, his eyes distant and thoughtful whenever she glanced his way. She hadn't expected him to reveal as much as he had about himself, so she figured she ought to be grateful and not focus on what he hadn't said.

At the edge of the circus lot, several members of the circus troupe were gathered around a horse-drawn cart. A pair of feet in men's shoes hung over the end and a white sheet covered the rest of the motionless form.

Harris rocked to a standstill beside her. "There must have been an accident," he said.

Gracie's knees wobbled beneath the many layers of her dress. Where was Jack? "Is it someone from the troupe?"

"We should go find out." Harris took her hand and pulled her behind him.

A woman in her mid-thirties looked up as they approached. She had an elongated face with sharp eyes and an even sharper nose. Her dress, yellow damask with brown trim, clung to her rounded figure. "Jack! Where've you been?" She pushed her way through the crowd to them. "Them coppers were here earlier, asking for you."

Harris's lips curled into a scowl. "Too bad for them, I'm not Jack, Charlotte."

"Sorry, Harris," she mumbled.

"What happened?" Harris gestured to the cart.

"It's Jonathan Detweiler." Charlotte sniffed and swiped her eyes with the back of her wrist. "He's dead."

Gracie felt as if someone had pulled three inches out of her corset ties. "Dead?"

Charlotte gave a small nod. "A street sweeper discovered 'im in an alley near the Chateau Versailles hotel. Barty was the one who realized Jon's dogs weren't let out this morning."

Gracie covered her mouth, afraid she might vomit. "Was he murdered?"

"Doubt it. If it was a murder they think the killer would have cleaned his pockets, and Jon had a lot of cash with him."

Harris's hands tightened into fists at his sides and his jaw tensed. "What do they think killed him?"

"Them coppers is saying it was a heart attack since everyone knows he was a heavy drinker. They were asking questions earlier since people at the hotel said he and Jack got into some kind of fight last night. They wanted to interview Jack just to be sure there wasn't foul play, except he hasn't been seen all morning either."

Gracie needed to splash some water on her face before she doubled over. "Please excuse me. I think I've been out in the sun too much today. I'm going to go rest."

Gracie took a few steps back, hoping the movement appeared more casual than it felt. As soon as she rounded the cover of one of the tents, she dashed for the train cars, upsetting displays and pushing her way through the loitering circus crew.

She locked herself in her room and threw herself on the bed. The image of Jack standing beside the coach, holding the door, made her heart pound against her sternum. Surely he wouldn't do something like . . .

Murder. The word tasted like chalk in her mouth.

If he had nothing to hide though, why had no one seen him since last night?

Gracie pounded her fist into the pillow until feathers started to fly into the air. Being alone in her room wasn't calming her nerves at all. She sat up and grabbed her stockings to go wash them.

If she saw Jack while she was out, she could simply ask him what had happened at the hotel after she had left. She would see the truth in his eyes. And if not, at least she'd have clean socks instead of an empty pillow.

BRIGHT light pushed through the train car window. Gracie yanked her pillow over her face, wishing it'd go away. Despite her brave effort to not seclude herself after the shock of Mr. Detweiler's death yesterday, she'd failed to learn what had become of Jack. While many of the other performers agreed it was suspicious that Jack seemed to be missing, quite a few shrugged off his scarcity as being perfectly acceptable for a non-performance day. She dreaded the idea that it was now Monday and she'd have to leave her room again to finally confirm if Jack was dead, missing, guilty, or innocent.

Asking around the lot, Gracie learned that early this morning that one of the twins had been seen at the pie car and then outside Vincenzio's stateroom. However, no one could confirm it was Jack and not Harris.

The grits she'd had for breakfast climbed up her throat. She swallowed the lump, but the dry, bland taste of starch remained in her mouth. Had the police arrested Jack? She had so many fears and worries and none of them were resolved with a visit to Vincenzio's stateroom. Neither Jack nor Vincenzio were there.

When Gracie changed into her costume, she removed one of Miriam's bust-enhancing soufflés and replaced it with her money sock. From what she'd heard from the fox-faced woman, Charlotte, the police weren't interested in her role at the hotel. There was no reason for her to make a run for the station yet.

Half an hour before the afternoon performance, Gracie had yet to speak to one person who knew Jack's whereabouts. They were holding the performance earlier today so they could pack up before it turned dark. Tomorrow the circus would perform in Buffalo. Would the circus's last show in Montreal be minus the dog trainer's routine *and* the knife-thrower and magician's act?

She paced inside the tent, digging a narrow rut into the dirt with the heels of Katherine's shoes. *Where is he?*

Gracie wrung the hem of her corset, putting several creases in the satin. The band would play the cue for their entrance at any moment.

She glanced toward the tent flaps, praying for Jack to walk through, fearing the worst.

If Jack wasn't hurt, detained, or in trouble, then he had abandoned his acts—and her. Vincenzio would kick her to the curb as soon as the curtains closed and once again, she would be unwanted and alone.

A hot breeze blew in as the tent flaps parted. Her heart leapt and then sank. A bunch of white-faced clowns rolled a cage containing a girl in an exotic bird costume into the cramped space. Feathers decorated the girl's neck in ruffs and even served as fluttering eyelashes.

The girl raised her mask and whistled Gracie over. "I saw Jack just a moment ago. He said he's running behind, but he'll be here in five minutes or so."

"But we're supposed to go on at any moment!"

"Don't worry, we'll stall for him with a quick run around the ring."

"Wait, what?" The hot, tangled ball of anger inside Gracie felt ready to burst like a popcorn kernel.

The trilled piccolo notes played for her and Jack's entrance. With a farewell nod, the clown at the front of the cage tugged on the wagon handle and they filed into the big top.

Gracie's teeth worried at her bottom lip.

Less than two minutes passed before the flaps at the back of the tent parted again. Jack emerged between the striped panels, dressed in his performance coat.

Her breaths came easier when he took his place next to her side, like when she unlaced her corset for the evening. "Where have you been?"

He smoothed his hair and counted the number of knives in his belt. "With Vincenzio, and around the lot."

"What about yesterday when the police were looking for you?"

The group of clowns, towing the girl in the bird cage, barreled out of the big top. Seal barks of laughter followed them.

Jack clapped one of the clowns on the back, ignoring her question. "Thanks, I owe you one."

It briefly occurred to Gracie that Jack *did* have some friends in the troupe. They hadn't all sided with Harris over Katherine's death.

The circus band played the high trilled note for their entrance again. "Smile, Gracie," Jack said, pulling her with him into the big top.

Gracie put on her overly wide performance smile and faked a ventriloquist act. "What's going on?"

"It's politics. Nothing you need to worry about."

"Mr. Detweiler died and the police wanted to question you. I think that's pretty serious."

"There's nothing to worry about, really."

"They don't think you're guilty?"

"You're just full of questions today, aren't you?"

Since her job required her to put her complete faith in him and he didn't have the decency to tell her where he'd been all yesterday, she found it impossible *not* to worry.

She stood in front of the backboard for the knife feats, wishing she had a blindfold. Why was it harder for her to trust him now than when they'd first met? She'd thought him a thief and a liar, yet she had stood straighter then.

She blinked several times, forcing her thoughts to the present moment. She was responsible for her own safety by posing accurately.

Jack took his place on the other end of the ring.

Gracie raised her arms high over her head, elbows bent to form a diamond. The flames in the kerosene lights shivered with the motion of air. The crowd inhaled as Jack raised his first knife past his ear. Gracie's breath caught and she couldn't bear to keep her eyes open.

He knows what he's doing. I can trust him . . . She recalled the warmth she'd felt in his arms two night ago and clung to that small bit of reassurance.

When a murmur spread through the audience, she reopened her eyes. Jack had lowered his arm and already crossed half the ring on his way over to her.

"What's wrong?" she whispered, lowering her arms.

Jack shoved the knife back into his belt. "Do you trust me?"

Everywhere Gracie turned, other expectant eyes met hers. Ringmaster Richard, over by the orchestra, had the most intense and sunken stare of all. Meeting her eyes, his message was clear, "Get on with it."

"You've already asked me once if I trusted you," she said.

"And I'm asking you again."

The patrons shifted in their seats, and Richard was now acknowledging the disruption by putting his hands in the air and motioning for everyone to settle down and keep quiet. He traced a line under his neck with his finger and then rubbed his fingers and thumb together. "Cut the nonsense or you won't get paid this week," his motions indicated.

Jack shifted between her and Richard. He took her chin in his long fingers. "Don't look at them. Look at me and answer honestly. Do you trust me?"

"I—I'm not sure . . ." Maybe she'd trust him if he'd just tell her where he'd been yesterday. Or if Harris hadn't told her to look at Jack's hands after the performance. Maybe she'd trust him again if she could see something in his eyes other than hurt feelings, as if Gracie had betrayed him somehow.

Richard cleared his throat. "Just a moment, ladies and gentlemen! The show will continue shortly."

Jack pinched the bridge of his nose and stared over the knuckles of his fingers. He let out a sigh then leaned in close until the space between her and him disappeared. Through the folds of his shirt, she felt the pounding of his heart increase against his ribs. His lips brushed her ear.

"I know you don't trust me, but that's all right. I'm gonna earn it back. Just promise me that you won't move."

The friction of their clothes brushing, something so infinitesimal she shouldn't even have noticed, felt as strong as a hailstorm as he took her hands and drew her arms up. He'd told her not to move, but if her blood didn't return to her head soon, she might not have a say in the matter.

The patrons applauded mildly when Jack returned to his mark on the opposite end of the ring. Light flashed and his knife somersaulted blade over handle until the tip landed in the mark on the board. The gasps and cries from the crowd gave audibility to the buzz of energy circling through the tent.

The knives flew at her and the board pulsed with each blow.

Jack wasn't a knife thrower this performance, he was a protector. Each toss pierced the heart of a beast nipping at her heels or sneaking up on her from the shadows. The show was not an act to him, it was a fight for her survival. And he was the blade forged in the fires of hell used to slay the beasts and shadows.

The last knife landed an inch over the crown of her head. She almost didn't want to step away from the target board in case the tickle on the top of her head was blood and not a few displaced hairs. The crowd roared.

If her shoes had been an inch taller . . .

"Thank you," Jack said when he came to collect his knives. The fact he had a hard time pulling some of them out confirmed her suspicion he'd thrown them harder than normal. "We can talk after the show when there aren't so many people watching," he added. It was in his silence afterward that Gracie heard what he'd really meant to say—I'm sorry.

Her heart pounded in her chest as if she had been running up a steep hill and had reached the crest. The fear she'd felt earlier was behind her, pushing her down the other side. Maybe he was tied somehow to Katherine's death, and who knew what he was up to yesterday? But at this moment, Gracie believed with every hair on her head that Jack desired her safety as much as his own.

Jack stepped away from the prop handlers as they removed the target backboard and brought the magic props forward.

Gracie stepped inside the vanishing closet and pressed her heels to the back wall. She started humming once he closed the door.

She sang every verse of "London Bridge is Falling Down," but the secret door did not move. Forget her earlier vote of confidence in Jack. He had his head in the clouds and had forgotten to set the mechanism.

She continued waiting, wondering how she should react if he opened the door. She'd likely try to play things off and scold him for not saying the "magic" words correctly and hope the mechanism worked the second time.

Four more minutes passed.

The vanishing act had never taken so long before. Perhaps someone in the crowd, boasting he knew the secret to this trick, was causing problems and Jack was stalling until the man was removed. Or maybe one of the horses escaped into the ring and needed to be caught.

Her ability to estimate time grew worse with each following minute. Nine minutes, or maybe thirteen. Singing no longer seemed an appropriate device to tell time. If Jack finally opened the door, no one would be impressed if she were gone. In all this time she might have dug a hole beneath the closet to hide herself.

Fifteen or twenty minutes. If something dreadful had happened, the band would have played the disaster march to signal an evacuation of the big top. Although she had a hard time hearing in the closet, she doubted she could miss such a cacophony of instruments. Her ears strained to identify the sounds of cracking peanuts or jingling coins. Or the sounds of twelve- and thirteen-year-old boys squirming in their seats because their mothers had made them wear their outgrown short pants to convince the ticket seller to charge the child's admission price.

Twenty-five minutes. A whole tent of people couldn't have evacuated without her hearing *something.*

By the time she estimated a half hour she'd given up standing against the back of the closet. She slouched against the side wall, one leg crossed over the other, and picked at her cuticles. If Jack didn't open the door in five minutes she'd let herself out.

She doubted the closet could still be inside the big top. The patrons would have gotten bored and have left on their own. If she was wrong and someone saw her step out, it'd serve Jack right for keeping her trapped for so long.

At the end of what Gracie estimated to be five minutes, she pushed on the door and was surprised that it swung open with ease. Strings of warm yellow bulbs appeared to float in a straight row in front of her, chasing the shadows to the edges of a long, narrow corridor. The setup looked nothing like the big top or the circus lot. If she had to guess, she would say the closet had been dropped into the basement of a hotel. That was impossible. Wasn't it?

The air, sticky and heavily humid, smelled dank and sharp. Every fifteen feet the corridor intersected another hallway. Galvanized pipes ran along the walls and bent around the corners.

She remembered the times Jack kept asking her if it had seemed like she'd been waiting in the closet a long time, and how his face had paled when she'd joked about meeting a sorceress. He'd *known* something was special about his closet.

"Hello?" Gracie spun in a circle. "Is anyone here?"

A few drops of water splashed in reply from the pipes overhead. If the pipes had steam in them, she could search for the boiler room and find help. Hopefully someone would know how to get back to the circus lot.

She tiptoed into the vaulted walkway, following the largest pipe as a guide.

She had the strangest feeling of déjà vu as she continued farther. At the seventh intersection, the pipe she'd been following turned upward and disappeared into the ceiling. A pair of French doors with peeling veneer awaited her at the passage's dead end.

A faint glow of light outlined the edges of the keyhole. The doors certainly didn't seem like they led to the coal room. Did she dare go further? She pressed on the handle and found it unlocked.

Better to ask forgiveness than seek permission.

Gracie stepped into a long corridor boasting handsome woodwork and tall, majestic windows. Intricate carvings embellished the stone pillars supporting the domed ceiling. A thick Persian rug filled the hallway, and lining the walls were sofas with upholstery so fine that it would stain if someone sneezed from ten steps away.

Soft music floated toward her from somewhere deeper in the building. She could hear stringed instruments and the singsong notes of a flute. The circus band?

Going through the door at the end of the hallway, Gracie found herself in a small vestibule. A pair of red velvet curtains trimmed in gold fringe separated her from the source of the music. Through the curtains, she spied a grand ballroom. There were no dancers, and as far as Gracie could tell, no musicians either.

A glowing chandelier hung in the center of the arched ceiling. Crystals, cut in shapes varying from stars to teardrops, hung in scalloped tiers. If this was some fancy hotel, she didn't want to be seen wandering around in her circus costume. She should probably go back the way she'd come and look for someone to help her.

It took Gracie two long steps to retreat to the French doors and a half second to fall on her face.

"Ow . . ." Gracie sucked in a sharp breath. The folds of the drapes must have caught her by the ankles. She rubbed her aching elbow. If she was in a dream, she would have awakened by now.

She kicked at the tangle of blue ruffles wrapped around her legs, and like quicksand, found that her efforts sank her even deeper in the trap.

Taking a moment to study the problem, Gracie realized that her first mistake was assuming that she had tripped on the red velvet curtains. The textile tangled around her feet was blue satin. Her second mistake: the fabric was caught on her corset, not around her feet. No—it wasn't caught on her corset, it was *attached*. At some point since she'd entered the room, her circus costume had grown a skirt, sleeves, and a full petticoat.

An illusion? She gave the folds of satin a few swishes. For so many yards of material, the fabric weighed less than a bolt of fine lace. However light, it did weigh something, which meant it wasn't a visual trick of smoke and mirrors.

Am I dead? Did she suffocate in the vanishing closet and go to heaven? If so, it wasn't like anything she'd imagined.

Gracie climbed to her feet and lifted the skirt layers. Katherine's golden shoes remained, unchanged from her original ensemble. She slipped her feet out and checked the soles.

Nothing, except another recurrence of déjà vu.

Gracie replaced her shoes and returned to the curtain for a second glance at the ballroom. *This isn't heaven.*

She no longer had any doubts that Jack was a real magician. No doubt if he caught her snooping around his magic castle he'd turn her into a rabbit. With some deliberation, Gracie decided eating carrots for the rest of her life was worth the risk if she could discover his other secrets. As the saying went, "Curiosity may have killed the cat, but satisfaction brought it back."

She crossed through the curtains into the ballroom.

CHAPTER XX

CLARICE GLOWERED at the forest green gemstone at the end of her tongs. Once again, she'd created a specimen of boring, common emerald. With a hundred elements to substitute, in thousands of combinations and volumes, there were just too many variables. She wasn't getting any closer to releasing her hidden heartstone from the desk drawer.

Two more heartstones had burned out in the chandelier since John's—Jack's—last visit. How many more could the fortress lose before it dropped out of the sky?

Clarice dumped the gemstone into a pail overflowing with her crystalized mistakes. A small landslide occurred, with gems spilling to the floor. Time to take the pail to the furnace room and dispose of the useless stones.

She hung her lab coat and goggles up and cleared away her notes and tools.

With the heavy bucket hooked on one arm and her notes tucked under the other, she decided not to take her particle extractor. She'd be back before the song ended on the gramophone. Besides, shades were attracted to shiny things. If any appeared, she could toss a few of the gemstones as bait and they'd leave her alone.

Clarice paused to glance at her reflection in the small wall mirror, making sure that even without her lab coat, her shirt concealed the rainbow of gemstones in her necklace.

Shades weren't sentient, but they did possess some sort of internal compass for gemstones. In every experiment she'd designed, shades consistently preferred genuine gemstones over synthetic ones.

The gems on her necklace were sufficiently covered, mere bulges in her shirtfront. Safe to proceed.

She opened the door leading out of her lab and froze. A young woman, dressed in a blue satin dress and wearing a guarded expression, stood in the center of the ballroom.

Oh good, the little chit is back. Leaving the gramophone constantly playing had worked. Like Hansel and Gretel's breadcrumbs, the music had led Gracie straight here.

"Excuse me, ma'am." Gracie had the expression of a small grub looking into the hungry eyes of a large bird. She held her skirt out to the side and folded at her waist. If Clarice had to guess, Gracie was trying to curtsy like a debutante, but she was doing it all wrong. "I'm a bit lost and was wondering if you could help me."

Clarice set the pail down and then straightened her bodice and smoothed her skirt. Since entering the ballroom, her sky blue shirt and bloused pants had turned into a formal gown cut from silk dupioni and trimmed with brown fur. A large bustle hung off her hips, and her breasts were uncomfortably squished by a corded corset. The low-cut neckline exposed her necklace, which flashed and sparkled with brilliant fire in the light of the chandelier.

From her previous encounters with Jack's new assistant, Clarice knew that the girl was afraid of this strange place and intimidated by her. Clarice also knew that the whelp had petty insecurities related to her flat chest and overall lack of "womanly" traits. Gracie's hidden jealousy created an additional obstacle Clarice needed to overcome in order to win her trust.

The girl would never directly help her, but people would generally help themselves. Thankfully, this time Clarice had thought of the perfect lie and a foolproof promise. During Gracie's last visit, Clarice had almost botched her objective by revealing her interest in the key too soon. If she played the part of a caring, motherly figure correctly, Gracie would trust her enough to give her the key. But if Clarice overdid it, Gracie might decide to destroy the key—or worse, give it to Jack. Manipulating the little twit required a delicate balance, but Clarice was determined to get it right this time around.

Clarice set her notes beside the bucket, crossed over to Gracie, and took her hands. "Gracie, it's so good to see you again. Don't worry, dearie, I'm here to help you."

Gracie withdrew her hands and tucked them behind her back. "I'm sorry. I don't recall that we've met before."

"We have, but I know you don't remember. My name is Clarice, and I'm Jack and Harris's aunt." Clarice leaned in to give Gracie one of those comforting hugs—the reassuring kind an orphan like Gracie no doubt craved. Gracie tensed during the hug, her body stiffer than dried resin. As for Clarice, the smell of rotten potatoes would be preferable over this awkward pretense. Her sister, Gladys, had been the sentimental one—too eager to squander her gifts and chain herself in marriage to some dim-witted imbecile. So selfish. Together, they could have achieved and created so much more, like time travel, but Gladys would have chosen to put science on the back burner in favor of producing whiney brats to feed.

Clarice broke off the hug. Gracie rubbed her arm and took a step back. "Jack never mentioned he had an aunt."

The effort to keep her voice soft required more concentration than Clarice cared to admit. "I imagine he hasn't told you a lot of things about me or this place. Otherwise, you wouldn't look so lost."

Gracie set her hands on her hips, her courage growing with her curiosity. "Where are we? What is this place, and how did I get here? The last thing I remember is being locked in the closet for the magic act. I waited for half an hour, but no one came to release me."

Gracie's wrinkled chin and scrunched eyebrows might have intimidated Clarice more if the girl weighed another hundred pounds or had spent the equivalent of hundreds of years in this place. As Clarice had. *"Half an hour."* The child had no idea.

Clarice circled to Gracie's side. "There is much we have to discuss, so allow me to tell you a secret word that will assure you that what I say is true." She leaned in and whispered the word. "Knossos."

Instant recognition colored Gracie's too-pale face. She raised a scolding finger and thrust it in Clarice's face. *"You* wrote that on my postcard."

If anyone else had made such a rude accusation, Clarice would've snatched their finger and turned it around to jab them right back in the eye. She smiled through clenched teeth. "No, dear. You did."

The narrow-eyed look of catty dislike that Gracie returned pulled at something deep inside Clarice. It was as though a taut cord ran had been strung up through Clarice's torso, and Gracie's wary disposition gave it a big *twang*. The vibrations shook Clarice's large frame, and she trembled with anger.

How *dare* this whelp stare at her with such ingratitude in her own home! Clarice ought to throw the girl in the attic with the shades for five minutes. Instead, Clarice tossed the ringlets of her hair over her shoulder and laughed tightly behind her hand. "I imagine this all must be hard for you to hear. Maybe it would help if I showed you around Knossos and let you see for yourself what convinced you before."

Gracie arched an eyebrow. "Knossos, is that what this place is called?" Her gaze circled the room once more, lingering on the chandelier. "Everything feels familiar, but at the same time it's like I've never seen any of this before."

There it was—the spark of familiarity. Gracie wanted to believe, but her suspicious nature needed some more convincing. And possibly a little flattery.

Clarice hooked her arm around Gracie's and patted her hand. "Accepting the reality of futuristic interdimensional portals would be a tall order for modern physicists, let alone an *intelligent* young lady like yourself. Come sit with me in my room and I'll explain. I'd offer you tea, but one of the side-effects of living here is my body has no need for food."

Gracie didn't pull away, nor did she move to accompany Clarice. "I think I'm more comfortable standing than sitting in a chair that might suddenly turn into a rose bush. What is this place? What happened to my costume?"

Clarice gestured toward the room with an expressive wave, her speech already refined by practicing on Katherine. "We are in a paradox called 'time compression.' The past and present together in a single place, but not at a single time. Everything here is in a fluctuating state between existence and nonexistence."

Gracie's head cocked slightly to the left. "You're making no sense—do you realize that? Is this real, or isn't it? Are we still even in Canada?"

The more helpless and stranded Gracie felt, the better. "We're nearly six thousand miles away from your precious circus. To be specific, we're nine hundred eighty meters above the Dusse-Alin mountain range in Khabarovsk, Russia."

Gracie blinked owlishly. Had she said too much, too soon? The process of spoon-feeding information grated on Clarice's patience. Mainly because this was the third time she'd given the exact same explanation to the same, stupid girl.

"How is it even possible to travel six thousand miles in a day, let alone in a few minutes?" Gracie asked.

Clarice's smile briefly slipped into a glower of impatience. The girl was a stubborn mule. Too many questions, too distrustful, too concerned with her own well-being. Clarice set a hand on Gracie's shoulder. "If you come with me, I can show you some things which may help you understand."

"I'd prefer to get back to the circus. There's something about this place that unsettles me."

She'd said something like this last time. As far as Clarice could figure, Gracie must be sensitive to the balance of light and dark energy—something Clarice had become desensitized to in all her time here.

"Fine," Clarice said. She picked up the bucket of gemstones and her notebook. If Gracie was going to continue to resist, Clarice would simply have to change tactics. Curiosity could work just as well. "I was on my way to take these to the furnace room. I can take you to the closet on the way back."

Gracie's eyes widened. Her fingers twitched acquisitively toward the large heart-shaped ruby on the top of the pile. "What are you going to do with them?"

Clarice swung the pail out of reach, resting it on her hip. "Use them for energy sources—same as always."

"Are they real?"

"They're real here, but they'll turn to coal dust if removed from the fortress." A trace of condescension slipped into her tone. "I explained all this to you on your first visit. I even let you take some back with you as proof. You wrote the name of this place on your postcard as a reminder. We really need to find a way to stop you from forgetting."

Gracie raised her chin, eyes fixed on the crystal chandelier while she twisted the fabric of her skirt. She turned back to Clarice. "Why do I keep forgetting this place?"

Clarice concealed her grin by turning toward the red velvet curtains leading out of the ballroom. "It's because of Jack. He uses hypnosis to make sure you'll never remember anything you see here. Just so he can continue to keep me here as his prisoner."

"Hypnosis?" Gracie's voice squeaked. Her shoes clacked the marble floor as she hurried to catch up.

Clarice stopped at the curtain. "Yes, and I'm beginning to tire of repeating myself. This is your third visit and the third time I've warned you against trusting him. I've told you that Katherine's death was no accident. If you don't want to end up dead like her, you need to listen more carefully. You've got to guard yourself. Never speak of our chats here with anyone."

Gracie's lower lip protruded in a pout. "I am listening. But I think it's unfair of you to act like I should know these things while also claiming I won't remember anything from my visits here. Those mysterious little notes you—I've—written and stashed in my costume . . ." Gracie tipped a nod at the notebook. "Why don't you send me back with a whole letter instead of a tiny strip?"

Clarice clutched the notebook to her side. "Paper, like many other inanimate things here, is too unstable to survive being bent through the time-compression field when you go back through the closet. Those notes I helped you write earlier were treated to have a specific pH balance. They were cut to a small size so they wouldn't dissolve or spontaneously combust before you got the chance to read them. They're hard to make and can only be used sparingly."

Out of all the things Clarice had told Gracie so far, this one was perhaps the most honest.

Gracie continued to eye the notebook. "My postcard didn't catch fire."

"Simple luck. Also, you don't have it with you now, and it's unlikely you'll bring it any time again since you said Jack warned you against having personal papers hidden in your costume."

Clarice made one final attempt to sell Gracie on the "concerned mother" persona. "Dear, I know more about you than you realize, and I know a lot about Katherine. She also ventured outside of Jack's closet and visited with me here. I tried to help her, just as I'm trying to help you now. *I* found out that her memory lapses were the result of hypnosis. *I* was the one who suggested she take notes back in her shoes. But she wasn't careful enough about the things she wrote in her notes." Clarice paused to let her words sink in the girl's fruitcake brain and then glared at the girl with complete seriousness. "Jack discovered Katherine's visits here. I told him that dropping her at a brothel in the middle of winter would be less messy than murder, but he feared she'd tell someone what she'd seen. He didn't like that she was trying to help me, so he used his hypnosis to send her out to buy a taller pair of shoes. He framed the murder as an accident."

Clarice parted the velvet curtain to leave. But Gracie closed her fist in the fabric. "If what you say is true, that Jack is a murderer and he's using hypnosis on me too, then why don't I remember being hypnotized?"

"If" *what I say is true?* Blasted girl. Katherine wasn't nearly so skeptical.

Honesty—it might be the only thing that could sway Gracie. Give her a little bit of truth mixed in with the lies. "I'm not entirely sure. Based on what Katherine told me, I'm assuming it happens during the vanishing-closet portion of your act with Jack and that he doesn't require physical or direct eye contact to put you into the hypnotic trance."

Gracie's head sunk tortoise fashion between her shoulders. "I'm not sure what's going on here, but I don't want to be involved. Please, can you show me the way back to the circus?"

If Gracie didn't want to be involved, she should've stayed inside the closet like Jack had told her to. Clarice set a hand on Gracie's shoulder and gave her best impression of sympathy. "You're already involved. You see, I need your help to get out of this prison. And if you don't want to die before you reach Chicago, you'll need my help."

Gracie looked defeated, a dried and withered husk. "What do I have to do?"

"First, be a doll and carry this pail for me. After that, you'll help me finish what Katherine started."

CHAPTER XXI

THE MOMENT they stepped through the curtained vestibule, Gracie's performance costume returned and Clarice now wore a shirt and pants. Gracie smoothed the front of her corset and gave the garter around her tights a snap. "Our clothes, they're normal again."

Clarice waved her gold and jewel-spangled wrist in the air. "Everything inside the ballroom is an illusion to some extent. Objects removed from the light of the chandelier will revert to their natural state."

The woman, who smelled a lot like strawberry bonbons, led the way back into the hallways of the fortress at a quick pace.

Gracie kept her distance at first. But, as the furnishings deteriorated and the lights dimmed, she shortened the gap.

If there was one thing Gracie knew to be true from all that Clarice had told her, it was that this was not the place to make Clarice her enemy.

Clarice opened the door leading into the dark basement utility area Gracie had originally come through. Now Gracie wished she had an oil lamp and a piece of chalk to put numbers, like street names, at each intersection. "Is this the prison you spoke of? Seems more like a maze."

Clarice huffed. "Knossos in its entirety is my prison. But technically the light from the ballroom chandelier keeps me healthy and young."

"You said Jack has you trapped here. What happened?" Jack seemed to have quite a bit of drama. Harris, his parents, and now his aunt.

"Years ago, he was my assistant—and forgive me for not knowing exactly how long ago. Time flows differently here—it varies from one room to another—and it's vastly different from what you know as the real world." Clarice held the door open for Gracie. "Jack weaponized one of my inventions and used it for horrible purposes. When I threatened to destroy it and the closet, he turned it on me and trapped me here."

"How are you trapped? Why can't you leave through the closet?"

Clarice stopped in front of the furnace room, identifiable by its ten-foot-tall door of reinforced steel. "The device I created extracts light energy particles from inorganic elements and converts them into carbon-based compounds. I intended to solve world hunger by converting rocks into food. Jack reversed the polarization and discovered that if he used my device on people, he could extract highly valuable gemstones from their bodies. These light-source extractions are called 'heartstones.' Jack stole mine, so if I leave Knossos for more than a few hours, the remaining physical elements in my body will rapidly decay and I'll die."

Only two comprehensible words stood out from Clarice's scientific jargon: "extract," and "heartstones." Bile climbed into Gracie's throat as she stared at Clarice's overflowing container of gemstones, which might as well have been roaches or spiders. "Is that what's in your bucket? People's souls?"

Clarice laughed, and Gracie thought the sound would perfectly suit a horse—if horses could laugh. "These are synthetic, as well as all the others in the furnace room. The real heartstones are in the chandelier and a few are in the laboratories."

Gracie's gaze settled on the lumpy necklace beneath the collar of Clarice's shirt. "What about the necklace you're wearing, are those real gemstones, or fake?"

"They're real. Gems can treat the symptoms associated with a missing heartstone, but they can't cure me."

"Can't you take one from the chandelier and use that?" Gracie hated herself for the suggestion. If heartstones came from people and

Clarice was the only person she'd seen in this place so far, Gracie must assume that once a heartstone was removed, the person died.

"It must be my own," Clarice said.

She opened the door to a room the size of a train station. Mining car tracks crisscrossed over their heads and beside them. Gemstones in all colors and cuts overflowed the wheeled carts. Conveyor belts fed the gemstones into an enormous furnace. All the lights, shiny bells, and spindly scaffolding gave Gracie the feeling she'd stepped into the circus's sideshow. "Knock me down with a feather—there are so many of them!"

"I've been here for what feels like an eternity," Clarice said, "yet I haven't been able to make a satisfactory replacement for my heartstone."

Gracie turned to Clarice. "You said Jack murdered Katherine because she was helping you, and you implied he stole all the chandelier crystals from people. If he's capable of such callous murder, why are you still here?"

"There are things he doesn't yet fully understand about this technology. I'll be his prisoner until his knowledge surpasses my own or until I find the formula to stabilize the synthetic stones so he can take them back through the closet and become rich."

Until now Gracie had thought she was taking everything in stride with a good dose of skepticism, but this she couldn't swallow. "That doesn't sound like Jack."

"I know you hold him in high esteem, but he's a master of deception. Why else would you forget this place if he wasn't purposefully hiding it from you using hypnosis? You don't have to fully trust me, but the sooner you realize we have the same goal, the better off we'll both be."

Gracie faced Clarice, square on, eyes beseeching. "This isn't really about money, is it? If Jack knows so much, he could do other things than pretend to be a traveling magician. Why is he really keeping you here?"

"You're very clever. Much more so than Katherine." Clarice picked up one of the gemstones, polished it with her sleeve, and then tossed it right back. "All right, I'll tell you. Over the course of time, the gemstones that light the chandelier in the ballroom grow dim and burn out. In order to keep the time-compression field in balance, they need to be replaced."

"Are you saying Jack killed Katherine and turned her into one of the chandelier crystals?"

"Perhaps I assumed your cleverness too quickly." Clarice's golden curls swished side to side as she shook her head in irritation. "A heartstone can't be extracted if the person is already dead. There's a chance during an extraction that the victim will die from the trauma of having so much light energy harvested at once. Their loved ones find them dead in bed and think they had a heart attack. Since Jack has the circus to help him keep the closet on the move, he can extract one or two stones from people in each town and no one is any wiser."

Gracie stepped back and leaned heavily against the wall, biting the tip of her thumbnail.

Jonathan Detweiler. The police had said he'd died of a heart attack. *If* Jack did need heartstones to preserve Knossos and keep his aunt here, and *if* Jack needed to take someone's life to do it, Gracie could imagine he'd pick Jonathan for his victim. Not out of spite, but perhaps from some noble idea that he was cleansing the population of undesirables?

Gracie pulled her hand out of her mouth. "What is it exactly you want from me? Where do I fit in all this?"

"I had a research journal on hypnosis methods which Jack took from me shortly before Katherine's death. He's locked it away with a special key that he hid in your bigger world, in the present time. Find that key for me, and I know I can reverse the hypnosis spell he put on you."

"Do I really need your help for that? As soon as I get back to the circus lot, I'm quitting. I'll never set foot in his closet again."

"How will you do that when you won't remember our conversation? Jack might not even allow you to leave, if he suspects you know something."

Gracie doubted that. He'd wanted her gone from the beginning. Her head hurt trying to figure everything out, yet the more she picked at the holes in this story, the larger they became. Nothing made sense. "Is there any reason I can't just walk out of this room and find my way back to the closet on my own?"

Clarice swiped the railing with her finger and rubbed the grit between her fingers. "Now honey, I can't let you do that. The shades will get you. You're safer with me than on your own."

"Shades?"

The golden goddess's smile turned cruel. "Jack's victims that don't die during the extraction process. They can't be left to run free—they'd tell someone what happened—so he brings them here. Within a short period of time they lose what's left of their sentience and revert to a form of dark energy."

Stay away from the shadows. Run or you'll be dead next.

So that thing that scared Barty was a shade, a monster from the dark horror of this evil place.

Gracie paced around the gemstone sorting table. Something was missing from the equation of the notes and this strange place. Her gut told her it was something big, yet how could the missing element be significant if it wasn't also easily apparent?

Gracie stopped walking. "Does Harris know about this? Earlier, he mentioned he was looking for something he believed Katherine last had."

"Yes, but you must be careful not to say anything about this to him either. I think Katherine was killed because she said something to one twin, mistaking him for the other."

It might be too late for her already. "When we went to the bakery yesterday I asked Harris if he knew what 'Knossos' meant. He never explained it, though he did say I shouldn't mention it to Jack."

"Harris is trying to protect you. Hypnotic magic is a complex process, woven through the subconscious layers of the mind. Jack can break a person's mind by stealing their memories and manipulating their deep-rooted thoughts. Harris is being careful, for your sake, to avoid getting involved. Also, Jack has stolen something precious of Harris's. Jack would gladly end his twin's life if Harris became meddlesome."

Gracie had just about had enough of this woman and her accusations against Jack. Some could be true, but Gracie suspected most were not. Either way, she had no desire to sort through the mess. "If I find the key you want, what type of assurance will you give me that you'll leave me alone and I'll never have to set foot in this place again?"

Clarice raised one of her finely-plucked eyebrows. "There's not much of value you can safely remove from this place, but after I get my heartstone back, I won't have need for this necklace. It can be yours."

"No. I want paper—enough to write a long letter to convince myself to quit the circus."

"If you take back more than a strip at a time, it will likely ignite."

She'd take her chances. There had to be a way to warn herself to stay out of this nightmarish alternate world, and she knew Clarice wouldn't volunteer the information.

Gracie turned away from Clarice, fussing with the front of her costume. When she turned back around, she held her sock purse in one hand. She poured the contents into her palm and panned through the pile of coins and wadded bills until she came across the silver key.

Clarice leaned closer. "You found it!"

Gracie closed her fist around the key and pulled it away. "Tear out a page from your notebook, give me a pen, and take me back to the closet. Then you can have it."

The stiffness of Clarice's movements as she tore out a clean page and handed Gracie a fountain pen conveyed her disapproval.

Gracie wrote quickly and folded the note several times before placing it in the sole of her shoe. She then stuffed the less bulky sock back into her corset, still holding the key.

Clarice wrapped her arm around Gracie's shoulders. "Let's hurry and get you back. While it would be fun to have Jack open the door in front of the audience and see you're still missing, it'll cause worse trouble."

"The audience? Haven't they gone home already? It's been over an hour."

"Time is in an expanded state here. An hour in the ballroom is only a few seconds under the big top. After you return through the closet, the next time the door opens it'll be Jack reaching in to escort you out. You won't realize you ever left."

The pressure of Clarice's hand on Gracie's back increased. Clarice shouldered the furnace room door open. Gracie fell into step beside her, only paying slight attention to the turns she made. Gracie couldn't get her mind off the situation with Jack and her worry over whether she'd made the right decision to give Clarice the key.

A few turns and intersections later, they arrived at the open closet, exactly as she'd left it. As promised, Gracie surrendered the silver key.

"Goodbye, Gracie," Clarice said, holding the door as Gracie stepped inside. "Give Jack my regards."

CHAPTER XXII

CLARICE SHUT the closet door, glad to be rid of the little twit. She should've thought to send the shades to the circus through the closet sooner. They hadn't spurred Jack to return, but seeing Gracie blanch when she'd mentioned them had been amusing.

Clarice moved back toward the ballroom through the cloisters with eel-like swiftness, the silver key squeezed in her fist. She turned left at one of the splits in the hallway, the path now headed away from the ballroom and her lab. She stopped outside an open doorway, a fizz in her blood.

The room was sharply square with shelves of books all the way up to the arched ceiling. A magnificent fireplace dominated the east wall, currently stuffed to the flue with broken furniture. Clarice went straight for the writing desk—a spindly thing with turned wood legs and a long skinny drawer. The metal trim around the lock was scarred and deformed from her attempts to force it open with the blade of a letter opener.

Clever, Gladys. Without the key, the drawer opened to nothing. With the key inserted, the quantum field would stabilize and reorganize the matter into something tangible.

Clarice probed the lock with the key.

She held her breath and opened the drawer.

At first, she thought it empty again.

No! It *must* be here!

She pulled the drawer out and reached into its dark depths. Her fingers brushed something brittle and dry, tucked in the back corner.

A letter?

Clarice ripped the seal and sliced open the envelope. She unfolded the parchment, wondering what had happened to the air in the room since none of it was reaching her lungs.

Clarice,

If you are reading this, congratulations, you're still alive—though it would seem I am not. Your heartstone is not here as you have likely ascertained. This letter is intentionally designed—I directed our brother to leave it along with specific instructions regarding the true location of your heartstone and the conditions for its return. Shame on you for thinking you could skirt your expiation. I hope our brother will be swift in fulfilling my last wish—that the closet and this place be destroyed. I would regret the forfeit of your life, but this is the price for your crimes. Heaven have mercy on you, for I have none left to give.

—Gladys

Clarice tore the letter in half and screamed.

All this time she'd chased the carrot Jack had dangled in front of her only to finally bite it and realize the blasted vegetable was wax the whole time.

Clarice stomped out of the room, knocking over chairs, tables, and décor in her rage. A wrathful hurricane, she left a wake of destruction behind her as she returned to her laboratory.

She slung her particle extractor over her shoulder and slipped her arms through the shoulder straps.

How many shades did she have locked in the garret? Three dozen, four? It was nearly impossible to keep an accurate inventory of the creatures because of their ability to phase through the seven states of matter. In their sublimation phase, she could easily corral them. The more destabilized ones oozed from the upper levels until they ran over the edge of the fortress's foundation and landed in the umbra, or she finished them off with her extractor first.

However many she had, there'd be a lot less after she sent them through the closet to Jack's time.

CHAPTER XXIII

L*ONDON BRIDGE is falling down . . .*

Gracie hummed all ten verses before the door to the closet opened and she saw Jack's blue cufflink wink and beckon her out. She tilted her head right and left to roll a crick out of her neck. She estimated she'd only been in the closet a little under three minutes total, but her muscles were tight like she'd been cramped in it for an hour. A sick, milk-turning feeling spread through her stomach and for some reason, the scent of strawberry bonbons lingered in the air.

Jack clenched her hand like she'd handed him a lemon to squeeze while they bowed to the audience. "You're hurting me."

He let go and then hooked his arm around hers and dragged her from the big top. "What happened in the closet?" He had a mulish set to his jaw that said he didn't give a flying rat's hiney about the "No talking under the big top" rule.

He released her arm after they stepped through the flaps. Gripping his right arm, he rolled his wrist in circles. "Jack, is something the matter with your hand? You didn't break it hitting Mr. Detweiler the other day, did you?"

He pulled his arm out of her reach and tugged his sleeve down. "My hand is *fine*." Gracie's mouth went dry as he stepped closer. His eyes were the color of black coffee without a single drop of creamer.

"You stayed in the closet, right?" he asked.

"The. Whole. Time. I think you'd have seen me if I'd come out!"

Jack ran his hands through his hair and stepped back. "Excuse me for asking something so stupid." His gaze fell to the side and he tugged at his cravat until it came free. "I've had a lot on my mind lately and haven't been able to properly focus."

Well, at least he admitted it. Gracie planted her hands on her hips and blocked his path to the men's dressing tent. "Where do you think you're going?"

"To change?"

No. He didn't get to run off and avoid her, not when he'd promised they'd talk. He had a bad habit of starting conversations and fleeing before they were over, which she intended to fix. Now. "I think I deserve some answers."

He looked away from the dressing tents and Gracie sensed it was not so much her request that he was considering, but the hardened tone she'd used to say it. "I did say we'd talk, though I don't see what's so urgent it can't wait until later."

Harris had told her to look at Jack's hands after the performances, not after dinner. Also, she suspected Jack thought she meant to question him about his activities yesterday. If she surprised him by changing the topic, he might let something slip if he didn't have time to come up with a lie.

All the older orphans know that in a fight when you're outmuscled and outnumbered, you go for the less defended targets.

"Show me your hands," she insisted.

He clenched his fists tightly and she thought he would refuse, but then he opened his palms and offered them to her without fuss. She scrutinized the lines in his palms more thoroughly than a fortune-teller and with one-hundred-percent less insight. He turned his hands over when she asked and didn't throw the slightest fit when her hand slipped inside the cuff of his jacket to feel his wrists.

His fingers were long, his palms a little rough. Each joint bent at her touch and the small tendons felt taut. He had healthy fingernails which weren't chewed off, bruised, or yellowed. Both thumbs extended to form ninety-degree angles and he had all his original ten digits.

The only thing wrong was her overwhelming urge to have him caress her skin with his strong, beautiful hands. If Harris wasn't a liar, she now had even less of a clue what to make of Jack's behavior.

"Through pawing?" He reclaimed his hands and removed his cufflinks. "Now what was so important about seeing my hands that it couldn't wait?"

Telling Jack that Harris had suggested the idea seemed inexcusably rude. Somehow, he'd turned the tables on her, and she needed a quick lie. "I've been worried about you. You were missing all yesterday and I, uh, wanted to make sure you're not injured from the night before."

"No," he said. While he spoke mildly, there was a distinct strength in his tone that left no room for argument. "You've been talking with Harris, haven't you?" Usually when she made a fool of herself Jack had a way of looking at her with one eyebrow raised higher than the other. This time he refrained, making her feel all the more horrible for lying to him.

His cheeks grew hollow—the way they had Saturday after the auction when Gracie had informed him she'd found his closet unlocked. "No matter," he replied to his unanswered question. "What else did Harris tell you to ask me?"

Words failed her, mostly due to her lack of mental preparation for this conversation. At the end of the knife act she'd have let him lead her blindfolded across a busy street. But after the magic act, she couldn't shake off a feeling of exhaustion and deep-rooted unease. What had made her think he'd welcome her prying into his personal life?

This subtle desire she felt to be open with him obviously only went one way. She might as well tell him the other question since she'd already earned his disapproval and scorn. "He told me to ask how your parents died."

"I don't know why he didn't tell you himself. It's not a scandal." Jack shoved his hands in his pockets. "My mother and father were trapeze artists, as I was. Mother died attempting to perform a triple flip on the trapeze for the first time in history. Father caught her, but he couldn't hang on. She landed on the safety net, so close to the edge the momentum dropped her over the side when it tossed her back in the air. She landed on her neck and died immediately. It's my fault they're both dead, because I knew my father shouldn't have been near the trapeze with a torn shoulder muscle. If I hadn't been such a coward, afraid that I'd drop her during her attempt to set the world record, maybe she'd still be alive. And maybe my father wouldn't have swallowed the barrel of a pistol."

He blamed himself for their deaths, though Gracie didn't agree that it was his fault. What Harris had said about their mother—doing things with passion or not at all—fit her overreaching ambition to set a fantastic trapeze record. As for Jack's father taking his own life . . . He hadn't ended his pain, only passed it on to someone else.

"I'm so sorry," Gracie said, each word stiff and clumsy.

"Yeah, well according to Harris, being sorry isn't good enough. I can say it was an accident until my voice goes hoarse, but he'll only forgive me after I die of thirst. I don't know what else he's said about me, but I'd hope in the future you won't take everything he says at face value."

Before she could explain the problem wasn't Harris, but Jack's own reluctance to be upfront about things, he walked off.

She returned to her room, disconcerted over the ruin of the recent closeness she'd felt with Jack. She should have kept her mouth shut and not been so nosy.

Gracie locked the door and checked under the bed before taking a seat on its edge. Before the performance, she'd stripped her shoes clean. If she found anything now, the Almighty himself must have put it there.

Gracie wiggled her toes and slowly slid her feet out of the shoes. Her stomach dropped when a large, folded piece of paper with cramped writing on it fell out. This ended her theory that someone in the dressing tent might have been dropping the notes at her feet or slipping them into her costume.

The writing on the paper was so scrawled she had to cross her eyes to read it—definitely hers.

Your full name is Gracie Anne Hart. You are a performer in a circus, and this is your handwriting. Your brother's name is Robert Thomas Hart and his birthday is April 10th. The silver key is gone as further proof that you must do as this note says.

The twins are liars. You must quit the circus. Run far away where neither can find you. Your life depends on it and

A strong, acrid scent wafted from the note. The edges of the paper blackened and curled in her hand, gray curls of smoke rising from the words. She jumped as the sensation of a hot spark forced her to drop the note before she'd finished reading. In a flash of fire, the paper turned to glittering ashes which fluttered to the ground.

Gracie scrambled backwards, tripping over her trunk and landing in a heap on her bed. To think she'd had such a dangerous article in her shoe. What if it'd ignited and burned her foot?

She poured her entire wash basin onto the floor over the spot where the note had disappeared and mopped up the slop with her blanket.

Who had designed that fiery warning letter? Hardly an ally, if she needed to read the message. Another puzzle—how could the warning contain personal information only she would know? Certainly, she herself couldn't be both the author and the destroyer of the message. Gracie mused over this paradox as she changed out of her costume, postponing the follow-up confrontation she wanted to have with Jack.

If not herself, then perhaps it was written by a really clever magician who could also read minds? On to the unsettling question—who in the circus wanted her gone, or who would benefit most if she quit? Jack seemed the most obvious answer, but then why would he call *himself* a liar? Harris, whom Gracie had pegged as the person who hated Jack the most, was also curiously named a liar. So, who else in the circus disliked both twins or wanted her to leave?

She unpinned her hair. The first note she'd pegged as an insult. The second note said to find Katherine's key and keep it secret or she'd die. The third note might possibly have warned her against the tiger attack and threatened death again. The fourth told her not to trust either of the twins and to quit the circus, at the peril of her life.

Who should she be more inclined to believe—the entity with the power to create a flaming warning, or her own skeptical nature telling her it was all a ploy to manipulate her? None of the threats mentioned a specific deadline, though Gracie didn't want to keep ignoring them.

She pulled out her money sock to investigate whether the key was safe or gone as the note claimed. Her throat clenched when she didn't see the key. Had it fallen out on her walk to the bakery or one of the hundred other places she'd gone while looking for Jack? Who could have known it was gone before she did? Had that person stolen it while she slept the night before? Harris, perhaps? Looking for something of Katherine's in *her* room?

Nothing was safe or sacred here. Tomorrow she could wake up and find someone had shaved her bald and sold her hair to a wig-maker. She dived for her trunk and yanked out the drawers with reckless abandon.

She was relieved to find her postcard where she'd left it, at the bottom of the top drawer. Gracie pressed the dry paper to her lips and mumbled a prayer of thanks. To anyone else it was a worthless piece of cardstock, but without it she'd be like a boat adrift. No anchor to her past, and no sail for her future.

She returned it to her trunk, locking it with the brass key.

When she'd finished tidying the room, she took a seat by the window and leaned her forehead against the glass. On the circus lot, the stagehands were already disassembling the canvas city.

Twenty men carried a rolled canvas tent to the flat cars. Their differing heights created a ripple of mountain peaks and valleys in the fabric roll, similar to the dance of a Chinese New Year dragon. Two clowns carried buckets of water into the men's changing tent for their post-performance make-up removal. A gypsy woman, dressed in colorful scarves and gold earrings big enough for a parrot to sit in, passed in the opposite direction. A blond-face, dark-tailed capuchin monkey sat on her shoulder.

Gracie sat straighter. Maybe that's who she needed to question—a real fortune teller who could see through the veil of death, into the future, and tell her what all this meant.

She pushed the thought out, angered she'd allowed it to enter her mind at all. If it was even remotely possible for a ghost to send a message to the living, then certainly her mother's spirit would have found a way to communicate her aunt's address.

However, Gracie might not have been completely honest when she told Jack she wasn't superstitious at all. She didn't believe that broken mirrors, spilled salt, black cats, or walking under ladders gave people bad luck. Life itself created hardship. However, Gracie wasn't so sure when it came to ghosts.

Mrs. Levenson had tried to scare the orphan children into staying in their beds by saying the upper floors were haunted at night by the ghost of the boy who had fallen down the stairs in the dark and died. Gracie had snuck out of bed several times and never saw anything, but there were others who swore they'd seen the boy's ghost.

If heaven and hell weren't too difficult for Gracie to believe in, then why should vengeful spirits with unfinished business be that much stranger?

Gracie hated to hope that she was being haunted by Katherine's ghost—but the alternative meant she was losing her mind.

Perhaps in her momentary lapses of sanity *she'd* murdered Mr. Detweiler and didn't remember it. She wondered what the police would think if she tried to use temporary insanity as her defense. They'd slap her in a pair of silver bracelets and haul her to an asylum, where she'd spend the rest of her life polishing the cell bars with her eyebrows.

In another hour, the train jolted and crept forward. With her gaze fixed on the window, Gracie watched the sky change from a pallet of colors to shades of violet. Before it turned black, she lit every oil lamp in the room. When she couldn't stand her corset stays digging into her hips a moment longer, she dressed for bed.

The note wouldn't leave her thoughts. Rubbish. Poppycock. A hoax.

She left one lamp burning and crawled into bed.

CHAPTER XXIV

GRACIE UNWOUND the sheet knotted around her legs. The lamp wick had drowned in the oil and darkness filled the room. The lack of vibrations alerted her that the train had stopped. She imagined this was the border inspection where the Canadian Immigration authorities looked over the manifest and documented any new names for their immigration records—a process she must have slept through on the ride to Montreal.

Swinging her feet over the side of the bed, the cold temperature of the floor sent shivers through her. She stubbed her toe on her trunk and slammed into the corner of the vanity as she moved around the room. That would leave a nice bruise. She searched every flat surface with her fingertips yet couldn't find the matchbox.

A sensible girl would climb back in bed and wait for daylight. However, Gracie didn't picture herself getting much sleep until she relit her lamp. She donned a thin robe over her nightdress and ventured into the train hallway. Most train cars had a single lantern burning near the rear door. She'd borrow it to relight her lamp and then return it.

Outside, the sky was darker than the opening of a gun barrel, even though the moon should be three-quarters and gaining. Squares of smooth, cold windows alternated with rough patches of wallpaper underneath her fingers.

The rear door flew open just before she reached it. Gracie could barely discern the outline of a man carrying something bulky on his back, like slain prey thrown over a hunter's shoulder. He let the door slam behind him.

How rude. There were others in the car that were undoubtedly trying to sleep.

"Gracie, thank goodness I found you. Come with me, it's not safe for you here." The tone and timbre of the voice indicated it was one of the twins.

Had the immigration officers recognized her name from a "Wanted Persons" list?

The twin linked his arm around hers confidently and walked beside her in a practiced manner, knowing exactly how much distance to keep between them without one of them tripping over her feet or his. Jack.

"I can't see a thing."

He repositioned his arm around her shoulders. "That's because they've surrounded the train."

"The authorities?"

He didn't answer, causing Gracie to wonder if she'd spoken loud enough. Attached to his hip, she let him guide her forward. His chin tickled the crown of her head each time he looked over his shoulder to the rear door. At the forward door, he took the lead which allowed her a glimpse of the article on his back—a rectangular box with sharp sides, similar in size to a telephone-transmitting unit. Round dials and pressure gauges were implanted all over it. As if reading her thoughts, he cautioned her, "Don't touch any of the buttons."

"What does it do?"

His firm hand, pressed into her lower back, herded her out of the car and down the steps of the porch. "Nothing until we find a fuel source for it, which is why we've got to reach Vincenzio's stateroom before they do."

Gracie couldn't follow Jack's logic at all.

"Who are 'they'? Indians? Train robbers?"

"I'm hoping that with your cooperation, you won't ever have to find out."

She slowed her pace. "If your box needs fuel, why would we go to Vincenzio's stateroom? The coal tender is at the front of the train."

"My box doesn't run on coal or wood; it's powered by converting gemstones into energy."

Gracie dug her bare heels into the drain rock, regretting she'd not put on shoes before venturing out. She twisted out of Jack's hold. "Don't tell me we're on our way to Vincenzio's stateroom to steal Katherine's jewelry?"

"Unless you have a diamond bracelet lying around, one which you don't need, that was the plan."

"No!" Gracie shoved him. What kind of fool did he take her for? "Saying things like you want to earn my trust back and then asking me to help you steal from Vincenzio the *same* night. The nerve! Where did you go after I left the hotel? Out gambling? Did you rack up a huge debt and now you need to pay your creditors? Since I'm the new person here, it'd be easy for you to pin me as the thief, wouldn't it?"

"That hurts, Gracie," Jack said, his shoulders hunching as though his backpack had gained fifty pounds. "I spent that entire evening and the following day looking for a lost item and searching for more evidence to explain the thing Barty saw." Jack's head scanned right and left as regularly as a metronome, his eyes guarded and on edge. "Yes, I am going to break into Vincenzio's stateroom, but I didn't bring you along to frame you. You're safer with me than you would be in your room or wandering around in the dark."

What rubbish. Gracie reached for the handlebar to climb back onto the train car. "Good riddance Jack, I'm going back to bed."

"Don't go in there." He grabbed her wrist.

The hot flame of her temper flared and she wrenched her hand free. "I'm not going to help you steal Katherine's jewelry, and I wish you'd leave me alone."

"Fine, we'll forget the jewelry, just come with me."

"I don't want to be seen with you if you're up to mischief." She hoisted herself onto the first step. "*Goodnight*, Jack."

As her foot touched the second step she was snatched backwards by her waist. Jack hoisted her over his shoulder, his arms wrapped around her kicking legs, much too close to her bum to be considered decent. "I can't let you go back in there, even if it means you hate me."

She pushed against his neck and pulled his hair. He still didn't let go. Her eyes fell to the box on his back. "Put me down, you brute, or I'll start pushing buttons!"

That got his attention. His hold relaxed, allowing her to slide down his front onto her feet. The moment her hands were free, Gracie balled her fist and swung. Because of his tall stature, she missed his nose and ended up knocking him in the jaw.

"Zut!" Jack staggered back with a hand clasped against his chin.

"Ouch!" Gracie shook the ache out of her hand. Men were built a lot thicker and hardier than young boys or teenage girls.

"Gracie!"

"Stay away from me!" For added emphasis, she drove the heel of her foot into his shin and scampered away.

A two-story maintenance shack stood near the front of the train, close to where the locomotive had stopped beneath the water crane. Gracie ran toward the brick building in hopes of finding someone from the train crew, who could escort her past Jack, back to her room.

Strands of her untrussed hair streamed down her back and her nightgown flowed behind her like a pair of white linen wings. The small pebbles digging into her feet made the ground feel like broken glass. She forced herself to ignore the pain in her feet because the building was only sixty feet away.

Twenty feet from her goal, Gracie suddenly halted. A thick, dark misty shadow emerged from behind the shack. Her eyes strained to focus on it as the figure shifted from one nebulous shape to another. It first took the form of a person, and then a large beast crouched low, stalking toward her.

"This isn't real." Saying the words aloud had no effect on the shadow. She blinked and rubbed her eyes. The ghostly mist was still there.

Stay away from the shadows.

In a split-second, she decided she'd rather take her chances with Jack than an evil spirit. Dust and gravel sprayed beneath her feet as she turned and bolted back toward the train car. Shadows nipped at the corners of her vision and her breath wheezed.

"Stand still!" A voice shouted behind her. The tone was harsh, masculine.

Jonathan's? The foreman's? Jack's? Gracie's body moved slower and slower, a clockwork toy running down. In another second, she could no longer move at all. A hazy fog settled over her thoughts so thickly she couldn't even find her voice to scream. The strength of the magic which had taken hold of her limbs had no bounds. She no longer had any control over her body.

The gray surroundings darkened until everything became a collage of varying shades of black. The train cars blurred into one long line as the light of the shack dimmed. Gracie blinked several times in a vain effort to clear her vision. If anything, it got worse.

"Please . . ." Gracie tried to speak, but her voice was gone.

Is this nerve damage? Did I get bitten by a snake? What sort of poison weakens a person so quickly, without prior warning?

Behind her, the whistle on the circus train howled and then a low rumble preceded the creaking of turning axels. She was going to be left behind.

Hopelessness numbed her remaining senses. Maybe this was what Jack had plotted with Vincenzio during their meeting this morning. In exchange for amnesty in the case of Mr. Detweiler's death, Jack would turn her into the "third act" by leaving her behind, giving Vincenzio a small headline because of her mysterious disappearance.

Whatever reason Jack had for wanting her off this train, he'd succeeded.

Something heavy moved behind her, grass stalks rustling as the thing drew closer. The clicks of a rifle being chambered echoed in the air. A low whining tone rolled into a shrill pitch. Gracie's lips moved in prayer. At the end of her life she was still alone.

The blast of the weapon was tantamount to getting hit by a freight train. It tore through her back and pushed its way out of her chest. Dirt and rock fragments danced around her. Pain exploded all over her body and pushed the air from her lungs. Something vaguely resembling her voice rose through the column of her throat, weaker than the chirp of a single cricket. A light glowed in front of her—the light at the end of the tunnel. Saint Peter mocked her by opening heaven's pearly gates, knowing plain well she couldn't drag herself to them.

Gracie dropped to her knees and fell over onto her back. Strangely, there wasn't any blood on the front of her night dress or any sign of an exit wound. The hovering light solidified into a diamond—a star with ten points, flat like a snowflake, and radiating the light of two suns.

She was definitely going to hell because her last conscious thought would be full of vanity—her soul was the most beautiful thing she'd ever seen. Scratch that, her last thought was that she should close her eyes, so she didn't look ghastly when someone found her dead body.

The ache from the cuts on her feet subsided and she grew deaf to the pounding of her heart. The lamplighter of her existence carried his ladder down the "streets" of her arms and legs, extinguishing one light at a time. There went the feeling in her fingers.

"Don't give up!" Jack shouted.

His words became an invisible anchor holding the remains of her existence to this world. She'd had a comfortable seat in Death's hearse and now was being dragged behind it by her hair.

"Open your eyes!"

Her eyelashes fluttered. Gracie could see the shapes of the train cars and Jack running toward her. Pain began to register all over her body again. She groaned, swearing a pact with everything unholy that if she ended up dying anyway, she'd come back and haunt him a year for every second he made her suffer longer.

Gracie knew little about guns but was able to recognize that the pistol Jack brandished wasn't normal. In place of a barrel it featured a revolver chamber large enough to hold bullets the size of cigars. The phone box on his back buzzed with the angry noise of a beehive knocked out of a tree. Aiming over her, Jack cocked the hammer and fired.

The pulse of heat that flew over her face carried the force of a lightning bolt, nearly scorching her eyebrows. The concussion of the shadow-thing's demise blew over Gracie—hot and energized. Her hair lifted away from her head and then went limp.

The glowing star crystal fell in the grass and she felt coldness in her chest. Holstering his weapon, Jack threw himself over it.

That soul-stealing pig! He'd only fought off the ghost so he could have her glowing diamond for himself. She'd have his teeth for pearls and his eyeballs for earrings before she let him get away with this.

Her head spun the moment she sat up. Despite this, Gracie arched her fingers into cat claws and pounced. The ground flew up to meet her, or was it the other way around? A moment later she realized Jack's arms were wrapped around her.

"Don't try to move." He eased her onto her back. With extreme rapidity, Jack shucked off his backpack and set it to the side. Holding her shoulder down with his arm, he pried the neckline of her gown down to just below her collarbone.

"Would you quit fidgeting? I'm trying to help." He pinned her legs down with one of his knees.

Would he make up his mind already? Either he was a gentleman or a scoundrel. The two characteristics couldn't live in the same body. Hot tears trickled down her cheek, but she didn't remember wishing to cry them.

Jack chewed on his lower lip and dug a brown leather glove from his rear pocket. He positioned the glowing crystal over her heart. The crystal radiated heat, warming her chest and then branding her as with a hot iron. His weight pushed on her like a millstone.

"If it's any consolation, this'll hurt me a lot more than you." He winced as he threw his weight onto it.

The crystal vanished in a flash of light. Her chest heaved, her stomach clenched, and she thought she would vomit. The fog lifted from her thoughts and she could feel her heart beating.

GRACIE jerked upright, astonished she could see in color and details again. Brightly-lit walls with patterned wallpaper surrounded her, not the open air of the outdoors. There was no weight on her chest from Jack, or anyone else, holding her to the ground. A steady rumble indicated she was aboard the train. Beyond the glare of her reflection in the window, she saw navy blue scenery highlighted by the waxing moon. Dark green pastures with cut timber livestock fences spotted the landscape. An occasional cottage passed, smoke from the chimney painting gray brushstrokes onto the background of a cloudless sky.

Had seeing that shadow-thing and her soul hovering in front of her been nothing but a nightmare?

The noise of rustling fabric drew her attention to the other side of the room.

On the pull-down bed across from her, Jack sat in a slump, asleep with his jacket draped across him like a blanket, his fingers interlocked over his stomach. Her room only had one bed, which meant they must be in Jack's.

Gracie clutched the front of her robe and jumped to her feet. She yelped as something sharp on the floor cut the bottom of her foot.

Her legs folded and she dropped back onto the bed. Examining the bottoms of her feet, she noted they were filthy and covered in shallow cuts. Her cheeks flamed and panic choked her as her imagination ran wild, filling the gap in her memory of how she ended up back on the train and alone with Jack in his room.

With shaky legs, Gracie crossed the room, wincing with each step. The door handle wouldn't turn as she gripped it. She whirled to face Jack's slouched, sleeping form.

"Why is this locked? What did you do to me?"

His voice was low and husky, each word dredged out of a deep, murky place. "Go back to sleep. I'll let you out in the morning."

"As if I could sleep with a man in the room!"

"I've done a lot of rotten things in my life, and some nice things, but plucking a lady's petals isn't on either list so don't tie your bloomers in a knot." He shifted slightly, digging his shoulders lower, trying to get comfortable. "No one saw me carry you in here and I'll make sure no one sees you leave. Your reputation will be fine."

On her coherency thermometer, his babble remained a silver blob of mercury at the bottom. Perhaps she had not made herself clear. "Where's the door key? I'm not spending the night in your room."

She watched his eyes with earnest as he opened them, hoping they'd betray the key's location with a wayward glance. Jack's gaze remained fixed ahead of him, and when he spoke, his lips were equally lazy. "I can't protect you if you leave."

"No one asked you to."

"Do whatever you want then, just let me sleep." The sound of dry leaves rattled in his chest.

Her hand slid off the door handle. "Are you unwell?"

He rolled his head to face her and cracked a weak smile. "I'm really tired. I don't usually lift so much weight in one evening. Exactly how many cakes did you have after dinner?"

Gracie situated herself in front of him, doing her best to imitate the stern expression Mrs. Levenson wore when she was in the process of divining a guilty individual out of a large group. He looked too bold for someone who claimed to be clapped out.

The room key was on him.

Her hand shot out with the speed of a pecking bird and snatched his jacket.

He scrambled to cover himself as if she'd caught him in the buff instead of just with his shirt open.

Jack's whole right arm, and even part of his shoulder, had turned glittering white—like he'd rolled his arm in honey then reached to the bottom of the sugar barrel. The contrast was heightened by the filthiness of his ruined shirt. Clusters of black bruises covered his chest, radiating from his shoulder.

Gracie fainted.

It was probably the best, most sensible thing she had done in a very long while.

CHAPTER XXV

G RACIE MOVED too abruptly and fell out of bed. Her bed, in her room. Morning couldn't have come at a better time. Her entire night had flowed from one awful dream into another.

She rubbed the sand from her eyes and stretched her legs. Her memory pieced itself together, starting backwards with the reason she'd worn her robe to bed. One glance at the underside of her feet put everything in place. The cuts and filth were still there—none of it was a dream.

Petticoat, bustle, corset, bodice, skirt, socks, shoes, hairpin—all the items she should have been wearing last night in the presence of someone of the opposite sex. Putting them all on this morning seemed to take longer than waiting for paint to dry. Gracie nearly tripped when she attempted to button her boots at the same time she bumbled from her room.

Most of the troupe strolled the circus lot in their performance costumes. She didn't know where they planned to hold rehearsal since the big top hadn't been pitched yet. She'd let Vincenzio and the stage-hands worry about that while she focused on finding Jack's room. He had some explaining to do.

Gracie found his room and pounded on the door until it opened. Her knuckles ached afterward, still tender from punching Jack the night before.

The door opened wide. The likeness of the statue of David greeted her (thankfully, only the top half) rendered in the flesh and blood of an Australian bushwhacker. One of the twins. His charcoal gray pants hung so low on his hips she'd almost mistaken them for chaps. He held his shirt in his left hand and one shoe in his right. There was nothing wrong with either of his arms. Harris.

"Where's Jack?" Gracie blurted, staring to the side when he didn't do anything to cover himself. He must have been expecting someone else or he'd have finished dressing before opening the door.

"Looks like I'll be having a dingo's breakfast this morning," he said, sitting on one of the beds. Out of the corner of her eye she saw him slip his arms through a shirt.

"A what?" Gracie moved into the doorway but didn't enter the room.

"A yawn, a leak, and a look around."

Watching him do the buttons with a practiced hand, Gracie wondered how the two men could share a room with all their enmity. "Have you seen Jack this morning? I was told you two share this room."

Harris nodded toward the opposite bunk. "That's his bed."

The sheets on the rear-facing bed were made and tucked under the mattress. No blood stains or sparkling white granules. Gracie drew her lower lip into her mouth.

This wasn't the same room as last night. Though Jack might have been able to change the sheets to hide the evidence of his condition, she doubted he could have changed the wallpaper and the lighting fixtures.

"What's the matter, Gracie? While I love having you stare at me, I wish you wouldn't frown when doing so. Did Jack steal your favorite pillow?"

If only it were that simple.

Not being able to think of anything else other than the ordeal, the truth came rushing out before she could consider the consequences. "Late last night, Jack tried to leave me behind at the junction and he had this weird buzzing box that shot lightning. The ghost Barty saw tried to steal my soul, but Jack put it back which made his arm ghastly white—like it'd turned to salt. He locked me in a room but this morning I was back in my own room like nothing had happened."

Harris stared at her like purple warts had spontaneously sprouted on her face. "Jack told me you had a rough night, but I'd say you sound like you're being followed by pink giraffes and bunyips. Are you feeling all right?"

A dam burst inside her and words poured out, her voice shrill beyond control. "Besides last night's near-death experience, Katherine's ghost haunting me with notes, and the fact that my confidant thinks I'm crazy—I'm *peachy*!"

Harris stood, crossed the room, and pressed his palm to her forehead. "You're a little warm, and you don't sound like yourself. I'd better tell Vincenzio you're too sick to be in the parade."

She swatted his hand away. "I'm not sick. And why do I have to be in the parade? You're not in costume."

"I'm staying behind to set up the tents, but if you want to get paid for the day, you'd best not be late."

"I'm not going anywhere until I get some answers. Where's Jack?"

Harris's lopsided smile leveled. "I saw Jack this morning, and both his arms were normal."

Gracie felt her resolute perception of "truth" weakening, however, the stinging pain from her feet demanded she persist. She tugged at the high collar of her dress. "I asked to see Jack's hands after the show yesterday—and about your parents' deaths. As far as I can tell, you've done nothing but lead me on a goose chase. Stealing my ticket at the station, buying me that trunk and taking me out to the bakery, then making me out as a fool with those silly questions to ask Jack—you're just one of those monstrous types who secretly finds pleasure in the suffering of others."

Harris's pause before speaking was calculatedly long. "I'm sure it'll disappoint you to hear me say, there was no special reason I stole your ticket besides the fact that I was bored. Our train was delayed while Vincenzio tried to find a replacement for Katherine. You caught my eye and I took it thinking I'd return it shortly after and you'd be grateful. But you realized I took it before I could do so."

He turned up his sleeve cuffs twice and looked Gracie in the eyes. "I bought you the trunk because I do feel guilty. Those questions I told you to ask Jack weren't meant to make you feel like a fool. He really is hiding something, but it doesn't matter anymore. I've got a feeling he's not going to be with the troupe much longer."

This was news to her and concerning because if Jack quit the circus, she didn't have any valuable skills to encourage Vincenzio to keep her employed. "Why is that?"

"Too many accidents, and he's always linked to them. Many in the troupe aren't too happy to have him here. I'd say the only reason Vincenzio hasn't fired him yet is that he's always got some excuse. Take last night as an example . . ."

She took a step closer to where he sat. "Do you know what really happened?"

Smooth as a symphony, his explanation flowed from his lips—careful, evocative, *rehearsed*. "All I can tell you is what Jack told me. Last night he said he saw you sleepwalk off the train at the Potsdam Junction. When he tried to help you back to your room, you punched him in the face and ran. If he hadn't used an emergency flare to get the engineer's attention, you'd have been left behind."

"I wasn't sleepwalking, and I punched him because he wouldn't let me return to my room even though I was half dressed and not wearing shoes."

Harris slipped his foot into one of the boots. "Now that is rude of him. If anyone deserved to see you undressed, it should've been me. Putting strangers before his brother. There's absolutely no sense of family loyalty in him."

Gracie stooped and picked up Harris's other boot, bounced it in her hand for a second, and then flung it at Harris's head.

"Hey!" He caught the shoe in midair. "What was that for?"

It had been a test to see whether he used his right or left arm to block it. He'd caught it with his right hand, his reflexes sharper than a barber's shaving knife, which proved it *was* Harris, not Jack pretending to be Harris. Also, lewd men deserved to be hit in the face with fast, flying objects.

She stood with arms akimbo. Whenever two people told the same lie—it meant they were working together. "I don't know what happened last night, but I'm through with your twisted mind games. You can tell Jack when you see him next that I want nothing to do with you two anymore!"

Gracie fled from the train car. Harris followed, calling for her to come back. Three stilt-walkers provided her an escape. She dashed between a pair of their tree-limb legs and cut in front of a moving wagon to lengthen the gap between her and Harris. The horses reared and the wagon master's curses followed her as she lost herself in the throng of flamboyant characters with their glittered eyelids, rouged cheeks, and candy-colored coiffures.

She took cover beside the toffee cart and listened for sounds of pursuit. Spots danced around the edges of her vision, and she was certain the pain in her side was because her heart had detached and fallen into her stomach. A minute passed, then another.

Legs quaking and the heels of her feet burning as badly as the bottoms, Gracie slid to the ground and undid the buttons of her bodice down to her collarbone. Hitching her skirt over her knees, she fanned herself with the hem.

Gravel crunched under someone's feet beside her. Gracie dropped the hem of her skirt and looked up to see Maria.

"Gracie, what's wrong?" Maria asked.

"Did Harris send you to talk to me?"

"No. I saw you cut in front of that wagon, and I was concerned. The parade is leaving shortly, and you're not in costume."

"I think something might be wrong with me."

"You look a bit sick. Is it the menses?"

Gracie shook her head, too embarrassed to say anything despite that not being the case.

"You're having problems with one of the men, or maybe several?"

"This is different." *I can't tell the difference between a dream and reality.*

Maria reached for her shoulder. Her hand fell before she made contact. "Tell you what. Come with me for roll call, and then after the parade, we'll sit down and have a chat."

"I'd rather not be seen by anyone right now. I'm a mess."

"Roll call is mandatory. There was some kind of incident after we crossed the border, so Vincenzio wants everyone to check in or else he'll scratch them from the books."

"I don't think I have enough time to get dressed." In truth, Gracie could dress in a rush; she just didn't want to.

"Then don't change, and just go tell Richard you're sick with the red tide. I promise he won't ask any more questions."

She'd rather walk ten miles on her cut feet than say such a thing. "I'll go change. Thank you for the advice." Gracie gave the woman a genuine smile.

While the twins pushed Gracie to the edge of her sanity and patience, at least Maria proved that not everyone in the troupe had amity issues and Gracie *could* make friends here if she wanted to belong. Even if she couldn't quite trust Maria fully, at least she had the possibility of becoming a friend.

Gracie changed into her costume in record time and then found her way to roll call by following the tipsy music blasting from the tall brass pipes of a calliope. The conductor, a gentleman in a white jacquard topcoat, sat on the slow-moving wagon, pressing the foot keys as if he were operating a treadle sewing machine. Beside the line of elephants, Gracie spotted Ringmaster Richard in his vibrant red coat, white jodhpurs, and top hat. He bellowed at a large, ridiculously curly-haired, man wearing a green waistcoat. "Start having the wagons pull around!"

Gracie tried clearing her throat to get Richard's attention, and when that didn't work, she tugged on his sleeve.

His voice roared, and she thought if his teeth were sharper he'd bite her head off. "I've already got you marked off. Jack informed me this morning you weren't feeling well."

"He was mistaken."

Richard gave her a second glance over. "Jack's wagon isn't on the parade list. Go find something to do out of my way."

"I'll see if Miriam has any laundry she needs washed."

"Whatever. Just go bother someone else."

Gracie set off to find Miriam and the dressing tent but gave up when she realized it hadn't been set up yet. Who else could she talk to, or where could she find the seamstress?

The backdrop of the sky was mottled by a flock of clouds in gray-edged tutus. Due to the threat of rain, the stagehands seemed especially preoccupied in their effort to unload the big top's support poles from the train car flats. Gracie turned toward the train cars, guessing Miriam might be in a meeting with Vincenzio.

She caught sight of Vincenzio walking the length of the train cars with two uniformed officers. Suddenly he bellowed her name. "Gracie!"

They found me!

She made a sharp turn away from the train cars, holding her hand up to cover her face, pretending she hadn't heard him. He called her again, his voice loud enough that several of the stagehands turned in her direction.

She dropped her hand and ducked around a cart loaded with folded tents. Then she sprinted for the line of unloaded stock wagons.

Gracie cursed under her breath for an entire minute without repeating a word once. In her rush to get dressed for roll call, she'd left her money sock in her trunk. But even if she'd remembered it, she couldn't run away dressed in her costume. She needed a place to hide.

Jack's fire-engine-red wagon stood out from the other colored wagons. Perfect! She checked over her shoulder for the police and Vincenzio before flinging open the back doors. The closet sat in the center, its black velvet cover in a heap to the side. Strange, usually Jack was careful to cover it after every performance.

Noises in the distance emptied her thoughts of everything— except the need to disappear.

How exactly did Jack set the secret compartment mechanism? She took a guess and jiggled the handle, and then she closed and opened the door. No movement. For her next attempt, she turned the handle counterclockwise.

A small click echoed from somewhere in the closet. She stepped inside, closed the door behind her, and then realized that if she covered the closet, it'd be less obvious she was hiding in it.

Turning the knob to let herself out, it broke off in her hand.

Crumbs.

Pushing on the door did nothing to release the locking mechanism. She picked up the broken knob from the floor but couldn't make it fit back into the door.

This might be a good thing. The broken knob meant the police couldn't open the door and find her hiding inside. In complete silence,

Gracie listened for the sounds of booted feet approaching and of handcuffs jingling. Seconds passed, then minutes.

Her stomach churned, and she regretted not eating breakfast. Another hour must have passed. She tried the handle again. The loose feeling in her belly turned to tightness. What if she couldn't get out?

"Hello?" Gracie said. After a moment, she shouted, "Can anyone hear me?"

No one answered. Of course, what had seemed the perfect diversion—everyone hurrying to get the tents up before it started raining—was now her undoing.

She fought the urge to panic. *Too late.* If the circus didn't have a performance tonight, she could be trapped here until the prop handlers came to get the disappearing closet for tomorrow's show. Or longer. Would anyone even realize she was missing? Would anyone care?

Jack had always warned her not to come out until he opened the door. That instruction indicated she had the means to let herself out. However, breaking the handle may have ruled out that option.

She searched the walls by touch, becoming convinced her teeth had more space between them than some of these wood panels.

The arches of her feet ached, and her eyelids grew heavy. The air had turned thick and humid, greatly assisted by the condensation of her breath. She slumped down, defeated and wondered if falling asleep would be so terrible . . .

She awoke some time later with a terrible crick in her neck. She was still locked in Jack's closet and only partly aware she'd fallen asleep.

"Is anyone there?"

Why did she even bother calling for help? If anything happened to her, Vincenzio and Jack would just find another starving runaway to take her place. No one cared about her. Her heart banged in her chest, and she wished the ache in her stomach was the sort that could be relieved with a bowl of porridge. The increased temperature in the closet made her clothes sticky under her arms and down her back. Groping the walls, she pulled herself up to her feet. She'd wait five more minutes, and then she'd break the door down.

One Mississippi. Two Mississippi. Three Mississippi . . . Sixty Mississippi—close enough.

CHAPTER XXVI

GRACIE PUSHED her shoulder into the door, and it swung open. When she toppled out, she met hard pavement. Darkness spread its chilled cloak over her. Goodness, evening already? And had she really not woken when someone moved the closet into this hallway?

Overhead, several pipes ran along the walls and ceiling. A string of yellow bulbs lit the tunnel.

I've seen this tunnel before.

Wherever this was, she didn't believe she was still in Jack's wagon, under the big top, or in any structure above ground.

"Hello?" she shouted.

Her voice echoed and then all was as quiet. Gracie tiptoed into the dark tunnel, keeping her right hand on the wall so she'd be able to find her way back. At the fifth intersection, the corridor ended in a large set of rusted steel doors.

The doors opened to a dim hallway lined with splintered doors hanging askew in their frames. A damp layer of leaves formed a spongy carpet beneath her feet. A long rug with frayed edges and the smell of wet wood lay beneath the leaves. On the ceiling, flakes of paint bubbled like a festering rash.

"Is there anyone here who can help me?" Gracie called into the hallway. "I'm a bit lost . . ." At this point, she'd welcome a scurrying rat or roach.

She might have gone back to the tunnels to keep searching for another exit, but the leaves looked as though someone had recently walked through and scattered them. The trail led her deeper into the maze of hallways, filled with identical thick carpets and soiled velvet chairs.

She followed the foot traffic marks to a section of halls where the wallpaper no longer resembled a peeling sunburn and the doors weren't torn off their hinges.

The improved interior maintenance did little to ease her concern. Whoever owned this rotting landfill of a building couldn't be a friendly sort of person.

"Please, is anyone here?"

Around the corner, beyond the end of the hallway, a door creaked open and then closed.

She turned the corner to go investigate, her sense of self-preservation screaming for her to reconsider.

Her instincts had a good point—whoever had moved the closet must have been incredibly careless to not have noticed she was in it, which meant they were inept and wouldn't be much help even if she found them. Or, they had known what they were doing, which made them dangerous.

The next hallway led to a windowless alcove with two chairs beside the single door. She reached for the door handle. The sharp zap of an electric shock went up her arm as she touched the handle. Ouch! She rubbed the dull tingle out of her arm.

When Gracie went to open the door again, black smoke began to seep from the gap beneath the door and she nervously jumped away. Confused, she watched as the black substance pooled around her feet. Unlike the smoke from a fire, this vapor smelled faintly of citrus and felt chilly against her skin.

She backed away farther from the door as a black oil-like substance began pouring out through the door's keyhole. It moved in slithering rivers, flowing over the carpet rather than being absorbed by it. The little snakes bumped into each other and merged into larger ones, congregating into a single, large pool. Around her, the lights dimmed. Shadows from the furnishings peeled off the walls and moved on their own.

Fear squeezed her chest in a vice, the clamp twisting tighter and tighter as the inky river approached. It followed her movements, weaving left and right as she backed away in short, shaky steps.

Gracie screamed as the blob took shape and grew more defined. The dark figure morphed and wavered. She turned to run and choked on a second scream—a shriek so much bigger than the first that it lodged in her throat, never leaving her mouth. A second shadow, far more defined, filled the hall behind her. Rotted flesh covered the apparition's gangly frame, studded with occasional clumps of mottled fabric and stringy fibers of something that might be hair—or cobwebs.

The horror lumbered forward, empty holes where its eyes belonged and a jaw full of pointed teeth that gaped in a sinister grin. "S-stay back," she whimpered, side-stepping toward the wall. The shadow circled her, its limbs in a crouch as though it might spring at her if she made any sudden movements.

Her foot bumped the wall. She dug her toe in and popped her heel out of her shoe. She didn't know where she'd find safety in this strange place, only that she'd get there a lot faster if she ditched her heels.

She kicked her left shoe off so hard that the heel gouged the wood paneling of the wall across from her. At the same moment, the blackened creature outstretched its twiggy arms.

Something pulled her back with a violent jerk, and her spine arched with the upsetting sensation of someone dropping a snowball down her blouse. The first shadow had her costume necklace in its blackened grasp. The clasp broke, and the necklace fell to the ground.

A gap formed between the two clashing shadows as though a breeze had blown through the hallway and cleansed the smoke and darkness.

Gracie took off in a sprint, not caring one lick about the spindly hallway furniture she overturned in the process.

In front of her, yellow light slanted across the hall from the crack of a partially open door. Seeing no one inside, she ran in, slammed the door behind her, and leaned heavily against it.

Ghosts. Real ghosts. Or rather, something worse than ghosts.

Run or you'll die next.

Gracie wrapped her arms around herself and hugged hard. Her mental state was a puzzle being lifted at the corners. In a moment, the surface tension would break and she'd be beyond reassembling.

She took several deep, fortifying breaths. If she gave up now it would make everything she'd suffered until this moment meaningless. The angels had spared her life on the ship ride from England. If Gracie didn't find family who cared about her, then what was the point of their mercy? Was she really meant to die alone in a strange, haunted hotel?

Not if she had anything to say about her fate.

Gracie peeled herself off the door. She could only be defeated if she refused to get up after she fell. As she'd done before, she would take whatever scraps of luck life gave her next and use more of her willful determination to make up the difference when the scraps ran out.

There had to be an exit somewhere, except she wasn't about to leave this room without a Bible or garlic cloves. A parasol wouldn't be too shabby either. After all, the only distinguishing difference between bravery and stupidity was a healthy dose of fear. Unfortunately, she doubted she'd find any protective items in this room.

Every flat surface was cluttered with delicate scientific instruments, the names and functions of which Gracie could only guess. The room had a smell of old books, alongside the unpleasant odor of discharged gunpowder. The whirring actuators of the various instruments hummed dissonantly. A bell chimed beside her, causing her to flinch and almost knock over a microscope. The inkwell next to the microscope wasn't so lucky.

The black liquid pooled on the tabletop, covering a surface area greater than what seemed possible for such a small bottle. The stain continued growing, only slowed by a stack of thin paper strips.

She picked up one of the soggy strips and frowned at the dripping mess.

Stay away from the shadows. Run or you'll be dead next. Find the silver key.

Two of the four notes she'd found were cut to this exact size.

The fact that the door to *this* room had been open, and there was an ink quill next to the paper strips, couldn't be coincidence. She'd come here before.

But if that were true, why couldn't she remember anything from her prior visits?

Gracie chewed her thumbnail as she tried to think of an explanation.

There were only two things she felt certain of. First, she'd forget whatever she saw here once she returned to the circus lot. Second, her only clue that any of this was real would be the message she wrote on this narrow strip of paper.

With limited space, she had to choose her words carefully. What should she write?

The twins are liars. Run far away where neither can find you. If she were to believe one of the notes, wouldn't she have to believe them all? What had she seen before that had convinced her that the most important message she could leave for herself was to find Katherine's key? She had no idea why she couldn't remember, or any significant new knowledge of the dangers that lurked here.

This last thought unsettled her most. How many more shadows were out there? What did they want with her and why had they attacked her at the junction? If she did as her last note said and quit the circus, would they leave her alone? To her knowledge, Barty wasn't involved in the matter of Katherine's death, and yet they'd given him a scare. If those things could leave this place, would she be safe anywhere?

Jack knows the answers, and yet he hasn't said anything to you.

Gracie stared at the blotted strip. Any sort of message would be better than going back empty-handed—if she could even remember the way.

She stepped back from the table as the inkwell spill began to run over the edge onto the floor. Several drops landed on the rug, narrowly missing a small, leather bound book. Gracie picked up the book and opened it to the first page.

The name "Gladys Harrison" was written in looped cursive on the inside of the cover. Gracie thumbed through the pages, noting several had been torn out. Most of the entries were gibberish comprised of words formed from a mixture of letters and numbers.

The door of the room opened without warning.

They've found me! Her thoughts flickered between hiding under the table and running to slam the door.

Except, it wasn't the shadow monsters. In the doorway stood one of the twins, dressed in a fitted white shirt, dark pants, and a black coat. "What did I tell you about snooping around the closet? Has anyone seen you here?"

Gracie would swear it was Jack, except his arms and hands appeared normal. But Harris had never warned her about staying away from the closet. At the moment, she had no desire to interact with either twin.

She edged her way out from behind the table and looked for something either sharp or blunt, her blood hot and urging her to fight instead of run. She grasped one of the smaller instruments. The twin's expression remained unchanged which meant the gadget wasn't expensive, valuable, or—most importantly—lethal.

Gracie dropped the object and eyed the table with the glassware. She grabbed a tall, glass cylinder and smashed the neck on the table edge. To her dismay, the glass broke without much of a pointed barb. "Don't come any closer." She held the broken article like a sword.

"You don't need to be afraid. I'm not one of them."

"Why should I believe you when you've lied to me about everything else?"

"Please listen. Last night you encountered a shade and nearly had your heartstone stolen. I don't have any more gemstones to power my extractor so it's important that we get out of here before we're found."

So, he was admitting he owned one of those soul-stealing boxes?

Jack reached for the cuff of his shirt. "I don't want to force you, but there's not enough time for me to fully explain."

Gracie chucked the cylinder toward his head, hoping to stall him from pulling a magic wand from his sleeve. It crashed splendidly into the door behind Jack, missing him by a whole yard. The flask with the bulbous bottom she threw next had a better spin on it but failed to make contact. She grabbed one of the triangular bottles, intending to verify its aerodynamics.

Jack's eyes were fixed on her, his chin raised like an Egyptian pharaoh. His wrist flicked up and his fingers snapped. "Put the Erlenmeyer flask down."

Gracie had her arm cocked back, ready to throw, but the glassware now became very heavy in hand. She set the flask on the table, simultaneously relieved and dismayed to no longer have it in her possession.

"Step away from the table and walk toward me."

When she looked up, it wasn't Jack standing in the doorway but the ghost of the poultry factory foreman. His mousy brown hair was matted with blood, which trickled down his face into cloudy eyes. His smile widened when he saw her, his gold front tooth shining. Fresh blood dribbled from his mouth and soaked into his rust-stained shirt. One of his sinewy arms extended toward her, his palm turned up, red and slick.

Her knees knocked together and she had no idea how her legs were holding her up. The ghost's fingers curled, and her left foot slid forward at the gesture.

"No! Get away from me!"

She fought the compulsion pulling her forward.

"Gracie. Come here," it growled.

Her right foot shuffled forward. The left was more obedient to the command and took a full step.

She stubbed her toe on the contraption she'd discarded earlier, causing a sharp pain to go zinging from her big toe to her pinky finger. Her eyes fell to the floor to inspect the broken instrument, and with choking horror, she saw it was the accordion pleated housing of a camera.

"I won't be in your pictures!" she screamed, picking up the broken piece and hurling it across the room.

The foreman's hollow face leered. "Gracie, walk toward me," it repeated.

She scanned the room for an escape. The window on the back wall!

She rolled her weight through to the ball of her foot. Feeling confident she had control again over her legs, she turned and sprinted for the window, clawing at the latch until it opened. A gale of wind caught the right frame and slammed it into the exterior wall, smashing several glass panes. Another gust sent raindrops rattling across the glass panes in the other window frame.

She climbed onto the sill and grasped the curtain rod to steady herself. Her toes curled around the stone ledge. She leaned out and then shrunk back inside.

She blinked several times, confused by the sight. The window hadn't opened to a back alley fire escape and rows of old brick apartments. Instead, she stood in an upper window in the main portion of a fortress—a rambling mishmash of stonework.

The entire fortress floated over a small lake that was darker and glossier than black piano lacquer. A wild region of flat-topped ridges and narrow valleys surrounded the lake.

"Gracie, wake up! You're having a nightmare!" The voice sounded desperate yet muted, like it was coming through a thick door. "I'll do whatever you want, just get down before you fall to your death."

In the room behind her, papers blew everywhere, the test tubes rattled, and the telescopes spun on their pedestals.

The foreman's ghost had vanished.

Her head felt hazy, like she'd stood too quickly after sitting for a long time. With effort, she picked out Jack's form in the room. He stood frozen a few paces away from her, next to an umbrella stand and holding some sort of strange bamboo and wire broomstick.

"Gracie, if you die here, you're not going to wake up in the closet."

The wind picked up with a force so strong it seemed that if she stepped over the ledge she could walk on the air. The gust inflated the curtain, blowing it into the room.

"Look out!"

The right window suddenly swung closed, knocking her off balance. Her arms windmilled and she scrambled to catch hold of the fluttering curtain. It brushed her fingertips and then waved goodbye as she fell.

CHAPTER XXVII

Jack's heart and stomach dropped.

He stamped the end of the bamboo pole into the ground causing two footrests to split away from the seamless shaft. A meter from the window, he jumped onto the pogo stick's pegs. The wire skeleton of a folding umbrella spread out across the top as Jack dived through the open window, the ripcord for the elementary parachute kite wrapped in his hand.

While Jack dove through the air, the rain had the illusion of falling upwards. The sheer face of the fortress smeared past, followed by its foundation—an inverted rock formation of stone blocks and steel I-beams. Gracie's hair blew around her pale face. In her falling form, Jack saw his mother. Life rarely gave anyone a second chance. If Jack didn't catch Gracie now, only his death would atone for his failures.

Jack fought the forces of gravity to unglue one arm from his side and extended it toward Gracie. "Take my hand!"

Their fingers touched and he stretched to take hold of her wrist. With a tug, she floated to him. Jack had less than three seconds to situate both of them on the foot pegs and deploy the rest of the kite.

"Hold on!"

Gracie clung to him with such fierceness Jack thought she might squeeze his lungs out through his nose. He yanked the ripcord.

A white canopy of silk fabric shot from the tube and expanded over their heads, slowing their fall. Jack aimed the parachute kite for the shore of the lake's east side.

The weight of their two bodies strained the umbrella's framework and threatened to turn it inside out. The joints of the foot pegs were slowly curling under. Fifty feet from the ground, one of the needle-thin kite supports broke.

The ground surged to meet them instead of water—they'd over-blown the shore by half a mile. Jack dragged his legs in the caked dirt to slow down. The bamboo support pole snapped in half as he fell on it. Caging Gracie with his body, they rolled over the jutting pieces of the broken kite.

A sensation like lighting grazed his back, a stick of dynamite that exploded on contact. He cried out, his voice sounding strange and frightful. He hadn't felt pain like this since . . . well, last night. It was enough to black out his vision.

Mist collected on Jack's face, forming a cold sweat. His damp clothes indicated he'd been lying here a while. The rain had turned to a driz-zle and the storm had passed for the most part. "Gracie?" Jack sat up with a groan.

She lay sprawled on her side a few feet away. Her chest rose and fell slowly. He watched her like she was a sick child on a hospital bed, uncertain if he could bring himself to approach.

What have I done?

Aside from her lack of consciousness, she looked unharmed. His only consolation was that since she wasn't awake, she wasn't subjected to the sight of their dismal surroundings.

They had fallen into the umbra, the darkest area of the shadowed wastelands beneath Knossos. Large boulders surrounded pitted, water-filled craters. To his left, Jack made out the shimmer of the lake and the enormous anchor chain rising from the center of it to Knossos. All around them, skeletal trees dotted the otherwise barren landscape. Tree trunks appeared to form openmouthed faces in their bark pat-terns. Roots covered the ground in a gnarled pattern, resembling the spilt entrails of a beast.

As if being stranded from civilization wasn't problematic enough, they'd fallen out of the boundary of the time compression field. Every minute that passed here equaled one minute on the circus lot.

"Gracie?" Jack nudged her shoulder with one hand, guarding his face with the other. She lay still, even after he rolled her onto her back. "Come on, Gracie, wake up. We need to get out of here."

He pressed her knuckles to his lips, cupping her hands in his. "Gracie." He rubbed her hands between his. "Gracie!" His breath sawed in and out. Fear that he'd broken her beyond revival seized him by the throat and tightened its grip each second she didn't respond.

While holding her hands, he felt the familiar tingle of dark energy prowling through her as it sought weakened places to burrow and entrench itself. He didn't need any special equipment to absorb it from her. Having only half a heartstone created a void in him that welcomed surplus subatomic energy whenever he came across it.

Ringed, purple bruises collected at his wrists and spread midway up his arms. Unlike previous times he'd absorbed dark energy from her, she had enough to indicate she'd come in physical contact with a shade before he'd found her. He'd have to find an outlet to release it before going to bed or else it'd give him terrifying nightmares.

The tight lines on Gracie's forehead relaxed slightly. With her dark hair strewn around her face and the low cut of her costume revealing the delicate line of her throat, she reminded him of a sleeping princess.

Jack pushed his sweaty palms down his trousers and took a slow, calming breath. Yesterday, when she'd hit him in the jaw, he'd not thought of her as some helpless and fragile damsel in distress. Quick to argue her opinion or recover after an upsetting event, Gracie was not someone lacking inner strength. Which meant he needed to increase his own by checking his unraveling emotions. She'd find her way back again. And boy, would he be in for a lashing when she did. Gracie had two modes of operation: annoyed and adamant, and Jack was sure she'd use a week's worth of stubbornness resisting his hypnosis back in his laboratory.

Her head hung forward as he tried to ease her into a sitting position.

Sheeze. He'd have to carry her.

Jack removed his coat and tugged the tails of his shirt out of his pants. Pain blossomed in his back and his heart threatened to pound through his chest. He reached to touch his skin in his lower back area, all too familiar with the feeling of his own blood.

He undid his cufflinks and peeled off his shirt, examining the size of the tear in the fabric. Swanning his neck, Jack stole a glance at his back. Although it hurt something terrible, his injury didn't look too deep. He replaced his shirt and jacket and then shoved his cufflinks and watch in his pants pocket.

Gracie cooed a protest of some sort when he hoisted her into his arms. His back blazed. He looked over the tangled mess of the kite and decided against turning it into a stretcher to drag her. Too many obstacles to navigate over.

He shuffled forward. She deserved better than to die here. Harris had brought her to the circus by stealing her ticket at the station, which meant that Jack was obligated to help her escape. It wasn't just for honor or chivalry. Over the past several days she had become his chance for redemption—whether he wanted to admit it or not.

When she'd first arrived he'd wanted nothing to do with her. Now, he dreaded the time when she would leave. Although she couldn't discuss exceptional things like false-axis repulsive field generator systems with him, she could sympathize with his emotional needs, and she counterbalanced the moral taint his family's legacy left on him. He wanted nothing to do with his so-called "family" and yet family meant everything to her.

Contrary to the standards held by most other young men, Jack didn't prize the companionship of a woman who was subservient and soft-spoken. His mother and aunts were anything but wilting flowers. Strong women were only an embarrassment to the eyes of society if they married weak men who didn't provide them adequate outlets for their ambitions.

Harris had managed to talk Gracie into a breakfast engagement and so Jack would eat his shoe if he would roll over and be bested by his twin. Jack could be just as charming and carefree if he didn't have to be the responsible twin. Once he got Gracie back to the circus lot he'd prove to her that he was the better man once and for all.

Jack walked half the distance to the shoreline before Gracie stirred. She coughed and her eyelashes fluttered. "Gracie?" He knelt and reclined her in his arms. "Come on, wake up for me."

Jack hadn't considered that his hypnosis might have played a part, but her eyes opened and lingered on him, widened and . . . terrified. "Jack?"

She goggled and babbled for a moment, and then he understood her. "Don't touch me," she said.

He leaned back, giving her some space. "Sounds like you've got the bushy end of a pineapple." Who between the two of them really had the more unfair situation? He tallied in his head whether this was the fifth or sixth time he'd saved her neck and she had yet to thank him. "Are you hurt anywhere?"

Her gaze zeroed in on her bare right foot. She'd lost the left shoe somewhere as well. "Your foot, is it sprained or broken? Can you walk with help?" He moved to help her up.

"Stay back!" She kicked air and gravel, scrambling away from him.

Her remark cut him deeper than the wound in his back. He'd jumped out of a window to save her, and yet she stared at him now like he'd pushed her. Was she still having a nightmare? This was his fault. He'd nearly killed her with his hypnosis spell because he was too weak to properly control it.

"Gracie, I made a mistake trying to force you to go with me. I'm sorry. Please though, you need to believe I want to help you."

"How can that be when you're one of those things too?"

"I'm not a shade, Gracie."

"In the room, you turned into his ghost. Rotted and dead—like that thing in the hall."

"Whose ghost, Gracie?"

She curled her legs tightly beneath her, huddling inward. Her voice was barely more than a whisper. "The ghost of the man I killed."

If he'd thought she looked broken before, she was shattered now. Jack wanted to crush her to him until the warmth of his body spread to her heart and healed the ice shards inside.

"You were having a nightmare. It wasn't real. I pushed your sub-conscious too deep when I tried to use hypnotic control over you. If you did run into some shades earlier, the exposure to their dark energy would've made the slip easier."

She tensed when he scooted closer but didn't run away. "Even if that wasn't real, even if you claim you want to help me now, what am I supposed to think about the fact you're involved with them at all and that you've been lying to me about this strange place all this time?"

"Do you really believe I'd intentionally hurt you?" He pushed a strand of hair that had blown across her face to the side. The breeze stole it right back.

Gracie turned away and smoothed it herself. "I don't know what to think anymore between all the lies you and Harris keep telling. This morning I felt certain that last night wasn't a dream, but Harris said you stopped me from sleepwalking off the train. I must be losing my mind because I can't tell what's real anymore."

Jack hadn't thought it possible he could be more confused at any point than she, except she'd just proved it possible. "I haven't seen or spoken to Harris since yesterday morning before the performance."

She studied him with an arched brow and leaned forward. "I want to believe you, but I was warned I shouldn't trust you."

Jack faced her with an expression hovering between resignation and impatience. "I thought I cautioned you before not to take everything Harris says at face value." Not taking precautions against his twin's involvement was the biggest oversight of his life.

Gracie watched him from beneath lowered lashes "Harris hasn't said anything," she amended. "The reason I find it difficult to trust you is because I wrote myself a note saying I shouldn't."

Every word was another kick in his ribs.

"Besides warning yourself against me, did you remember to mention that if Clarice finds you here, she'll add your heartstone to her chandelier?" Gracie continued to stare at him as though he were speaking Chinese, and not English. "Last night, at the junction, you nearly had your heartstone stolen. That crystal you saw is similar to the hundreds in the chandelier in the ballroom, or didn't you pass through that room on your way to my laboratory?"

Something he said must have finally resonated with Gracie because she grew quiet. Her expression went bland and indistinguishable, the way it usually did when she was about to be stubborn about something.

She glanced up toward the fortress. "I think I know what you're talking about, but even when the occasional image comes to me, like the chandelier you just mentioned, it puts me in a stupor when I try to focus on it."

If only there was a way to reverse his hypnosis and compel her to remember everything it had made her forget. He'd thought he was keeping her safe from Clarice and the shades in the cloisters. Instead he'd prevented her from remembering things that could save her life. "Don't worry yourself about it. What's important now is getting back up to the fortress."

"Unless you can pull a hot air balloon out of your sleeve, I think we ought to think about finding a town instead."

"There's nothing for miles." With a groan, he eased himself to his feet. He took one swat at the grit on his pants and decided clean pants weren't worth the skin-stretching discomfort it caused his back. "Once Clarice anchored the fortress, she stole all the heartstones of the people who'd helped her, and those of all the villagers in the area, to preserve the secrecy of Knossos. We'd starve to death before finding help, so it's a good thing there *is* an emergency balloon."

Gracie pulled herself up with his help and wobbled on one shaky leg, treating her right foot as if someone had strapped a hot coal to the bottom. "I don't fancy the idea of returning to the lair of a ruthless murderer."

"Can't be helped. It'd take weeks to travel from where we are back to America by normal methods. I'm more worried Vincenzio would sell my closet if I wasn't there to perform with it than I am about running into Clarice. The fact that I have something she desperately wants has preserved me so far."

Her lower lip quivered as she stared at the anchor chain rising from the lake. "She won't kill *you*, but what about me?"

He shrugged. "I never said going back was risk-free."

"So, where's this balloon of yours?" She picked a small rock out of the bottom of her foot and tried putting weight on it.

"Over there." Jack nodded toward the lake. Unlike the water-filled craters in the area, the lumped shapes clustered at the edge of the lake were not boulders, but tarped crates. Each contained a large barrel and a canister full of a special gas-emitting compound that would fill a thin rubber-coated balloon.

Her face turned ashen. Jack thought it was an indication of her own hesitancy until she extended her palm out to him. It was smeared with his blood.

"You're hurt?" her voice squeaked. He cursed the fact he had nothing in his pockets to clean her trembling hand.

"It's just a scratch." He took her hand and used his sleeve to wipe it.

"Between you and Harris, you're definitely the worse liar," she said, pulling back. Her arms slipped inside his jacket and pushed it off his shoulders. "You should take a moment to bandage yourself properly, so you don't lose more blood."

She helped him out of his shirt and her face paled further when she saw the gash. She audibly swallowed and then started to tear his bloodied shirt into strips.

"Gracie, you don't have to, I can do it."

"Please, let me. You did save me, after all."

The rejected and abandoned feelings he'd been quietly harboring combusted into a firestorm of emotion.

"Turn around until I tell you it's okay," she instructed.

He did so, shifting his gaze to the nearest rock formation. Several seconds passed. What was she doing? He peeked over his shoulder. In her hand she held two white . . . mushrooms?

"You can look now," Gracie said. The way she clenched her elbows tight to her side was familiar. "These are a lot cleaner than that torn shirt of yours, and they're filled with cotton so they should help control the bleeding."

Good gracious, were these pancake stuffers what she'd been desperate to hide from him that night at the hotel?

Gracie placed her bust-enhancing pancakes over his wound and wrapped the shirt strips around his side. He leaned into her touch, hungry for more of her gentleness and disgusted that he'd caused her to remove a piece of her armor. The gash in his lower back throbbed but stopped bleeding.

"Thank you." He bent to pick up his jacket, his limbs protesting like an old, rusted bike. Her frown deepened. "Don't worry about me," he said. "I'll recover faster once we get back to the lighted areas of the fortress."

Gracie laughed dryly. "What kind of medicine works so fast? Simply add light and you are suddenly cured? Are you even human?"

"Of course I am."

"Are you alive then?"

Now her questions were getting silly. "Would you think me in danger of dying if I weren't?"

"You'd know best." She turned toward the lake and hopped three steps, her eyes full of suspicion and her lower lip thrust out with disappointment.

He caught up to her in one long stride and pulled her arm over his shoulder. There wasn't anything else to do but push through the pain and keep walking. The longer he spent outside the time compression field, the slower his injury would heal. Once they got back to the fortress, he'd return Gracie to the safety of the circus lot then he would loll in a corner of the fortress until he had the strength to join her and finally settle things with his dirty dish of a twin.

CHAPTER XXVIII

Each step toward the lake and crates wore at Jack like a piece of sandpaper. At least they didn't have much farther to go.

Gracie's breath tickled his chest. "Those shadow things I saw in the fortress. Where do they come from?"

"Shades are people who had their heartstones harvested but didn't die during the extraction. The absence of light energy in their body is what causes them to become shadows—pure dark energy."

The corner of Gracie's lips twisted into a frown. "I'm not certain now if you are explaining things or making them more confusing."

What part of flying castles and shadow-people did she expect to ever be understandable?

Gracie's head titled away from his neck as she looked at her filthy feet. Her small face was drawn thin from all she'd suffered, yet her eyes were resolute with a quiet dignity—a quality Jack knew no one could touch without her permission. "You've had your heartstone stolen before," she said, looking up at him. "It would explain how you know so much."

He nodded.

"But you got it back, didn't you?"

He turned his gaze forward. "Just half."

Having half a heartstone, one cufflink out of the set, was the only reason he'd not turned into a shade.

THE rain resumed briefly, turning the ground into squishy mud that smacked with each step. The bottom of his trousers had turned three shades lighter from the muck by the time they reached the lake.

Out of eight balloons, one had already been used. A few weathered wood slats from the opened crate littered the ground—though most seemed to have been washed or blown away years prior.

Jack picked the crate with the most well-preserved tarp and set to unpicking the knot on its tie-down cords.

"Some of these other crates don't look so good," Gracie said, working on the knot on the other side of the box.

"They're wrapped on the inside too. It'll be apples." So he said, yet her unspoken fear matched his own—that the crates had sat here too long and the balloons were damaged or that the inflating compound had turned inert. He imagined they hadn't been touched in the fourteen years since Gladys had died. The single opened crate was also a curiosity. He knew the balloons existed because of the entry he'd read in Gladys's journal, not because he'd made use of them before.

Once they uncovered the crate, Jack found a crowbar tucked between the slats and set to prying off the lid. The sides of the crate folded down, and to his relief, the interior components—a large oak barrel, rope, sand bags, netting, the fuel canister, and the ignition burner—showed minimal signs of weather damage. Dirty was better than broken any day of the year.

His back blazed and he cried out when he lifted the balloon parcel to spread it out.

"Jack!" Gracie hobbled to his side.

He leaned over, breathing heavily. "I'll be fine. My aunt designed this, and I know she wouldn't have made anything heavier than what she could lift on her own."

"Clarice is your aunt?"

He may have forgotten to tell her that part, or he might have been ashamed. "She is, but I was referring to my other aunt, Gladys. They're my father's sisters. Gladys and Clarice created bits and pieces of Knossos together before they had a rough fallout. And then Gladys died. I was six when it happened. Afterwards, my father emigrated from Australia to America with the closet. I was a bit older before he first took me through the closet."

Gracie allowed him an unusual moment of silence by not asking a follow up question. He welcomed the chance to rest his voice as he tasted brussels sprouts every time he swallowed the spit in his mouth. The darkness he'd absorbed from her was spreading in him.

With Gracie's help, he unrolled the silver material of the balloon. She brushed his hand in the process, and he noted with dismay that her skin felt papery and moist with sweat. *This is hard on her too. You're not the only one in physical pain.* He hated himself for placing such a burden on her.

She wiped her brow. "If your aunts were smart enough to make a fortress fly, you'd think they could have installed a dumbwaiter to hoist us back up instead of making us assemble this impracticality."

A smile cracked on his cheek, forming into a laugh, the sound of which came out like the hybrid of a sneeze and a yawn. A throbbing spasm attacked his lower back and he doubled over, clenching his stomach although the pain originated elsewhere.

"Are you all right?"

He wiped the corner of his mouth, adding a rusty smudge to the back of his hand. "I can't lie, I've been better." She did that pouty thing where she set her hands on her hips similar to one of his knife poses.

She might have stayed rooted to that spot for the rest of the night if he hadn't passed her the utility knife from the tool box and set her to work cutting the excess cords. "Knossos was never meant to fly," he explained while he knotted the cords to their correct eyebolts. "My aunts miscalculated the anti-gravity formula, which caused the facility to uproot from its original location."

She sawed the cords slowly, and he sensed she did so out of fear of doing something wrong and ruining the balloon. If she did make a mistake, he'd simply open another box and take what he needed.

She handed back the knife. "If Knossos wasn't always a floating castle, what was it before?"

"It used to be a hospital, in Sydney." He twisted four sections of conduit pipe together. "The light energy of the chandelier is what gives it the appearance of a fortress. Location-wise, we are now somewhere in Russia, in the Dusse-Alin mountain range."

"That sounds pretty far from Australia."

"Yeah, well it took Clarice and Gladys a few weeks to gather the resources to catch the hospital after it started migrating." He twisted the support shaft for the igniter until it clicked into place.

Gracie helped him mount the silver balloon over the igniter at the top of the pole. "What's so special about this place that they anchored it here? Is it just that it's in the middle of nowhere?"

"The towns nearby used to be centers for mining and metal refineries. As big and heavy as the chains needed to be to keep the fortress anchored, it saved a lot of trouble having a shorter distance to cart them into place."

"And then Clarice killed everyone who helped her."

"Yes. Clarice didn't see it as barbaric or cruel. To her, their lives were necessary sacrifices for science." He stepped back from the contraption after connecting the fuel canister. "This is ready to be inflated."

The contact points beneath the igniter lever sparked when he turned it on. White hot flames with blue tips spread in a circle around the device and a blast of hot air funneled into the balloon. The fabric took form, rising from the center of the barrel in a shiny silver column.

He painted himself down the side of the oak barrel, sliding into an exhausted heap at the base, grateful to be able to take a break while the balloon inflated.

Gracie sat next to him and rested her head on his shoulder. He noted her legs and arms were covered in goosebumps.

"You're cold." As he lifted his arm to draw her close, she caught his wrist.

"What's this?" She pushed his sleeve up for a better look at his bruises and darkened veins.

He shrugged his sleeve back down. "An imbalance of light or dark energy always leaves a mark."

She shifted her head out from under his chin. "Can't you fix it with magic, like you healed your arm from last night?"

Before now, Jack had never met anyone with such a talent to see the world as they wished it to be. Her fanciful thinking seemed to be the source of her inner passion and the reason he admired her tenacity.

She took his hand and pressed it over her left breast. "Tell me how to help you. Do you need my heartstone? Would that make you better?"

Beneath the crooked icicles of her fingers, he felt the blazing warmth of her heartstone.

"I won't take it from you." Without his particle extractor, he couldn't take it from her.

Her fingers curled around his and she attempted to push the tips of his fingers into her chest cavity. "You wouldn't be taking it because I'm giving it to you."

The dark energy which had grown to occupy the empty space of the missing half of his heartstone growled and pushed at his fingertips.

He wrenched his hand away, but not before his nails had left crescent shaped marks in her silken skin. Without a full heartstone, he would always feel in want. The plague of misery would never end until he recovered the other half. No matter how much he suffered, he would never allow her to feel the same. The pain she felt now would be nothing compared to his if he had to print her name for the stone carver to engrave on her tombstone.

Her voice grew softer. "You often get cramps in your hands after a show, are the two related?"

So she had noticed, even before Harris told her to look at his hands after yesterday's performance. "After each show, you are usually carrying residual traces of dark energy. I've been absorbing them, so you don't have nightmares when you go to sleep."

Beneath her long, dark lashes, she blinked her doe eyes at him. "You did that, for me?"

Jack cupped her chin in his hand and brushed her jaw with his thumb. The breath which escaped her lips, lighter than butterfly wings, made his own heavier.

"Of course." He pressed his lips to the corner of her eye. She exhaled slowly.

She burrowed into his chest, wrapping her arms tightly around him. "Jack, in case we don't live through this, I just want to say thank you for giving me the chance to be your assistant, even reluctantly. If I never make it to Chicago, I'm at least glad I met you."

He wrapped one arm around her shoulders and pulled her tighter to him. His heart stretched in his chest and sang. Finally, he'd done something right.

Too bad he didn't think he'd be around much longer to enjoy this victory.

CHAPTER XXIX

GRACIE TRACKED the balloon's inflation progress based on the hissing of the fuel canister as it emptied. The noise almost drowned out the shallow sound of Jack's breathing. If it weren't for the reassuring thud-thud of his heartbeat, and the gentle pressure of his arm around her shoulders, she'd have thought him dead.

Jack, I'm not afraid to die, not as long as you're here. Chicago, the rosewood trunk—she'd give up everything if they could somehow get out of this place alive.

Jack stirred as the barrel shifted and the base lifted off the ground. His arm slid off her shoulders, and he struggled to his feet. She missed the warmth of his touch and the feeling of safety that accompanied it.

"Time to climb in," he said.

The barrel was scarcely big enough for both of them to stand in without stepping on the other's toes. The rest of the fuel canister emptied in a burst and jolted the balloon into the sky.

The directional control for the balloon was primitive as it relied on shifts in its center of balance to steer it. Gracie held tightly to Jack as he held the center support, both of them trying to move as little as possible to keep the balloon from tipping to one side or the other as it ascended.

Jack's fingers slid into her hair as he pressed her head into his chest. His breath warmed her neck and his nose brushed her ear. "The wind will get worse as we gain altitude. I might need your help to reel in the balloon after I throw the grappling hook."

She nodded.

They rose higher, the trees transforming to little specks. Small dots of light shone in the face of the fortress from the occasional open window. But the backside, where the wind pushed them, was entirely dark. The destruction to the south end resembled a four-tiered cake for which someone had used a shovel to cut and serve.

The barrel rocked as the wind howled, whistling and wailing as it snaked through the open rooms and halls. Jack wasn't kidding about things being windier—they were almost losing more distance to the wind than they gained.

He lifted the grappling hook from the side of the barrel and uncoiled the length of rope. "Hang on," he warned.

The basket rocked with the swing of his toss. The teeth of the hook scraped the stone and clattered as it skipped over the floor of a balcony. The teeth caught on a protruding decorative cornice, but the weather had damaged it, and it broke when the rope pulled. Her heart fell with the broken piece and hook.

"Almost." He coiled the rope for another toss. On his second try, he managed to hook the balustrade of another balcony. The wind jerked and pulled at the balloon, as if angered by their arrival.

The gritty dirt on the rope colored her hands orange-brown as she pulled the rope, hand over hand beside him. Her breaths came hard, her hands burned, and the muscles in her arms threatened to tear from her bones.

"You go first!" Jack said with a grimace, trying to tether the balloon and hang on at the same time. "Once you step out, the reduction in weight is going to rocket this thing to the stars."

"We should climb out at the same time, then."

"It's too windy, and I can't let go to tie it off. Just get out fast."

The barrel lurched the moment she leaned over the edge to grip the balustrade, throwing her onto the balcony and dumping Jack chest-first into the balustrade. The balloon tore away and shot for the clouds.

"Gracie!" He clung to the rail. His legs kicked the air as he scrambled for purchase on the wet, slippery stone. His wide eyes elicited a muted shriek in her throat. She threw herself over him, pulling him up with all her strength. The blood from his injury bled through the bandage and smeared the satin of her costume. Ignoring the impropriety, she wrestled and pulled on whatever part of him she could until he was on the safe side of the railing.

She joined him in a tired heap on the stone floor of the balcony.

"Thank you," he said, a hint of panic threading his voice. He lay on his back with one hand across his stomach. "I didn't know if I had the strength to hold on."

She rolled onto her side to face him. "You didn't have to, because I was here."

His dark hair was a mess, though she supposed it always had a bit of a windy look. She smoothed his hair against his head and then pressed her hand to his forehead.

He's like stone. "Come on, you need to get inside," she said, digging her arms under his shoulders to help him to his feet. Groaning and straining to lift him, she wanted to say, "Just how many cakes did you eat after dinner last night?" But she decided her efforts might be better used to encourage him. She tried to brighten her voice, like a nurse might have in the old Sydney hospital before it was Knossos. "If we hurry, maybe we can make it back to the circus in time for lunch. The menu said they'd be serving meat pies. Won't that be nice?"

"Count the zoo animals first," Jack said, a tiny smile on his face.

THEY entered a large open room. The ceiling was made of rectangular windows, all broken, and the interior walls on two sides had collapsed, creating a landslide of chunky debris. Gracie could see into several of the rooms at once, like looking through the open back of a dollhouse.

"What happened here?" She followed him around the perimeter of the room, avoiding piles of bricks and the dark murky water in the center.

Jack scanned the room as though he were looking through the walls to a past time, seeing the room as it had been before the destruction. "This is where Gladys died," he said.

Something about the ruined room trapped sound and amplified Jack's voice and even the sound of their clothes brushing as they walked. He lowered his voice. "She tried a risky experiment to bring her fiancé back to life after Clarice stole his heartstone. It appears she got carried away. This whole place defies logic and reason, yet here it is." He stared at the rubble near his feet. "I'm sorry she suffered, but part of me is reassured. At least there's still some constancy in death. Toying with the power of life . . . something so powerful doesn't belong in human hands."

Small, jagged rubble pieces and bits of broken glass covered the floor, giving it the appearance of alligator skin. Gracie winced, the pain in her injured ankle increasing as she walked. Jack kicked a small rock into the large puddle. It sank without a splash, ripple, or any sort of sound. She moved closer to the wall, away from the strange water.

Jack kicked another rock in. Again, it disappeared without a splash. "Gladys knew what she was doing was wrong, and she knew the risk before she attempted the experiment." He frowned at the water. "Guessing it would kill her, she wrote a long letter to my father with instructions on how to settle her affairs."

Gracie stopped hobbling. She gestured first to the room and then to the entire fortress towering around them. "How does something like all this even happen? Where does someone get the idea they're going to make a flying fortress or change people into gemstones? It seems like something from a fantasy book or a dream."

He held her hand to help her climb over a twisted I-beam. "Calling this a dream world might not be too far from the truth. Clarice and Gladys were two, out of hundreds of children, who received an experimental treatment serum to find a cure for scarlet fever. The serums were most often ineffective, but in their cases, not only did it cure their fevers, it chemically altered the way their brain processed information. When they went to sleep at night, their brains stayed awake—and kept learning—so they woke up smarter than the day before."

His explanation left her feeling a bit colder inside. All this destruction and disaster was of human design.

Jack entwined his fingers in hers and led the way into the next room through a gaping opening in the wall.

"And your father. Was he smart too?"

Jack laughed. "He never had any interest in science. While Clarice and Gladys took control of the hospital and turned it into a research facility of their own, he ran off and joined the circus. I think the pressure of being compared to his sisters was too much."

They'd reached the far wall, with a set of double doors that creaked open at Jack's touch. The solid stone walls of a long tunnel greeted them. The stones had a repeating diamond pattern, and the lights were mounted to the walls instead of hanging from the ceiling.

"You seem to have a knack for grasping new concepts though," Gracie said, following him inside. "You assembled that balloon without any instructions."

"I've been reading in Gladys's journal but I can never hope to know as much as she did."

Under the lights, Jack's skin lost its sallow cast and he began to regain his usual coloring. As he'd said, he seemed to be faring much better. The tunnel soon took an uphill turn. She slowed her pace, the muscles in her legs aching with each step and her ankle crying out in protest. Jack waited for her to catch up and then wrapped his arm around her shoulders. Gracie leaned into the embrace, savoring the moment and praying Jack would recover so she didn't have to think this was the last time he would hold her like this.

"So how is it that your father ended up with the closet?"

"Gladys left a will entrusting the closet to my father, and her wishes regarding Knossos and Clarice."

"And what exactly is her wish for Knossos and Clarice?"

Jack took a deep breath, needing to draw on more of his unknown inner strength before he related the next bit. "Gladys's last wish was that I find a way to dismantle the time-compression machine, her legacy. I can't do that until I satisfy her other request—that I return Clarice's heartstone once she's paid her penance."

Jack stopped at the halfway point in the tunnel, leaning a hand against the wall as he caught his breath. Gracie welcomed the chance to rest her sore ankle. She gazed at him, her eyes imploring him to tell her more.

"Gladys invented the particle extractor because she wanted to turn rocks into food and solve world hunger. Clarice made the extractor work the opposite way, and used it to turn people into gemstones. Gladys was enraged when she learned what Clarice had done and threatened to destroy Knossos. They got in a huge altercation, which ended with Gladys using the extractor to steal Clarice's heartstone. Gladys took the extractor and the stolen heartstone through the closet back to Australia, imprisoning Clarice in the fortress. But Clarice had made a second extractor and lured Gladys's fiancée to Knossos to steal his heartstone—attempting to force Gladys to trade hers back for his."

Jack peeled himself from the wall. At the end of the tunnel Gracie could see a door. He extended his arm for her to resume walking with him. "Gladys's fiancé died immediately; it's a rare but possible reaction to having your heartstone extracted. Gladys tried an experiment to bring him back but, well, you saw the room."

They arrived at the door. Jack gripped the handle and wiped his forehead with his sleeve. Gracie reached out and laid her hand on his shoulder. "Thank you for telling me, even though I suspect I won't remember," she said in a hushed tone.

The edges of his mouth lifted in a smile, while creases of regret appeared between his eyes. "Don't thank me until I've gotten you out of here," he said, opening the door.

At the end of the tunnel a door led them into the maze of the cloisters. After the ninth turn, they saw the vanishing closet just ahead with its door ajar. The broken handle glinted from the floor.

"You buggered my closet." His forehead furrowed as he examined the piece.

She longed for another window to throw herself out of, or for a mountain to fall on her. "Can you fix it?"

He turned the piece over in his hands. "The actuator is cracked, and all the quantum flux has solidified."

She wished he'd offer her a simpler explanation that didn't sound like he was quoting his aunt's journal. "Does that mean we're trapped here?"

Jack ignored her question, fitting the handle back into the door. He kneeled next to the lower corner of the box and used his index finger to spin one of the nubby sprockets on the side of the box.

This must be how he set the secret compartment mechanism.

Jack opened the door of the closet and stepped in. Gracie hovered in the doorway behind him, seeing the closet with its hidden panel in place for the first time. The panel had been masterfully painted to create the illusion of an empty box.

Jack examined the upper corner of the closet. Digging his nails under one of the panels to remove it, he exposed a mess of colored spaghetti wires and glowing lights. He handed the small, paneled cover to her and tore out a mysterious metal contraption and then threw it aside.

From his pocket, Jack withdrew a small vial of blue liquid. "This should work until I can find another benitoite stone." He wedged the vial into the space of the old piece and replaced the cover piece she'd been holding.

"If you've got enough magic liquid in that vial to get us back, why do you have to replace anything? Can't you just lock it behind us?"

A shadow fell across Jack's face. "Gladys originally left the task of fulfilling her last wishes to my father, but he couldn't handle the pressure with my mother gone. It's my responsibility to set things right now." He said these last words with more regret than pride.

Gracie hugged his arm. "I wish you didn't have to carry this burden alone. When we get back to the circus lot, I hope you'll tell me the truth so you don't keep suffering by yourself."

His head dipped to touch hers. "I know you too well to believe you'll stay out of trouble if I tell you."

Gracie didn't like his answer. Not one bit. Her lips trembled. "Jack, because I won't remember any of this, can you do one thing for me?"

"What's that?"

"When we get back to the lot, and I go back to being a stubborn brat, don't give up on me. Please?"

"I promise." He gathered her into his arms, and she felt his full strength—not just the strength he used for his chores but the muscles he held in reserve so that at the most pivotal moment in time, he could hold on to the one thing he held most dear and never let go. "I'm not going to disappear," he added, guessing her thoughts.

Jack's eyes, the color of a plowed field after a storm, were the most distinguishing of his facial features. There were times she felt as though he'd never done anything to earn the hard, determined lines of his mouth, but when looking in his eyes she could see him as a young boy, ready to face any challenge, and still believe that he'd come out on top.

He brushed her temple with his fingers, and tucked a stray hair curl back behind her ear. "I'll rest up a bit, then once I get a chance, I'll fix the handle and join you on the other side."

From the unnatural lines of exhaustion covering his face, she knew he was putting on a brave face for her. She shook her head. "I don't like your plan at all."

"I can't risk having Clarice find you here, and I can move faster through the cloisters on my own."

Jack's jaw was set, a shadow of stubble delineating it from his neck. He saw her as a burden, a liability, but also as something he wanted to protect, to keep safe. The opposing emotions made her chest ache as though it could not hold all the emotions she felt.

She stared directly ahead, squeezing the fabric of her costume, only allowing the whiteness of her knuckles to show how much his dismissal hurt. "You promise you'll come back?"

"I will," he said, putting his hands on her shoulders and looking directly into her eyes, "because you're the most important thing in the world to me, and I know you'll be there waiting for me." He drew her to him and pressed a kiss to her forehead. Then he steered her to the back of the closet. "Now, close your eyes, and when I snap my fingers, this will all have been a forgotten dream," he said. She heard the door close between them.

CHAPTER XXX

G RACIE BLINKED awake, feeling as though she'd just had a strange dream. Her heart felt heavy in her chest, beating quicker than usual. With excitement? It almost seemed like the feeling of falling.

The light coming in through the window above her indicated she was not in the closet and that it was sometime in the afternoon. Her gaze darted around the room and settled on the rosewood trunk at the foot of the bed—she was in her own room.

Slowly, her memory sharpened. She'd gone to confront Jack about the strange events at the junction and his salt-encrusted arm but had found Harris instead. Richard had excused her from the parade, so she'd gone looking for Miriam. On her way, she'd found Vincenzio walking with two police officers and had gone to hide in Jack's closet until they left. The handle had broken off, trapping her inside. She must have fallen asleep or fainted, and someone must have found her and brought her here.

The floorboards outside her room creaked. She flinched as her mind flashed back to several days earlier, when she'd woken up in the caboose and Vincenzio had let himself in.

Whoever it was this time had the decency to knock—but not to wait long enough for her to respond. The door opened.

Seeing one of the twins in the doorway set her scrambling to pull the sheets higher. Since he was dressed in a white shirt, boots, and dark gray pants, she assumed it was Harris. Also, his arm wasn't white and granulated.

"What are you doing here?" How dare he come into her room without her permission!

He shut the door behind him, his mouth twisted in a grimace. "You say that like you're trying to pick a fight. I'd rather hoped you might've said it more gently."

Smooth-talking and a shameful flirt—definitely Harris. Had she not made herself clear when she'd thrown the boot at him that she didn't want anything to do with him or Jack?

"You have three seconds to turn around and open that door before I scream."

"I wouldn't if I were you. Richard already thinks you've gone crazy with the menses, and screaming will only convince him more."

Embarrassment tangled in Gracie's stomach. "Why would he think that? I told him this morning that I was well."

"It might have something to do with the fact that you were covered in blood when I found you in the closet," he said, nonchalantly.

Gracie pushed the sheet down from her chest to her hips, immediately alarmed to see she was dressed in her nightgown rather than her costume. Turning from Harris, she stole a glance down the neckline. Her skin from her chest to her abdomen was covered with dried traces of blood.

Harris crossed the room to her vanity and pulled out a wad of blue fabric from the wash basin. "Here's your costume." He handed it to her.

The rust spot covering the corset was the same color as when someone mixed all the paints in the paint box. She scratched at the stain. Her stomach churned when it came off in flakes.

Dried blood.

Unspeakable horror choked her breath. Women were supposed to take great care never to expose any ailment, and it seemed she had been covered in blood worse than the mud on a pig in a mud trough. Was this the blood of someone else? Was it related to why Vincenzio had the police on the lot and had called out to her? Her memory was disturbingly hazy.

These thoughts swirled around her head until she realized that Harris hadn't stopped talking. His tone had turned sarcastic, with an undercurrent of anger. He also seemed like he was borrowing some of Jack's fancy vocabulary words. With his eyes averted from her, Harris didn't seem to have noticed her inattention. ". . . An imbalance of any one of the four humors: phlegm, water, bile, or blood must invariably create an equivalent form of mental illness. Conversely, strong emotions can cause menstrual obstructions, leading in turn to insanity and death."

Gracie knew little about "Eve's curse" besides what Mrs. Levenson had shared with her the first morning she'd woken up with blood on her sheets. The only thing Gracie knew for certain was that if Harris didn't stop talking about her delicate, private lady affairs, she'd die of mortification. She dropped her ruined costume on the floor.

Gracie sat upright, clutching the blanket to her chest. "Go away! I am *not* discussing this with you."

"I understand you're not feeling well. A doctor has been called, but before he arrives and makes his diagnosis, I hoped to see if there might be another explanation."

Gracie had always thought it a bit ironic that doctors were supposed to be the authority on women's health, yet none of them were female. "You don't think this is my blood?" Harris shoved his hands in his pockets. "If you were tampering with my closet, it's possible there could've been something which caused the gear lubricant to leak. As you may recall, it has a very potent smell, which could explain why you lost consciousness."

My closet? All this time she'd been speaking to Jack and not Harris? How likely was it that they both had dressed in gray pants, white shirts, and boots this morning?

When Jack had crashed into her outside the laundry tent the other day, she hadn't thought to scrutinize the timing of their crossed paths beyond the normal scope of a life-saving coincidence. Last night at the junction, she'd left the train car under his direction. And now, when her costume was covered in blood, he was by her bedside.

Three similar events indicated a pattern, not happenstance, renewing her suspicion from this morning that she was tangled in something dangerous, at which he was the center.

Accusing Jack of facilitating the strange occurrences made the most sense—after all, the success of a magician was defined by his mastery of tricks, deceit, and pretense. But accepting that Jack's prior expressions of concern were only carefully practiced deceptions rubbed at the already-raw spot in her heart.

If she lost her trust in Jack she would lose more than an income with the circus or a free ticket to Chicago. She'd lose confidence in her judgment, in her hope for a profitable future, but most humbling— she'd lose the friend she had apparently never made.

Why would Jack care if she were covered in her own blood or in his closet oil if he wasn't trying to divert the doctor from realizing something else was going on—that she was neither crazy nor covered in machine oil? She needed to be careful what she said around him.

"I might have accidentally broken the handle, but I didn't touch anything else," she said.

Jack stepped forward, his lips pressed into a razor-thin line, yet his eyes glistened. "What were you looking for in the closet?"

The ache in her chest grew in intensity and pushed at her rib cage. Gracie pressed her hands to her chest, wishing she could channel the pain into something physical that she could remove and discard permanently. It was just an act; he wasn't really worried about her—he was afraid of having his mischief exposed.

"Who says I was looking for something?" Her voice felt small coming out of her. She felt trapped and vulnerable, the same as she had in the foreman's office. Was Jack also the monstrous sort of man who would betray the duty of his sex and use his superior strength to hurt her if she didn't do what he wanted?

The door stood only a few feet away. If she took Jack by surprise, she might make it out of the room before he hexed or drugged her again. She scanned the top of her vanity, her emotions twisting into fear faster than she could detangle them from plausibility and truth. *Something sharp, something blunt, a pair of scissors, anything.* A parasol would be marvelous right about now, but it seemed the only thing at her disposal was her hairbrush and a near-empty perfume bottle. She'd have to run for it.

Gracie swung her feet over the edge of the bed and stood.

"Gracie!"

Pain zinged up her leg, like a bear trap snapping shut around her ankle. The sudden wish to have her foot amputated drove everything else from her mind.

Jack scooped her into his arms before she had a chance to scream or reach for her hurt ankle. He held her close, with her knees draped over his arms, and stared deeply into her eyes. The rise and fall of his chest was oddly noticeable, as was his sigh of relief, like he'd saved a jade vase from toppling off its pedestal.

She wouldn't let him distract her with his false sincerity. Gracie clenched her fists, gearing up for a struggle. "Put me down!" She pounded on his chest.

"I'm well aware how much you dislike it when I handle you like this." His voice hiccupped with each battering. He caught her hands and pinned them to her chest. "That's better." He continued, "You had your foot caught in the door of the secret compartment when I found you, and it looked like you'd badly twisted it. I suggest you stay in bed until the doctor gets here."

More lies. His heartbeat, heavy like a horse, betrayed him. Something strange was going on, and Jack wanted it buried.

She wriggled and squirmed. "I didn't twist it. You maimed me so I won't be able to run away next time!"

"I've only wanted to keep you safe."

She glared at him. Giving Jack a proper stare-down might have worked better if she didn't have to crane her neck so far back to face him. "You told me to trust you, but I'm not even sure *who you are* right now. When you first walked in, I thought you were Harris. Even now, I'm not entirely convinced you're Jack."

"Though I personally would rather regret trusting someone than regret doubting them," he said, his voice stoic and calm, "I understand it is not fair to expect the same from everyone else." He lowered her onto her bed, and she felt his offense in the heaviness of his footsteps beside her.

After a few seconds, he paused in front of her. The intensity of his gaze drew her eyes to his, and she was surprised at the pain she saw reflected in their depths. She blinked and it was gone.

Her gaze then turned toward the door. For the sake of her foot, she might have to sit here and listen rather than attempt to escape.

She gripped the edge of the bed. "What's *your* version of what happened at the junction last night? And I don't want the watered-down, risisble version involving sleepwalking and flare guns."

Her bed creaked as he took a seat. "I'm afraid I don't know what I should tell you . . ."

"Should we just take a look then?" Gracie leaned forward and snagged his shirt by the collar. She split it down the front in one vicious swipe. The buttons scattered all over the room.

"This was my last good shirt . . ."

Leaning forward, she ran her hands over each of his arms. He watched her with curiosity, his lips pressed together in a sharp line. He was right-handed, so the circumference of his right arm felt a smidgen larger than his left. Nothing else unusual. No sign of the white substance that had covered his arm the night before. Truly, she was going mad. From Jack's bicep, her hands ran down his chest and circled to his back.

He flinched away as she touched something that felt like an old scar. He grasped her hands. "It's my first time having a young lady undress me. Shouldn't you be gentler? I don't fancy you'd think much of me if I let my hands search you in the same manner." Jack stood and resumed his spot, standing across from her.

Gracie determinedly turned her face away from Jack and stuck her nose in the air. "How can I be sure you didn't already? I wasn't wearing my nightgown before I got locked in your closet."

Tugging at the ends of his ruined shirt, Jack overlapped the pieces and tucked them into his pants. "You can thank Maria for that and for cleaning you up. And you might want to stop by and apologize to Miriam when you're feeling better; your costume is ruined, and she's a bit upset." He moved toward the doorway, stiff and formal again. "My apologies for the intrusion."

Gracie twisted on the bed, faltering for words. "Wait!" she called after him. "You haven't told me what really happened at the junction."

When he didn't turn around, her temper flared. The fear of remaining indefinitely confused sent her into heady action. Gracie snatched the perfume bottle from the vanity and threw it at him. The vial grazed his shoulder and shattered on the floor.

He turned around slowly. "Has anyone ever told you that your aim is terrible? I'd be happy to spend some time training you, after your foot gets better, of course."

She pounded her fists on the mattress. "I don't want knife-throwing lessons. I want the truth, Jack."

"Are you inviting me into your room?"

"As if I could stop you from doing whatever you want."

"I can come back when you're feeling better."

"I want to know what's going on, and I want to know now."

"Very well, then." He moved to her vanity and perched on the edge. He took a deep breath. "Last night you were attacked by a shade."

Gracie knew she should be shocked by the strangeness of his answer, but it somehow felt like she'd already had this conversation with him. She surprised herself with the calmness of her response. "Then it was all real. The darkness, the pain, having my soul stolen . . ."

"Your heartstone, not your soul," he interrupted. "You should know its proper name if you're going to insist I explain everything to you."

"What did the shadow want with my sou—heartstone?"

"Leverage. The woman facilitating the attack, Clarice, wants something only I can give, and she's using Harris to get it."

"Harris shot me last night?" How many times now had Harris deceived her? Gracie feared that if Jack chose to follow in the same suit, she'd not know until it was too late.

Jack crossed his knee over his leg, the vanity squeaking beneath him. "To be fair, only a small portion of those who have their heartstones extracted die immediately. Most survive a few hours before becoming shades. I think he only did it because he believes his own life is at risk if he doesn't get what he's after."

"I hope it brings him nothing but misery."

His narrow lips sunk at the corners. "We may both agree on that aspect. He wants me dead, but Clarice needs me alive—at least until I give her the item she wants."

Gracie's face twisted as she tried to see how all these new facts related to each other. "I'm not sure I believe you have my best interests in mind. Even before Harris extracted my heartstone, you were trying to get me away from my room."

"You told me Harris thought that Katherine was the last one who had the item he wanted. Your room would be the first place he'd look, and if he were going to use force to obtain it . . . Well, I wanted you to be out of harm's way."

Gracie shifted as if she was about to get up, which caused Jack to flinch. "Aside from the fact that I have no idea what any of this means, is that what happened to your arm last night? Harris turned it into a heartstone?"

Jack rolled his eyes. "The thing you saw with my arm was a side effect of handling your heartstone without proper protection."

Gracie was tempted to stick her tongue out at him for his ridiculous answers. Jack opened his mouth like he was going to say more and then closed it.

"And the buzzing box you carried?" *What impossible thing does it do?*

"My particle extractor is one of two remaining devices which can remove a heartstone."

Gracie angled herself away from Jack. He knew too much about these strange events and he'd just admitted to owning the machine that could extract her heartstone.

"Where'd you come by such an invention?"

Jack shook his head. "If you want specific details, I think I'm entitled to an explanation in return. Your excuse for being in my closet would be a good start—and preferably not the jaded one that you were trying to figure out how the secret compartment works."

Her eyes drifted to the door. She wanted to tell him that she was hiding from the police, to be open and honest with him. But she realized she cared what Jack thought of her. As long as she kept her secret, she'd never have to find out how dark his deep, brown eyes could turn. At least she didn't have to think hard about what she'd tell him—her alibi had written itself the moment he walked into the room. "I'll admit I was looking for something."

Jack leaned forward. "Something my twin asked you to find?"

Gracie folded her hands in her lap. "I didn't find anything, so does it matter?"

"What did he promise you in return?"

She met his eyes with intrepid confidence. Jack, despite all his attempts to only appear controlled and confident, had a glaring flaw. He was far too curious and invested in his twin's affairs. "He promised to tell me something you'd never tell me otherwise."

"A lot has changed in a very short time. I never planned to tell you the truth about what happened last night, and I just did."

Gracie sucked on her lower lip. "Harris promised to give me a foolproof method for telling you two apart."

Jack stood from the vanity and leveled his face with hers. In a scowling match with Mrs. Levenson, he would have won—which is saying a lot since that woman raised headstrong orphans for a living. "No, he didn't, because that's impossible."

Jack leaned forward, and the bubble of her false confidence burst. She grabbed the only thing left on the vanity, her hairbrush, and thrust it in his face. "Stay back!"

He blinked once, then again. "Strike me if you wish, if that's what would make you most happy right now. But I don't think you really want to hurt me. You're scared and confused. You don't realize that you've just been through a rough ordeal, but your body is stressed, and so every little thing feels compounded. Why don't you put the brush down and we can continue our conversation civilly?"

The calmness of his voice and something about his hand atop hers—when had that happened?—undid the cord knotted around her ribs. His straight smile urged her to listen, to obey. Her grip on the brush relaxed and her arm grew heavy. Sensing her weakened resistance, Jack calmly removed the brush from her hand and set it on her vanity. "What were you really doing in my closet?"

Noises from the hallway reached her room. Jack turned toward the door then retreated to the opposite side of the room. "Sounds like the quack is here."

Gracie breathed a sigh of relief.

The physician was a man with more wrinkles on his face than ridges in a fingerprint. His silver hair lay plastered to his head as though he'd dunked it in a barrel of water. A smell of wet wool wafted from his long gray coat as he removed it, revealing a plaid suit vest. Gracie stole a glance out the window. The storm clouds in the sky were like bruises above her. The weather had worsened significantly since this morning. If she tried to run away, she wouldn't make it far before it started raining.

The doctor took one look at her and reached into his carpet bag for his stethoscope. "Is she running a fever?" He asked, setting the device around his neck and pressing the cold end over the swell of her left breast.

"She's still delirious," Jack said. "Talking nonsense about shadows and diamonds and ghosts out to steal her soul. Last night I caught her sleepwalking off the train at the Potsdam Junction, completely delirious and hallucinating. She's still confused this morning. Best be careful around her. She threatened me with her hairbrush a moment ago."

"You lying sack of rat tails!" Gracie batted the physician's hands away. "I'll show you deliri—" she lunged toward the vanity to snatch at the hairbrush. If he was going to charge her with threats on his well-being, she would make sure she at least had the enjoyment of committing the crime.

The doctor restrained her, holding her in place on the bed. He turned to Jack. "I think it would be best if I examined her alone. Your presence seems to aggravate her symptoms."

Jack moved to the doorway, his lower lip stiff and the hollow area in his cheeks even more depressed than usual. If he ever quit the circus, he'd make a superb actor. He had almost fooled her into believing he was sorry to leave her alone with the doctor and his bag of mysterious devices.

"If I hear trouble, I'm inviting myself back in," Jack said, exiting into the hall.

Rather than feeling relieved to be rid of Jack, Gracie felt caged and baited. She tucked her legs up to her chest and rocked back and forth, wishing this was all another nightmare.

"How are you feeling this afternoon, Miss Hart?" the doctor asked, digging through his bag.

"Scared, sir."

"Not of me, I hope."

"A little, actually."

"And why is that?"

"I'm not crazy like he says."

"I never said you were."

"I'll be the first to admit that things haven't seemed normal in the last few days, but I'm certain there's a logical explanation for it."

"That's what I'm here to find out. Your gentleman friend was very concerned for your health and most insistent I pay you a visit."

Her cheeks flushed. "I don't know if I can call him a friend."

"My mistake." The doctor resumed rummaging in his bag. He emerged holding a rolled bandage in one hand.

"Can I ask you something?" Gracie asked, watching his every move and waiting for him to plunge a syringe into her arm. All he did was wrap the bandage around her foot.

"Of course you may, Miss Hart."

"Do you believe in ghosts?"

CHAPTER XXXI

THE DOOR to Gracie's room opened. The physician stepped out, clutching his bag and hat. Jack quit his agitated pacing. "How is she?"

The doctor shut the door behind him. "The good news is that her temperature is normal, so it's not brain fever. I also don't believe it's a woman's uterine condition."

Jack put on a performance of exhaling a sigh of relief. He'd already known it wouldn't be any of those things.

The doctor continued, "Based on your earlier stated observations—anxiety, delusions, hallucinations, rash behavior . . . I thought this would be a case of *démence précocem*, or early dementia in plain terms. However, during my interaction with her, I noted no disintegration in her cognitive and mental functioning."

You do realize she's a person and not a machine, right?

"What do you think it is then?" Jack scrunched his face. His tolerance for dealing with these birdbrained "experts" only extended as far as he could spit.

"Based on her age, I'm inclined to say she suffers from the biphasic mental condition of dual-form insanity. Luckily, although the condition is not treatable, it is also generally not life threatening. Most patients can function normally and learn to cope with the occasional oscillation between mania and depression. However, should she develop an inclination to harm herself or others, then you might see about having her committed to an asylum."

The doctor proceeded to give his recommendations for various persons who specialized in psychology and facilities that might take her in. Jack politely waited for him to finish. "How's her foot? Is it broken?"

"Only sprained. She should keep it wrapped and stay off it for several days."

"Thank you, Doc." Jack reached into his pocket and withdrew a gold coin.

The doctor bit down on the coin. Noting the impression of his tooth, he pocketed it. "She's refused my offer to prescribe some laudanum and would prefer to be left alone for a while. Perhaps in an hour or two you might see if you can get her to eat something. I wouldn't say she's malnourished, but she looks like she could use some meat on her bones."

"I'll see to it." Jack shook the doctor's hand.

With a nod, he pulled his coat tighter around him and left.

Ignoring the quack's remark about Gracie wanting solitude, Jack turned the handle and leaned his shoulder against Gracie's door, pressing it open a crack.

Her melancholic countenance assaulted him with invisible daggers of guilt. She sulked by the window with hunched shoulders and her blanket tucked around her. Taking an unnatural interest in the fuzzy fabric pills on her wool blanket, she picked them off one at a time and dropped them on the floor.

Jack entered, setting his hands on her shoulders. All the vivacity of her spirit had departed with the doctor, and she lacked the will to shrug him off.

He kneeled at her bedside and took her hands in his own. They felt so small and fragile, like he was holding brittle leaves. Jack held his breath, fearing it might be the wind that blew them into oblivion.

"It's going to be okay. I won't let anyone put you in an asylum," he told her.

Gracie withdrew her arms and tucked them at her sides. "I don't know anymore. Maybe that's where I belong."

He'd hurt her, deeply, and he'd caused her to doubt her sanity. He wanted to spend the rest of his life trying to make it up to her—after he made sure she'd still be around to share it with him.

"I should let Vincenzio know we can't perform tonight." He lifted the blanket over her shoulders, guilt sitting heavily in his stomach. He needed to hurry and end this before he broke her beyond recovery. "I'll be back to check on you in a bit."

He crossed the room and closed the door, but she never looked up.

RAIN splattered against Jack's shoulders in intermittent drops. Hopefully the train crew would manage to get the big top up before the ground got too muddy. He dug his chin into his collar and shoved his hands into his pockets.

Jack changed into a new shirt in his room then went searching for his twin. He found Harris lurking near his wagon again. Jack's blood boiled. Patience and mercy were dispatched with a single, swift blow. Grabbing Harris by the collar, Jack pushed him into the wagon and slammed his head against the vanishing closet door. Harris's teeth clacked together. "No more games, Harris. This ends now."

Harris rubbed his head. "What if I disagree? As far as I'm concerned, this is just the beginning."

"Your time is up. Now that I know you're the one who's been helping Clarice, I'm gonna send you the rest of the way to hell." Jack gripped Harris by the throat, watching his face turn from pink to red. The bruises began collecting at Jack's wrists, and his arms burned as though his blood had turned to acid.

Through gritted teeth, Harris flashed him a smile of glistening white piano keys. "What will Gracie think when she finds out you killed me?"

"She's kind of pissed you shot her at the junction. Who knows? Maybe she'd thank me."

Jack squeezed harder. The fire in his arms spread to his shoulders as Harris's eyes began to bulge and water. His twin's skin turned from beet red to mauve. Harris's dark energy spread to Jack's chest and mushroomed. His chest tightened, barely leaving enough clearance for his lungs to expand and contract. Jack dropped one hand to loosen the top button of his shirt.

Harris clawed harder to free himself. "You're just jealous she came to me first about the note," he choked.

Yes. In fact, Jack was *incredibly* jealous.

With a growl, Jack released Harris and slung his twin's limp body across the small space. Harris hit the side wall with a clattering noise like dice shaking in a cup.

While Harris wheezed and gasped for breath, Jack shook his arm out.

"If it's any consolation," Harris said, his face back to its normal color, "Katherine never told me about her notes or that she'd found the benitoite key. I had to find out from Clarice."

Jack's jaw unhinged. Katherine had found the key and written herself notes? Could this nightmare get any worse?

When Jack regained feeling in his fingertips, he hauled Harris to his feet by his shirt front. "How long have you known about this?"

Harris rubbed his throat. "Only this week. I thought something was odd after Miriam said something about Katherine's old shoes being in good condition. I went to Knossos and ran into Clarice. She admitted she'd been helping Katherine write secret notes to herself and she'd deduced you were using hypnosis to prevent your assistant from remembering anything. Katherine found the benitoite key but wouldn't hand it over to Clarice until she helped break your hypnosis spell. Clarice suggested you had used the rhinestones on the costume shoes as the channeling medium, so Katherine went and bought a new pair."

Guilt rose like bile in Jack's throat, bitter and scalding. He released his grip on Harris's shirt. "It was an accident." The words sounded pathetic, even to him.

Harris rolled his eyes. "Sure," his voice grew stronger, more rounded in tone, "just like Jonathan's death was an accident. Poor bloke never saw it coming. You never directly killed either of them, but it's still your fault they're dead."

Jack's whole body trembled, and cotton grew in his mouth. In the alley outside the hotel, he'd transferred to Detweiler some of the dark energy that he'd absorbed from Gracie after the performance. It wasn't much, just enough so he'd have a grand nightmare when he fell asleep. But Jack hadn't considered that the man's heart would be too weak to handle it, or that he'd be too drunk to wake up.

Harris sneered, "You're awfully quiet. I suppose that means I'm right?"

Jack paced the back of the wagon while he collected his thoughts. His hypnotic suggestion that Katherine and Gracie should never leave the closet should've kept them safely hidden while in Knossos. Were they even falling asleep in the closet before they woke up and wandered deeper into it? He didn't think his hypnosis had failed entirely since Gracie and Katherine didn't remember anything. But whatever was going on, it certainly wasn't working the way it should. Were his commands not direct enough, or was there interference from a gemstone on the costume hairpiece or necklace? Perhaps—except Gracie hadn't been wearing either during her first rehearsal. The shoes? Possibly, but . . . no. Katherine wore her old shoes in Knossos and Gracie wore the newer pair.

Jack twisted his cufflink in the button hole of his shirt, wondering if the black inclusions could affect the hypnosis. Perhaps using his cufflink as the channeling medium wasn't such a good idea. He quit pacing. Regardless of why his hypnosis failed, there was nothing he could do to remedy the matter now.

Jack turned to Harris. "Where's the key?"

"Maybe I'll tell you if you ask nicely."

Jack drove a punch straight into Harris's abdomen. "Please."

Harris's mouth turned into a smirk, one that made Jack wish he'd elbowed him in the throat instead. "Clarice has it, and she's furious that it turned out to be a red herring. Now she has it in for Gracie too."

Jack whirled at Harris with a pointed finger. "Gracie has nothing to do with this. Clarice's vindictive nature is exactly why she's not ready to have her heartstone returned."

"No, it's because you're so selfish." Harris eased himself onto the edge of one of the floor trunks. "If you weren't keeping Clarice from collecting heartstones, she might be able to reverse the damage to our cufflinks—maybe even find a way to clone the pieces and create two instead of one."

Jack couldn't allow that—not when each heartstone she stole in the process of perfecting her formulas destroyed an innocent life. "It won't happen in our natural lifetime. You're a fool if you believe Clarice will still be interested in helping either of us after she gets her heartstone back."

Harris's expression softened, and his smile lost some of its smugness. "Maybe so, but it's not like you left me with much of a choice. Heartstones weren't meant to be kept outside the body long term. We've had ours apart for over a year and a half. If we wait too much longer to have her reunite the halves, there may come a point when they can't be rejoined."

Jack rested his forehead against the closet, letting the coolness of the metal ease the heat from his skin. "I know." He straightened, crossing his arms. "I also know the process of reuniting them would be as risky as the one that killed Gladys. I'll take half a life over no life."

Harris stood from the trunk, and Jack puffed out his chest and pulled himself up to his full height too—a pointless gesture since they had the same build and height. His twin kicked the trinkets on the floor out of the way and cracked his knuckles and then linked them behind his head. "Gladys didn't have fifty grams of moissanite."

Fifty grams!

Moissanite, or space diamonds, were the rarest gemstones in the world. The only place they had previously been found was in meteorites. Gladys had chipped out a total of 1.7 carats to create the time-compression field. If Clarice had over 250 carats of it, that must mean she'd found the moissanite as a heartstone.

Harris dropped his hands, his teeth glinting in a wide smirk, confirming Jack's suspicion.

Gracie's heartstone is a moissanite.

Droplets of sweat formed on Jack's forehead. How big of a time field could Clarice make if she used all of Gracie's heartstone? Or she might cut it into pieces and make several smaller time fields on the ground, working in populated areas where she'd have access to thousands of heartstones and unlimited resources for her research.

He'd learned from Gladys's journal that Clarice believed she'd been blessed by the angels, and as such, it was her divine responsibility to preserve and develop the technology. If she harnessed the power of that much moissanite, there'd be no way to stop her.

This was exactly why Gladys wanted the closet destroyed. The particle extraction technology was too dangerous to be left intact.

Harris leaned against the wall, arms crossed over his chest. "From your brooding silence, I can tell that you're starting to realize you've got two options: return Clarice's heartstone and let her continue to experiment and find a way to clone our pieces, or refuse, and Clarice will take Gracie's heartstone to make a new time field in an area where she can keep experimenting until she circumvents the compatibility issue and can finally make her own heartstone."

Jack rubbed his temples with his fingers then tugged at the roots of his hair until he was sure he'd give himself a bald spot. "You're forgetting the third option: we both die."

Harris stuffed his hands in his pockets, wearing a stupid smile. "I don't much like that one, though I'm okay if it's only you. If Clarice hadn't promised to make my life miserable if I killed you before she gets her heartstone back, you'd be dead by now."

Harris leaned away from the wall. "How many more people are going to get hurt before you can accept that Clarice will get what she wants, with or without your cooperation?"

Of all the things he hated about his relationship with Harris, somewhere close to the top of the list was the way they could usually tell what the other was thinking.

Space diamonds were rare, but now that one had appeared as a heartstone, Clarice would certainly focus on getting her own heartstone from him. With it, she would not be compelled to remain in Knossos to stay alive and could easily increase her harvesting efforts in the hope of coming across another space diamond. However, if she set her priority on obtaining Gracie's heartstone . . .

If Clarice stole Gracie's heartstone, Gracie would become a shade. And it would be his fault.

Jack swallowed hard, though it did nothing to get rid of the knot in his throat. "Tell Clarice I'll give her the pages I ripped out of Gladys's journal if she promises to leave Gracie alone."

"You've got to give me more than that. She's seething mad because you've known where her heartstone was all along and lied about it."

"I never lied to her. I told her what I knew at the time. I didn't realize Gladys left *two* keys behind—one physical and one like a riddle—until I started reading Gladys's journal more in depth."

Harris straightened his collar and then crossed his arms, trying not to appear upset by the news. "I've read the letter she left with her last wishes. It never mentioned a second key."

That's because the second key wasn't referenced in the letter; it was in Gladys's journal, which she bequeathed to their father in the letter. "The second key is that Gladys hid Clarice's heartstone not only in space, but in time as well. In the present time, the benitoite key opens to a drawer with a scathing letter. Clarice needs the second key to align the time-compression machine, combining the past with the present. Once she does this, she'll find her heartstone and a different letter."

"Now I know you're bluffing. Time flows at different rates between room to room, so it's impossible to measure and track."

Now Jack folded *his* arms. "Gladys had a formula to do it, which is in the pages I'm willing to give Clarice in exchange for Gracie's safety."

"Why don't you tell Clarice yourself? She could be stealing Gracie's heartstone as we speak."

The knot in Jack's stomach tightened and his heart felt as though he had an anvil tied to it. Harris wasn't just lurking around the prop wagon—he was guarding the closet for Clarice. "Do you really not care about Gracie at all?"

"I do," Harris said, his tone holding less of its usual asperity, "but what good will that do me if I'm dead? I can't continue living with half a heartstone. It's all or nothing for me now." He looked directly at Jack, almost compassionately. "The chances Gracie will die during the extraction are low. If you're quick to trade Clarice her heartstone, Gracie will probably be okay in the long term. What happens to her is now your choice."

Jack could feel his accent creeping through. "The condition for me to return Clarice's heartstone was that she makes penance for her crimes. Sneaking behind my back to get it just proves she isn't ready. I'll never give you my cufflink, and I'll die before I let either of you hurt Gracie."

In the short time period he'd known her, somewhere in between the teasing and all the times she'd hit him, he'd fallen in love with her. When it seemed everyone around the lot was whispering behind his back, calling him a murderer—she'd still stood in front of the knife board and allowed him to redeem himself. He couldn't tell exactly when it had happened, but he at least knew now that any world would be empty for him if she wasn't in it.

Harris's jaw tightened, and he clenched his fists. "Why do you care so much? If you were to help Clarice, she might eventually be able to clone your half of the heartstone. You could be free."

"I won't ever be free until you're gone. You're a mistake, and you shouldn't exist."

Harris was silent for a moment as he fossicked through the contents of one of the trunks. He found a deck of cards and shuffled it, his eyes fixed to a spot on the floor. "When Mother and Father died, you wanted someone to take all the pain of your guilt away. And when you went to Clarice for help, she did just that. She cut the dark inclusions of your heartstone off—the part permanently blackened by your nightmares of their deaths. You can't blame my existence on anyone but yourself."

Heat flushed Jack's cheeks at the memory. If there was one moment of his life he wished he could change, that meeting with Clarice would be it. The shame he carried from that choice stared back at him in the mirror every day.

Jack's jaw tightened. "The particle extractor was never designed to cut heartstones. I should've known better than to let her try. Now I'm stuck with you for an evil doppelganger, and ironically, I got the half with the inclusions."

"You talk like I don't have my disappointments too." Harris moved in front of Jack so their chests touched. "My life could go on if you didn't keep getting in the way. Just take Clarice's offer!"

Jack curled his upper lip away from his teeth. "I told you before, *over my dead body*."

Harris smirked and then patted Jack on the shoulder. "That's the spirit. Lucky for you, I don't think you'll have to wait long."

Jack turned for the door. He had to hurry and find Gracie before Clarice did. He turned back to face Harris. "I'll find a way to end you first, if it's the last thing I do."

Harris pantomimed a bored yawn. "I've heard that one before. I'm still waiting to see it. Watch your back, Jack, but especially, watch hers."

"I hate you."

"The funny thing about that is, I am you." Harris's dark laugh rang in Jack's head, long after he was out of earshot.

CHAPTER XXXII

GRACIE DUG her postcard out from the top drawer of her trunk and shook her pillow out of its flour sack case. She wiped a tear from her face. When she'd made the resolution to leave, she'd done so despite all her conflicted feelings—anger, betrayal, loss, confusion. Yet somehow, it was the thought of leaving Jack that had started her tears.

"None of that now," she scolded herself. He'd played her from the start, and she'd been a fool to fall for him. "He's the one who's crazy, not me," she said, though she wasn't sure that was true.

She had little to pack in the flour sack and justified keeping one dress for herself in exchange for leaving behind her seven-dollar trunk.

"Dual-form insanity. A danger to myself." Gracie shoved her postcard into her skirt pocket and reached for the door handle. She had to get out of here before Jack returned with asylum wards to collect her.

Ever since she'd jumped on board the circus train, she'd started to lose her mind. She needed to get away from this living nightmare. No more haunted messages. The time had come to spend Mr. Detweiler's money and buy a ticket to Chicago.

Getting to the train station wouldn't be easy since blood pooled in her foot and worsened the pain in her ankle whenever she stood. If she could make it to the street, she could get a hackney to take her to the station. If not, she'd crawl there—whatever it took.

Because of the rain, the stagehands hurried to finish pitching the tents. Although no one paid any particular mind to her, Gracie was convinced her limp made her stick out like a blonde in China.

She arrived at the train station within the quarter hour.

"One ticket to Chicago," she told the man at the ticketing counter. Thank goodness she didn't have to worry about travel papers on top of everything else.

"The next train leaves in a half hour. You'll have to change trains in Toledo," he said.

"I'll take it."

The red ink on her ticket, still wet from where he'd stamped "paid," transferred to her fingers. It looked like blood.

The polished wood floors of the train station's waiting room and the cut planks used for walls reminded Gracie of a packing crate. Long mahogany benches lined the sides and dissected the room in rows. Overhead, gray light streamed in from the greenhouse-type windows.

Gracie edged her way through the crowds, which were much thicker inside because of the brewing storm. Smoke from cigarettes writhed in the air and curled around the flickering kerosene lamps.

Gracie found an unoccupied bench and sat. The pounding of a second heartbeat pulsed in her foot. She'd had to unwrap the bandage to fit her foot in her shoe, and now she doubted she'd ever be able to pull it out.

She bent over to loosen the laces and buttons on her shoes. She glanced up when a pair of shiny black Oxfords shuffled in front of her. Her gaze followed the soggy hem of the man's charcoal pants up to the French cuffs of his clean white shirt. A bright blue cufflink winked at her from his outermost crossed arm. A small dark speck, a blemish in the gemstone, stared at her like the pupil of an eye.

"You followed me!" She glared at Jack. Clearly, she'd not ruined his last good shirt since he still had this one.

"I didn't have to. Gary by the duck shoot saw you leave, and I had a feeling you'd come here. Now, why don't you come back with me to the lot?"

Gracie grabbed her sack of belongings. If he knew she'd try to leave, he should also know she wouldn't go back without a fight.

"Trust him," he'd told her, but where had that gotten her? Nearly in an asylum.

"I'm leaving the circus, Jack. You were right—I never should've taken the job. When you see Vincenzio next, you can tell him he has my permission to make up any sort of story he wants about my disappearance."

Jack looked at Gracie, his mouth in a loose smile—more smug than apologetic. "You're in a lot of pain and aren't thinking clearly. Running away and traveling as a single young woman is very unsafe. Come back to the circus with me, and after your foot is better, I'll see what I can do to get you another train ticket."

He reached to take her bag from her, and she swung it out of his reach. Like she was falling for *that* trick again. "Keep your hands off!"

The undercurrent of warning in her voice carried much further than she'd intended.

A barrel of a man with big-knuckled hands and a flattened nose approached. The rest of his form was hidden beneath a driving cloak with several short capes. He placed a callused hand on Jack's shoulder. Half the station now watched them.

"Miss, is this young man bothering you?" cauliflower-hands asked.

"It's just a slight misunderstanding—sorry to disturb you," Jack said coolly. "I offered to carry her bag, and it seems she thought I meant to steal it."

Jack's warm eyes and the strong curve of his jaw naturally made him appear trustworthy. Gracie doubted anyone else would be able to see the glint of cunning in his eyes if they didn't know to look for it.

The coachman's hand slipped from Jack's shoulder. "My apologies . . ."

No, don't fall for it!

Gracie threw herself around the man's burly arm. "Don't listen to him! He wants to sell me to the whorehouse to settle his gambling debts. I beg you—don't let him take me!"

The man stared at her, eyebrows leveled and his chapped lips pressed firmly together. He then pulled her behind him, rolled up his sleeve, and threw his gnarled fist into Jack's stomach.

The sound of Jack's outcry stabbed her squarely in the chest with a sharp pain. Without thanking the gentleman or looking back at Jack's crushed form, she hobbled toward the door.

"Wait, Gracie!" Jack called after her, still doubled over and his breath wheezing.

Outside the station, drops of rain pricked at her skin and darkness leaked around her like paint spilling between stones. With her sack clutched under her arm, she sloshed through the spreading puddles. Just as the lights from the station behind her began to fade, a woman stepped out from the darkened alley at Gracie's side, blocking her path. The woman was dressed in fitted trousers and a gold brocade dress coat.

"Did you miss me, *dear?*" From behind her back she produced a telescope-like tube from the machine strapped to her back. Gripping it by the handle, she tucked it against her shoulder. The woman pointed the dark orifice of the tube at Gracie, her finger hovering over the trigger. A solid green light glowed on the side of the contraption.

Gracie turned to run, but two words from the woman's rosebud lips held her in place. "Don't move."

This must be Clarice, the woman Jack had spoken of.

The low-pitched drumming of the gun grew into a shrill whine.

"This might hurt a bit." Clarice gave a tinkling laugh. The gun fired.

The force crushed Gracie, like a piano falling on her from a hundred-foot height. Each of the piano's eighty-eight keys forced their way through her body, one agonizing note at a time. A scream rose up the column of her throat. The pain ripped through her back and collected itself in the form of a glowing crystal—the heartstone Jack had told her she'd imagined.

Her knees buckled, and Gracie fell onto her stomach. She had to be dead and burning in hell. How else could she still register pain of this magnitude without losing consciousness? She tried to tell herself it wasn't real. Her body didn't believe her.

She fell facedown on the ground. A dampness spread over her chest and skirt, followed by overall wetness. Was it her blood, or just the puddle she lay in? She realized with some disappointment that she might drown in it because she lacked any strength to lift her head.

In front of her nose, her train ticket and postcard grew soggy in the puddle. The ink on the postcard already resembled a smudge of rouge.

Her heart sputtered, and her eyes bulged with tears. Her postcard would never arrive at the orphanage. Everyone she left behind would never know she'd made a future for herself outside the sweatshops and slums. Mr. Levenson had won the bet.

A wave of the puddle sloshed over Gracie's face as the bronzed woman kicked through it. The ebbing sting in her chest worsened when she coughed and spit the water out.

In an act of compassion or spite, Clarice grabbed Gracie's hair by the roots and flipped her over onto her back. "When you see Jack again, tell him I'm offering him a trade. Your heartstone for mine. He has three hours, and then I'm going to start cutting pieces off." Gracie's heartstone disappeared into one of her many pockets. All the warmth in Gracie's body vanished with her heartstone and Clarice.

An inkwell had spilled inside Gracie, its dark stain taking the place of her blood.

Heavy raindrops continued to crash on Gracie like a catapult bombardment. A hollow feeling settled in her fingers and toes. How much longer until her life ended?

In a feverish blur she saw her brother, Robert, going off to his first day of school. She saw her mother and father having a picnic outside on a bright red blanket. She saw Robert at the bow of the steamship, the wind whipping his dark hair into his face. Then, her mother lying in bed, lifeless. The bodies of her father and brother, wrapped in blankets on the floor. Her fevered memories ended there.

She missed them terribly, but she didn't want to join them.

Not like this.

CHAPTER XXXIII

GRACIE OPENED her eyes to a squint. Jack hovered over her with a sodden newspaper clutched over his head. "Gracie!" Jack shrugged his coat off and laid it over her.

Blood and spittle spotted his shirt. The open collar of his shirt revealed a mottled ring of dark bruises around his neck. The man who'd allowed her to escape must have been a veteran boxer. That didn't surprise her since the gentleman's nose had obviously been broken a few times. Jack looked so beaten he might have been run over by four horses pulling a carriage.

As Jack picked Gracie up, her sopping wet clothes saturated Jack's dry shirt. His touch was warm, as welcome as a field of sun-kissed daisies blooming over her skin. He shielded her from the downpour with his coat as he carried her the short distance back to the circus lot.

Why did he bother? She'd slandered his character and had left him at the mercy of a man who undoubtedly slaughtered pigs himself for the ham on his breakfast plate.

"Hang in there, Gracie. You made me promise not to give up on you," Jack said.

His accent had regressed enough to brand him a descendant of an original Australian settler. Gracie puzzled over why he seemed to think she'd survive when that woman had given her a three-hour death sentence.

Gracie tried to speak, but her voice made only a weak gurgle.

"Save your breath," Jack spoke softly into her ear. "Once we get back, I'll give you some amethyst, to help you find your tongue and take the edge off. And maybe some quartz."

Quartz? Was he trying to help her feel better by offering her gifts? What was he talking about?

Jack's sodden shoes squished and smacked with each step down the train car hallway. The movement added to the sickening feeling building in Gracie's stomach. Her head rolled to the side, coming to rest on his chest. His labored breaths pushed his chest out in a slightly nonrhythmic pattern like the crashing of ocean waves. She wrapped herself in the water and let herself float.

He carried her through the doorway to his room and placed her onto the bed. He rested for a short minute before standing again. Taking his coat from her, he used it to mop up the water trail in the hall.

"You'll be safe in here for a while," he said, tossing the wet coat aside.

Jack approached her, elbows tucked against his tense body, his left hand wrapped around his right fist. He frowned at the way her wet clothes clung to her body. "I don't want to invade your privacy again, but you'll catch your death if you don't get into some dry clothes. Do you have a preference if Miriam or Maria dresses you?"

She shivered. He could burn her clothes while she wore them, and it'd only warm the air in her room, not her skin. She shook her head, "No."

He turned toward the door. "I'll be right back with some dry clothes. I'm gonna have to lock you in since I can't count on you not to run away."

"I'll be here." Her throat ached like she'd gargled gravel.

With a *click*, the door shut behind him.

Gracie strained to turn over onto her side, pulling the blanket of the bed around her tighter. She had aches and cramps everywhere, plus an overall sense of gloom. Would he have a straitjacket with him when he got back? Yet, she wouldn't let herself lose hope, no matter how bleak things seemed. Until she found a way to gain control over the situation, she'd do her best to keep a level head.

Jack returned a little while later with a suspicious bundle under his arm. He entered the room one limb at a time, as if he feared an ambush from Gracie.

"Miriam and Maria are both busy," Jack said. "You might have to let me help you dress." He spilled the contents of the bundle onto the vanity. "I didn't have time to sort through everything, so I took it all." The dim light revealed the glimmer of mulberry purple, blush pink, sky blue, and coral red stones affixed to shiny gold and silver necklaces, rings, or bracelets. There was a broach with a forest green stone and a large heart-shaped pendant with a white stone. Timid Harold would grab a gun and shoot them on sight if he caught them with Katherine's reserved jewelry collection.

Jack rummaged through the pile of glittering jewelry until he found a ring with a violet stone surrounded by small garnet rounds. "Do us a favor, and after I put this on, keep your mouth closed for a bit. If you go squawking like a galah for help, someone's gonna find us here, and Vincenzio already thinks you're the one who stole the ring I used to get rid of that shade last night." He measured the size of the ring on his smallest finger.

His jaw clenched, making a muscle in his cheek twitch as he reached for her hand. "You were right about him accusing you because you're new. I suppose I need to apologize for that."

Jack pried her index finger from her fist and pushed the ring on. The gemstone's effect was instantaneous. Warmth tingled in her toes, and she felt her voice begin humming in her throat.

Gracie sat up, her limbs sluggish but responsive.

Jack released her finger. "Better?"

"Yes." Her voice sounded like a young woman instead of a cat in heat.

With an approving nod, he began hanging a bedsheet between them to act as a divider. "I don't imagine we have a lot of time, so the quicker you change clothes the better."

Jack tossed the dress he'd rummaged over the top of the divider . . . The ecru one.

Gracie's blush darkened even more when she saw a dry set of her underthings too. Like she would take off any piece of clothing with him in the room—divider or not. She tore down the sheet and fixed a cold scowl on him. "Jack, what's really going on?"

He stopped unbuttoning his shirt in order to fix the divider. "Either dress yourself, or in three minutes, I'll do it for you."

"You'd like that, wouldn't you?"

He was smart enough to know not to answer *that* question. Gracie wrung as much water out of her dress as she could, leaving the ecru dress untouched. Glancing at the divider, Gracie saw Jack's silhouette seat itself at the small table and begin sorting jewelry. If he was planning on handing her over to an asylum, why was he worried about the jewelry? She wished she could figure out what to make of him, one way or the other.

"Did Clarice give you a time frame or an ultimatum when she stole your heartstone?" Jack called through the sheet.

Gracie fanned the skirt of her dress to air it out. "I'm not sure I should answer that, because to have the slightest clue what you're referring to would also be admitting I'm insane."

Jack let out an exasperated sigh. "You're not insane, and it wasn't fair of me to let you believe you were. I told you I wasn't a liar, but I haven't always told you the complete truth either. Since I met you, I've tried to protect you from all this, but I've only managed to put you in the center of it."

She peered around the sheet, hoping for a glimpse of his face. However misguided his previous efforts were to keep her safe, she felt stupidly compelled to trust him every time he promised to protect her. Relying on her own devices—running away at the junction, hiding in the closet, buying another train ticket—had hurt her situation, not helped it.

Realizing he was dressed, she pulled the curtain down again.

"You didn't change," he grumbled. "How can you expect your body to avoid sublimation when you won't help it maintain homeostasis?" He spelled it out for her when she only blinked in reply. "The colder your body temperature, the faster you'll turn into a shade."

"That woman said you have three hours to return her heartstone before she starts cutting mine into pieces—or something like that. If I'm not dead before then, Miriam will definitely kill me if I trash yet another one of her dresses."

Jack simmered down as he considered her point. "That's less time than I'd hoped."

"She threatened to cut *my* heartstone to bits. Why does it bother you?"

"It doesn't matter what she promised; she can't be trusted at all."

"Sounds terrible for me." Her brave front did little to ease the quaking in her legs.

Jack stood and then extended a pink necklace. The teardrop gemstones hung on the golden chain like a line of laundry strung between an alley.

Gracie swatted the necklace away. "If you're trying to buy my forgiveness for all the times you've lied to me and for dragging me into this, it's going to cost you a lot more than *stolen* jewelry."

"If we're keeping tallies, you owe me at least *four* apologies, so I don't owe you a thing. Besides I'm looking for your cooperation, not your forgiveness."

She scowled at the necklace. "What will someone think if they see me wearing Katherine's jewelry, even for a minute? Exactly when are you planning on returning them, Jack?"

Jack untwisted the necklace's chain, straightening out the kinks. "If you are wearing some of this jewelry, I predict people will think you more agreeable." He nodded toward the glittering mound on the table. "Certain types of gemstones can simulate the effect of a heartstone. For instance, amethyst helped with your speech and motor capabilities, and this pink gemstone, kunzite, should help with your irritability . . ."

Gracie lifted a shaking finger to his face. "If I'm angry it's because some old woman is performing voodoo on me, and yet you think you can help me by dressing me up for a ball!" Gracie shook her head and shrugged. Regardless of how silly the idea sounded aloud, she'd felt loads better since putting the amethyst ring on. "Of course, none of this matters since I'm crazy and this is all a figment of my imagination."

Holding the pink necklace toward her, Jack said, "You know this is real and not your imagination. I know you can feel the darkness spreading, *bleeding* inside you. If you don't let me help, it will take over you entirely."

How could he possibly know that? Had he helped Clarice create the drug that left her body weakened and her brain feeling like a streetcar rail ran through it?

"I don't know what I know anymore." She wished she could clear the mist of confusion away. "Are you really trying to help me? Or yourself?"

Jack stopped trying to hang the dazzling noose around her neck. "I'd like to help *both* of us, since she's already done to me what she's threatened to do to you. I know you're not feeling like yourself. We've both been hurt by Clarice, so if you can't cope with trusting me again, at least believe we're on the same side. Then, when this is all over, if you still want to leave, I won't try to stop you. I'll buy you a ticket to Chicago or even California if you want. But now, we've got to get your heartstone back from Harris and Clarice."

"So you're just going to give her what she wants? Her heartstone?"

"I could, but it'd be a short-term solution and I'd still have Harris to deal with."

Gracie tilted her chin up and challenged him with her eyes. "What other choice do you have?"

Jack's lips pressed together, and it looked as if his eyes were more shadowed than a second ago. His silence was like a dark expanse of water and she didn't know if she dared attempt to cross it. She might find it too deep and full of sharks. What if Jack had no other options? Was her life already doomed? In her mind's eye she saw a dark, ruined castle with an inky-black pond in the floor. She imagined drowning in it, like when she'd fallen in a pond as a child. This water didn't splash when she fell but engulfed her, filling her mouth, her nose, her lungs. Killing her in complete silence.

"Don't feed the nightmares," Jack interjected, his eyes piercing. "It'll make the darkness spread faster."

Somehow, his voice cleared away the water. She breathed in deeply, easing the pressure in her chest.

Jack ran a hand through his hair. "There may be another way to persuade Clarice to return your heartstone. If I destabilize the time-compression generator, creating a catastrophic problem, she'll be too busy to retrieve her heartstone. Several years ago, I took pages from her sister's research journal with important formulas she'll need to make repairs. I'll make her trade your heartstone for the pages, and I'll keep her heartstone hidden. Then, while she's fixing the generator, we'll escape, and I'll dismantle the closet before she can follow us back."

He had a plan, but how could Gracie help? She felt like a bird with a broken wing, twisting on the ground in the midst of a pack of hungry cats. "How does this new plan of yours resolve the problem with Harris?"

"I have something in mind, but I'll have to work out the details along the way."

"I hope it involves him rotting in jail for a few years." Anger and hurt laced her voice. "I can't believe I went out to breakfast with him. He bought me the trunk and made me think he was sorry for stealing my ticket. All along he was just trying to gain my trust to use me against you."

The muscle in Jack's jaw twitched.

"There's something you should know about Harris which I want you to consider carefully before passing judgment on him."

"You're defending his behavior?"

Jack's lips thinned. Gracie had seen this look before, on the group of orphans whose parents died in an apartment fire. Every time someone lit a match, they hunched and cowered.

"I'm not defending him," he said, "but I hope you can try to understand. I'm afraid I'm not so different. Harris and I are two sides of the same coin. My—I mean our—real name is John Harrison. We adopted the nicknames Jack and Harris to distinguish ourselves after we separated."

"Wait. So, your brother's name is Harris Harrison?"

"No." Jack sighed. "Harris isn't my brother. He's me, or rather, we're the same person."

CHAPTER XXXIV

O F ALL Jack's lies, this one was the mother lode. Gracie scowled. "You can't be the same person. I've seen you stand right next to Harris."

"We aren't the same person now, but we can't continue living separately much longer. We were one person until Clarice experimented with cutting our heartstone in two, and we each ended up with a half. If we wait too long to reverse the process, we could lose compatibility with the other cufflink and neither of us would be able to claim both pieces." He raised his arm, turning his wrist so she could clearly see his cufflink. "Harris and I each have one half of a set of cufflinks, which is one of two pieces of our original heartstone. The hypnosis method I used on you is channeled through my cufflink. It explains how Harris was able to exercise hypnotic control over you at the junction since his cufflink half is almost an identical specimen to mine."

As she took a step forward, Jack positioned himself in front of the door. It wasn't his imposing frame that stopped her but the look in his eyes promising that he'd run after her again, and as many times as it took until she believed him.

She crossed her arms over her chest. "What do you mean? You hypnotized me?"

His shoulders hunched. "Do you recall me telling you that if anyone asked how the vanishing closet worked, you should tell them you didn't remember because I hypnotize you before each performance?"

"I never thought for a moment you meant it!"

Jack lowered his voice. "It's always been my desire to keep my assistants away from the world on the other side of the closet door. The first time you stepped into the closet, I shut the door and put the hypnosis on you using my cufflink. Except gemstones from your costume or maybe the inclusions in my cufflink have been interfering, since you didn't stay asleep in the closet. You've been leaving the closet each performance and exploring Knossos on your own—and because of my hypnosis, you've forgotten every visit."

"You claim you rescued me from the closet this afternoon, but we didn't have a performance where you could hypnotize me. Without hypnosis, why don't I remember that visit?"

"I used the same hypnosis spell afterward to suppress your memories, but they're more likely to resurface than if I had hypnotized you before you went into the closet."

Something about Jack's story struck a chord in Gracie. It sounded like the truth. Already, visions of dark corridors and a flying fortress poked at the corners of her thoughts. "One of my notes told me to look for Katherine's key. I found a silver key with blue and white stones in her trunk, but then I lost it. Do you know what happened to it?"

"Clarice convinced you to give it to her, and you don't remember because it happened in Knossos. She thought it was the key she needed to retrieve her heartstone. She didn't realize Gladys had a second key."

Gracie's stomach rolled. "She tricked me, didn't she?"

"If you want to get even with her, help me, and we can put an end to this insanity."

Gracie only pretended to understand everything Jack had just said. After all, only someone who was genuinely naïve, and maybe insane, would *want* to believe they had traveled to a different world through a magician's vanishing closet and had been writing notes to warn themselves of the dangers there. The moment she stopped hoping there was another explanation was the moment she completely lost her sanity.

That moment occurred when she lifted her hair from the base of her neck and turned around so Jack could hang the kunzite necklace on her.

The necklace felt like ice, smooth and cold.

"You don't have anything in that pile of jewelry that will make the pain in my foot go away, do you?

"Sorry, but the rest is fake," he said, taking a step back. "We might as well let Vincenzio catch us with it since there's nothing in here worth more than a dollar. That's the best I can do."

Gracie found it easier to think now that every cell of her body wasn't bursting with anxious nerves. "So," she said, squaring her shoulders for the upcoming battle, "what needs to be done first for this plan of yours to stop Clarice and Harris *and* get my heartstone back?"

Jack took a seat on his bed. He shoved a foot into a shoe and began tying the laces. "As soon as I finish dressing, we're going to sneak back into Knossos. I'll sabotage the time-compression generator—the machine that keeps the time field intact and the fortress floating. In exchange for your heartstone, I'll offer Clarice the repair formulas from Gladys's journal."

"It sounds like it might work," Gracie said. In reality, she had no clue.

Jack gave her an encouraging smile. "I'm certain it will."

Gracie pulled herself straighter. "I think I understand enough. Let's go before my three hours run out."

She reached for the handle.

He grabbed her hand. "Just a second."

"I thought we were rushed for time! You have your shoes on already. Don't tell me you need to put on your cravat—you're always tying it too tight or wearing it crooked."

He blushed and raked his hand through his hair. "I thought I should warn you. Clarice has Harris helping her, which means they'll have strong hypnosis control over you. If they manage to claim my cufflink, they'll have absolute hypnotic control over you. She will kill you if you get in her way. If you don't want to chance it, tell me now so I can try to come up with another plan."

Gracie took a deep breath. "It's a risk that can't be helped. I'll just do my best to avoid her."

"If things go according to plan, you won't even have to meet her."

Gracie hated to ask, but she needed to know. "And if our plan fails?"

Jack turned his face away from her before he answered. "You'll be nothing more than a shade by morning. However, since Clarice won't be happy you tried to assist me, she'll make sure you don't make it through this evening."

With the terrible fate of becoming a shade hanging over them, Gracie understood now why Jack and Harris always fought. "Is there another option then? Can I get a new heartstone somewhere?"

"No, heartstones aren't interchangeable. You'd be trapped in Knossos like Clarice. The gemstones she wears fill some of the void of her absent heartstone, but without the light energy emitted by the chandelier, she'd die within a few hours away from Knossos."

"How have you and Harris survived with half?"

"Half isn't nothing. It's difficult, and I have nightmares almost every night, but it's manageable. For Harris, it's a lot worse. It's not good for the long term because I tend to collect dark energy whenever I come across it." Gracie's lower lip trembled, and she knew if she started crying, she wouldn't be able to stop. Although she felt more in control of her emotions since Jack had given her the pink necklace, every stupid little thing activated her tears.

Jack gathered her into his arms, his cheek pressed against the top of her head. His chest moved as he drew a deep breath and released it. "This may be hard for you to understand, but Harris and I cannot both exist. He will die, or I will."

CHAPTER XXXV

THE CLOISTERS in Knossos were dark and noiseless—like death. Jack stepped out of the closet, followed closely by Gracie. He gazed into the darkness, staring at nothing yet taking in everything. He patted his watch in his pocket and adjusted the straps of his particle extractor on his back.

"Look familiar?" he asked.

"Maybe?"

He pulled Gracie's arm over his neck. "We should hurry before either Harris or Clarice realizes we're here. If you lean on me a little more, I think we can move a bit faster."

Eleven intersections and about two minutes later, they arrived at a dead end. A tall, steel ladder, barely visible in the dark shadows, disappeared into a small square cutout in the ceiling. If someone didn't know to look for it, they might never have noticed it.

Gracie took one glance up into the dark shaft and planted herself against the wall as if she were trying to become one with the bricks. "We have to go up there?"

"I know your foot hurts, but if you hook your arms around each rung, you can make it up on just your left foot if we go slowly. I'll go second, so if you do fall, I can catch you."

"Somehow, that last part doesn't seem reassuring." Gracie twisted the end of her hair around her finger. "That's also not what I'm most worried about."

"You can't tell me you're scared of heights after jumping out of a window almost a thousand feet up."

Her right eyebrow formed a perfect arc on her forehead. "Perhaps I have an evil doppelganger too, since that doesn't sound like something I'd do. And it's not the height that scares me as much as how small and dark it is."

"So you *are* claustrophobic." Jack stole a second glance at the ladder rungs. It did look like a tight fit. If she was nervous now, then she wasn't going to like the size of the crawl space they'd have to cross to reach the other section of the attic. "I hope you can come to terms with your fear because if we want to avoid Clarice, we don't have any other choice."

Gracie uncrossed her arms and left the safety of the wall. "Where does it go?"

"This shaft leads to the top level of the fortress. From there we'll enter the garret and cross over to the north section using the crawl space that spans the two attic sections."

"That doesn't sound too difficult."

"The garret will be full of shades. I brought my particle extractor, but I might not have enough fuel to neutralize them all. If that happens, I may have to focus on luring them away and leave you to sabotage the generator on your own."

Gracie turned to face him, hands clutched in front of her. "I've never even seen this machine before. How will I know what it looks like let alone how to use it?"

Jack turned his sleeve cuffs up twice. "If it becomes necessary, I'll tell you what to do."

"How about this instead? Why don't I deal with the shades and you break the generator?"

If he had unlimited gemstones, he might've considered it. "I'm worried I don't have enough fuel to take care of them all as it is. Besides, if I have to lure them away, I can move a lot faster than you. Plus, once I deal with the shades, we have to worry about Clarice and Harris. Since she already has your heartstone, there's no reason for her to keep you alive if you become meddlesome. But she won't kill me until she has her own heartstone in hand, on the slight chance I collected it already and hid it somewhere in our time."

"Fine, we'll do it your way," Gracie said with a frown. She reached for the handrails of the vertical ladder and stepped onto the first rung. "Don't you dare think about stealing a glance up my skirts," she added.

What crime had he committed that the universe would now jinx him with such thoughts when he had to ascend a ladder with more rungs than seats in a theater?

"I can't guarantee anything," he replied, eyes fixed downward.

"I'll kick you if you do."

He scoffed. "You don't have eyes on your bum."

"I'll just know it."

THE ladder ended at a small landing the size of a double bed. Upon arriving at the top, he saw three doors. A short staircase of five steps led to the one in the center. On the other side of the door, shades lumbered and the floorboards creaked.

Jack opened the back of his particle extractor and reached in his pocket. He withdrew a pendant necklace with teardrop-shaped stones arranged into small flowers around ivory pearl centers.

Gracie watched over his shoulder. Despite the low lighting from the single bulb on the wall, the diamonds sparkled. The reflection in Gracie's eyes reminded Jack of staring into the night sky.

"Is that also Katherine's? It's beautiful." She caressed the necklace.

"This was my mother's," he said, dropping it into the fuel chamber.

Gracie slipped her arm through his. "I'm sorry I'm the reason you have to part with it. Maybe after we get back to the circus, we can sell my trunk and you can buy a new necklace with the money."

"It's okay." He screwed the fuel chamber lid on tight. "It's not like I was ever going to wear it myself."

Gracie unlinked her arm from his. "This machine we're going to sabotage—are you certain Clarice needs it enough to give you my heartstone for it?"

"The moment you tweak anything on it, the time-compression field will begin to collapse. The harmony between all the new and old technology will be disrupted, and everything will be all over the place like a Tasmanian devil's breakfast. If Clarice doesn't want this fortress to fall into the lake, she'll give me your heartstone—and Harris's cufflink."

"There's no one else who can fix it, like Harris?"

Her attempt to grasp a deeper understanding of the situation amused him. She knew so little about what was going on, yet she was trying so hard to make sense of it.

"When things start falling apart, they'll go down fast. Clarice is very smart, but she's not a genius in every aspect. Since Gladys created the foundation for the time-compression generator, there are a few pieces of the mathematical equations that Clarice struggles to fully understand. She'll need the advantage of having the formulas from Gladys's journal when the roof starts caving in."

He squeezed Gracie's hand. It felt sweaty, and electric. "Stay close behind me. The ladder leading up to the crawl-space access is on the far side. If there are more shades than I can neutralize with the extractor, find a safe place to hide until I can lure them away."

"Stop talking such nonsense. We're both going to be fine."

He hoped so. They'd need a miracle to make it past the shades. He hoped her belief in dumb luck would be good enough.

CHAPTER XXXVI

L IGHT POURED out when Jack opened the door, so bright he had to raise his arm to shield his eyes. Timbered beams held up the large, triangular trusses of the roof. A planked walkway ran on the right side over the crossbeams. The shades came into focus more slowly. Monsters with scales, dinosaurs covered in rotting flesh, creatures walking upright on bifurcated legs. Some were more solid than others, and some Jack could only sense as an aura of something otherworldly. At a glance, he counted fourteen.

Had he thought they were entering the garret? Because it looked more like they'd walked into Pandora's box.

He fired three shots and cleared the right side of the room. "Come on!" he pulled her behind him and fired two shots at the puddles forming on the floor.

The crawl space was framed up high, close to the ceiling of the supporting side wall. A catwalk, suspended in the roof trusses, led to it. To reach the catwalk, they'd have to climb a spindly wooden ladder leaning against the railing of the walkway.

Jack launched shots at the shades while Gracie hopped one rung up the ladder at a time.

The shades continued to climb out of the spaces between light and dark. They slithered over the floorboards and took shape as clouds of black mist or as monsters. He ran out of fuel by the time Gracie had made it three-quarters of the way. At least she was high enough she'd be safe from their parasitic touch.

"Looks like you get to do this on your own," he called to her.

"Don't you dare think about leaving me!" She wrapped one arm through the rungs. With the other she tugged on her kunzite necklace. "Here, use this." She threw the necklace to the ground. His stomach plummeted when he saw her next trying to twist off the amethyst ring. He was certain she'd fall once her limbs returned to the over-cooked noodles they'd been before she touched the amethyst.

"Not the ring—you need it more!" She paused a moment, as if debating the idea, and then resumed her climb without removing it.

He grabbed the kunzite necklace and loaded it into the fuel chamber. It gave him four more shots. Not nearly enough. She'd reached the catwalk and was now waiting at the crawl-space entry. Why did she delay? He'd warned her he might have to lure the rest of the shades away. Without the kunzite necklace she was less appealing to them, but they'd still be able to sniff out her amethyst ring. They wouldn't hesitate to follow her through the crawl space if he didn't stop them. Or he could offer them a more delicious morsel . . .

The remaining shades pooled together, forming one large shadowy figure. It glided across the floor, furtive and fluid. Leathery wings pro-truded from its back like shredded voile curtains. A long tail dragged a barb of spikes behind it. The body was muscular with backward-jointed legs, like a horse. The finer details, like whether it had sharp teeth, talons, or hooves remained elusive. One detail, of which he was certain, was that its soulless eyes were locked intensely with his.

"Jack, come on!" Gracie motioned for him to join her.

He couldn't. Not as long as she had her ring and he had his cuf-flink. He slung his particle extractor off his shoulder and discarded it on the floor.

Hunched and staggering, he advanced to confront the shade. Everything around it turned hazy. He spread his arms wide and stood stationary in the middle of the room. "Come to me. I will end you."

"Run, Jack!" Gracie screamed behind him.

The shadow reared and charged. It crashed against him like waves against the bow of a ship. He stood as still as the captain at the helm while the sea raged around him. The darkness tried to push its way around him and then through him. It grated against him, shreds of black ribbons fraying from its body and dissipating into a misty fog.

He dropped in a heap on the floor. He heard Gracie slide down the ladder then fall at his side. His breath came in wheezing gasps. The effort it took to form coherent sentences taxed him so much Jack could almost hear his own accent. "I won't be able to contain it very long, so listen carefully."

She shook her head in protest.

He reached into his pocket and withdrew his watch. Familiar welts and clusters of darkened bruises mottled his skin. His voice bubbled in his throat. "Go through the crawl space. On the other side, open the floor hatch and descend the spiral staircase into the art gallery."

She took his hand and pressed it against her cheek. "I won't leave you. You made it this far, you can make it the rest of the way."

"You have to. I can't hold onto this shade much longer. Harris will have heard all the noise, and he'll be here soon for my cufflink." He pushed the watch into her hands. "You'll need this to gain access to the generator."

She clutched it tightly. "What am I supposed to do with this?"

He gulped and licked his dry lips. "That watch shows the true time. Position the watch in the center of the clock motif on the floor, look at the time, then enter the four numbers on the keypad—it looks similar to a typewriter. It changes every minute, so you need to do this last step quickly."

Jack coughed, and black specks painted his hand. He took a raspy breath and wiped his mouth. "Once the access panel slides open, you'll see a gearbox with several moving parts. That's the adjustment mechanism for the time-compression field, and it's essential you disable it before Clarice or Harris stops you."

"How do I do that?"

"You'll figure out a way, you're naturally good at breaking stuff."

"The closet handle was an accident, I swear I didn't—"

He cut her off with a choked cry. A biting pain coursed through him, causing his muscles to twitch and spasm. His back arched and bent in half—backwards.

Gracie flinched, but didn't run away.

He screamed in anguish. Had he any fillings in his teeth she might have counted them all. Then, as suddenly as it had come, the pain eased. He grabbed her wrist with his blackened hand and pulled her to him.

"Do as I've told you, and don't come back for me," he gasped. He had to get her out of here, away from him, even if it meant using his hypnosis on her again. Since she didn't have her heartstone, she wouldn't be able to resist the compulsion if he did.

"And one more thing, Gracie—"

"Yes?"

His throat tightened as he whispered the words, "I love you." Her eyes shone with tears. Something about the controlled, subtle gesture she made to wipe them away made him feel even worse for what he had to do next. He pulled his hand out of hers and squeezed her hand around his watch. "Go," he said, snapping his fingers.

She ripped her arm free. Confusion filled her face, then anger.

"No! Take it back! Jack. *Jack*!" She scrambled to her feet and sprinted for the ladder, compelled by his hypnosis.

Tears streamed down her unhappy face as she disappeared from his sight through the crawl space opening.

His only regret was that with all the chaos going on recently, he'd never gotten the chance to show her the best of him. He felt like that postcard she carried around, warped at the edges and about to tear through the middle from the creases. If only second-rate and weak was what she desired, he would have given all of himself to her. And in turn, he wished she would have given him the same: the fears she had about the death of the man she said she'd killed, the insecurity she felt about her figure, the loneliness she felt since losing her family. Then, like Japanese kintsugi—broken pottery pieces mended with gold—he would have taken all her pieces and crafted them into a work of art more beautiful than the original.

CHAPTER XXXVII

Somewhere in the fortress, Clarice must have split Gracie's heartstone in half. Gracie could think of no other explanation for the ache in her chest at leaving Jack behind.

When this was over, she'd make him pay dearly for forcing her to do this alone.

Behind her it sounded like a one-man bloodbath. Jack screamed, and each agonizing wail rang in Gracie's ears. She crawled on her elbows through the small space. She couldn't make herself turn around—not that there was enough room to do anything except inch forward. Good thing she hadn't changed into the ecru dress. Its excessive bustle would have trapped her in the access strip.

When she pulled herself out the other side, the front of her dress had turned the color of a baked potato from the dust caked on it.

"Curse you." She slumped to the floor. How could he say he loved her then push her away?

The longer she sat, the worse the hazy fog of confusion muddled all her thoughts, except for one. She needed to find the floor hatch and climb down the spiral staircase into the art gallery. Once she got to her feet and started moving, her thoughts cleared and the spinning in her head stopped.

"Hold on, Jack." Gracie tugged the rope in the middle of the framed box on the floor. Dust flew into the air, sending her into a coughing fit. The pull of the hypnosis throbbed in her head, forcing her down the rickety steps, bringing her more relief with each step. The massive domed ceiling of the room turned each sound into a symphony of echoes.

At least thanks to Jack's hypnosis tugging on her mind, she knew she was headed in the right direction.

The staircase led to an alcove on the balcony level of the art gallery. It didn't look like a room for industrial machinery, but she knew it was the right place since the invisible blacksmith was no longer using her head for an anvil. The furniture was split almost evenly between heavy armchairs and spindly side tables. A large marble staircase connected the balcony to the main floor. The room's only other exit appeared to be a set of French doors on the lower level.

Dozens of paintings hung on the wall, each with a polished frame and its title inscribed on a plaque nearby. The smallest frame belonged to a dark black sheet of glass the size of a piece of parchment. Gracie noticed the small, typewriter-like keypad on the desk beneath it. That must be where she was supposed to enter Jack's numbers.

In the center of the floor on the lower level was the clock motif he'd spoken of. Floral vines intertwined with flourishes engulfed twelve Roman numerals.

"Stand in the center of the clock," he'd said.

She hobbled down the marble stairs. The parts of her body responsible for recognizing pain were so burned out and numb that someone could cut off her foot and she'd only realize it was gone when she went to tie her shoelaces again.

She aligned herself at the center of the motif.

A *tick-tick-tick* noise pounded in her ears alongside her heartbeat, though the sound seemed to be coming from above her rather than from the pocket watch. She craned her neck back and almost fell over at the sight overhead.

A large machine sprawled across the domed ceiling. The whole unit reminded her of a printing press. It had more gears than spots on a leopard. Clouds of thick steam rose and collected at the top of the funneled ceiling. The ticking sound came from a large, carriage-wheel-sized pendulum swinging above her.

Now *that* was a clock.

She opened Jack's watch and held it in her palm as though it were a perched budgie. The hands moved slowly and with purpose.

The hour hand of the watch stopped just before XI. The minute hand placed itself at VII. The second hand skipped forward a quarter-way around and then began ticking. One second passed with each breath she took, in perfect synchronization with the pendulum swinging overhead.

Ten thirty-five.

She ran to the chair by the desk and slid into it so fast it almost tipped over.

Urgency, fear, concern. All her emotions clouded her thoughts and made it difficult to study the keypad and pick out the numbers from all the other letters and fancy symbols.

"Hour first, then minutes," she said to herself. She typed the four numbers, "1-0-3-5." When nothing happened, Gracie pressed the largest key.

The sound of heavy movement and the hiss of air escaping behind her made Gracie turn around. A split had formed between two of the bookshelves.

The shelves swung outward to reveal a small room with polished marble floors and surgically-clean white walls. The heat of the air rushing from the room burned against her face as Gracie stepped inside. Pipes of different diameters climbed the walls like ivy, overlapping and crossing over each other. Each pipe connected to a riveted metal firebox in the center of the room.

Was this the generator mechanism Jack wanted her to break?

Gracie glanced at the open bookshelves behind her, praying that they would remain open, so she could make a hasty exit if needed. Swatting at the heavy mist, she walked around to the back of the machine.

The gauges on the pipes whistled and released more steam into the hazy room as their needles climbed into their respective yellow zones. All over the mountain of pipes and parts there were plenty of little knobs and switches for her to snap off. However, the only unique bit of machinery, the only thing that actually looked irreplaceable, was a spinning glass gyroscope above a row of gearbox levers.

Gracie eyed the moving parts and filigree cog wheels turning the gyroscope, which reminded her of the inner workings of a music box. Her heartstone was already gone, so it wasn't like she had much of a life to go back to if she jammed something into the midst of all those gears and somehow ended the world as she knew it . . . A hammer or wrench would be ideal.

Of course, neither was available.

Why was it that a young woman could never find anything menacing and blunt when she needed it?

She pulled out Jack's watch. Did she have enough time to go find something before Clarice came to stop her?

In answer to her question, the French doors behind the staircase slammed open.

Gracie jumped and her stomach twisted at the sound of someone storming into the other room. "Gracie!" a female voice shouted from the back of the staircase.

Clarice rounded the staircase, coming into view of the control room and Gracie.

"Get away from there!"

Gracie couldn't fight the command. The hypnotic demand allowed her no leeway to resist it. Her hand recoiled from its place above the gyroscope as though she'd grabbed the glass chimney of a lit oil lamp—but not before she'd dropped Jack's watch into the intersection of moving parts.

CHAPTER XXXVIII

T HE PARTS in the gearbox continued turning only for a moment before emitting a tremendous noise like an elephant having its trunk wound around a taffy machine. All at once, the pressure gauges changed their tune to a cacophony of screams.

Gracie ducked her head and ran from the room as rivets bulleted from the machine. Glass fragments danced around her as the gyroscope shattered. In the main room, colored lights flashed across the ceiling and buzzing noises echoed from one part of the room to the other. The outcry of agonized machinery continued as the bookcase doors sluggishly thudded shut behind her.

Clarice wrung her hands. "What have you done!"

Her gaudy jewelry clinked as she ran over to the hidden doors and tore every book off the shelf.

If Gracie had any moisture in her mouth, she'd have spat on her.

Clarice shoved Gracie to the side and hurried over to the keypad where she tapped at the keys. The machine on the ceiling yowled like a pack of hungry cats. Clarice whirled toward Gracie, murder in her eyes.

Gracie smiled grimly and hoped the tricks she'd picked up at the orphanage would be enough to defend herself. With her swollen ankle, she wouldn't get far running.

Clarice charged, and with a quick sidestep, Gracie grabbed a handful of Clarice's hair. Her own scalp tingled as a handful of Clarice's golden locks ripped free.

Clarice shrieked and her sour smile twisted into something feral. "So, you want to fight dirty?" She flipped her hair out of her face. "How about this? Don't move."

Gracie stood frozen in place, her thoughts echoing Clarice's command. Clarice's instructions held twice the potency of anything Jack had ever made her do, which Gracie assumed was an indication that Clarice now had both Jack and Harris's cufflinks in her possession. The words had a stricter governing effect that lingered in her thoughts even after her body had obeyed. Her thoughts continued in circles, ending up at the same conclusion—she should do nothing except remain still as Clarice whipped the tube of her particle extractor off her back. Cackling with laughter, Clarice swung the tube, knocking Gracie solidly in the face. She fell atop the typewriter pad, her cheek burning as though she'd landed on a set mousetrap. Strange symbols ran across the black glass, and a long beeping sound followed. Fire ripped through Gracie's arm as Clarice grabbed and twisted it.

The next hit grazed Gracie's temple and turned her sight to double vision. She'd been *very* wrong to think she'd have an easy fight with Clarice.

The golden woman dived on top of her, knee first into Gracie's sternum. In a swipe, Clarice tore off her own rainbow necklace.

"Now, the real fun begins," Clarice said, unscrewing the back of the particle extractor and dropping the necklace into the fuel chamber.

She raised the gun to her shoulder. The tube roared like rushing wind as it powered on.

There's no way out.

"Gracie!" Jack's voice sliced through the background of the chirping alarms.

In the dark shadows under the awnings, Jack moved like a shark through water. When he ran into the light, Gracie could almost see the colors at his edges shift into hues of blue. The light bent around him in slow motion and then darkened as it passed through him. The sight of him eased the weight on her chest long before he crashed into Clarice, knocking her to the side.

Clarice stumbled for balance, arms swimming in air. Jack took advantage of her disorientation by pulling Clarice into a close grappling hold. He knocked her out cold with a jab of his right elbow to her temple. She dropped to the floor in a heap.

Gracie rolled onto her side and coughed, sucking as much air as she could through her crushed lungs.

Jack wrapped his arms around her, helping her into a seated position. "Are you all right?"

She should be the one asking him that question. Gracie pulled away and massaged her chest. "I'm fine. But I can't say the same for your machine. I only meant to break it a little, but Clarice showed up and I think I did too much."

He laughed, the tension melting from his shoulders. "I knew you'd do great." He hopped to his feet, buoyant in both body and spirit. Taking her by the wrists, he helped her up. Jack's hand in hers was like solid steel, but the rest of him was a shadow. He was a ghost, flickering in and out of existence between two worlds.

His smile turned cold as old bathwater when he brushed her hair aside for a better look at the injuries on her face.

The sound of a door closing caused Jack's chin to raise sharply. They both turned to face the tall mahogany doors in the back of the room. Harris had arrived. Gracie noted that Jack and Harris were identically dressed and neither had the telltale dark spots and bruises on their skin.

"Get out of here while you still can," Jack instructed, pushing her to the side. She felt no hypnotic compulsion to obey him though. Without the cufflinks, there was no chance.

She would not leave him twice.

"Looks like we get to finish our fight from the big top after all." Harris said, and threw himself into Jack.

Harris sailed his fists into Jack's stomach. Their grunts and cries blended into a dull background noise, as indistinguishable as the sounds of a busy market street. Considering how intensely the two brothers were fighting each other, in a matter of seconds there would be some injuries Gracie could use to differentiate them, if she paid close enough attention.

From across the room, a bolt of lightning shot through the air—Clarice had regained consciousness and discharged the particle extractor. Disconnected wires dangled above them, intermittently shooting sparks. The air carried the burning metallic tang of a blacksmith's shop.

Gracie's nails dug into her palms. She wasn't a physical match for any of them, and if Clarice took notice of her again, she'd command her to stand there as a human shield. But doing nothing seemed worse.

After a split-second deliberation, Gracie charged toward Jack and Harris, latching onto the twin she thought was Harris from behind. She pulled his arms and made herself enough of a nuisance for Jack to worm his way free.

"Get off, Gracie, it's me!" the twin swatted her away.

Harris might have fooled her if she had her heartstone, but without it, she could sense the darkness of the lie. She continued to cling to his back, giving Jack the chance to engage Clarice and disarm her of the particle extractor with a well-placed kick. The tube flew out of Clarice's hands and spun across the floor. Harris elbowed Gracie in the stomach, knocking her to the ground, and ran for it. He only made it a few feet before Jack latched onto his legs and sent him crashing to the floor.

"Get the extractor, Gracie!" Clarice commanded from where she sat on the floor, nursing a split lip.

The muscles in Gracie's lower body reacted involuntarily, and she stumbled to reach the long tube before Harris or Jack.

Although the generator was broken, there were still a few lingering effects of the time-compression field. The view of Jack and Harris from behind had a red tinge to it. In the shadows, they moved too fast for her to visually follow them. In the light, their movements slowed. The sound of their voices even changed tone, much like a train whistle rolling full speed past a station. Trying to watch them move gave her the dizzying feeling of watching a housefly zipping through a bright field.

Their fighting styles mirrored each other's—strength and intention with every punch, no effort wasted in unnecessary movement. Slender at the waist and built solidly at the shoulders, Harris and Jack moved like hunting panthers as they took their fight to the second landing.

The particle extractor lay on the floor in the open.

"Get the extractor, Gracie!" Clarice repeated.

Gracie reached for it, but before her fingers could close around it, Jack stepped in and kicked it back to the other side of the room. He had a cut on his knuckles that had started to bleed and had given Harris a few small blood spots on his shirt. "Clarice has both cufflinks." In the blink of an eye, he was in a duel with Harris on the upstairs balcony. He shouted to her, "Run away while you still can!" His movements happened so fast he seemed to be in two places at once.

Even if she could resist Clarice's hypnotic commands, there was no way she was abandoning him.

On Gracie's third attempt to reach the tube, per Clarice's lingering command, the fortress intervened. The floor lurched and the lights flickered. Pieces of plaster and paint flecks dropped from the ceiling. One of the paintings fell from the wall.

The ground abruptly tilted, and Gracie found herself sliding toward the left wall. All the furniture, except for the desk with the keypad, tumbled into a messy pile around her. The remaining pictures leaned away from the wall. Half of them dropped and skidded across the room. By the time they reached the other side, many had reverted to their original forms of hospital beds, the magic all worn off.

Over by the staircase, Jack and Harris clung to the banister like it was a life raft. Wrapped around the desk leg, Clarice stretched to reach the particle extractor, which was wedged in the jumble of chairs and tables near her.

A deep groan reverberated throughout the entire fortress, as though the sound had traveled from the center of the earth.

"What's going on?" Gracie cried.

"The anti-gravity balance has been disrupted, and it's straining the anchor chain," Jack answered, or at least Gracie thought it was Jack. "If this keeps up, the whole fortress will fall into the lake."

The floor jolted and seesawed. Gracie skidded right and then rolled over a few times to the left. The furniture and books cartwheeled with her. Before she could pull herself up, something weighty pressed into her back—Clarice's foot. She knew the object jammed into the back of her head had to be the end of the particle extractor.

"Fix the generator, Jack, or she dies."

With her cheek pressed into the floor, Gracie could hear Jack's voice but couldn't see him. "If you kill her, I have absolutely no regrets dying as well."

The pressure on the back of Gracie's head increased. Clarice was trying to make a round biscuit out of her flesh using the end of the tube as the cookie cutter.

"You're too vain to let yourself die in this mess," Clarice said, but the shoe pressing into Gracie's back trembled.

"That was the old me. If I die now, it'll be with the peace of knowing I've finally found a way to atone for the mistakes I've made and to fulfill Gladys's last wish. I think you'll find you have more to lose in death."

"You're—"

The floor heaved and Clarice fell on Gracie, crushing the air from Gracie's lungs. They were weightless for a second, and then gravity glued them to the floor.

"Give me the heartstones," Jack shouted from across the room. How he'd gotten over there so fast was a mystery. Why couldn't she learn his trick of disappearing and reappearing elsewhere?

Clarice rolled off her, yet Gracie still gasped as though she only had a straw to breathe through.

Somewhere to her right, Clarice's voice sounded over the buzzers and bells. "You can have the cufflinks, but you can't have her heartstone until the generator is fixed."

The twin with the small blood splotches on his shirt—Harris, by Gracie's calculations—shook his free fist at Clarice. Jack stood behind him, twisting his other arm "You promised to give both cufflinks to me!" Harris shouted.

"All or nothing," Jack said flatly.

The ground lurched again, and a large gear fell from the ceiling. Gracie scrambled out of the way and took refuge at the bottom of the staircase.

"Make up your mind, Clarice. You're out of time!" Jack insisted, now the one with his arms held by Harris.

Clarice screamed and rolled the two cobalt cufflinks across the floor.

Acting as though he'd been faking submission the whole time, Jack flipped Harris over his back and snatched the cufflinks.

The ground shook like a spoke-wheeled cart rolling over a pumpkin patch. A bookcase tore from the wall and collapsed to the floor. Ruptured pipes gushed water, steam, and pressurized air. Sparks jumped from wrenched cables. Another gear dropped, inches from Clarice's head. As she dived out of the way, the particle extractor slipped from her grasp. It sang a high-pitched note as it slid across the floor that was tilting on its axis. Gracie continued to cling to the stair railing while Clarice, Jack, and Harris chased the device.

Jack emerged from the pile first, fist still folded around the cufflinks, but otherwise empty-handed. Clarice crawled out, defeated, shortly after.

"Looks like I win," Harris leered, training the particle extractor on Jack.

Time seemed to slow to a standstill around the twins, and the noises in the room softened to dull whispers. An invisible force stirred Gracie's insides with a fork.

"Don't kill him! He has to fix the generator!" Clarice begged.

"What's done is done," Harris said. "You lied to both of us, and now you're the fool—there's no way to undo the damage, and I'm going to take care of my unfinished business."

Jack raised his hands over his head. "You'll never get a cleaner shot."

The particle extractor trembled in Harris's hands. Even from where she was, Gracie could see sweat beading on his temples. "You'd do the same." He fixed a scowl on Jack.

The sharp features of Jack's face softened. "Which is why I won't begrudge you for it. We've always known it'd come down to this."

Jack turned to face Gracie, his eyes misty. He looked the way she'd felt when the immigration officer had stamped her orphanage paperwork with his official seal.

Jack turned back to Harris. "Just promise me you'll take care of her after I'm gone."

Harris flipped up the scope and pulled back on the muzzle of the gun. The low drumming turned into an ear-piercing whine. "I will."

"No!" Gracie choked back a shout of dismay and clambered over the debris.

Whatever she'd wanted when she'd first gotten into this mess, none of it mattered now if Jack wasn't there to share it with her. Even finding her lost family in Chicago would be empty if she lost the young man that she knew, without a doubt, she wanted to one day start her own family with. The sun rose and set on his head, bringing the morning with it.

The particle ray blazed like a lighthouse beam. The heat from it rivaled the inside of a volcano.

Gracie closed her eyes and threw herself into Jack's embrace.

CHAPTER XXXIX

G RACIE ANTICIPATED the pain with such eagerness that when it did not arrive, she figured she must have already died. She squinted one eye open and then the other. Jack's arms were wrapped tightly around her, like a second corset.

Clarice was gone. Charred bookcases occupied the space behind where she had stood. Several books belatedly fell from the top shelf. The ashes from their burned pages drifted through the air. On the floor, in the middle of the black heap, lay Gracie's heartstone.

Harris had obliterated Clarice.

Gracie slipped to her knees. Harris stooped and picked up her heartstone. Kneeling beside her, he pressed it into her palm. In the soft lines of his face, she could see that a great burden had been lifted from his shoulders. Jack, although silent, also seemed to stand straighter.

"You two don't have much time. I'll see if I can buy you some, though." He closed her fingers around her heartstone. Immediately, the crystal warmed her hand.

"Harris?" Tears pricked at the corners of her eyes.

He wiped the corner of her eye with his thumb. "Let's just pretend that we'll meet again."

Gracie threw her arms around his neck and let her full weight lean into him. "We're not saying goodbye, because you'll always be next to me—*John*."

A wistful sigh escaped his lips. "I wish I had another seven dollars—I'm going to die and all I get is a hug?" His hold lessened. "You'd best hurry before the roof comes crashing down."

"You did steal my heartstone, but—" She pulled his face to her and lightly kissed his lips.

Another large gear fell from the ceiling. Harris stood and repositioned the particle extractor on his back. "The closet is on the other side of the ballroom, which is going to be full of shades since Clarice thought you'd enter from there. Run as fast as you can, and I'll cover your backs." He unscrewed the back of the unit and poked at the necklace still rattling around in the fuel chamber.

"And take this," Harris said, producing a silk handkerchief from his pocket. He wrapped her heartstone with it. Thank goodness—it was getting *hot*.

"I'll keep this safe for you," Jack insisted, tucking her heartstone into his pants pocket. He stared at Harris with unspoken gratitude in his eyes, as if seeing his own face in his twin's for the first time, yet memorizing it for the last. Jack then ushered Gracie toward the back of the room.

The set of French doors led into a giant ballroom. The chandelier had fallen and its crystals lay scattered on the marble floor.

Jack clenched her hand, and Gracie realized the room was growing darker because of the swarming shadows. The shades greedily feasted on the chandelier pieces. The heartstones caused the darkest shades to grow defined edges, but they weren't turning back into people, they were becoming *beasts*. Sharp-angled jointed limbs, winged bodies, and scaly tentacle appendages blended into one another, only distinguishable by their beady eyes and gleaming teeth.

Jack squeezed her hand. "We can't do anything to help them. We might not make it out as it is."

She nodded and gathered the hem of her skirt.

The whine of the particle extractor started behind them. Harris took aim and fired at a scaly horse-lizard.

The beam of energy tore through the shade. Had Gracie taken a breath next to it at that moment, the whirling flames would have scorched her lungs.

For three brief seconds, the ballroom grew quiet. Then, the shades turned from the chandelier, their slanted and bulging eyes fixed on Harris. His plan to distract the shades might have worked a bit too well.

Harris stepped forward to meet the herd and fired again. A spider-legged avian beast writhed as white flames engulfed it.

Harris called over his shoulder, taking another measured shot. "Take care of her like *you* were the gentleman."

"I promise." Jack squeezed her hand.

Jack ran in front, and Gracie threw her legs forward in leaping strides to keep up. Her right foot throbbed as though she were running through scalding water, but she was past the point of acknowledging the pain.

A second set of doors had fallen off their hinges on the far side of the ballroom. They ran across the ballroom and through the doors, climbing over the shredded curtains of the vestibule as they exited.

She looked back, searching for signs of Harris, but the ballroom had vanished into complete darkness.

Jack's voice echoed in the empty hallways. "I think we'll make it!"

The last stretch was the hardest.

The fortress began to spin—they were sometimes running on the floor and other times on the walls. They moved quickly but carefully as they sidestepped light fixtures, aware that any misstep through one of the broken windows would send them falling out of the fortress. In the cloisters, the pipes from the ceiling had fallen and created a turbulent log drive. Jack reached the closet first and pulled her inside.

In the cramped closet, Jack stepped on Gracie's feet several times, and she elbowed him in the gut in equal measure as they turned toward the disintegrating hallway. Jack pulled Gracie to him. He held her head and tucked it under his chin, his heart threatening to punch through her chest. "Hold on tight."

Jack closed the door, and when he opened it again, a gust of wind swept them out.

GRACIE blinked awake. She was lying on a chaotic tumble of sheets and pillows, and it took her a moment to realize she was in Jack's room. The pillow was damp.

Have I been crying?

The sight of the empty bunk across from her caused her grief to rear inside her. The memories hadn't vanished this time since Jack hadn't hypnotized her to forget. At the moment, with her emotions varying between extremes, she didn't know if he'd done her a favor or an injustice.

Her insides churned, and she felt utterly sick. But she knew vomiting would not make her feel better. Harris was gone. Even though he'd betrayed her, in the end, he had saved both her and Jack.

The door handle shook, followed by the sound of a lock turning. The door opened, and Jack stepped through. His eyes met hers, his forehead lined with concern. "You're awake." He removed his jacket. "How are you feeling?"

There was no doubt in her mind that his sacrifice had been greater, but no matter how much she wanted to be happy for him now, she couldn't hold a smile, even a weak one.

Jack crossed the room to her side in one step. "No, Gracie." He sat beside her on the bed and pulled her into his arms. "You don't need to be brave now."

She remembered the moment he'd held her close at the hotel. His heart beat even faster now.

"Not having the kunzite necklace is making this seem worse than it really is, but don't worry, it's all over," he breathed into her ear, sending shivers throughout her trembling body. "Nothing will hurt you now."

Gracie buried her face into his chest while he stroked her hair, smoothing it down her back. He pressed his lips into the crown of her head. "During this last visit, I didn't hypnotize you to forget anything. I wanted you to remember that Knossos is no longer real." His gaze shifted to the floor. "But if the truth is too much for you to handle right now, I can do it," he offered, with a hint of resignation in his tone.

"No." Her voice came out too high in pitch. "I'm just sad because . . . he's gone."

Jack cupped her cheek in his palm, a smile tugging his cheeks higher. "It'll take some adjusting, but soon you'll see that things are the way they should be. You'll feel better once you have your heartstone back where it belongs."

He flipped back the bedsheets and picked up the folded handkerchief with her heartstone in it. He pressed it back into her hands and folded her fingers around it. Joy and warmth spread through her as if she held a kitten or puppy. He returned to his seat beside her on the bed.

Gracie loved how Jack ran his fingers through her hair. No one had handled her hair like this since her mother had brushed it for her when she was young. She tucked her head to his chest and breathed him in. He smelled like fresh-baked bread, and she knew it would be her new favorite scent.

His fingers slowed and slid out of her hair. He eased himself off the bed, and she let out a whimper in protest. "Is something the matter, Jack?"

He paused. "I'll let you call me Jack for now, but soon I'd like you—to start calling me John."

"Sorry. *John.*" The name tasted foreign to her, almost as if he'd asked her to learn to write with her left hand.

He crossed the room to his dresser and opened the drawer. From it he retrieved a thin, wrapped parcel. "Here," he handed the gift to her, "I got these for you. I guess now is as good a time as any for you to have them."

Gracie set the warm heartstone in her lap. She unwrapped the paper and fanned a stack of postcards across the bed. At first, she didn't understand, but then she recognized a theme among the dozen cards: a steamer ship, a crowded beach, a lighthouse, a harbor. All featured locations with water, except for the last card, which had white tents and colored flags dotting a grassy field with a train chugging along a set of tracks in the lower corner. "A Day at the Circus" was scrawled across the top in red and yellow.

"What are all these for?"

"I recall you said it was none of my business, but when I saw your postcard at the bottom of the puddle, I felt responsible—except I couldn't find one exactly like it."

Gracie shuffled the circus postcard to the top of the pile and pressed the stack to her chest. "This one is my favorite."

"If anything happens to it, I want you to let me be the one to replace it. And if there's anything else that would make you happy, I want you to tell me first."

Gracie bit her lower lip to contain her smile. She wound her fingers into his shirt and drew him to her. His weight, leaning heavily into her, pressed the cards flat between them and squeezed the last bit of emptiness and loneliness out of her chest.

"Thank you, Jack."

The beat of Jack's heart echoed in the room, its sound a faint undercurrent to the rattle of rain on the train car roof. Gracie turned toward the window and set the stack of cards to the side. "It's really pouring outside, isn't it?"

"It's been on and off for the last several hours."

Hours? "How long have I been asleep?"

"Since we got back. That last trip through the closet was a bit rough, to say the least. We missed the evening performance."

Foggy details of landing on the floor in Jack's wagon lurked at the corner of her thoughts. She remembered feeling severe pain in her foot again. Possibly she'd blacked out because of it. Jack must have brought her back to his room. He was always taking care of her. When her own strength came up short, somehow he always had enough for both of them.

"Did you happen to see Vincenzio when you were out today? Do you know what he plans to do about me?"

Jack took a seat on the opposite side of the bed, extending his feet. "Vincenzio's not going to pay you if you don't work, but I believe Miriam might be interested in having a laundry girl. You could do that for a start and do some dressmaker training with her on the side. The pay won't be much, but with Harris gone, Vincenzio is likely to acquiesce if I ask him to find something for you to do. He'll be short three acts if I don't fill in for Harris."

Gracie's heart panged at the reminder of who was missing. "What will we tell the crew about Harris?"

Jack nodded pensively for a moment. "I'll tell them he stole Katherine's jewelry then ran off to join the Ringling Brothers. With your testimony that he stole your ticket at the station, I'm sure I can paint him as a gambler with a big debt to repay."

He picked up the pillow, fluffed it, and fixed it behind his back. "It'll be interesting to see how my first rehearsal goes since I haven't touched a trapeze since the accident that claimed our mother. Hopefully I'll retain the best skills of both Jack and Harris and overcome my fears. Of course, if your foot gets better and you want to resume the magic act before the circus reaches Chicago, Richard will have to move the acts around a bit to give me enough time for the costume change."

Gracie bit her lower lip. "Actually, if Vincenzio hasn't replaced me by then, I was thinking I might stick around with the circus—if it's all the same to you."

Jack ran his hand through his hair and sucked his cheeks in. "That may be a bit of a problem because I was planning on resigning once we reached Chicago. I remember what Harris did to you at the train station, and I don't want to see you fall into misfortune again. So, with your permission, I'd like to escort you around in Chicago, at least until you find your family."

Her lips parted in surprise. Jack put a hushing finger against them. "The morning I missed rehearsal, I was in Vincenzio's stateroom letting him know of my intent. But if you decide you prefer a traveling life, I imagine he'll let us both stay on."

So much had changed since she'd first gotten involved with the circus—not having to worry about meals or shelter foremost. Having Jack as a friend and the closest thing to a family she'd had in years added to her gratitude. Mr. and Mrs. Levenson had taken care of her, but they'd never been more than her caretakers. Not like *real* family. Not like the circus crew. Not like Jack.

Gracie huddled closer and nestled her head under his chin. She wrapped one arm around his waist and squeezed. He softly stroked the back of her head.

"I should say though, if you still plan to be my assistant, we may have to work out a new magic act or I'll have to modify the closet into a simple magic prop that no longer risks transporting you somewhere."

"Is Knossos gone for good then?"

Jack's fingers worked to separate the soft curls of her hair. "With Clarice gone, I'm confident the fortress won't be resurfacing from the bottom of the lake anytime soon."

"What about the shades that were there?" Gracie didn't dare ask if Harris could possibly be among them. She pressed herself more into Jack's chest. He tightened his hold.

"I'm not actually sure what's become of them. They could've been converted into neutral energy, or something else. Whatever the case, I'm sure you'll not have anything bothering you tonight."

"And no one's going to try and take my heartstone again?"

"With the time-compression generator destroyed, there's no need to worry." Jack took the handkerchief with her heartstone from her lap. "Go ahead and lie down."

"Where are your cufflinks?" Her eyes skimmed over his many jackets scattered around the room, on chairs, coat hooks, and the floor.

"I've already removed the heartstones from their settings and taken care of my business."

She wrapped her hands around his hands, recovering the heartstone with the handkerchief. "I feel better when I'm holding it. I can wait a little longer. You've been through enough for one evening."

His hand found its way to the side of her cheek. "I promised Harris I'd take care of you. I won't be able to say I've done that until I return your heartstone."

"Won't it hurt you?" He traced the contours of her face with his finger, pausing at her lower lip. She pursed her lips and kissed his finger. From her lips, Jack's finger ran across her cheekbone to the place where her jaw met her neck. It made her chest tickle.

"A bit, but you'll be there to nurse me back to health, won't you?"

"And if I don't?" She smiled coyly, grabbing the pillow and holding it up with the clear intention that she'd give him a well-deserved thumping with it if he was going to insist on having things his way.

In hindsight, now lying pinned to the floor with Jack leaning over her, Gracie should have known better than to think he could be bested in a pillow fight.

Feathers littered the floor as though the entire pigeon population of Central Park had decided to hold their seasonal molt in Jack's room. Jack laughed, carefully pulling a few feathers out of Gracie's hair and then shifting to kneel close to her hip.

"It's time." From his back pocket, he withdrew a glove that looked like it was made of the same material as the covering for his closet.

When he unwrapped her heartstone from the handkerchief, everything inside the room warmed and grew more vibrant—except the glove, which radiated darkness. She took his free hand in hers and guided his fingers to the neckline of her gown. Brushing her hair over her shoulder, Jack leaned in. Her heartstone warmed her skin as he positioned it over her chest. She held her breath as he pushed it back into her body.

The crackling ice she'd been dancing on broke and she fell in. A fiery river swept her away, making her head feel as though her hair might light up in flames at any moment. Then, with the swiftness of a door closing, the walls she'd built inside herself to cage the darkness tumbled, and there was nothing. Not darkness, or light—simply herself.

She let out a long breath.

"Better?" He removed the glove. His hand appeared pale and drained of color—though nothing like the crystal-covered spectacle she'd seen the night at the junction.

She drew her lower lip into her mouth and nodded. He smiled and brought his face close to hers. His nose drew feather-soft circles on her neck while his kisses crept to her collarbone. She let out a small whimper when he stopped.

"Until I can be certain you're not still under my hypnosis, I'm sorry to say I can't accept any further solicitations from you. Having two heartstones in one body might take a while for me to get used to. And because I'm not sure which stone will dominate at any given time, I can't guarantee to be a perfect gentleman."

"I trust you." She fluttered her eyes. He leaned in, taking the bait.

"Me, Jack, or Harris?"

"Yes."

He kissed her forehead. Then, tilting her head back to meet his lips, he stole her breath.

He tasted like sunlight—a bright Australian sunrise and sunset.

Sound, sight, and touch blurred into one physical sensation in their kiss. It was the blue color of the sky, or the taste of wine, or the feeling of being genuinely loved—a mesh of experiences anyone could relate to, but that no two people could describe exactly the same. For her, it was home.

END

EPILOGUE

CHICAGO, WITH a population nearing one million, still had many citizens who wanted to see a circus performance on a Tuesday night.

"Don't count the audience," Gracie chastised herself and closed the curtain at the staging tent doorway.

"Just think—this could be our last performance. No more cramped, suffocating secret compartments or target board bull's-eyes," John said over her shoulder.

The band played the notes for their entrance.

In his thundering voice, Richard announced her name to the crowd, and she smiled the whole time. Since she'd confessed to murdering the foreman to John, he'd done some long-distance inquires and found several New York newspaper reports about an Albany factory supervisor being found dead in an office strewn with licentious materials. There seemed to be more interest in the nature of the materials than in how the man died. No wanted persons report was filed with the police mentioning her by name.

John had teased that he should put "Albany poultry factory foreman" on his list of unsuitable future careers. She'd elbowed him in the ribs, at which he'd complained that her limbs were too bony and she should eat more.

Miriam had said the same thing while measuring her for a new costume, and because Gracie, waiting for her foot to heal, had assisted

Miriam in the weeks since they'd left Buffalo, she'd been able to convince Miriam not to cut the chest of the new costume quite so big.

Once again, Gracie stood against the backboard while John flung his silver bullets at her. She hummed "London Bridge is Falling Down" seven times inside the vanishing closet, and she knew without a doubt, there was nothing except John waiting for her on the other side of the door and the secret panel. She'd not found a single note in her costume since Montreal, and John no longer had cramps in his hand after the show or nightmares when he slept.

After the show, Gracie changed out of her costume and hurried to the dressing tent to find Miriam. Since Gracie had lost the costume necklace and shoes in Knossos, Miriam insisted she return her costume items directly after each performance.

"I've been waiting for you," the seamstress said, her eyes narrowed in a squint. "Come here." Miriam gestured for her to follow her out of the dressing tent.

Gracie's chest tightened. What had she done wrong this time?

Miriam led her near the ticket booth and gestured to a girl and boy, both a few years younger than Gracie. The girl had dark hair, golden brown eyes, and a thin frame. Her head resembled an egg balanced on a straw. The boy was younger. His hair, a color just dark enough to disqualify him as blond, nearly covered his bushy eyebrows. Brother and sister, Gracie guessed.

"They came to the dressing tent looking for you after the show and insisted I introduce you to them."

Gracie stepped forward hesitantly. "Can I help you?"

The girl looked to the boy for encouragement and then spoke in a quiet voice. "Is your name really Gracie Hart?"

Gracie smiled at the girl. "For a little longer." Soon she hoped to change it to Gracie Harrison.

The girl stirred dirt with her feet and then twisted the ends of her shawl, not meeting Gracie's eyes. "We'd like to know if you have a brother named Robert."

Gracie's knees trembled at their inquiry. "I did. He died eight years ago."

The brother talked so fast Gracie almost couldn't understand him. "Our mother is Mary Blackington, and she had a sister named

Eleanor Hart. Eight years ago, she was supposed to come visit us but never arrived—"

The girl interrupted, "Mother heard your name and remembered her sister had a daughter with the same name who'd be about your age now. We think it's possible you might be related to us."

Gracie's eyes welled with joyful tears. "Eleanor was my mother. She died on the crossing from England, along with my father and brother."

The girl threw herself at Gracie in a sudden embrace. "I'm Tillie, and this is my brother, Lincoln. We're your cousins, Gracie!"

Gracie's blood coursed through her with the force of white water rapids, and she would have collapsed if it weren't for Tillie's firm hug. So many questions bubbled up in her she didn't know where to begin.

Gracie gripped Miriam's arm in a vice. "Hurry and find John. Tell him to come here immediately and that it's urgent!"

Miriam freed her arm with a frown. "You know I am Vincenzio's seamstress, not his errand girl, yes?"

"I'll hem two skirts for you tomorrow if you do."

"Three," Miriam said heading toward the men's dressing tent.

Gracie turned back to Tillie. "Is your mother here? Can I meet her?"

Lincoln answered. "She's waiting with Father over in the menagerie—she didn't want to get her hopes up in case you were just a stranger."

John raced across the lot to her as though on his way to put out a fire. When he arrived, he had his cravat in one hand, and his shirt was half-unbuttoned. "Are you all right? Are you hurt?"

"I'm fine, though I do have some bad news. We'll have to cancel our dinner with Vincenzio tonight."

Though John must have been annoyed for the false sense of urgency, he gave no sign of it beyond an initial hesitation in his response. "Oh? Do you have something else in mind?"

Gracie made the necessary introduction with contagious enthusiasm filling her voice. "Mr. Harrison, may I have the pleasure of presenting to you, Miss Tillie Blackington and her younger brother, Lincoln—my family."

Dear Mr. Levenson,

I hope this letter finds you well. You said my stubbornness was the reason I had to be employed at the poultry factory instead of in a respectable, technical trade. That same stubbornness has led me to a wonderful family and job as a performer in a traveling circus, and it has helped me find my real family here in Chicago. Please share this note with the orphans and tell them to have hope.

Sincerely,

Gracie Hart

ABOUT THE AUTHOR

KIMBERLEE TURLEY grew up in California where she earned a degree in Fashion Design from FIDM in 2005. Soon after, she married her husband, and they moved six times in the next ten years before settling in Utah and starting a family. Kimberlee is currently a stay-at-home-mother of two and a freelance cosplay costume seamstress. She is passionate about aerial circus arts, historical clothing, and writing clean fiction for teens and the young-at-heart. Her favorite books to read feature a touch of magic, silk gowns, and romance.

Scan to visit

www.kimberleeturley.com

ACKNOWLEDGMENTS

FIRST, I am so grateful for Angela Johnson and the rest of the Cedar Fort team for their hard work on my novel, especially Shawnda Craig and her ability to design such a beautiful cover based on my scattered and numerous concept ideas. Prior to Cedar Fort, I was blessed to work with an amazing group of women who are now graduates of Brigham Young's Editing & Publishing bachelor's degree. A huge thanks to Alayna Een, Alice Card, Becky McKee, and Monica Bullock for forcing me to stretch myself as a writer and make this story great. My gratitude also goes to Brigham Young University's Suzy Bills for her professional instruction and oversight of the young adult fantasy novel capstone course.

I owe so much to my older sister, Jennifer. Your faith and belief in me and Gracie's story kept me going when I was ready to quit. You gave me the encouragement I needed to apply to "just one more person." You always made time to answer my questions and helped me brainstorm and work out plot holes. Your addiction to historical romance novels helped make this book what it is.

Thanks to my super analytical mother, who spent many late nights sacrificing time to help me find all the plot holes and inconsistencies. I'm sorry I didn't fix all the ones you found. Along these lines, this story wouldn't exist if not for the sacrifices of my loving husband who went to bed alone many nights because I was up late writing.

This story had been over ten years in the making, and so I need to express my appreciation for my early critique partners Kimberly Ann Miller, Jackie Felger, and Jordan Elizabeth and to my later writing group friends and beta readers JoLyn Brown, Rachel Hert, and Jacque Stevens. Each of you made it a little better and some of you made it a lot better, particularly Caitlin Sangster. You're a great author and friend.

A quick shout out to Shem Flitton and Scott Applegate for your help with the French translations . . . the closest I've come to learning French is ballet lessons.

I also need to thank my Heavenly Father for His guiding hand in my life and for blessing me with the things that I need, but not necessarily the things that I want.

Last, to my readers: I wrote Gracie's story for me, but mostly I wanted to share it with you.